D1191107

DEAD
SOULS

D.I. KIM STONE BOOK SIX

ALSO BY ANGELA MARSONS

Angela MARSONS

DEAD SOULS

D.I. KIM STONE BOOK SIX

Bookouture

Published by Bookouture
An imprint of StoryFire Ltd.
23 Sussex Road, Ickenham, UB10 8PN
United Kingdom
www.bookouture.com

ISBN: 978-1-78681-161-5
eBook ISBN: 978-1-78681-160-8

This book is dedicated to my partner Julie Forrest
who holds my hand every single day.

And one day you will come to understand how
invaluable you are in this process.

PROLOGUE

Justin looked down at the blade as it hovered above his wrist. The knife was his mother's; the trembling was his.

For a second he was overcome by the practicality of the task. Had he chosen the right knife for the job? There were so many of them. Knives in the cutlery drawer. Knives sticking out of a wooden block. A set of sterling silver knives left to his mother that lived in their own decorative box.

This knife was not his first choice. Initially he had reached for the biggest, baddest knife in the drawer. Its edge serrated. A row of sharp teeth like a mountain range.

The handle had felt good in his grip but the thought of those teeth ripping across his skin had made him wince. Ironic, that he was ending his life, yet worried about the pain involved.

He had put it back and reached for another. A long sleek number with a thicker, meatier handle. He'd seen his mother slice the Sunday roast with it many times.

A pang of sadness, mixed with regret, coursed through him.

He remembered sitting down every Sunday, beside his little sister, eagerly awaiting the most anticipated meal of the week. His mother would place each dinner plate, carefully, ceremoniously. Her face tinged with pride. He swallowed as he realised that she would never again look that way when thinking about him.

The knife faltered as he wondered if there was any way back to those days; his early teenage years when belonging within his family had been enough. The days out, the seaside holidays, the takeaway and film nights.

He swallowed deeply.

He wasn't that boy any more. Had not been for years. The rage that had seeded within him had been fanned to a roaring inferno.

He knew what he had to do.

His mother's face planted itself in his mind. The pain he felt was almost physical.

He cried out as he pulled the blade across his wrist.

The action left a scratch that criss-crossed some of the other poor attempts he'd already made. This effort was rewarded with a small bubble of blood at one end of the cotton-thin line. It was progress.

Her face remained in his mind. It was filled with understanding and forgiveness. The way she had looked when he had earned a detention for punching a boy in the school playground. Or the time he had taken another kid's bike and damaged the front wheel. These were mistakes and he had been forgiven.

This would not be one of those times.

Never before in his eighteen years had he wished to turn back the clock. In the last two days he had wished it on the hour, every hour. The regret was not for himself. He would never marry. He would never bring a girlfriend home to meet his mum. He would never have children. But his regret was for his mother. He took with him her only hope of a grandchild.

In his mind the face of his mother changed and looked puzzled, confused, almost questioning.

The pain of her pain ripped through his heart.

She would question herself. She would wonder what she'd done wrong. If it was her fault.

Tears stung his eyes at the thought.

'This is all wrong,' he whispered, as he began to shake his head.

He couldn't bear the thought of his mother blaming herself. It wasn't her fault. None of this was her fault. It was his own.

His hand let go of the knife and reached into the top drawer of his bedside cabinet and took out a notepad and pen.

He knew there was no other way for him. Had known it for two days. But his mother did not have to live the rest of her life with guilt due to his choices. He would never forgive himself for what he'd done and, try as she might, she would never forgive him either.

He paused as he remembered the helpless, terrified face that had looked up at him, confused, searching for the reason; the motivation for his actions. It was a question he had suddenly been unable to answer, and it sickened him to his core. Those eyes, oh God, those eyes, full of fear, found the shame in his heart. It was only then he'd realised exactly what he'd become. The blackness of his soul had taken away his breath. He had turned into a monster.

It would not end with him. In truth, it was only just beginning. Death and hatred were coming, and he was too cowardly to stop them.

He placed the note to his mother on top of the pillow and reached once more for the knife.

His grip was firm and his hand was steady as he focussed on the vein in his wrist.

He slashed at the skin with the blade.

This time, he meant it.

CHAPTER 1

'Bryant, take this left,' Kim cried, as she heard sirens in the distance.

The brakes screeched as he did a Clarkson around the bend onto a trading estate.

'I'm pretty sure we were on our way home,' he grumbled.

Kim ignored her colleague as she swept her gaze left, forward, right and back again, her eyes peeled for any movement between the darkened buildings.

'Guv, you do know there are other officers on the West Mid—'

'We were less than a mile away from an armed robbery with injury and all you can think about is your pie and mash?' she snapped. It was his own fault for keeping his radio on.

'Fair enough,' he conceded. An evening meal paled against the vision of an innocent male bleeding profusely from a stab wound to the stomach.

'I'm willing to bet he's on here somewhere,' she said, narrowing her eyes against the darkness.

She already suspected from the description that they were searching for Paul Chater, a nineteen-year-old prolific shoplifter she'd been hauling into the station since he was eleven.

The lad was banned from every shopping centre and high street shop that were members of an intel-based partnership scheme, and his photo had been passed around more than a reality star's sex tape.

'Why would he come on to here?' Bryant asked.

'Because it's like a small town,' she answered. 'This place has over two hundred units and three miles of road.'

They were less than a quarter of a mile from the shop, and the kid was still riding a crappy old moped with a dodgy exhaust muffler. He would want to be off the main roads as quickly as possible.

'We could both be driving around here for an hour and not meet,' she said.

'So, he probably knows we're gonna look here?' Bryant said.

'Not in an Astra Estate,' she answered. 'He'll be paying more attention to those bloody sirens.'

In recent years, Paul Chater had focussed his shoplifting and theft from small shops with limited or no CCTV. He took his frequent stretches inside as an occupational hazard and a well-earned rest. But the report of a knife was an escalation.

Kim rolled down her window, hoping the tinny sound of his bike would give him away, but the sound of the approaching sirens was doing nothing to help her.

'Guv, we're not gonna find—'

'There he is,' she cried, pointing through the windscreen.

Bryant put his foot on the accelerator.

'No, don't chase him,' she warned. 'He's looking for somewhere to hide. If he drops the bike and goes on foot, we'll never catch him.'

She tried to think quickly. 'Carry on to the end of the road, do a right and then a left.'

If Chater had any sense at all, he'd be riding to the far west of the site that backed on to a steep bank leading to the canal towpath, but the way he was heading meant a half mile of straight road first.

As they cut across a hardware store car park and landed on the stretch of road, Chater came into view, aiming right for where she'd thought he would.

'Catch him up,' she instructed.

Bryant hit the accelerator again.

Chater looked behind.

'Faster,' she barked.

The sound of the sirens told her that squad cars had entered the estate, but she knew they would never catch up with him now.

It was just them.

'Get alongside him,' she said, letting down her window fully.

The bank was two hundred metres away.

'Guv, what are?—'

'Pull over,' she screamed once she was level with Chater.

'Pull over,' she repeated, shouting into his surprised face.

One hundred and fifty metres.

'Guv, don't do anything—'

'Stop the fucking bike,' she cried.

One hundred metres until he dropped the moped and ran.

The moped nudged ahead.

'Get me closer,' Kim said, breathlessly.

'Don't do what I think—'

'Bryant, I already asked him nicely,' she said, turning in her seat.

Fifty metres and she was back level with his upper arm.

She hesitated for just a second and then remembered the radio message that had described Mr Singh bleeding back at the shop.

Twenty-five metres.

She grabbed the handle and opened the car door, nudging him in the thigh.

Bryant hit the brakes as the moped was falling to the left away from the car.

She threw open the door and scrambled out. Chater got to his feet and began to run towards the bank.

The sirens were coming at her from all directions as she closed the three metre gap between them.

She launched forward as he reached the foot of the hill.

'Gotcha,' she cried, tumbling on top of him. The solid zip of her leather biker jacket dug into her stomach and his back.

He groaned and struggled to get out of her grip.

She turned him over and looked into the face behind the Perspex visor.

'Okay, you little shit,' she said, straddling his stomach. 'What you been up to this time?'

'Gerroff me, bitch,' he said, wriggling his hips like Ricky Martin.

She tightened her thighs around his ribs. 'Where's the knife, Paul?'

'Weren't no knife,' he protested.

The denial from his lips was quick, but his eyes did not agree.

'Where is it, Paul?' she asked, tightening her grip on his wrist.

'Told yer, weren't no fucking knife,' he shouted now that the courage of his conviction had caught up with him. 'Just wanted some fags, didn't I?'

Kim felt the anger surge through her at the picture of an innocent man bleeding back at his own shop. His life hanging in the balance because this little scrote didn't want to pay for smokes.

'So get a job and buy some,' she said, tightening her grip as a squad car pulled into the kerb at an angle.

She looked to her colleague who was now standing against the car with his arms crossed. 'You know, Bryant, I bloody hate people who think the world owes them something.'

'Shall we take him, Marm?' asked one of the arriving constables as a second squad car pulled up.

She nodded and raised herself from the ground to her five feet nine height and picked a twig from her spiky black hair. She turned her attention back to the man on the ground. 'You've always been a dick, Paul, but now you're a dick with a knife and that's gonna put you away for a long, long time,' she hissed, handing him over. 'The knife will be on this estate somewhere, guys,' she said to the constables.

'That ay gonna solve all yer problems, pig,' Chater smirked. 'There's plenty more like me out there and they'm coming...'

'Oh, I know that, but as one supermarket likes to say, Paul: "every little helps".'

She walked over to her waiting colleague, who was quietly shaking his head. She rubbed the dirt from her hands and smiled. One less scumbag on the streets.

'Okay, Bryant. Now you can go home to your dinner.'

CHAPTER 2

Doctor A surveyed the row of faces before her and tried not to sigh out loud. Her colleague from Aston University was on his way to Dubai to advise a group of newly appointed police officers on the first stages of excavation.

And she was in the middle of a field in the Black Country with a group of apathetic students wearing the Monday morning expression that she was too professional to show. Oh, where were the eager young minds with spongy brains desperate to soak up new information? That would have made the job allocation easier, she thought. The next request for archaeological consultancy in a warm, sunny climate had better have her name on it.

'Okay, gathering round,' she said, waving her hands forward.

'She means gather,' offered Timothy, her assistant.

She pursed her lips at him. Yes, she sometimes mangled certain words in the English language but if they hadn't understood that simple instruction, there was going to be trouble ahead.

While she had been busy spraying the outline, two metres by one metre, the fourteen students had broken away, forming small groups and huddling together, hands deep in pockets, shoulders hunched against the early November seven degree temperature. Although the wind was chilly, it was not biting. She would like to take these youngsters to her home in Macedonia on the Balkan Peninsula where cold air masses travelled from Russia and hung in the valleys, plunging the temperature to minus twenty.

'Who can name me tools in the forensic archaeologist's toolbox?' she asked, opening the bag beside the shovels.

'Camera,' said one, yawning.

'Sketchpad and pencils,' offered another.

'Tweezers and swabs,' said yawner.

'Torch.'

She nodded as the most obvious responses were called out to her. The enthusiasm was short-lived as their brains needed to change gear to search for more answers.

'Don't forgetting we are crime scene,' she prompted.

'Tape.'

'Disposable clothing.'

Doctor A nodded again, and looked down at the rectangle of grass.

'So, are we ready to begin?' she asked, reaching for the shovel.

They looked from one to the other as they stepped forward.

'*Da mu se nevidi*,' she whispered under her breath.

Doctor A stole a glance at Timothy, who made a cross-eyed expression at her. He had learned enough Macedonian to know it was her cry of frustration.

'Is there anything we should be doing first?' she repeated.

'Clean your tools,' called out one student.

'One would hoping they are clean,' she said, shortly.

She was beginning to hope that none of these students took the forensic route.

It was time to spell it out a bit, she thought as she began to dig.

'Normally you would examine the topsoil area. There is no crime here so I shall dig as I explain.'

Timothy stepped forward and began to dig alongside her.

A few people stepped forward at the promise of activity.

'At ancient sites, relevant layers are generally completely buried. At forensic scenes the existing surface is a relevant layer too.

'The burial feature opens directly onto the present ground. This meaning that the ground you walking on simply to get to the scene is part of the site and your presence may alter or destroying evidence.'

She paused for any questions. When none came she continued with the lesson plan. 'Forensic evidence is more subtle. A forensic archaeologist must be sensitive to the presence of such evidence as cut roots, dry leaves, dead vegetation, tool marks, shoe prints, even fingerprints.'

The pile of turf began to grow just outside the white paint border.

'Artefacts at forensic sites are often perishable and rarely encountered at normal archaeological sites: paper, cloth, tobacco, insect evidence, hair, fingernails, other soft tissues.'

Doctor A looked around at the bored faces as the hole gaped at a foot deep.

She passed the shovel to a brunette to her right and indicated to the man beside her to take the second shovel from Timothy.

'Dig, please,' she instructed, and waited until they were throwing down the shovels to dig before speaking again.

'There is also the possibility of encountering biohazardous or dangerous materials…' She hesitated. 'Like a loaded gun.'

The woman student hesitated. Suddenly that word had attracted everyone's attention.

She nodded towards her audience. 'Yes, it has happened.'

She walked behind the diggers and motioned for them to pass the shovels along. It was time to warm these kids up.

She laced her fingers behind her back as she continued to walk and talk.

'Any evidence found must be entered into the proper legal chain of custody. Pass the shovels, please. And all must be accounted for and protected until officially…'

Her words trailed away as she glanced down into the pit.

'Stop,' she cried at the top of her voice.

Every single person jumped back, startled.

'Step away,' she said, not taking her eyes from the hole.

She moved around to the long edge of the feature and knelt down.

She peered closer and held out her right hand. Like every good assistant, Timothy knew exactly what to do.

A soft brush was placed into her palm.

'Getting out of my light, people,' she shouted, without removing her gaze from the object that had caught her attention.

She brushed gently, her heart beating loudly in her chest.

Gasps sounded around her as the smooth, round shape began to emerge. It appeared these students knew something after all.

Doctor A paused to turn and speak to her colleague.

'Timothy, get everyone away from this area. And then get me the coroner and Detective Inspector Stone.'

CHAPTER 3

Stacey Wood struggled hard to process the scene around her. There was something obscene about the volume of blood that appeared to have reached every hard surface of the tiny box room at the back of the small house. But that wasn't the only problem. She'd seen blood before. The real issue was the memory that had been pushed to the back of her mind.

Her gaze met Dawson's over the space that was littered with trainers, football boots, car magazines and tee shirts.

A normal boy's bedroom – except for the body of the teenage boy that was slumped against the wall, and the bloodstain on the carpet. The metallic smell of blood fought against the aroma of sweaty clothes.

His head had dropped backwards, his open eyes appearing to stare at the blood spatter on the ceiling as though either stargazing or looking in awe at what he'd done. A white scar that ran beneath his left eye was the only interruption to the smooth, youthful skin. One sleeve of his hoody was rolled up to his elbow, displaying the fatal wound. His grey skinny jeans were covered with drying bloodstains.

The kitchen knife had fallen just inches from his right hand.

Stacey tried to keep her breathing even and unaffected as her gaze rested on the knife. She didn't want Dawson thinking she couldn't hack being out in the field. And he could smell her weakness a mile off. But that knife was tugging her mind towards somewhere she did not want to go. Not here and not now.

She mentally shook herself and concentrated her thoughts. The mother had found her son and hysterically called for paramedics. A call had been funnelled through to the station, and subsequently a call for the pathologist to attend at the same time. Stacey guessed the boy had been dead for a couple of hours.

The key reason for their attendance was to establish that it was not a murder staged to look like a suicide. A swift agreement between the detective and the pathologist would aid a speedy process in allowing the family to make funeral arrangements.

'He meant it,' Keats, the resident pathologist offered. 'Eventually.'

Stacey knew that. Despite the false attempt scratches running across the wrist, the tear in the skin ran down the arm. The vein had been sliced.

Stacey couldn't stop her mind wandering beyond the sight before her to the knowledge that the moments prior to death had been painful, emotional, laboured. Bad enough that this youth had felt there was no other alternative than to end his own life, but the hesitation cuts echoed his suffering.

Stacey had no clue what had been torturing this young man but she did know that many teenage problems were not as insurmountable as the person thought they were. Perhaps if he'd been able to share his problems, he would not have felt this was his only course of action. She shuddered and swallowed the rising sickness away.

Keats would continue to process the scene but from her view there was nothing to indicate anyone had been involved in the death of Justin Reynolds. The small room would have shown some signs of a struggle if that had been the case, but the only conflict had been in the young man's head.

'You happy to call it, Sergeant?' Keats asked quietly, glancing at Dawson.

He nodded. 'I'm satisfied this young—'

Stacey didn't hear the rest of his words as she stepped out of a room that she could not leave quickly enough.

CHAPTER 4

Kim took a sharp left off the A456, a dual carriageway that separated the West Midlands force with that of West Mercia.

She followed the satnav's instructions when it told her to turn left onto a dirt track behind a garden centre.

'Is this thing on drugs?' she asked, when the electronic voice announced they had reached their destination. Kim had thought the contraption was taking her on a shortcut and that they would eventually rejoin civilisation or at the very least a tarmac road.

Bryant shrugged as the right tyre hit a pothole that bounced them both like a trampoline.

'Oops,' she said, as she spotted three police vehicles next to two minibuses on a gravel parking spot by a field gate. Luckily for her, electronic gadgets did not require apologies.

She parked ten feet back, blocking the single-track road.

As they headed towards the gate, a few fragmented groups of students reached the minibuses, talking animatedly.

Thank goodness someone had had the sense to start clearing the scene. She was sure this was a training session these kids would not forget in a hurry.

Both of them flashed their identification at the police officers guarding the entrance gate, even though both constables were known to them.

A part-worn path continued into the field, gouged by farm vehicles entering the space. It continued for approximately fifty metres before disappearing.

The wooded area to their right thinned to expose a flat, grassy field that stretched a quarter of a mile in each direction, bordered by dense green hedges separating it from the crop fields beyond.

Kim spotted the activity at the tip of the trees.

'Aw, shit, guv. You could have told me it was her.'

Kim smiled. 'Thought you liked surprises.'

'You call that a surprise?' he said, sourly.

Kim shook her head. She knew the scientist was an acquired taste. Her directness did not sit well on everyone's palate but to Kim the woman was a breath of fresh air. She said what she meant and meant what she said. Not always correctly, but close enough.

Kim watched as Doctor A paced the length of the hole. Her one hand was thrust into her front jeans pocket while the other held the phone to her ear. The left leg of her light blue jeans had broken free from the confines of the Doc Marten boot.

What may once have been a tight ponytail holding up her long ombre hair had now loosened and dropped to the back of her neck.

'Doctor A,' Kim said, offering her hand as the woman ended the call.

The nickname had been fashioned by the scientist herself after witnessing too many annihilations of her Macedonian name. Kim wasn't even sure what it was any more as she had used the shortened version for as long as she could remember.

A brief smile accompanied the handshake as she moved her gaze along.

'Bryant,' she said, thrusting her hand forward.

Her colleague had no choice but to take it.

'She got my name right,' Bryant mumbled, as the woman turned towards the hole.

'Where is Keatings?' she asked, suddenly.

'Handing over a suicide scene,' Kim explained. 'He'll be here shortly.'

'Come, come,' Doctor A said, beckoning them forward to the edge of the pit.

Kim saw immediately the chalky white bone protruding from the soil. Experience told her exactly what she was looking at.

'A skull?' she asked.

Doctor A nodded.

Kim stepped back and looked at the hole in the context of the flat land.

'A foot and a half deep?' she asked.

'Approximately, yes. Very shallow.'

Kim stepped forward. 'Can we?…'

'No, no, no, no, no,' Doctor A cried. 'We cannot rush. We must have Keatings and my team firstly and foremost. We do not know condition or circumstance before you start tramping the scene.'

Kim understood. At this point there was no way of knowing how long the skull had been in there. Doctor A's job was to preserve the evidence and remove the skull as carefully as possible.

Like most forensic archaeologists, Doctor A held a PhD in Anthropology and understood how to read any clues left in the bones.

She would need to ascertain firstly that the bones were human. Kim had seen enough skulls to hold no doubt about that.

She would then attempt to identify biological characteristics: i.e. age, sex and race. Kim already knew that establishing the time since death was beyond problematic when dealing with bones without tissue. The rate of decomposition of the flesh, factoring in both the biological and climate conditions, could have at least landed them in the correct ballpark. It was unlikely that entomology would assist either. Judging by the cleanliness of the bone, she could see the insects had long since left the party.

Most importantly for the investigation, Doctor A's knowledge would hopefully assist them to identify a cause and manner of death.

Kim knew there were four manners of death: natural, accidental, suicidal, and homicidal.

As yet Kim had no clue what they were looking at, but she knew one thing: this poor soul had not buried themselves.

'Aww… double shit,' Bryant said, causing her to turn.

A horde was heading along the treeline towards them. Most of them she was expecting. One she was not. She groaned.

'Thank you for keeping my crime scene warm but I'm here now,' said Detective Inspector Travis, her arch nemesis from West Mercia Police.

Never, since she had made DI had he ever referred to her by rank.

She turned to face him, fully, and returned the favour.

'Tom, by my count, this is the third time you've intruded on a crime scene of mine and walked away empty-handed.'

'I make it one all,' he said, referring to the body of a young manager of a Leisure Centre found in West Hagley.

'Fair enough, and so pleased you solved that case. Oh, hang on, *you* didn't,' she said, realising, as the smile spread across his face, that she'd given him exactly what he'd been seeking. A reaction.

Now she sounded just as childish as he did. If not more so.

He continued. 'I think you'll find that Hunnington is under West Mercia.'

'And Hayley Green is West Mids, so just leave it, Tom. We'll let the grown-ups sort it out.'

'Stone, you know…'

'Tom, over here,' she said, taking a few steps away from the audience that was suddenly more focussed on them than the skull in the ground. 'Are you ever gonna just grow the hell up?' she stormed.

'Stop trying to steal my crime scenes and we wouldn't have a problem, Stone,' he spat back.

'Oh, I think we both know that statement is bollocks,' she said. 'While there is breath in both of our bodies there will be a problem – but stop turning it into a sideshow for the masses. It's childish, unprofessional and beneath even you.'

He glared back at her with a coldness she knew well as more people arrived at the scene behind him.

She turned away and headed back to the activity around the pit.

Doctor A's team members were assembled and changing into white protective suits.

Kim ignored everyone around her and watched as more of the skull was exposed by the techies. It appeared to be lying on its side in the dirt.

One eye socket was exposed confirming, beyond doubt, that it was a human skull they were looking at.

The techs continued to move the soil painstakingly away from the bone. Soon a gaping hole appeared where the nose would have been.

More brushing and gentle trowelling revealed the socket of the other eye.

Kim frowned as the work slowed and then ceased.

A tech took photos of the skull.

'What the hell?…' Bryant asked, as his gaze rested in the same place as hers.

Something unnatural was protruding from the eye.

CHAPTER 5

'It's a bone,' Doctor A said as she stepped down into the hole.

Kim was relieved that hers was not the only expression of confusion around the pit.

How the hell was a bone protruding from the eye socket?

Kim looked to Bryant, who shook his head. Clearly, he'd never seen anything like it before either.

'I don't know which bone it is,' Doctor A continued. 'But this just got a whole lot difficulter.'

No one corrected her.

If the bones were anatomically correct there were clues for the direction of excavation and recovery. Normally the skull would lead to the vertebrae and so on. If the bones were not in their proper place, the process for removal was far more complicated for the scientists.

And for themselves also, Kim thought, turning to Bryant.

'We need to speak to Woody. There's a lot to sort out.'

He nodded his agreement.

Kim leaned forward and explained their departure to the scientist.

'About time, Stone,' Travis said, as they began to walk away. 'You've encroached on my crime scene—'

'It is *my* crime scene, Sergeant Travis,' Doctor A barked. 'You will do well to remember that.'

'It's Detective Inspector,' he corrected frostily.

'My mistake,' Doctor A said, although Kim knew it was no mistake. It was her way of telling him to act his rank.

Kim chose not to look at him as they headed back towards the car.

Her mind was already making a list of requests for Woody. First and foremost was the need to survey the rest of the area. They had found body parts, and the whole field would need to be checked for more.

'Do you think we'll get it?' Bryant asked.

She shrugged in response. She hoped so. Woody had come through for her every other time. Had she never known about the bones she would not have been so determined but once she visited a crime scene it was there in her head. It was now hers.

As they neared the gate, Kim could see that the additional vehicles had taken the place of the minibuses that had transported the students back to class.

The road out was clear except for a gleaming white Audi.

As if by magic, Tracy Frost appeared at the gate just as they reached it.

'Hello, Frost. You're back,' Kim stated.

'Miss me, Stone?'

'Only if my aim was off,' Kim quipped.

Tracy laughed.

There was less animosity between them than there used to be. Saving each other's lives could do that to a relationship.

To be fair to the woman, Tracy had been busy investigating a drugs supply chain that led from the Midlands to the nation's capital.

Kim looked her up and down and was pleased to see the five-inch heels still in place. Good to know things hadn't changed that much.

'So, Inspector?...' Frost said, holding up her notebook.

'I'll save us some time,' Kim said, walking past her. 'No comment, no comment, no comment.'

As she expected, Tracy followed.

'Police presence is excessive for a university training session, eh?'

Kim ignored her.

'I'm guessing you've found something that shouldn't be there. Am I right?'

Kim continued to ignore her.

'Why are there two police forces here again?'

Kim reached the car and stopped walking. 'By my count that's three questions, and I've already given you my answers.'

Bryant coughed to hide his chuckle.

'Okay, just one more,' Tracy said, tossing her long blonde hair over her shoulder.

'You know I'm not going to…'

'How the hell are you going to decide who gets this investigation?' Tracy asked, anyway. 'We're right on the border of the two forces.'

'Are we really?' Kim asked, feigning shock.

'So, you tossing a coin, pissing contest or arm wrestling?' Tracy goaded.

Kim smiled. 'Okay, this one gets an answer. We're gonna take turns kicking you across that field and see who gets the furthest. Best of three. Now move your car.'

Tracy folded her arms over her breasts. 'What if I don't feel like?…'

'Frost,' Kim warned. She'd had enough. 'Your car is gonna move if I have to ram it all the way back down the dirt track.'

Her arms dropped. 'You wouldn't.'

Kim nodded. 'Oh, I would. It ain't my car. It's his,' she said, nodding towards Bryant.

She got in and started the engine.

Tracy hurried backwards.

Kim gave her a little wave and revved the engine three times.

The reporter got into the Audi and began to reverse.

'You wouldn't have, would you, guv?'

Kim said nothing.

There was a body in the ground, and she needed to get back to the station.

Had Bryant really felt the need to ask?

CHAPTER 6

Kim didn't pause at the office before heading straight up to the third floor.

She had no doubt that news of the skull uncovered at Hayley Green would have reached her boss, DCI Woodward, already.

She knocked on the door and waited only a second for his call. He was expecting her.

She stepped into the office and held back the smile that teased at her lips. Never would she get bored of seeing that man sitting behind that desk. Although his six feet height was hidden behind the mahogany desk, his straight back and vertical torso were no less imposing; nor the smooth caramel skin accentuated by the crisp whiteness of a uniform he had earned.

Only six weeks earlier it could have been a very different story. They had never spoken of the incident in Welshpool and they probably never would. But a week after the case that had almost cost his granddaughter her life, Kim had received a solid gold miniature replica of a Triumph T100 motorcycle, her favourite model. With it was a colourful handwritten note from Lissy. And that was as much discussion as there would be.

'Sir, I take it you know that…'

'You found a skull in a field, Stone?'

'Well, it wasn't actually me,' she corrected. She got enough shit for her own shit.

He sat back in his chair. 'Sit down.'

She realised this conversation was going to take longer than she'd hoped. All she wanted to hear was 'it's yours, Stone'. Surely, she didn't need to sit down for that?

'Sir, we need to organise a full survey of the site, GPR equipment and—'

'Slow down, slow down,' he said, holding up his hand. 'There is a geographical issue to deal with first that I gather you and Travis discussed at the scene.'

She just about stopped her eyes from rolling.

Travis must have called his DCI the second she was out of view. She added 'telltale' to the list of his unenviable qualities.

It wasn't important. What was important was the fact that the two DCIs had already spoken, and Woody was not looking pissed off. It boded well for possession.

'Stone, I'm curious to know what happened between you and Travis. Weren't you close once?'

Kim frowned. Close was not a word she would have used in relation to Tom Travis, or anyone else for that matter. But they had been partners and almost friends before he'd defected from West Mids to West Mercia.

But that was before he'd placed her in an untenable position. A few months after the incident he had transferred to a smaller force. Within a month of her making DI before he did.

She had never spoken of it to anyone. And she never would.

She shrugged. 'Just force rivalry, sir,' she answered.

There was no doubt that he didn't believe her but he accepted her response. He laced his fingers. 'You already know the location of this one is a complete nightmare.'

She nodded. She still wasn't hearing those magic words.

'The field itself lies right on the border. West Mercia's Hunnington at one end and our Hayley Green at the other. No one actually knows exactly where the boundary falls.'

Kim knew that Hayley Green consisted mainly of owner/occupied housing stock. It was made up of Causey Farm Estate, St Kenelms Avenue, Squirrels Estate and an estate off Uffmoor Lane.

Hunnington was a village that fell under the Bromsgrove postcode. Originally a township in the parish of Halesowen, it had been transferred to Worcestershire in 1844.

And clearly no one seemed to know where it ended.

'Now, we could get caught up in a pointless fight with our neighbouring force, which serves no purpose to anyone, especially the person who is in the ground.'

Kim's earlier conviction was fading fast. That was way more words than she wanted to hear.

He continued: 'So, having spoken to DCI Walsh at West Mercia and to Superintendent Shaw at Lloyd House, we have reached an agreement that satisfies all parties.'

Kim frowned. The case of the skull in the field was either theirs or it wasn't.

'This will be a joint investigation, led by both yourself and Detective Inspector Travis.'

He sat forward, awaiting her response.

She laughed out loud. 'Oh, sir. I'm sorry, but for a moment there I thought you said "joint investigation".'

'Yes, Stone. I did.'

She stopped laughing.

'Sir, you can't possibly believe…'

'Actually, Stone. I do. As you know, I have long held the belief that forces could and should work more closely together.'

'But—'

He held his hand up to silence her. 'I believe that each police force should maintain their own identity but there are practices and methodologies that could be shared across police in general. We're all trying to do the same job.'

'One team, one vision?' she asked, testily.

'Not quite. But we can all learn from others, Stone. All of us,' he added meaningfully.

She ignored the remark. Her mind was already trying to process the logistics. Two investigating teams, two forensic labs, two pathologists, two SIOs. That was all one more than she was comfortable with.

'But it's doubling up on everything,' she said, wondering how this was a sensible use of anyone's budget.

'It's not going to work that way, Stone. Travis gets operational and you get technical.'

'Technical?' she questioned.

'Laboratory and forensics.'

She frowned. 'So my team?…'

'Will not be joining you on this one and will be working on other cases,' he said, confirming her worst fears.

'Supervised by whom?' she shot back.

'You're a very resourceful individual, Stone. I'm sure you can work it out.'

'But…'

'Travis has the larger team but our forensic services are more efficient than theirs. And they know that.'

Kim was stunned. The details had been arranged. She sensed there was no wiggle room on this at all, but she had to try a token movement.

'You do understand that Travis and I can barely work in the same county, never mind—'

'You are both professional adults,' he stated.

Well, half of us is, she thought to herself.

It had been almost five years since they'd worked together, and it had not ended well. She wondered if Travis was feeling the exact same way as she was right now.

'I'd like for *the record* to reflect that I don't think this is a good idea,' she offered.

'Stone, *the record* had no doubt that's what you'd think but this is evolution. We have to try new things. If you want involvement in this investigation it is on these terms. This is a test case for inter-force collaboration.'

'I'm a guinea pig?' she clarified.

He thought for a second and then nodded. 'Yes, I suppose you are.'

'Sir, do you want this project to fail?' she asked, seriously. Her reputation for playing poorly with others was legendary.

Woody shook his head. 'Why would you think that?'

'Because you're sending me out to work with another force, without Bryant. It's almost like you want me to fu… mess up.'

A brief smile settled on his features.

'Or am I sending you because I know you won't allow it to fail?'

Oh, that was low. How was she supposed to fight that?

Woody handed her a piece of paper. 'This is Tom Travis's address. Pick him up first thing in the morning, make your peace with him in the car and then get on with this case.'

Kim hesitated before taking the offered paper. This was her last chance to refuse. To let someone else take her place, or just hand the investigation to West Mercia.

Could she work with Tom again? she asked herself. After all the bitterness and animosity that had built between them over the last few years? Could either of them let it go?

She could walk away now and work the current caseload with her team. Was she really that desperate to uncover the identity of a skull found in a field and meet the challenge that had been set out before her?

Kim reached out and took the address.

CHAPTER 7

'Righty folks, we need to have a little chat,' Kim said, as she entered the squad room.

She noted that the board had already been wiped clean and the words 'unidentified skull' had been written across the top.

She had taken a walk outside and around the building to work off her irritation. It didn't need to follow her into the squad room. Her team would pick up on her negativity, and she didn't want that.

'So, you guys are going to get a bit of a rest for a while.'

'Really?' Dawson asked.

'Not really,' she offered, smiling. 'The skull case is going to be a joint investigation with West Mercia.'

Three surprised expressions turned her way.

'I'll be working alongside Detective Inspector Travis and his team while maintaining contact with forensics.'

There, the great big ball of tension rolling around her stomach could be explained in one simple sentence.

'So, we have no involvement at all?' Dawson asked, looking up at the board.

Kim shook her head, feeling the dissatisfaction travel around the room.

'You're working with Travis?' Bryant asked.

Kim silently thanked him for noting the obvious.

'What's wrong, Bryant, feeling left out?' Dawson asked.

Bryant smirked. 'Nah, just wondering where I can buy tickets.'

'So, what are we supposed to do?' Dawson asked.

She glanced at his untidy desk. 'I think you have enough to be going on with. Find out if the guy that was assaulted on Friday has regained consciousness yet, and I want Bryant on that with you.'

'You want any follow-up with Paul Chater?' Bryant asked.

She shook her head. The CID team at Brierley Hill had made it clear they required no further involvement from her on that case. Because of her, their questioning had been delayed by three hours awaiting medical authorisation after she'd knocked him off his moped. She had not hesitated to remind them that it was only because of her they had the little shit to question at all.

Dawson rubbed his hands together. 'Fantastic. I get a partner. But we're the same rank so who's in charge?'

'Me,' Kim said. 'And Stacey will continue to be your hub, okay folks?'

They all nodded.

Kim checked the clock on the wall. It was almost five.

'Okay, enough for today,' she said, not sure how much longer she could keep up the pretence. 'We'll brief at seven in the morning,' she added, before stepping into The Bowl.

The frustration was not leaving her as quickly as she'd hoped. If it was her case, her team, they would all have been assigned jobs and tasks by now. Her team would be animated, keen and eager to unearth the clues.

The potential problems were already beginning to stack up in her mind.

'Good sell, there, guv,' Bryant said from the doorway.

She shrugged. There was little point trying to lie to him.

'So, I guess this is goodbye,' he joked, as her phone signalled receipt of a text message.

It was from Doctor A confirming that all facilities were now on site and that recovery would continue in the morning. She knew full well that if it were up to the scientist she would work all night to extract the bones but, like herself, Doctor A had the welfare of a team to consider.

She sent back a short message acknowledging the information, and then dropped her head to the desk and groaned.

'How the hell are you gonna cope with this?' Bryant asked from somewhere above her.

Once again, he appeared to be reading her mind.

CHAPTER 8

17 October 1989

Jacob James opened his eyes and instantly knew four things.

The room was dark around him.

A searing pain surged from the side of his head.

His wrists were bound.

And he was naked.

The panic that seized him was immediate as thoughts and questions flew into his mind but he forced himself to consider one terrifying detail at a time.

The darkness was resting heavily against his bare skin. He blinked twice. He felt the physical action of his eyes opening and closing but the dense blackness of his vision didn't change.

Another dart of panic speared him. He blinked once more and raised his bound hands from his lap in front of his eyes. There was a slight shadow. He was not blind.

The pain in his head was thick and travelled around the entire contour of his skull. He narrowed his eyes, trying to focus through the pain and remember what had happened.

An interview. He knew he'd had an interview.

After so many months of looking, he'd met with the owner of a new printing company in Perry Barr. He'd been hopeful.

After the interview, he'd been going to buy chips for the two of them. To celebrate.

He carefully retraced the steps in his mind, looking for the missing information like a set of car keys.

He had turned into Shaft Street and then… nothing.

He tried to force the memory by picturing himself walking down the familiar road. But it wasn't natural. It was like a film that he was directing instead of a recollection.

As his mind lost focus and wandered from the trail of his memory, the questions flew into his mind.

Where was he?

Who had done this to him?

What the hell had he done?

Why was he being treated this way?

Anger grew inside him as he felt the binding around his wrists, and his naked skin against the wall. He wished his captor were here, now, in front of him. Just one opportunity was all he needed. Although age was no longer on his side, he had learned to fight on the streets back in Jamaica.

But those years were far behind him now. England had given him work, a wife. Family.

A picture of his daughter's face came into his mind.

'Adaje…' he cried out loud.

CHAPTER 9

Bryant rubbed his hands together, sighed, accepted the inevitable and turned to Dawson.

'What we got on that assault, Kev?' he asked.

The guv had popped in before heading for Kidderminster and reiterated her instructions from the previous day. As though he could have forgotten. Her expression had been tight and closed, and he had known her long enough to leave well alone.

During the time he'd worked with Kim Stone he had wondered about the rumours that had whispered through the corridors of the station around five years ago, when she'd been promoted to DI. He had known her only by name and reputation back then but had still not played in the gossip pit. It helped no one.

But what he had seen during the last two years was the tension in her jaw whenever the two of them had collided or even at the mention of Tom Travis's name.

Bryant's daily workload normally involved a slice of tolerance with an extra helping of patience thrown in for good measure. And as he looked towards Dawson he had a feeling his tolerance in both those areas was going to be tested during his boss's secondment.

It wasn't that he particularly disliked his colleague. Yes, he was reckless, sometimes, and yes, he defied authority other times. He was cocky and confident and full of his own opinion. None of this bothered Bryant. Most days he was entertained by it. He had no issue with the kid making mistakes. His problem was that he never seemed to learn from them.

Dawson pulled at the top three folders of the stack in his filing tray, opened the top one and spoke as he read.

'Polish male named Henryk Kowalski, early thirties, found in the car park next to the Job Centre, in town,' he said, nodding his head across the road towards Halesowen.

Bryant knew the car park. It was single storey and full of concrete pillars and dark corners that had seen their fair share of drug deals.

'Is he a user?' he asked.

Dawson shrugged. 'Haven't got anywhere near him since Friday. In and out of consciousness. Nurse said we can have five minutes.'

Bryant frowned. 'Serious injuries, then. Any witnesses?'

Dawson nodded. 'A young kid named Marie, who had just closed up a jewellery shop for the night.'

'Witness first?' said Dawson.

'Victim first?' said Bryant.

'Permission to just follow yow two around for the day?' Stacey asked, smirking at them both.

'Victim first,' Bryant confirmed. 'Need his full account of the incident so we know what needs corroborating.'

Dawson thought for a moment.

'Okay, victim first,' he agreed.

Bryant wondered if every minor decision was going to result in disagreement and debate.

He stood up and grabbed his jacket.

God help them when it came to deciding on lunch.

CHAPTER 10

Kim pulled up at the address given to her by Woody, the day before. The semi-detached property, complete with box porch, lay on a small housing estate in Blakedown, an area between Hagley and Kidderminster. The house was as she'd expected it to be: bland and uninspiring; completely reflective of its owner, she decided grumpily.

The morning had not started well due to a sudden freeze during the night which had left her eleven-year-old Golf GTI wearing an ice jacket. Cars with a decade under their belts didn't do anything automatically so she'd grabbed the scraper and de-icer and broke it free.

The pipes in her house had frozen as though this first freeze of the winter had taken them by surprise, and her last bottle of water had been poured into Barney's bowl.

If she believed in kismet, she'd think the universe was preparing her for the day ahead with Detective Inspector Travis.

Their text conversation the previous evening had been brief and direct, the syllables counted on the fingers of one hand. Clearly, he was as excited as she was at the prospect of them working together. But like her, had probably been told there was no choice.

Travis's familiar form stepped out, attired in black trousers, black tie, white shirt and navy fleece: the uniform that had followed him throughout his career as a detective.

Kim couldn't help but feel that a fleece prevented any clothes from looking smart.

His height was similar to Bryant's six foot, but Tom was much broader, more bear-like than her colleague. His hair was now more salt than pepper and the short beard almost white.

He turned his back on her as a woman appeared in the doorway. They hugged briefly before he turned her way.

There was no acknowledgment of her presence, and his face was set as he strolled down the path.

Kim sighed heavily.

He opened the car door and folded himself into the passenger seat.

Kim glanced his way. 'Look, Tom, I'm sure we feel the same way about—'

'Don't speak to me about anything other than the case,' he said, staring straight ahead.

'I'd be happier not to speak to you at all,' she retorted. 'But I'm not sure that's what our bosses had in mind.'

Happy that the olive branch had been well and truly snapped in her face, she put the car into gear and pulled away.

Yes, kismet had definitely been trying to give her the heads-up.

Kim decided to remain in her own head as she headed towards Kidderminster Police Station: a thin sliver of a building that was flat-faced, three storeys high and eighteen windows to its length.

West Mercia was the fourth largest force in the country. Covering 2,868 miles of Herefordshire, Shropshire and Worcestershire, serving a population of 1.19 million, with almost two and a half thousand officers.

It differed from her own force as it covered both densely populated areas, like Telford and Shrewsbury, as well as sparsely populated rural areas.

* * *

She parked the car and followed Travis into the station.

He stopped at the front desk to pick up her temporary identification, which she took without speaking and jammed into her pocket.

He offered a few nods as they worked their way through the building, pausing to introduce her to no one. The strange looks she received made her feel like a curiosity or a suspect at his side.

The low hum of conversation stopped completely as they entered the detective's squad room.

Kim was immediately struck by the difference in layout to her own set-up.

For a start, the room was four times bigger than the one at Halesowen. The wall opposite the door held a total of eight wipe boards fixed together to make one long board. Two doorways were cut into the top wall like a pair of ears.

The left led to an office, and the right appeared to be a small kitchen.

But what she didn't like was that the eight desks, four on each side of the room, all faced towards the front, like a classroom.

There were no prizes for guessing who stood beside the small square table at the top that was holding a single pot plant with purple blooms.

Five of the desks were occupied, and ten curious eyes rested on her as she followed Travis down the aisle that separated them.

'Weird floor plan,' she said, following him inside the solid walls from where he could see a whole lot of nothing.

'All eyes focussed on the boards,' he said, shortly.

Like detention, Kim thought.

Her own view was that if it took staring at a wipe board to keep their concentration they were in some bloody trouble.

'Do you always?…'

'Look, Stone. You run your team and I'll run mine, okay?' he snapped.

She'd only wanted to know if he always briefed at nine o'clock. It was beginning to feel like half the day was already gone.

She offered no reply and waited while he gathered papers and a clipboard.

Eventually he headed out of the office and across to the head of the room. Kim put her hands in her front pockets and leaned against the door frame.

Travis began the briefing by introducing her. She guessed he'd explained the situation to his team, as she had to hers. Once he had offered her a name for each of his team she nodded in their general direction. She received a half smile from the single female in the room. The ratio saddened her.

Travis rubbed his hands in front of him. 'Okay, guys and… girls,' he said, nodding towards Lynda with a smile.

She rolled her eyes in response.

'We'll do a quick catch-up before I ask you all to hand in your homework. And first we'll go to… Gibbs,' he said, casting his eyes around the room and landing on the smartly dressed man in his early forties.

'Yeah, pick on the guy in the suit,' Gibbs offered.

Travis held up a hand and addressed the team. 'I think we can all work out that Gibbs has court this afternoon,' he said, raising one eyebrow.

A few chuckles sounded around the room.

'Go on,' Travis urged.

Kim could not tear her eyes away from her former colleague. This was not the man she had fought with across crime scenes for the last few years. It was not the man who had shown up yesterday, and it certainly wasn't the man she'd driven in to work ten minutes earlier.

But it was the man she remembered working with.

'Finally got a full confession last night from Dalglish,' Gibbs answered. 'Admitted to driving the car in three of the four robberies. Insisted he didn't do the fourth but gave us the name of the kid that did.'

Travis nodded with satisfaction. 'And?…'

Gibbs growled. 'Yes, you were right, guv. Revealing his mother was waiting for him outside loosened his tongue quite a bit.'

Travis smiled. 'I met her. I'm not surprised. I'd be more frightened of her than court, if I'd been in his shoes.'

'Still waiting for a decision from CPS on the Turner rape case,' Johnson offered, from the second row. His attempts to hide a prematurely receding hairline were not wholly successful.

Travis's mouth tightened. 'Chase them again, I don't want him back on the streets any time soon.'

Johnson nodded.

'Okay, homework time,' Travis said. 'And it's back to Gibbs.'

'The land where the body has been found is leased by the Cowley family,' Gibbs said. 'Which consists of father, Jeff; daughter, Fiona, and son, Billy. Originally leased around thirty years ago by Jeff Cowley's father.'

Travis nodded and turned to the only other female in the room.

'Lynda?'

'The Preece family own the land and have done for fifty-seven years. Robson Preece is head of the family and has one daughter, named Mallory. She has two sons, Bartholomew and Dale. All live together at Donnay Hall.'

'Does Mallory have a husband?' Kim asked.

Travis threw her a murderous look, as Lynda turned to answer.

'Killed in a boating accident years ago.'

She nodded and closed her mouth, as Travis turned to the guy with ginger curls being held back by a Union Jack bandana.

Kim swallowed her irritation. Clearly she was not allowed to speak.

'Penn?' Travis asked.

'Started compiling a database for missing persons. Working backwards until we have some idea of time frame and description.'

Kim was impressed. That was one hell of a task to start with no physical details of their victim.

'Okay,' Travis said, picking up the pot plant. 'Wilma goes to Penn today for his proactive thinking.'

He strode across the room and placed the purple flower on the edge of Penn's desk.

A murmur of good-natured dissatisfaction rumbled around the room as Penn performed a mock bow to his audience.

'Okay,' Travis said. 'Focus is on learning everything there is to know about these two families. We have to rule them—'

'Yeah, sorry to interrupt, guv,' Lynda said, looking at her screen. 'Just had a report come in about an attempted abduction.' She continued to read the information on the screen. 'Apparently some guy tried to haul a woman into a van on the Worcester Road.'

'Well, as our newly appointed Detective Sergeant, Lynda, I suggest you get on it. We don't have the luxury of working one case here at West Mercia.'

Kim smarted at the misinformed arrow that was aimed at her and wondered how long her mouth would obey her brain during these briefings.

'Will do, guv,' Lynda answered, chirpily.

It was as Travis began reallocating tasks that she felt her phone vibrate in her pocket.

The text message was short, direct and from Doctor A.

'Get here, now.'

CHAPTER 11

Bryant hated the smell of Russells Hall hospital. Or any hospital, for that matter, but this one in particular. The ever-present aroma of disinfectant always tugged at his memories, and he had lost too many people in this damn place.

His father had died in the ambulance outside the building when a second heart attack in twenty minutes had pushed his heart beyond repair. His mother had lost her life to breast cancer in the Intensive Care Unit, and it was where he and his wife had lost the two baby boys that should have been born before Laura.

It was those two losses that came to mind every time he stepped into the building.

And today, as he walked silently beside Dawson to the Surgical Ward, was no different.

The six-mile journey from the station to Russells Hall had also passed without conversation. It was woefully obvious they had never worked together closely before, and their working practices could probably not have differed more. Bryant knew his methodical, logical approach was viewed as 'slow and boring' by his younger colleague. And he himself didn't ascribe to the gung-ho style of investigation adopted by Dawson. He had already wondered if he would spend all his time carrying out mental risk assessments.

Dawson's methods often bordered on impetuous, and normally that would be the guv's problem. But right now it felt like his.

Dawson spoke into the intercom at the entrance to the Surgical Ward. He had called ahead and the staff were expecting them.

They approached the desk, and Ward Sister, Jane, smiled.

'You have five minutes. He's still in pretty bad shape,' she said, firmly.

'How bad?' Dawson asked, offering her a charming smile.

'Better now he's back in the land of the living. He's in a lot of pain from the seven broken bones in his legs and arms.'

'Seven?' Bryant clarified.

She nodded. 'There's a lot of soft tissue damage as well so he's going to be hurting for a good few weeks.'

'Thank you,' Bryant offered.

'Bed two, bay three and your time starts now.'

Bryant immediately altered his walking pattern to reduce the sound of his shoes on the floor. Dawson did not and strode into the bay before him, his heels heralding his arrival.

'Jesus Christ,' he said, as the man slowly turned towards them.

The face was swollen and bloated, as though parts of it were being inflated at different speeds – and it appeared to have been coloured in by children daubing his stretched shiny skin with shades of red, purple and black.

Bryant could make out a row of about seven stitches above his left eye and another railway track along his jawline. His left arm and right leg were encased in plaster.

'Henryk Kowalski?' Dawson asked, although no clarification was needed.

He nodded and winced.

Dawson introduced them both and took the easy chair to the man's left.

'I won't even ask how you're feeling,' he said, quietly. His sympathetic smile and lowered tone caught Bryant by surprise.

'Can you tell us anything about what happened to you, Henryk?'

If it was up to him, Bryant thought, he would be asking short, direct questions to get as much information as possible in the time they had available. Additionally, the effort required by this man to answer open-ended questions was too much.

'Henryk, how many people hurt you?' he asked before Dawson's follow-up.

He shook his head and held up one finger, two fingers then a shrug.

A few yes or no questions would have served them better.

'Did you know them?' Dawson asked, assuming there had been more than one.

He moved his head to the left slightly to indicate no.

'Did they say anything while they were hurting you?'

He nodded.

'Can you manage a few words, just to give us an idea of the kind of things they were saying?'

He swallowed three times.

'Polish… bastard… scum…'

Bryant was puzzled. 'They knew you were Polish?'

He nodded.

'I know it's difficult for you to speak, Henryk, but have you been having problems with anyone recently?' Bryant asked. This was beginning to look more personal than a random attack.

His voice was barely more than a whisper. 'Normal… insults… we ignore… my wife… worries…'

Bryant held up his hand. Too much effort and too much pain for no useful information. He didn't want to cause the poor guy needless suffering.

'Could it have been someone from the pub?' Dawson asked.

Henryk shook his head. 'No drinking… no money,' he said with a weak attempt at a smile.

'What exactly were you doing there, Henryk?' Dawson asked, finally favouring the direct approach.

Bryant knew they were thinking the same thing. Drugs.

'Job,' he said, simply.

Dawson looked up, and his confusion was clear.

'Henryk, the Job Centre doesn't normally open at ten o clock at night.'

He shook his head and winced again. 'Not… that… kind,' he said quietly.

His good thumb and forefinger rubbed together.

'Cash… pay.'

Ah, thought Bryant. That made much more sense.

Immigrants, both legal and illegal, used the underground work channels to make money. It was estimated that as many as half a million migrants were being used by rogue gangmasters to supply cheap labour to the hospitality, construction and farming industries. Men and women were being placed in dangerous conditions with no training and low pay because they had families to support.

'No… choice,' he said with despair. 'Wife… children… hungry…'

Bryant put aside his feelings of outrage. As a man, a taxpayer and a police officer he hated the underground cash working trade. But he'd also been the primary breadwinner for his wife and daughter for twenty years and could not be sure he wouldn't have done the same thing to feed his family if he'd needed to.

Perhaps they were looking for people who knew where these workers were collected.

'Did they say anything else at all?' Bryant pushed.

He shook his head. 'If that… lady… had not…'

'Don't think about that now, Henryk. You got a damn good beating but you're going to be—'

'But… I saw… the knife,' he said, as a tear fell from his eye.

'Your attackers had a knife?'

He nodded.

'Henryk, how did you know to be there at that time?' Dawson asked.

'Text… message,' he said. 'I receive… text message.'

The ward sister signalled to them from the end of the bay just as Henryk's eyes began to droop.

Boy, she had called that good. It was five minutes to the second.

'Do you have the phone?' Bryant asked, moving the chair back. Stacey might be able to track the sender.

Henryk shook his head, wearily. 'Lost… stolen…'

Dawson nodded his understanding. He would check with the attending officers if a phone had been found.

They said their goodbyes and headed out of the ward.

Bryant paused as the door closed behind them.

'A knife and a text message to lure him to the location,' Dawson said.

'You thinking what I'm thinking?' Bryant asked.

'Tell me what you're thinking.'

Bryant sighed. 'This is no ordinary assault. What we have here is attempted murder.'

CHAPTER 12

Kim felt herself calming down once they were back in the car. Her car.

Now she felt like she was back in control. Driving the case forward at her own speed.

Travis made notes beside her.

The personable, pleasant man she'd seen in the squad room had been left there. The greyed out substitution had followed her to the car.

She couldn't help wishing it was Bryant beside her. They would have been tossing ideas about, spouting theories, discussing, debating. Moving the case along.

Kim took the left turn towards the dirt road, sharply. His pen slipped, and he shot her an irritable glance.

He should already know that she ought not be left alone to make her own fun.

He slid the pen into the spine of the folder and closed it as she passed the pub car park that was holding the press. Tracy Frost was positioned at the front, talking to a kid in a colourful shirt beneath his Firetrap jacket. Tracy paused and offered Kim a slight nod as she passed by.

'I certainly don't miss that poor excuse for a human being,' Travis said.

Kim bristled. Three months ago it might have been the one single thing they could have agreed on.

'She's not that bad,' she said, remembering everything she'd found out about Tracy Frost.

'The woman has no redeeming qualities at all,' he insisted.

She knew his game. He could tell he had touched a nerve and now he wanted to prod it with a metal fork until she bit. He would happily lure her into an argument and then go running to his boss claiming she was being difficult. His boss would believe him. Hell, even her boss would believe him. She hated the joint investigation as much as he did but it wouldn't fail because of her. Not on the first day.

'And setting the precedent for the majority of this investigation, Tom, we shall agree to disagree.'

She saw the flash of disappointment as she parked the car.

She got out and headed towards the site, not caring if he caught up with her. When he did he was clutching the leather document holder like a safety blanket.

'No one here needs insurance,' she said, looking at his wallet.

'You do it your way and I'll do it—'

'As awkwardly as you can,' she interrupted.

Kim observed that there were at least twenty people milling around the small area, and yet, the voices were hushed, reverent, respectful. Ultimately they were dealing with a grave.

A white tent had been erected around the pit. This was for the purpose of preservation and privacy. The techs would be able to investigate the immediate area without the added complication of the elements. And although the press had been cordoned half a mile away, it was not unknown for a news helicopter to suddenly appear in the sky.

Black clad officers appeared to be searching the outer perimeter of the field, while the white suited techs had claimed the immediate area around the pit. She knew they would be looking for footprints, tyre tracks, even cigarette ends. Anything that might offer them a clue. It was procedure but she had to wonder at how much value this held when they had no clue how long the skull had been buried.

Kim would have liked to see the GPR team on site. They needed to know if there were more bones, but she understood the ground could not be further contaminated until the surface of the field had been thoroughly combed for clues.

Kim headed for the pit that had deepened by more than a foot since she'd last seen it, but little progress seemed to have been made with the excavation itself. The bones were not coming out of the ground, and without them she had no hope of moving this case forward.

Currently her victim had no name, no identity. A cause of frustration for her on any case.

She found the scientist kneeling in the middle of the hole, talking earnestly to a white-suited female beside her. The upper part of the white protective suite was tied around her waist by the arms.

A forensic photographer was taking pictures from every angle.

Kim cleared her throat.

Doctor A turned and narrowed her eyes.

'I do not understand this English habit of throat cleaning to announce one's arrival. Why not a hello?'

'Hello, Doctor A,' Kim said.

'So, finalling you are here,' she said, looking beyond Kim. 'And I see you brought your friend.'

'Doctor A,' Kim warned.

The scientist had witnessed their exchange the day before and knew they were not friends.

Travis offered no response. His attention had been caught by something to their far left.

Doctor A gave her a devilish smile before guiding her towards the hole.

'Please, come take a look at Lesley, our victim.'

The scientist had a habit of giving victims ambiguously sexed names until she had a true identity.

Kim peered down into the pit as Travis appeared beside her. She heard the slow scratch of the zip as he opened his leather wallet. She had a premonition that sound would be really annoying to her by the end of the case.

Kim took a closer look and frowned. She had expected more progress.

Doctor A caught her expression. 'Frozen,' she explained.

It was almost ten thirty, and the temperature had now reached a balmy six degrees.

Kim nodded her understanding but her frown remained. The team had exposed more bones but the placement was unlike anything she had seen before.

'That's a metacarpal bone, protruding from the eye,' Doctor A said, taking her hand. She pressed on the bone between her knuckle and first joint. 'This one. And I think the proximal phalanx is still attached,' she said, pressing further down Kim's hand.

'You're telling me our victim has a finger in the eye?' Kim asked.

Doctor A nodded.

Kim tried to imagine any scenario where that made sense.

There was none.

'Any idea how long he's been in there?' Kim asked. For now she would presume a male identity.

Doctor A shook her head. 'Not yet but there is something you should know before we go any further.'

'Go on,' Kim said, following Doctor A to the edge of the pit.

'Do you see that bone sticking out of the ground over there?'

Kim nodded, as Travis stepped to the edge of the tent and looked outside. Fair enough that he didn't like Doctor A all that much but he could damn well respect her expertise.

'That appears to be a radius,' Doctor A said, now taking her arm and tracing a line from her elbow to her wrist.

Kim was unsure when she'd turned into a presentation aide but she allowed it to pass.

'It seems to be a long way from the rest of the body,' Kim said. The physiology of this skeleton was not making sense to her.

'Initial analysis of the soil is throwing up anomalies. There are elements that do not belong here. Samples have been sent to the lab.'

Kim was puzzled.

'Doctor A, what are you trying to say?'

'I'm saying I don't think this is the first place our victim was buried.'

Kim was confused. 'But, why?—'

'Excuse me, Doctor, but is that man one of yours?' Travis asked from the tent doorway.

Kim followed Doctor A to where he was standing and looked out.

In the middle of the field stood a solitary male dressed from head to toe in dark clothing.

Doctor A began to shake her head. 'He is not one of mine,' she said.

'Are you sure?' Travis asked. 'He was here when we arrived.'

'If he was one of mine he would not be standing still,' she said, simply.

Kim looked at Travis and they exited the tent together.

She primed herself to start running as the gap began to close between them and the trespasser. As he was not supposed to be there she expected him to start moving away at the sight of them.

He remained still, staring in their direction, his hands wedged into the pockets of the long coat he was wearing.

'Not exactly field attire,' she observed from a distance of thirty feet.

'Cashmere overcoat, looks like Dunhill, and I could probably just about buy you lunch with the change from two grand,' Travis replied.

'You'd buy me lunch?' she asked, sarcastically.

'Well, no, but…'

'Excuse me, sir,' Kim called from fifteen feet. 'You have no business being here right now.'

The man offered no reaction as she came to rest directly in front of him.

She guessed him to be mid-thirties. His hair was black with just a touch of grey at the temples. Thick, dark lashes framed piercing blue eyes that were serious and cold.

'I have every reason to be here, officer. You are standing on my land.'

'Mr Preece?' she asked.

'Dale Preece,' he confirmed, making no effort to remove his hand from his coat pocket for a handshake.

'How did you get here, Mr Preece?' she asked, looking around.

He remained silent and looked beyond her to the white tent.

'I must ask you to leave the area,' she said, reasonably. 'This is a police investigation, and you could be contaminating a crime scene.'

'I would like to know what exactly has been found,' he said.

'You will know in due course, sir. We will be along to speak to you during our investigation.'

'Have you spoken to the Cowley family yet?'

Kim opened her mouth to answer when Travis stepped forward. 'Mr Preece, you really need to leave the area. Now.'

Kim bit her tongue as Dale Preece appraised them once more before turning and heading to the far side of the field.

Kim was under no illusion that he had left because it suited him to do so.

'Don't you ever do that to me again,' she rasped. 'It was in hand,' she said, turning back towards the tent.

He made no effort to catch her up or respond to her instruction.

'Inspector, a moment,' Doctor A said, as she passed by the tent. She took two steps back and entered.

The scientist reached for a long bone lying at the far edge of the pit.

'This is a femur,' she said, quietly, as Travis entered the tent. She took a pencil from behind her ear, and pointed at the rounded ball shape at one end.

'This is the fovea capitis, and down here is the medial condyle and…'

'Doctor A, I know what a femur is, and I would expect to find two here so why the fascination?' Kim asked, impatiently.

'Because, Inspector, this is femur number three.'

'I'm sorry, Doctor, but what exactly are you saying?' Travis asked, unnecessarily.

The doctor didn't hide her irritation as she spelled it out.

'What I'm saying, Inspector, is that unless Lesley had more than two legs, we are dealing with a second victim.'

CHAPTER 13

Bryant stopped the car outside a tiny terraced house in Coombs Wood. The property overlooked the valley that had once been home to the Stewarts & Lloyds tube works. Back in the 1950s the site had supplied more than 3,000 local jobs and had been known for looking after their workforce. The 56 acre site had been swallowed up by the British Steel Corporation in 1967 when the steel industry was nationalised for the second time. The works had eventually closed in 1990.

A twelve-year-old white Mini parked along the street confirmed their witness was at home.

'Anything?' Bryant asked as Dawson ended his calls.

'Nothing,' Dawson confirmed. 'Definitely no phone collected at the scene.'

'Damn it,' Bryant said. He still wasn't convinced that Henryk's story was true, but if it was, the phone message could have offered them a clue as to who had arranged to meet him at the car park.

'And let me do the talking on this one,' Dawson said, as Bryant locked the car.

'Why?' he asked.

He shrugged. 'A young girl…' he said, as though that explained everything.

Bryant knew his colleague was young and good-looking. How that helped with interviewing a witness he wasn't sure.

The door was opened by an attractive woman who appeared to be early thirties. Long blonde hair was tied up in a ponytail, and grey jeans hugged a shapely figure.

'Marie West?' Dawson asked, holding up his identification.

'My daughter,' she said, standing back for them to enter. 'I'm Christie West.'

Bryant hid his surprise. How old had she been when she'd given birth, twelve?

As he stepped inside, his nostrils were assaulted by a smell he knew well. Dogs. No matter how well you tried to eradicate the aroma they insisted on leaving something behind.

Two Jack Russells hurtled down the hallway towards him, yapping excitedly.

The woman leaned down and expertly caught one in each arm.

'Marie, police are here,' she called up the stairs.

A quick look around told Bryant it was just the two of them. Ladies' trainers were parked beside the mat. A collection of hats, scarves and gloves erupted from two hangers behind the door.

'She's not going back to that shop,' the woman said, as Marie appeared at the top of the stairs. 'Having one staff member on for late-night opening,' she said, shaking her head. 'Not happening.'

'Mum, I have to go back.'

'Try it, love,' Christie said, putting the dogs down and scooting them in the direction of the kitchen. 'If I have to lock that door and physically restrain you, I will.'

One look at her face and Bryant believed her.

'I wasn't hurt,' Marie said, rolling her eyes.

Christie looked his way, sensing a fellow parent in him.

His own daughter was the exact same age as Marie, and he allowed the smile to rest briefly on his lips.

Marie would never understand that her mother was now consumed with nightmarish visions of what might have been. Men, darkness, violence – and her daughter, all alone. He got it.

'I've disagreed with members of staff being alone late at night. Kids given the responsibility of locking the premises. She wouldn't let me fetch her just to be safe and—'

'Mum, please, I'm fine,' Marie said, reaching the bottom of the stairs. She looked at her mother and smiled tolerantly. Side by side, they looked more like sisters.

A look passed between them. These two were a team.

'Okay, okay, I'll make coffee,' Christie said.

Marie guided them into a front room that was small but furnished tastefully and to scale.

A two-seater sofa and a single chair huddled around a fireplace. Two occasional glass tables were placed either side. A matching glass unit supported a flat-screen television and DVD player. The laminate flooring helped to add to the illusion of more space.

Bryant remained standing behind the sofa while Dawson took the single chair.

'I know that last night must have been quite a shock for you,' Dawson said, surprising Bryant. The kid's interviewing skills were not as coarse as he'd expected.

Marie placed a bright smile onto her face.

'It's okay. I'm okay,' she said, nodding vigorously.

A deep swallow gave her away.

'Did you sleep much?' Dawson asked, perceptively.

Very few people could witness what she had and bounce back immediately.

Bryant remembered the first major incident he'd attended as a police officer. A kid had been stabbed in Lye High Street. When he'd arrived the paramedics were struggling to stop the blood flow from the male's inner thigh. He had concentrated on his own job of questioning witnesses and had eventually finished his shift and gone home, feeling fine and unaffected.

His dreams had been filled with images of streaming blood-filled rivers and waterfalls. Eventually he had risen early, headed for the gym and beat seven shades out of the punchbag.

Feelings had to come out. And they would find a way. If this young girl held in negative emotion for the sake of her mother, it would bite her in the end.

'Can you tell me what happened?' Dawson asked, gently.

She nodded and sat forward in the seat, her hands neatly folded.

'The first thing was the sound. I had my back turned. I was locking the door.'

She made the motion with her right hand.

She kept her eyes on Dawson. 'It was sickening, the cry, like an animal being hurt. At first I thought a dog had been hit by a car. It took me a minute to see where it was coming from. I didn't know it was a person.

'I crossed the road, and I could tell the noise was coming from the car park, but at the back. And then I heard a voice…' Again she swallowed the emotion down her throat and into her body.

The door opened and Christie entered with a tray that she placed on the glass table beside Dawson.

Dawson offered her a smile of thanks then turned back to her daughter.

The woman stepped back but didn't leave the room.

'Go on,' Dawson urged.

Bryant watched with interest as she continued.

'I know I should have stopped and called the police, but I just kept moving forward. I could hear punches and kicks landing,' she said, as her fists began to clench. 'And horrible names…' she said, shaking her head.

'Was there any accent to the voices you heard, Marie?'

She thought for a moment and shook her head. 'Local, I think.'

'What happened next?' Dawson asked.

'I stood still for a second, not knowing what to do. My phone rang. The noise stopped.'

Bryant looked to the mother. She offered a wry smile that acknowledged it had been her calling.

'There was a pause and then I heard footsteps running along the back of the cars.'

Bryant knew the layout. It was single storey, one lane in, one lane out.

'Did you see them at all?' Dawson asked.

Marie shook her head.

Bryant imagined they were running away along the exit aisle, and Marie's viewpoint was blocked by cars.

They were going to get no description from her.

Marie looked to her mother for reassurance.

Bryant knew he was looking at a good kid who had never been any trouble. She would have wanted to do nothing that would make her mother's life any harder.

'What did you do next?' he asked.

Dawson shot him a look that said they had everything they were going to get from this witness. And they had. Almost.

'I called out. He groaned quietly, and I ran over. I knew they were gone so I knelt down and… I told him it would be okay, and then I called the ambulance.'

The hesitation between actions was what he'd been waiting for.

Bryant leaned forward and spoke gently. 'Marie, do you have his phone?'

Her face coloured instantly 'His phone?' she repeated.

Bryant nodded. 'You've not done anything wrong. I've seen police officers instinctively pick something up without considering the evidential repercussions. But it could help our investigation.'

She hesitated.

'You've done nothing wrong,' he emphasised.

Her lip quivered but she nodded and pushed herself to her feet. She left the room and her mother's concerned eyes followed her.

Bryant turned to her mother. 'Has she cried yet?'

Christie shook her head. 'She rarely cries. She's a very brave girl.'

'She's holding it in,' Bryant said, kindly. 'Get her to keep talking about it.'

'How do I get her to let go?' she asked.

'Ask about his injuries,' Dawson piped up from the sofa. 'And get her to talk about the noises she heard. Those are the things that will keep her awake.'

Bryant nodded his agreement as Marie re-entered the room.

The old cream Nokia had been wrapped in cling film.

'I thought…'

'It's okay,' Bryant said, taking the phone from her.

From a useable evidence perspective this was as good as a confession written in pencil. But they could look at it for clues.

'Thank you for your help, Marie. If we need…'

'There was something I heard that seemed strange,' Marie said, 'but I don't know if I heard it right.'

'Anything at all,' Dawson offered.

She scrunched up her face as though listening to the words in her mind once more.

'The attacker… I'm sure he was telling the man on the ground to close his eyes.'

'Close his eyes?' Bryant queried. Seemed like a strange request to him.

She shrugged and shook her head. 'I think I must have heard wrong,' she said.

They said their goodbyes and got into the car.

'So, what do you think of that?' Bryant asked.

Dawson shook his head dismissively. 'She must have heard wrong. Why would the attacker tell him to close his eyes when he had every intention of killing him? Makes no sense,' Dawson said, taking out his phone.

Bryant agreed with his colleague; Marie must have been mistaken.

But a very small part of him wasn't so sure.

CHAPTER 14

Stacey replaced the receiver and sat back. For a moment there had been some animation. Some activity to cut through the silence of the squad room. It hadn't lasted long and the air had once again fallen silent around her.

The phone from the incident was on its way to her and that was about it. Her whole job list from Dawson and Bryant had taken approximately seven and a half minutes.

Stacey couldn't help but feel her skills were not being fully utilised. If her fingers were still, she was underworked.

Normally, the peace and quiet of the office was filled by the activity in her brain. She didn't notice it as her thoughts whirred from one task to the next and her tapping keyboard tried to keep pace.

And although she spent many hours working alone while the rest of the team was out in the field, the days rushed by; the end of shift normally taking her by surprise. Already she was missing the constant calls from the boss; check this, research that, analyse this, dig into that. She knew this was not the boss's choice but she resented the fact those calls were going somewhere else.

She sighed heavily and checked her emails again. Nothing new. She drummed her fingers on the desk and looked around the office.

Her eyes rested on an eerily empty whiteboard. She had already wiped away the 'unidentified skull' title daubed by Bryant.

With little else to do, she stood and stepped around to Dawson's desk. How he found anything in this mess just astounded her. Bryant's desk was not clinically organised and tidy, like her own, but there was an order that matched his methodical mind. Dawson's desk was Armageddon, and she couldn't stand it a minute longer.

Stacey pushed away his chair and began separating the papers, matching them to the relevant case file. She rolled her eyes as a few stray baguette crumbs fell from a stack of leaflets.

Within ten minutes the piles were orderly except for his bottom tray. She knew it was where he filed 'don't know what to do with it so I'll leave it until later' stuff.

She pulled out the pile and began to sort it. Perversely, he wouldn't even notice what she'd done. For an astute detective, Dawson missed a lot.

She moved a half completed expense form to reveal a handwritten page. The toner mark along the top told her it was a photocopy.

The two words at the top of the page caught her attention.

'Dear Mum'

Her stomach turned when she realised it was the suicide note of Justin Reynolds. Dawson had removed it from the scene, copied it to attach to his statement, and returned the original to the family.

The simplicity of those two words being written as though leaving a note about football or a reminder to pick something up for tea. Especially when it was the last thing he would ever write, the last thoughts he would ever communicate. The vision of his youthful face and teenage existence at odds with the blood spattered wall had not yet left her mind.

Stacey felt she should do him the honour of listening.

She slid down into Dawson's chair and began to read.

'Dear Mum,

I am sorry for everything. I'm sorry I couldn't explain it to you. Whatever happens, whatever you find out it's not your fault. It's mine and it's who I've become. I just can't live with myself and what I've done. I'm not the person you think I am. Not any more. I'm sorry, mum, so sorry for everything'

Stacey ignored the slight tremble in her hand as she placed the letter back in the bottom tray on the desk.

It was no longer their case, as there were no suspicious circumstances.

The boy was dead and it was not their problem. A family was broken, stunned and bewildered but it wasn't their concern.

Oh, but she recognised elements of the letter.

The first few words were written strongly, neatly, with conviction; smaller letters, more focussed concentration. As the letter progressed the words got bigger, more untidy as emotion controlled the pen. The last few words, scrawled, messy, at the heart of the pain and then nothing. A half page of white nothingness. Acceptance and death.

Stacey bit back the tears forming in her eyes.

Oh yes, she recognised the letter all right.

CHAPTER 15

'So, what did you think of our landowner turning up at the site?' Kim asked, weaving through the traffic. She could no longer cope with the interminable silence of the car.

'Sorry, are you talking about the guy I spotted and you did not?' Travis asked smartly.

Kim gripped the steering wheel harder, wishing he was not correct.

So, clearly she was presented with the choice of complete silence or petty little digs.

'Seemed very interested in whether we'd spoken to the Cowley family,' she observed.

Travis shrugged. 'He's bound to be interested. Human remains have been found on his property. Wouldn't you want to know what was going on?'

'Yeah but there was an arrogance there, an expectation of getting his own way. A sense of entitlement.'

'Not surprised you'd pick up on that, Stone,' he mumbled as he opened his leather folder and made a note.

Okay, perhaps complete silence was better after all, she thought, biting her tongue. She wondered if four hours was really too soon to drive back to her boss and concede defeat? She decided it probably was.

The ringing of Travis's phone startled her.

He answered, listened, looked her way, cursed and hung up.

'What?' she asked.

'The Cowley residence,' he said.

'Yeah, we're on our way,' she snapped. What did he want from her? Travel at the speed of light in an eleven-year-old Golf.

'Well, step on it because someone there has just been shot.'

CHAPTER 16

Bryant pulled up outside a mid-terrace house with heavy green velour curtains suffocating the small downstairs window and a board in place of glass upstairs.

'You sure this is the address?' he asked Dawson. The property looked abandoned.

'Number twenty-three,' he confirmed.

Bryant got out of the car and almost heard the swish of net curtain as people had a nose out of their windows. He took a look around. It was a small street. The houses had no front gardens so the upstairs windows faced each other across the narrow road.

He approached the door and knocked. He heard a female voice shout something in Polish.

'Jesus, look at this,' Dawson said, peering closer at the door. Although painted over, scratch marks into the wood were still evident. The new paint had simply settled in the lines.

Bryant counted seven different profanities and insults that had been scribed into the wood.

The door opened to reveal a slim mousy woman dressed in a washed-out grey tracksuit. A baby was climbing over her shoulder.

'Mrs Kowalski?' Dawson asked.

She nodded but didn't step back as she continued to pat the child on the bare back.

The aroma of a soiled nappy wafted towards him.

'Who are you?' she asked, suspiciously.

Dawson introduced them, as the baby offered a loud and satisfying burp and immediately began to cry.

'May we come in?' Bryant asked, eager for the door to be closed. The child would catch its death.

She stepped back as a toddler came hurtling towards them. He ran into her calf and fell to the ground. The toddler began to cry. She leaned backwards and pulled him to his feet by the wrist with her free hand.

Bryant guessed the toddler was around eighteen months old.

'*Niech to szlag*,' she breathed, as she ushered him away from the door.

He stopped crying and continued on his journey, rustling a nappy as he went. A lime-green potty was visible amongst the building blocks, books and soft toys that stifled the carpet.

A third cry sounded, and Bryant saw there was another baby, a twin, in a rocker beside the sofa.

The woman placed baby one on the sofa then lifted baby two onto the sofa, placed baby one into the rocker and then put baby two onto her lap.

She lifted her sweatshirt and positioned baby two accordingly.

Bryant felt himself blush slightly and kept his gaze firmly on her face.

Dawson coughed.

'Sit, sit,' she said.

Dawson stayed where he was, and Bryant didn't blame him. A jam-covered blanket and a rolled-up dirty nappy took up most of the sofa. He pushed them to one side and sat.

'We've been to see Henryk,' he said.

Tears immediately sprang to her eyes but she blinked them away.

Baby one began to grumble. Her left foot slid to the side and began to nudge the rocker back and forth.

The tears in her eyes were replaced with hostility.

'So, it takes almost him being killed to get your attention?' she asked.

'I'm sorry?' Bryant said, trying not to focus on the black patch of damp he could see crawling up the wall.

'We have called many times, many problems, but no help.'

'What kind of problems?' he asked.

'Vandalism, insults, threats…' she said as her voice began to rise.

The toddler looked up from the toy he was banging against the side of the sofa.

Bryant wanted to calm her down. There would be little co-operation at the moment.

'It's a nice house,' he said, ignoring the crack in the wall above the fireplace. 'How long have you lived here?'

'Shit hole,' she said, looking around. 'But landlord give no care. No interest. No listen.'

He could see where she had made the effort to keep the house as nice as she could. Framed flower prints livened up the stark walls. There were no layers of dust on the surfaces, and the vacuum cleaner was stationed behind the door. Despite her efforts, the aroma of damp was evident.

He got the feeling this woman was tired of being ignored.

'Go on,' he said, patiently.

'Henryk and I moved to UK seven years ago. We want to start a family but not in Poland,' she explained. 'We both have jobs to come to in my uncle's building company. Henryk labourer and me in office. We earn money, we pay taxes,' she said, defensively.

Bryant felt saddened as he wondered how it must feel to have to explain yourself. They had done nothing wrong. They were legally in the UK and had followed the rules.

'Sounds perfect,' Bryant smiled.

The smile in return was brief but it gave Bryant a glimpse of the woman beneath the rage.

She shrugged. 'There was occasional insults for the first few years but we just ignored them. The babies started coming,' she said, sweeping her eyes around the room. I gave up my job but business was suffering anyway.

'A year ago the business died and Henryk lost his job. At first he refused to get help. He did not want to drain a country he had grown to love. We lived on our small savings and began to sell our possessions.'

Bryant had only just noticed there was no television, music centre or evidence of any other technological gadgets.

'Eventually we ran out of items, and Henryk had no choice but to get state help. Then the insults and threats became worse. Neighbours were shouting nasty things, telling us to go home and take our bastards with us.'

She swallowed deeply, as Bryant felt the anger growing inside him.

Her face had softened with sadness.

'We found insults on our door. New ones every day. We had a brick through the window, and Henryk spat at many times.'

Bryant had the urge to apologise but he wasn't sure on whose behalf.

'Did you report the incidents?' Dawson asked, unnecessarily. Of course they had.

She nodded. 'And then two days ago we received the letter.'

'What letter?' Bryant asked.

The woman removed the child from her breast and pulled down her sweatshirt. She stood and reached for a single folded sheet on the fireplace, passed it to Bryant.

He opened it and began to read.

'Fuck off you Polish bastards. Go home and stop taking our money and our jobs. You've been warned. We will rape your wife and stab your kids.'

'Any idea who might have sent this?' he asked.

She shook her head. 'Pinned to the door, no envelope,' she replied, wearily.

Bryant felt sickened at the words. Someone had possessed enough venom to actually put these words to paper with the sole intention of terrifying a young family.

And now this poor woman was here alone.

'Any witnesses?' he asked.

Her expression said it all.

He raised the letter. 'May I take this?'

She nodded.

'Is there anywhere else you can stay; your uncle?' he asked.

She shook her head. 'He moved back to Poland three months ago. And we will do the same once Henryk is well enough.'

Bryant felt saddened that this family had been driven out of their home. He saw Dawson's head shake and knew he was feeling the same way.

'I'll inform the station that any calls to this address are to be treated as a priority,' he said, standing.

She nodded dejectedly. No, it didn't give him much comfort either.

He wished he could do more.

At the door, Bryant offered her his hand.

'Thank you for your time,' he said.

She adjusted baby two on her shoulder as the toddler grabbed her knee. She returned the handshake and offered him a tremulous smile in return.

'And thank you for yours,' she said.

Bryant stepped out of the house and took another look around the street.

'You didn't mention the texts on Henryk's phone,' Dawson said as the door closed behind them.

'You think she needs anything else to be frightened of?'

Dawson nodded his agreement.

Bryant strode from her front door to the front door directly across the road. It took him eight paces. He stopped, surveyed the street from the other side of the road.

Bryant counted three BNP stickers nestled into the window corners.

'Stretching your legs?' Dawson asked, standing beside the car.

Bryant ignored him. The family had had offensive comments scratched into their door, broken windows and anonymous letters posted.

He looked around the street one more time.

No fucking witnesses, indeed, he thought.

CHAPTER 17

Two more lefts through a residential estate and they hit another lane which she guessed was north-west of the dig site.

'Up here?' she checked. This road was narrower than the single-track road on the other side of the property.

'That's what…'

'Shush,' she said, lowering the window. 'Do you hear that?'

'It's called a siren, Stone,' he said. 'They're used by Police, Fire…'

'And ambulance,' she said, putting her foot down.

The narrow road turned and increased in gradient before levelling out at a small farmhouse with a view of fields to the west and the M5 to the east.

'Bloody hell,' Kim said, hitting the brakes.

Ten feet in front of her a man was on the ground, another leaning over him.

Stone and Travis launched from the car. Travis got there first and hauled the leaning male to his feet.

'What the hell?…'

Kim saw the man's hands covered in blood.

'Please, help him,' he cried, trying to escape Travis's grip.

'Sir, step away,' Travis said, moving him backwards.

'What's his name?' Kim shouted.

'Billy. It's my son. His name is Billy. Please help him.'

Kim leaned down and saw what must have been the father's handprint on the victim's neck. She guessed he'd been applying pressure to stop the blood that was now oozing from his son's wound.

An occasional flinch and moan confirmed that he was still alive. His eyes were closed but his breathing appeared strong and even.

'Billy, it's okay, help is coming,' she said, whipping a latex glove from her jacket pocket.

The proximity of the siren suggested the ambulance was heading along the single-track lane.

Kim placed her hand where his father's had been and felt the stickiness trying to seep around the shape of her hand. She pushed harder, applying more pressure to the wound.

Billy moaned.

Kim could hear Travis trying to establish if there was anyone else in the house and the direction of the shot. He was getting no answers from the man, who just wanted to be back beside his son.

'They're almost here, Billy,' she said, looking behind as the ambulance pulled onto the property.

'Just hang on, the medics are here now and they're going to take care of you.'

Another moan as a gloved hand touched her shoulder.

'We've got it, miss, thank you.'

Kim stepped backwards and allowed them to step in and do their job, unable to recall the last time she'd been called miss.

The paramedics performed a couple of quick checks but wasted no time transferring him to a stretcher that elevated to a gurney. They then pushed him as gently as they could towards the ambulance.

'Is he going to be okay?' cried the father from behind Travis.

'We'll take good care of him, sir,' said the older paramedic as they expertly transferred the patient to the rear of the vehicle.

The older male tried to break free but Travis was too quick for him. 'Let me come with…'

The ambulance door closed behind them.

'Mr Cowley?' Kim asked, walking towards the farmhouse.

He nodded as his eyes followed the ambulance leaving the property.

'Is there a bathroom where I could just clean up?' she asked, placing herself between him and the ambulance.

'First on the left,' he said.

Kim got her first chance to observe the short, chubby man. His bald head was emphasised by the grey stubble on his chin. Oil-stained jeans were tucked into wellington boots, and a dirty blue tee shirt strained around his stomach.

His face was creased with fear and worry.

As she stepped into the farmhouse the stench of rotten food and damp almost overwhelmed her. She ducked into the room on the left which held a toilet and a tiny sink that was full once she placed her hands into it. The toilet was cast iron with a pull chain.

Kim swilled her hands quickly and chose to wipe them on her jeans rather than the towel that was not grey by design.

She stepped back outside to find Travis on the phone by the car and Mr Cowley waiting impatiently with car keys dangling from his finger.

'What exactly happened here, Mr Cowley?' she asked.

'I don't... I'm not... please just let me...'

'Mr Cowley, we need to know how your son was injured.'

'Please, officer, let me go to him. I have to know he's okay.'

Kim looked to Travis, who was off the phone. He nodded.

'We'll meet you at the hospital, and we'll talk there,' she said.

He smiled gratefully and ran towards an old pickup van.

Kim strode towards her own car, ready to follow. She paused as she opened the driver's door and glanced back to the side of the barn and the pool of blood from which Billy Cowley had just been removed.

Lying right next to the red stain was a brown-handled rifle.

Which she would swear hadn't been there when they'd arrived.

CHAPTER 18

'Stone, I'm not sure what you're hoping to achieve,' Travis said, dourly, as she parked the car outside the A & E department.

She had tried to attach herself to the ambulance, but without flashing lights and a siren on her Golf she'd had to let it go a couple of miles back.

'It's called investigating, Travis,' she said. 'I'll explain it to you later.'

'What are you hoping to gain?' he insisted.

Okay, it looked like she was going to explain it now.

'A man has just been shot on the same land where bones have been discovered,' she said slowly, as she approached the entrance.

'You're getting distracted,' he said, testily. 'It's probably unrelated to our old case. We should continue to focus…'

'Are you kidding me?' she asked, stopping short of the automatic doors. A man sporting a brand new plaster cast had to be pushed around them. She ignored the flash of irritation from the woman pushing him. 'You don't think it's a bit coincidental? Your instinct isn't burning a hole in your leather wallet?'

'I think we should leave this family in peace and…'

'Did you see that gun next to the barn when we first arrived?' she asked, pointedly.

'No, but…'

'Neither did I,' she said.

'We were both distracted by the commotion that was going on at the time,' he reasoned.

'We're both trained investigators and neither of us noticed it right there?' she asked with wide eyes.

Travis shook his head. 'You're turning what might be a simple accident into a conspiracy to—'

'Oh Travis, shut up,' she snapped as she spied Mr Cowley standing at the reception desk. She headed towards him, leaving Travis to look for his gut reaction.

'They won't let me through,' Mr Cowley raged when he saw her. 'Said he needs to be assessed before I can see him.'

Kim glanced at the middle-aged receptionist behind the glass panel. Her face was colouring as a line of sick and injured continued to form behind them.

'Come with me, Mr Cowley,' she said, trying to edge him away.

He shook her off. 'I want to see my son.'

Kim could understand, but the security officer who was peering at them from the edge of the reception was not going to let it happen.

'They need to be able to do their job, Mr Cowley. Please step to the side.'

She successfully moved him a foot to the left, and the receptionist was now taking the details of the next person in the queue – a young man who was holding his right hand in the air wrapped up in a bloodstained tea towel.

Mr Cowley shot her an angry look.

'Please, just come over here. They'll let you know as soon as there's any news.'

He hesitated but then allowed himself to be guided to a row of vacant chairs nailed to the periphery wall.

'Thanks for your help,' she growled at Travis, who appeared beside her.

'Bloody hell, Stone. Make your mind up. One minute you don't want my help and then…'

'My colleague here will get you a cup of tea,' she said, sitting beside Mr Cowley.

She didn't look at Travis but sensed his bulk moving away from them.

'Mr Cowley, can you tell me what happened to your son?' she asked, trying to ignore the stench of body odour that emanated from him.

Jeff Cowley shook his head and ran a hand over his unshaven chin.

'I don't know,' he said. 'I heard a shot and ran outside. Billy was on the ground, by the barn. I ran over. There was blood everywhere.' He patted the side of his neck.

'He'd been shot in the neck?' Kim asked, as Travis held a plastic cup towards the man. He shook his head at Travis and nodded towards her. 'And his shotgun was lying beside him.'

'Was he conscious?' Kim asked. Had he been able to say anything? she wondered.

'Stone, we need to step away and let…'

Kim followed his gaze to the door. The West Mercia squad car had finally caught up with them.

'Back them off for a minute,' Kim said. Travis was eager to hand this off as an unrelated incident. She was not so sure. Coincidences unnerved her. And the timeliness of a shooting incident on the property where bones had been discovered the previous day was setting off her senses like a street full of house alarms after a power surge.

'Did your son manage to say anything at all?' Kim pushed. She needed to know if this was some kind of accident.

'His eyes were closed,' Cowley said, swallowing deeply.

'Stone,' Travis said again.

Kim shot him a warning glance. The two black clad officers were fidgeting by the door. Illnesses, injuries were momentarily forgotten as every gaze in the waiting room was on them.

'Mr Cowley, you do understand that we need to search your property?'

He looked confused. His mind only on the life of his son.

'Not because of the shooting,' she clarified. 'But because of the discovery by the woods. Do we have your permission?' she asked.

He nodded absently, as a woman charged through the waiting officers and headed straight towards them.

Kim assessed her quickly. She was five two in heels with a petite frame. She wore a navy trouser suit with a plain white shirt. The curtains of an auburn bob were separated by a blunt fringe.

'What happened?' she asked, ignoring both Kim and Travis.

'It's Billy. He was shot... I don't know what...'

'And you are?' the woman asked, turning to Kim and then looking at Travis.

'The officers investigating the discovery of human bones on Mr Cowley's property,' Kim answered shortly.

Kim turned back to the man with his head in his hands but had no chance to speak before the woman stepped closer.

'What have you told them?' she barked.

Mr Cowley looked dazed. 'They want to look... search the property,' he said, looking towards the entrance to the treatment rooms.

'Mr Cowley has given us permission,' Kim clarified.

'Has he?' the woman said, through a tightening jaw. 'Well, my name is Fiona Cowley; Mr Cowley's daughter. It's my name on the lease and that permission has just been revoked.'

She looked towards Travis whose expression remained impassive. Surely that instinct had to have kicked in now.

As though reading her mind he stepped forward.

'Miss Cowley, we *will* get permission from the landowners or with warrants. It would just be helpful...'

'I am not here to assist the police, so if you take one step towards that property I'll have you in court. And good luck with the Preece family. You'll get nothing from them.'

Despite her hostile manner, Kim couldn't help her own interest at the venom in the woman's tone when she referred to the landowners.

'Why do you say that?' she asked, as Fiona's hand came to rest on her father's shoulder.

'Because they are a bunch of robbing bastards,' she said.

Kim would have liked to pursue the matter further, but the phone in her pocket began to ring.

'Doctor A,' she said, taking a step away from the smartly dressed Rottweiler.

'Inspector, I need you at the lab, now,' she said, solemnly, before ending the call.

Kim shoved the phone back into her pocket and checked the clock on the wall. What could she possibly have discovered in the three hours since they'd last met?

By the sound of the scientist's voice, Kim knew it was nothing good.

CHAPTER 19

'Anything from the boss, Stace?' Bryant asked, as they entered the squad room.

Dawson's tie was immediately removed and discarded onto his desk.

Stacey shook her head. 'Not a peep.'

'Busy day, Stace?' Dawson mocked.

'Fuck off,' she replied, tersely.

Bryant sighed. It was obvious from her set expression that she'd had a shit day, and he had no clue why Dawson had to needle her.

'Kev's got a present for you,' he said, narrowing his eyes.

Dawson tutted and took the phone from his pocket. He skidded it across the desk.

She caught it. 'Whose phone, Fred Flintstone?' she asked, turning it around.

'It's not that old, Stace,' Bryant said. It wasn't so long ago he'd had that same model himself.

'In technology terms we're talking early Victorian,' she quipped.

'Phone belongs to Henryk Kowalski,' Dawson said.

'Why isn't it logged?' she asked, turning his way.

Evidentially, it should have been bagged, recorded and sent to forensics. Had the phone been available immediately at the scene, Marie West's fingerprints could have been taken and eliminated.

'It's been MIA since the attack,' Dawson answered.

No court would allow it as evidence now. The attacker's sweat, saliva and semen could be all over it but that information would never be admissible.

The tiny screen sprang into life as Stacey pressed the power button.

'Henryk received a text message about casual work,' Dawson explained. 'Can you crack it?' he asked, as the password prompt appeared on the screen.

'Yowm kidding?' Stacey asked, disgusted he would question her about such a basic request. 'Can you take a witness statement?' she retorted in response.

'Debatable,' Bryant offered with a smile. There was a line of tension stretching across their desks.

'Bloody hell, Stace. Are you not getting enough?—'

'Finish that sentence, Kev. I dare yer,' she snapped.

Dawson closed his mouth.

Bryant watched with fascination as the constable hit a few keys in quick succession before powering it off and on again. The menu appeared on the screen.

'Nice one, Stacey,' he said.

She offered no response. He did wonder sometimes if she had any clue of her own value. The task had posed no challenge for her but neither himself nor Dawson would have been able to do it in a month of Sundays.

'I've got the text message,' Stacey said. 'Received from an unknown number.'

'Damn,' he said.

'Shit,' Dawson added.

'I'll see if there's anything I can do,' she offered, continuing to look around his phone.

Her fingers paused as she began to read. The frown on her face turned to a look of horror. She looked from one to the other.

'Guys, you'd better come and have a look at this.'

CHAPTER 20

'You know, Travis, either step in or don't step in but at least be consistent about it,' Kim said, taking the stairs down to the morgue.

Travis shook his head. 'Stone, I find women in general a complete mystery but you should come with a bloody instruction manual.'

Kim ignored him as she buzzed through to the lab.

'Hello again, Doctor A,' Kim offered, brightly. It was good to see a friendlier face.

The scientist offered a brief smile as she signed something on a clipboard and handed it back to the man beside her.

In a few short hours Doctor A had traded the white suit for a white medical jacket that fell just below her knees. Her legs were encased in grey denim, and the trademark Doc Marten boots were on her feet.

'It is about time you are coming,' she said.

Kim held back her smile. The call had reached her less than ten minutes ago. She moved around the doctor and saw what the fiery figure had been obscuring.

Then she looked back to the doctor, who nodded.

Three separate gurneys contained bones.

She moved towards them.

'You're sure?' Kim asked, quietly.

'Definite,' Doctor A responded.

The first gurney held the largest collection of bones. Both legs, a right arm and part of the left arm.

The second gurney held some bones of the lower limbs and a pelvis.

The third gurney currently held a single arm.

'Three victims?' Kim asked.

Doctor A nodded as she came to stand between gurney one and two.

'Yes, there are too many bones of the arm. We have a second skull en route right now.'

Kim noted a box on the metal counter still holding the first skull and a collection of small bones.

'We do not know yet which victim it belongs to.'

Kim was reminded of a jigsaw puzzle and fitting pieces by the process of elimination. That piece cannot fit there and so on until you whittle it down to the only place left where it can fit.

The method only became a problem if there were pieces missing.

Kim prayed there were no pieces missing.

'You're sure there are no more than three?' Kim asked.

Doctor A shook her head. 'We cannot yet be certain. The remains are not in any particular order so until the excavation is complete…'

Kim prayed there were no more than three.

'It is clear that this was not the first burial site. These bones have been moved. We are having two types of soil in the pit. Both have been sented off for analysis.'

Kim ignored the mauling of the English language. She got it.

'Any idea how long the bones have been in this grave?' she asked.

'It is hard to say at the moment but they were already skeletonised when they were dumped here.'

Kim found the use of the word 'dumped' a little jarring, but then she remembered the bone protruding through the eye and realised it was very accurate indeed.

'I have seen no evidence of tissue on any of the bones.'

Kim understood and realised this was an investigation into time. How long had the bones been buried; how long since the bones had been moved. How old were the victims?

Crime scene investigators tried to use evidence to create linkage, like a hair on the clothing of a suspect; a fibre from the victim found in the home of a suspect. All to create an association between a perpetrator and a crime.

Kim moved to the foot of the first gurney, the one with the most bones but still without a skull. Travis sidled along the other side.

Had these bodies been buried separately? And then thrown together. Why three bodies all in the same grave?

She suspected that Locard's exchange principle was not going to help them here. His theory of leaving trace materials picked up from elsewhere, like hairs from dogs, and children etc, would be a challenge to execute if the bodies had already been moved.

'Can you tell us anything about victim one?'

Doctor A reached for the clipboard that was hanging off the end of the gurney. Kim was reminded of a medical doctor doing rounds and checking progress of their patients. Live ones.

She hoped to God the scientist had something for her. Identifying the victims was always her priority, for both personal and professional reasons. She detested anonymity in her victims. Every one of them had been a real life person and deserved the respect of their own name. And professionally it was the beginning of the crumb trail. It was the centre of the investigative wheel. Spokes pointed out in every direction from the identity of a victim; family, work, friends, lovers, activities, enemies, past. Without an identity they had nothing.

Kim knew that there were ways to sex an adult, but not a child or juvenile. She knew the skull was not good for age estimation in adults.

'Victim one is a male aged between forty-five to sixty. I would estimate approximately six feet tall with…'

'Hey, slow down,' Kim said, taken by surprise. It looked as though she was going to get more detail than she'd expected. If only Keats was around to take notes.

Travis had his leather folder open and ready.

'You can pinpoint his age that accurately already?' Kim queried.

Doctor A pointed to the long bones of the arms and legs.

'The growth plates in here are closed. They remain open as the bones grow and close when growing ends, normally no later than twenty-five years of age. X-rays indicate that the level of bone calcium is consistent with a male older than forty.'

'Okay,' Kim said.

'And here,' she said, pointing to the ribs. 'The sternal areas are pitted and sharp through ageing. The level of pitting at the junctions would suggest early fifties to approximately sixty years of age.'

Travis continued to scribble furiously.

Kim wondered at the level of detail he was recording. She could quite easily remember middle-aged male.

'And the height?' she asked, dubiously.

Doctor A frowned at the doubt in her voice.

'For that we are consulting the long bones again. Height is usually equalling to five times the length of the humerus.'

Kim found herself looking at her own arm. She hadn't known that.

Travis stepped forward, holding his pen aloft. 'Can you give us an idea of the man's build?'

Doctor A narrowed her eyes.

Travis read this as a communication issue but Kim knew the doctor better than that. She knew what he was asking.

'Physique,' he clarified.

'I understand the question, Sergeant, but I don't understand why you would ask it.'

'Because the last bones person I worked with was able to offer an idea of build based on the bone size and thickness,' he challenged, imperiously.

Kim considered asking Travis if he would like his genitals gift-wrapped when they were handed to him.

'Then your bones person was a cock head,' the doctor said, simply.

Kim suspected she meant dickhead but same difference.

'Thicker bones can indicate thicker muscles, but this is not reliable as bone thickness is also dependant on nutrition, heavy physical activity. Your so-called expert was guessing. I give you only facts and leave the guessing to you.'

Doctor A had come to stand before him. The size difference was laughable. Doctor A's head was tipped back at seventy degrees to meet his gaze.

The scene reminded her of a Chihuahua barking at a Doberman. Dogs had no concept of their own size. For the first time in her life she actually felt sorry for Travis.

Kim stepped forward like a referee at a boxing match. 'Anything else for us, Doctor A?'

The scientist offered one last look as she took a step back. Kim would not have been surprised to hear her growl.

'Aah, delivery,' she called out as the doors opened, but it was not pizza coming through the door.

Two techs entered, each carrying a white plastic box. The shorter male had a bouquet of colourful blooms clutched in his armpit.

Doctor A frowned. 'Flowers, Timothy?'

'Marina said to bring them here,' he said, nodding towards the gurneys. 'Brought to site by Mr Preece.'

Kim's head snapped up. 'Dale Preece brought flowers?' she asked. He hadn't appeared the flower-giving type to her.

Timothy shook his head. 'No, this one introduced himself as Bart. Offered no trouble. Said a prayer, and left when we asked him to.'

'You moved the flowers?' Doctor A asked.

Timothy nodded towards the gurneys. 'To be with the victims,' he said.

The Doc shook her head. 'They are to mark the grave,' she said. 'Never mind; now, who has the skull?'

The first tech that had entered shook his head as he placed his box onto the metal counter.

'Marina said to give you this first,' he said, removing the storage box lid. He handed her the smallest possible evidence bag, which was an inch square.

Both she and Travis leaned forward as the doc held it up to the light.

'Dirt?' she queried, as her voice rose. '*Mame mu ebam*, I have enough dirt, Timothy,' she said, impatiently.

'Look again,' he said, evenly. The man was clearly used to the Macedonian outbursts from his boss.

She grabbed a magnifying glass from the desk and huffed as she inspected closer. The deep frown changed to a look of surprise like a CGI graphic.

'No ways,' she breathed.

'What?' Kim and Travis asked together.

'A fibre,' Doctor A said, wondrously.

'No way,' Kim said, realising she had repeated the scientist's words.

Doctor A was still shaking her head as she placed the bag onto the counter.

'Aren't you going to open it?' Kim asked. Anything she could tell them would be helpful.

The doc shook her head. 'This will go to the laboratory. If it is our only one we must ensure we get everything we can from it.'

Kim understood. They did not have the necessary equipment at the morgue to glean everything the fibre could offer.

It would take longer but it would be worth it.

Timothy took out a much bigger plastic bag containing one long bone and handed it to the doc. 'And she said you were to have this one second.'

Doctor A turned it in her hands and then held it up to the light. A beam shot straight through a section of the lower part of the leg. The hole cut clean through the bone.

Doctor A looked her way.

Kim let out her breath and nodded at the same time.

She knew exactly what she was being shown.

That hole had been caused by a bullet.

CHAPTER 21

Stacey walked through the door and into the distinctive aroma of chip fat.

The café was located just off Dudley High Street and had been frying for the masses for over twenty years. She had first graced the place in her teens when there was little else to do in Dudley on a rainy Saturday afternoon once the activity of window shopping had been exhausted.

It was also the place she'd been when she'd first had the notion to end her own life.

In the years since, the ownership had changed hands but the décor and menu had not. A few of the usuals were in their normal spot, and her preferred table was free.

Hank Brown sat at the window table. He spent most evenings in Betty's Bite's. Having lost his wife of thirty-seven years he ventured to the café a few nights each week for a hot meal. She had once made the mistake of offering him a smile. That was an hour of her life she would never get back.

'Hey Stacey, what can I get you – toasted tea cake and diet coke?'

Stacey nodded and fished into her purse. It was her theory that the one cancelled out the other. She suffered a diet Coke to spread the packet of butter onto the warm, fruity dough. And after receiving a cup of tea, suffocating beneath a film of grease, she'd chosen a sealed bottle ever since.

Priscilla held up her hand. 'Already balanced the till,' she said, with a smile. 'It's on me.'

'Thank you,' Stacey said, returning the smile. Genuine acts of generosity were few in her personal life and even less in her work.

Priscilla nodded towards the corner table. 'I'll bring it over.'

Stacey thanked her, hoping she didn't offer too many free snacks. Manny wouldn't like that.

Manny was the owner of the café and so nicknamed after the woolly mammoth in the *Ice Age* films. He was big, hairy and Romanian. He had inherited Priscilla with the fixtures and fittings from the previous owner.

Stacey wiped the table and took out her iPad.

Priscilla placed the small plate and a knife onto the table.

'There you go, lovely,' she said.

'Thanks a lot but…'

'Shhh…' she said, resting a hand on Stacey's shoulder. 'It'll be our secret.'

The woman headed to the door and turned the 'open' sign to 'closed'.

She was the most unlikely Priscilla that Stacey had ever seen. Not a common Black Country name, Priscilla tended to stand out. Stacey guessed her to be late twenties. Her lips were full and shapely but her eyes seemed too small for her face. Her large forehead was exaggerated by the dyed red hair pulled back into a bun. And yet there was a quality to the features that Stacey found intriguing.

Priscilla caught her appraisal and smiled.

Stacey blushed and turned her attention to her snack. She spread the butter onto the teacake and watched as it disappeared.

People came into the café for any number of reasons. Her own was to provide a buffer between work and home. The six miles between the station and her flat were not normally enough to erase the events of the day. On the days she went straight home she entered one doorway as fraught as the one she'd left. Eventually, the traumas of the day would dissipate but by then it was time for bed. If she used the café as a pit stop it became an event, a separation between work and home.

Tonight she was struggling to leave work behind. The vile texts found on Henryk's phone were still rattling round in her head. Despite his attempts to delete them, perhaps to hide from his wife, she had managed to retrieve the messages that had escalated in to vicious, sickening threats. The last one she remembered word for word.

'Fuck off or we will gut you, gang rape your wife while your little bastards watch and then rip their limbs off one by one'

Her mind could not compute the level of hate needed to send such a message. At the very least it was designed to terrify human beings who had done nothing wrong. At most it was a credible threat.

She pushed away the teacake, unable to stomach food as she glanced at the *World of Warcraft* icon on her phone. A smile hovered around her lips as she imagined the smirk and eye-roll if Dawson could see her now. It would confirm everything he ribbed her about: that she had no life and spent most of her time in a fantasy world full of goblins and ogres.

And he was right. She didn't have a life. Not since her relationship with Trish had died in a lacklustre way. The initial spark between her and the forensic tech had never ignited in the way both of them had hoped. There had been no great scene or argument; there hadn't even been enough passion for that. The period of time between phone calls just got longer and longer until they were no longer calling or texting at all.

She took a moment to check her emails. Nothing new.

Her whole day consisted of four messages. She'd been tagged in a photo of a relative on Facebook. She'd received a daily email voucher, and got three new followers on Twitter. The fourth was someone trying to sell her more followers.

She put the phone away.

Tonight she wasn't trying to cut off her emotions from work, this time she was trying to distract her mind from the feelings that had engulfed her upon reading Justin's letter.

And those same feelings would not now let her go.

CHAPTER 22

Kim let out a low and prolonged groan as the darts of water pricked her flesh before rolling over her skin and down the drain.

Although symbolic, she did actually feel as though she was cleansing Travis from her flesh.

After leaving Doctor A, Travis had pointedly looked at his watch. They had been half an hour past the official end of shift. Personally, she had wanted to crack on and visit the Preece family or pore over the missing persons reports, but Travis's set expression had told her neither was an option. So, she had delivered him safely back to his wife, who was twitching behind the net curtain. Probably fearful of burning the meat and two veg.

She stepped out of the shower and into a beach towel. A rub of her head with a smaller towel followed by a quick shake and her short black hair was damp and spiky.

She dressed in loose jeans and plain black tee shirt, and smiled as she saw Barney sitting patiently at the bottom of the stairs. Kim had no clue why the dog had never even tried to venture upstairs. There was no gate or barrier and yet he never crossed that invisible threshold.

She rubbed his head and continued through to the kitchen. She looked behind but he hadn't moved a muscle.

He wasn't waiting for her at all. He was waiting by the front door.

Kim laughed out loud. Even her dog was developing a sixth sense about the arrival of visitors.

She moved to the coffee machine and took down two mugs. Plain black liquid for her and milk and sweetener in the other.

The front door tapped as she was pouring the second cup.

'Enter at your own risk,' she called.

Her colleague pushed the door open and walked straight into the furry welcoming committee.

He was holding up his identification.

'The name's Bryant. You might not recognise me but…'

'Jesus, I only saw you this morning,' she laughed, pushing his drink across the breakfast bar towards him.

'How do you do that?' he asked, handing Barney a tripe strip. 'I didn't call; I didn't text; I didn't send a pigeon, so how?…'

'Bryant, you visit me unannounced for one of two reasons. Normally it's either to see if I'm okay or because you're being nosey.' She raised an eyebrow. 'Today, I've been forced to work alongside a man I despise on a case that you know nothing about. You turning up tonight was a pretty safe bet. Even the bloody dog knew you were coming.'

'Fair point,' he conceded. 'So, how was it?' he asked, wasting no more time.

'Like watching a game of cricket in slow motion. He is methodical to the point of laborious. There's no fire in him unless he's arguing with me. He writes everything down and his greatest act of impulsiveness so far has been to add a caramel shot to his skinny latte.'

Bryant almost spat out his drink.

She sighed. 'Oh, all right, it wasn't a skinny latte but you get the picture. Around his own team he's personable, amusing, just as I remember him but with me, well…'

'Didn't you two get on once?' Bryant asked, quietly.

'A long time ago,' she replied.

He looked at her. 'What was it – four or five years ago? There were a lot of rumours, back then about…'

Kim crossed her arms in front of her. Yeah, she'd heard the rumours too, and she hadn't responded to a single one of them. She opened her mouth to explain to Bryant the type of police officer Tom had been, but she couldn't. The very example she'd been about to use was the thing of which she'd promised never to speak. And she never would.

'He wasn't always like this,' she said.

He shrugged. 'Some people just work differently more er… organised than…'

'Are you saying I'm not organised?' she asked.

'In your own way, eh? Let's just leave it at that.'

She narrowed her eyes. 'That's one of those things you'd only dare say to me as Kim, right?'

'Hell yeah. Now tell me about the case.'

'Doctor A suspects three separate victims, buried elsewhere first. We have a fibre and a bullet wound.'

'Guns?' Bryant asked.

She nodded. Any crime concerning firearms was still an exception in their neck of the woods.

'We have a possible description of our first victim. We still have no clue how old the bones are or how long they've been buried. She's briefed her colleague, Marina, who will continue the excavation at site, now that Dr A's transferred to the morgue to start putting it all together.'

'Oh, Keats will be pleased,' Bryant observed.

'No less pleased than Doctor A. She contacted the HTA but they wouldn't issue—'

'Back up,' Bryant interrupted. 'What's the HTA?'

'Human Tissue Authority. They issue licenses for morgues, even temporary ones. But there's no building on-site with running water, one of the basic requirements, so the remains have to be transported back to the morgue. Trust me, she would have preferred to stay on-site.'

Kim knew that Doctor A was very much like herself and would have preferred all aspects of the forensic operation in the same place. Where she could better control it.

'Anything interesting about the site?'

'Actually, yes. The farm is leased by the Cowley family. Father, son and daughter. I have no idea about the mother yet. The daughter is a terrier who refused permission to search the property, and her brother was involved in a shooting incident earlier today.'

Bryant's eyes were wide.

'Exactly that,' she exclaimed, pointing to his face. 'That's exactly what I'm not getting from Travis.'

'And with all that you're home and showered before half seven?'

'Precisely,' she said.

Armed with so much information, her team would have been investigating, researching, prodding and probing until either they or the options available to them were exhausted.

'Oh, and I get the feeling there's no love lost between the Cowley family and the Preece family who own the land.'

'Bloody hell, Kim. It's even got me excited. Are you sure you can't wrestle this case away from West Mercia?'

Kim had thought it a hundred times. If only she'd had a pound for every time she'd been tempted to call Stacey or wished that Bryant was in the car beside her.

Only her respect for her boss had stopped her.

'I gave Woody my word that I would try to make it work,' she said.

He nodded his understanding. 'Must be killing you not being in total control, though,' he said, with mild amusement.

'You have no idea. Anyway, enough about me. How are the kids? You and Dawson bonding?'

'Oh yeah, he's coming for a sleepover at the weekend,' he offered, drolly.

'How about Stacey?'

'What do *you* think?'

Yeah, Kim had thought as much. Stacey was a detective that worked better under pressure. When pushed, her brain created magical friction that transferred to her fingers.

'Can't you two involve her more?' she asked.

Bryant sipped his coffee. 'Trying to but we need to give her a starting point and we haven't got that yet.'

'I heard that Henryk guy was beaten pretty bad,' she said.

Bryant nodded. 'His family has been threatened. Wife and three young children. Text messages are beyond vile and clearly from a total sicko. There have been threatening letters, vandalism and insults scratched into their door.'

'Is the family safe?' she asked.

He coloured slightly. 'Yeah, they're safe,' he said, pushing himself off the stool. 'Anyways, I'd better…'

'What have you done?' she asked. 'I know that look.'

Bryant shook his head, and started to back away.

She joined the dots together. A woman on her own with young children, receiving vile and violent threats and a husband incapacitated in hospital.

'They're at your house, aren't they?'

'On the basis of plausible deniability for you, I'm going to choose not to answer that.'

He didn't need to. She was tempted to remind him of protocols and rules and witness distance, but that would have been hypocritical and it wouldn't have changed a thing. Nothing Kim said about his career would have trumped children in danger.

'Just be careful,' she warned.

'Of course,' he said, as he got to the door.

'Can you hold the morning briefing tomorrow?' she asked.

'No problem,' he said, as he stepped through the door.

He paused and turned. 'Oh, and Kim, just because you're not in control doesn't mean you can't be in control.'

Kim smiled as she closed the door behind him.

The smile didn't last long.

There was a sense of foreboding growing inside her, and she knew it had something to do with her team.

CHAPTER 23

Dawson had the sudden urge to roll up little balls of paper and flick them across the desk at Stacey. The set expression of her face told him she wouldn't appreciate it, but he was convinced eventually she'd lighten up and they could exchange knowing glances behind the backs of the adults, like they normally did.

He knew his irritation was from Bryant leading the briefing. They were the same rank, yet he hadn't been asked to do it. His colleague was standing there trying to fill a boss-sized hole and it wasn't working.

He knew he was being unfair but he couldn't rid himself of the phrase 'Be careful what you wish for.'

Not so long ago he'd confided in his boss that he was sick of working alone and yet one full day of being stuck with Bryant had disabused him of that opinion. Around his colleague he felt constricted, like the man was judging his every move. It affected the way he was doing his job. He just wished the boss would come back and take Bryant off his hands.

'Any luck with the number that offered Henryk the casual work?' Bryant asked.

Stacey shook her head. 'No, but I'm almost finished with tracing the number that sent the racist messages.'

'Great,' Bryant answered.

But Dawson knew it wasn't good news. If one contact was difficult to trace and the other wasn't, he would bet they'd been sent by different people. And much as he wanted to know who had sent the sick threats to Henryk and his family, he suspected it wasn't the same person who had attacked Henryk in the car park.

'Check with forensics, Stace. See if they have anything at all.'

'Okay.'

'Is it worth going back to our witness? See if she's remembered anything else?' Dawson asked.

Bryant shook his head. 'I think our time is better spent checking the CCTV.'

Great, Dawson could hardly wait. Hours of poring over grainy images, looking for an average-looking white guy dressed in black. They'd have him by lunchtime.

'It's the neighbour,' Stacey said, suddenly.

Dawson frowned. 'Huh?'

'The text messages. The filthy, threatening ones came from the Kowalski's next-door neighbour, Gary Flint.'

Bryant sat back in his chair. 'You're joking?'

Stacey offered him a sharp look.

'Right next door?' Dawson asked, feeling the nausea rise in his stomach. The texts had been graphic, violent, sick – and all the time he'd been right next door?

Initially, Dawson had been mystified by Bryant's decision to move the family into his own home. He didn't officially know, and he preferred it that way. But he'd overheard the phone calls Bryant had made to his wife. He'd thought his colleague was overreacting, but now he wasn't so sure.

Bryant grabbed his jacket from the back of the chair. 'That'll be our first port of call this morning,' he said, with an authority that caused Dawson to grind his teeth. 'And Stace, can you check on the rest of the neighbours? See if they've got any markers for violence.' He paused. 'Particularly numbers twelve, sixteen and twenty.'

Dawson recalled they were the windows with the BNP stickers.

'Yeah, more busywork,' Stacey muttered as he and Bryant headed out the door.

Dawson waited until they were outside the building before he spoke.

'Hey, Bryant, any idea what's up with Stace?'

Bryant shook his head. 'Seems okay to me.'

Dawson hid his smile as he got into the passenger seat.

Looked like this wannabe boss didn't notice everything, after all.

CHAPTER 24

Kim idly wondered how many times she could bounce her head off the table before it began to bleed. She had deliberately placed herself at the back of the room so that the frustration on her face would go unnoticed, although the thunk of her skull on wood would definitely elicit a glance or two.

So far, the day was replicating the day before. She had collected Travis from his home, watched the awkward embrace between him and his wife, and spent the journey to the Kidderminster briefing in silence.

Being a ghost at the briefings of a case she was co-heading was beginning to grind on her nerves. She could feel questions bubbling in the back of her throat, despite the silent instruction from Travis that this was his playground.

'So, are the warrants through for the Cowley family?' Travis asked, from the top of the room.

The guy with the bandana nodded.

'Johnson, Gibbs, go along and oversee the search. Remain sensitive to the family and let me know if anything develops.'

The last sentence was completely unnecessary, Kim observed.

'Lynda, keep in touch with the hospital and let me know when Billy Cowley wakes up. We need to know what happened there.'

Thank goodness he'd seen sense about investigating the so-called shooting accident.

'Penn, start looking at the description from Doctor A and see if you can match it to any of the missing persons reports.'

'Any indication of how long back we're talking?' Penn asked hopefully.

Travis walked towards Penn's desk and took back the pot plant from the previous day. He placed it on the top table. 'And that's for expecting everything to come to you on a plate, wanting an easy life,' Travis said, smiling.

Oh, she was trying so hard to stay quiet.

'What do we know about the Cowleys?' she asked, taking herself by surprise.

Six heads turned her way. Kim suddenly felt like the naughty kid at the back of the classroom. She realised that analogy was a little too close for comfort.

Travis coloured with rage. She considered for a moment his anger versus her boredom and frustration, which would manifest as rage for the rest of the day. She ignored him and continued. He could thank her later.

'The family, what do we know? Where's the mother? Why the obstruction from the daughter? How long have they leased the land? Who?…'

'Twenty-seven years,' Lynda offered, answering her fourth question before glancing at her boss.

'It's all in the briefing document,' Travis said.

'Pretend I can't read,' Kim said, ignoring the little darts of hatred coming her way.

Lynda continued: 'Not sure about the mother yet, but the daughter is a solicitor and the son is a bit of a loser. He's had a dozen jobs, not lasting in any of them and has been between jobs for the last three years. He still lives at home with his father. Fiona Cowley does not.'

Everyone in the room was now looking at Lynda.

Kim nodded for her to continue.

'For the first fifteen years of the lease, Cowley farm was a thriving, successful business supplying mainly beef to local supermarkets. The foot-and-mouth outbreak decimated their stock, and they haven't recovered since. They've tried different things to gain an income from the property. A farm shop from one of the barns was closed down by Environmental Health, and one of the lower fields that brought a small income from camping flooded three years ago.'

Kim saw the interest on the faces of her colleagues.

It was now a possibility that the Cowleys were a desperate family.

'Thank you, Lynda,' Kim said.

Now she'd succeeded in getting one of them to speak to her, she considered shutting up and then changed her mind. Travis was raging now anyway.

'What about the landowners, the Preece family?' she said to no one in particular.

Bandana boy turned towards her.

'Robson Preece is the fourth Preece heir to expand the land fortune owned by the family for the last two hundred years. He's in his mid-seventies now but the family fortune has almost quadrupled under his control.'

'What type of land?' Kim asked.

'Anything. There's barely a square mile of Staffordshire, Worcestershire and the Midlands that the family hasn't owned at some stage over the last two centuries. The portfolio includes plots big enough for a decent-sized supermarket up to vast estates of farmland.'

'And what do they do with it?' Kim asked.

He shook his head. 'Nothing. They buy it, hold it and sell it. The family has profited heavily from the housebuilding boom in the last twenty years.'

'Okay, thank you, Penn,' Travis said, sharply.

Kim considered asking him to continue, but that would have been deeply unprofessional and it helped the team not at all to see blatant division in the line of authority.

But the briefing had finally become interesting.

'Lynda, anything on the attempted abduction from yesterday?'

'I've spoken to the woman, Mrs Umgabe, and let me tell you they picked the wrong one there,' she offered with a wide-eyed smile. 'She said a van pulled up beside her and two men jumped out, one grabbed her arm and, to quote her accurately, "I maced the bastard".'

Kim smiled along with everyone else. Except Travis.

'Circulated the description of two average-sized white males and started checking local CCTV.'

'Share the load with Lewis,' he said, nodding towards the youngest, quietest member of the team. 'And stay on top of the hospital.'

Lynda wheeled her chair across as Travis headed back into his office.

Just for a minute it had felt like she was doing her job, but it had been short-lived. Kim began to wonder if Travis's hatred towards her trumped the need to solve this investigation.

As he closed the office door behind him, she questioned if he would cling to his animosity, whatever the cost.

CHAPTER 25

Stacey breathed a sigh of relief when they left. Yesterday she had welcomed their interaction. Today she did not.

She had the distinct feeling that Bryant was giving her busy-work, but unlike Dawson she didn't resent the work instructions coming from the older sergeant. To her it was the natural order of things. Despite both her male colleagues holding the same rank, there was a seniority in Bryant. She wasn't sure if that was because the boss chose to spend most of her time with him or because of his age and experience. But the man had her respect.

Although, she had to admit that seeing the barely concealed petulance on the face of Dawson had brightened her morning.

Oh well, she thought, firing up the electoral roll website. She'd find out about the people at the addresses Bryant had requested. She'd do some digging into their backgrounds. The email to forensics had left her inbox before the two of them had left the building.

Yes, she would complete the tasks she'd been given, she thought, with a feeling of delicious mystery. Because today she had a purpose.

She lowered her head and focussed.

Once she'd completed these requests, she could begin the secret project of her own.

CHAPTER 26

Kim pulled off the car park into a line of traffic. All animation in the face of her passenger had been replaced by red hot rage.

'Let it out, Tom,' she offered, calmly.

He ignored her.

'You'll feel much better,' she insisted, finally reaching the traffic island.

'Shut up, Stone,' he growled.

'Tom, are you really prepared to let—'

'No, Stone, seriously, shut up,' he said, winding down his window.

She could hear sirens in the distance.

Travis switched on his radio and listened carefully.

He turned to her. 'Hit-and-run just up ahead.'

She wound down her window and listened. The sirens were behind them. 'They're never gonna get through,' she observed.

'Agreed,' he said.

She indicated left and beeped her horn twice before pulling the Golf onto the pavement and then onto a car sales forecourt. Travis was out before she had switched off the engine.

She scrambled out of the driver's side and threw the car keys at a stunned car salesman.

'Move it if you need to,' she shouted, setting off after Travis.

She ran through the slowing crowds of pedestrians who were stopping to wonder what was happening.

She crossed the dual carriageway through stationary traffic and headed for the next exit from the island. The road was smaller, with two-way traffic.

She sprinted towards the clutch of heads gathered behind a supermarket delivery van. As she approached, she searched for Travis's head above the rest.

'Move,' she shouted as she headed to the centre of the huddle.

She could hear the sirens but they weren't getting any closer.

She assessed the scene quickly.

Travis was on his hands and knees, performing CPR on a black male with scratches across his cheek.

But that wasn't where Kim's gaze rested. She stopped dead at the sight before her. For a second, no sound penetrated her ears and no movement caught her eye.

To Travis's left lay a woman who stared up into the endless sky. Her broken body lay at impossible angles, reminding Kim of one of those chalk figures daubed on the ground. The top of her skull had been cracked open by the impact, and brain matter seeped from the open wound along the edge of the pavement and into a storm drain. Clumps of blonde hair were being lifted and moved by the breeze.

Travis had been forced to make an immediate choice and had chosen to try to save the person who at least had a chance.

She would have made the same call. There was nothing they could do for her now.

Kim swallowed deeply and the action around her unpaused.

She turned right into a man recording with a smartphone. She raised her hand and brought it down on top of the phone. It plummeted to the ground and smashed.

'Now fuck off before you get nicked,' she growled. That footage was not going on Facebook.

The male grabbed the remains of his phone and scarpered.

'If you're not involved or can't help, move away,' she shouted at the crowd. 'Right now.'

Two men wearing roofing contractor jackets stepped forward. 'Can we help?' they asked.

Although they were pale and shocked, she could use all the assistance she could get.

She nodded. 'Do you have anything to cover?…'

The taller man nodded and sprinted back along the pavement.

'Did you see anything?' she asked the other roofer.

He shook his head. 'There's an old lady over there that was walking by. I think she saw something,' he said. 'And a couple of folks in that group said something about seeing the delivery van.'

Kim glanced towards the woman being comforted by a younger woman over by the wall.

'Can you start to move everyone back?' she asked. 'Try to identify witnesses and keep them separate.'

He nodded as his colleague returned with a dust sheet. Kim took it from him and carefully draped it over the dead woman.

She moved closer to Travis. She could see that he was exhausted.

'Tom, do you want me to take over?' she asked.

He shook his head without looking at her, keeping his concentration on the count of compressions between breaths.

She would have been the same. Despite the fatigue, during CPR you found a rhythm and blocked out the pain in the arms and shoulders. The movement became automatic but he would know about it later.

'Sirens are getting closer,' she said.

Although he offered no acknowledgment, Kim knew he had heard.

She took a few steps along the pavement to the elderly woman.

'You saw what happened?' Kim asked, gently. Damn, if Bryant had been with her he would have thought to ask if she was okay first.

The woman raised her head and nodded as a fresh batch of tears escaped from her eyes. Kim looked to the younger woman who was gently supporting her.

'Did you?…'

The woman shook her head. 'I was at the bottom of the road,' she said, pointing to the corner approximately one hundred metres away.

'Do you know this lady?' Kim asked, as she saw a squad car pull in at the bottom of the road.

She nodded. 'She's a neighbour of mine. Her name is Mrs Harper, Enid Harper.'

Kim moved closer and touched the older woman's arm. 'Enid, can you tell me what you saw?' she asked, gently.

From the corner of her eye Kim could see paramedics running towards her from the bottom of the street. Travis would be relieved momentarily.

'It all happened so quickly,' she said, shaking her head. 'I was walking just down there,' she said, pointing with a trembling hand.

Kim nodded and stepped forward as the paramedics rushed past her. Black uniforms had arrived and were starting to bark instructions.

'Did you see what kind of vehicle it was?' she asked, hopefully.

She nodded and pointed across the road.

Kim followed her finger. 'It was a grocery delivery van?' she asked, confused.

'That delivery van,' she said, staring right at it.

Kim had been led to believe it was a hit-and-run; she needed to clarify before she went any further.

'You're sure the driver of that delivery vehicle over there knocked down these two people?'

She nodded as she wiped at her eyes.

Kim thanked her and headed towards the van parked fifty metres along the road.

One person dead and another one close to it.

It was definitely time to talk to the driver.

CHAPTER 27

Dawson was not sure what he'd been expecting as they had travelled towards the residence of Gary Flint, but the man that answered the door was certainly not it.

'Mr Flint. Mr Gary Flint?' he asked, to make sure.

The man was early forties, dressed in smart black trousers and a plain white shirt. A faint mark around his neck indicated that the shirt collar had not long been loosened. Despite the early morning shadow appearing on his chin, Dawson recognised skin that was tended to by its owner. His hair was tidily cut, and his face was open and friendly as he looked from one to the other.

Dawson couldn't help wondering if Stacey had made some kind of mistake. But the man nodded, confirming she had not.

'May we come in?' Bryant asked, holding up his identification.

He yawned and stepped back. 'Of course,' he said, pleasantly. 'I've not long got back from work but please, come in.'

Dawson entered a room that was exactly the same layout as the house next door. Except this front room was awash with gym equipment instead of children.

He noticed the brand new Life Fitness Club Series treadmill facing the curtain-less window. His own gym had recently purchased a few of the machines for just under five thousand a pop.

'Please, come through,' Flint said.

They followed him to a small kitchen diner with a patio that looked out onto a poky thirty feet garden made smaller by a seven feet fence barrier fronted by conifer trees.

This man clearly liked his privacy out back but had unfettered windows at the front. To see but not be seen, Dawson couldn't help but think.

'How may I help you?' he asked.

Looking closer, Dawson could tell that the open expression was now forced, tentative, tense.

'We're here about your neighbour, Henryk,' he said, stepping forward. He would lead this one. 'You know that he was badly beaten the other night – almost killed actually?'

Flint folded his arms and leaned back against the cooker, causing the ignition to click repeatedly behind him.

'I'd heard something,' he said, moving to the side.

'Yeah, he's in a bad way. Attempted murder, we think.'

'Shame,' Flint said, with no emotion at all.

'You don't like Henryk very much, do you?' Dawson asked.

'I don't like any of them, to be honest,' he said.

'You mean the whole family?' Dawson asked.

He shrugged.

'Or do you mean Polish people in general?' Dawson asked.

Again he shrugged. 'I mean Poles, Pakis, Jews, N—'

'I think you'd better stop right there,' Bryant advised, and then nodded to Dawson to continue.

The shock quickly turned to anger, and Dawson had to force it back down. Way down.

'So, you're openly a racist?' he clarified.

Gary Flint smiled. Dawson hated that the smile was pleasant, personable. Such ugliness inside should flash like a beacon and not be clothed in average normality. There should be horns, warts, disfigurement and scales to reflect the putrid person within.

'If that's what you want to call it. I prefer to think of myself as a nationalist.'

'An honest-to-goodness card carrying member of the EDL?' Dawson asked.

'Absolutely. Keep Britain white, officer. We have become infected by so many races we no longer know who we are.'

'And how far do you take your views, Mr Flint?' Dawson asked through a jaw that was beginning to ache.

He shrugged but said nothing.

'Where were you Sunday night?' he shot out. He wasn't sure how many more minutes he could remain in this man's company.

'At work,' he shot back. Amusement was dancing in his eyes. 'I supervise the night shift in a supermarket.'

'You think this is funny?' Dawson asked.

He could see Bryant's warning glance to his left. He shrugged in response.

Flint tipped his head. 'I honestly have no feelings on that, whatsoever,' he said. 'What does amuse me is your noticeable change towards me since I mentioned my political views.'

'You must get that a lot?' Dawson said, trying to keep control of the rage building inside him. Oh, how he wanted to retaliate. Give this man his real thoughts.

Bryant stepped forward. 'Those views are your own, Mr Flint, and they are your right, however abhorrent they may be to a normal, sane person. Although, sending threatening, abusive messages is not your right.'

Dawson felt himself reacting just as badly to his colleague's measured, reasonable tone. There was nothing reasonable about this disgusting piece of shit.

'Threatening to rape his wife, slit the throat of his children,' Dawson raged, taking a step forward.

Flint looked unapologetic. 'The end justifies the means in my book. If they pack up and—'

'They're fucking human beings,' Dawson interrupted, aching to wipe the satisfied smile from the bastard's face.

'Not my kind of human beings, Sergeant,' he said, imperiously.

Dawson found himself moving towards the man. 'What the hell gives you the?—'

Bryant stepped right between them and started speaking.

'Gary Flint, I'm arresting you on suspicion of…'

Dawson turned away in frustration as Bryant calmly stated the caution and applied a pair of handcuffs. He took a few deep breaths and worked to compose himself. He was by far the most agitated person in the room.

'You're not even bothered that you're in some serious shit?' he asked.

Flint smirked. 'Officer, you want me to be sorry for what I've done, and I'm not. I will take the consequences for my actions, but it won't change a thing about how I feel whether I'm here or in prison.'

'But at least it's one more scumbag off the streets,' Dawson spat.

Flint surprised him by laughing out loud.

'Oh, Sergeant, I can assure you that you have much bigger problems than me.'

Dawson was prevented from replying as his colleague turned Flint and pushed him towards the door.

CHAPTER 28

Kim took a good look at the vehicle as she crossed the road.

Her eyes widened as she got closer and saw the full impact of the damage. Bloody hell, no wonder the woman had stood no chance. The entire driver's side front wing had been smashed and crumpled into the middle of next week. The mangled metal reminded Kim of an unironed white shirt. Pieces of orange and clear glass littered the floor and the front bumper hung down, sadly.

Kim paused for a moment before continuing. She looked up and down the road. It was a 40 mph zone leading up to the traffic island. Something wasn't making sense here.

A suspicion began to build in her stomach.

A man, who she assumed to be the driver, attempted to get up from his seated position on the pavement. She indicated for him to stay where he was. If the two pools of vomit to the left of him were anything to go by, he would not be stable on his own two feet.

'Detective Inspector Stone,' she said, showing him her ID.

'I didn't do anything,' he said, immediately.

She appraised him slowly, leaving his statement hanging between them. She guessed him to be late fifties, with a greying stubble evident on his chin. Glasses had been pushed on to the top of his head and left there.

Kim leaned down, bringing herself to his level.

'Are you okay, Mr?…'

'Brady,' he answered. 'Allan Brady.'

Kim had opened her nostrils when he spoke but she detected no obvious smell of alcohol. He would be tested for that shortly but her initial feeling was that he was not driving under the influence.

She raised herself back to a standing position as the smell of the vomit began to waft towards her.

'Mr Brady, can you tell me exactly what happened?'

He rubbed at his head and realised his glasses were there. He popped them back to their rightful position.

'H… how is she?' he stuttered, pleadingly.

'I can't answer that right now, Mr Brady. If you could just tell me…'

'She's d… dead, isn't she?' he cried, searching her face.

She gave away nothing. 'Mr Brady, I can't…'

'She's dead, I know it. I know she's dead and it's my fault. I should have seen… I sh… should have stopped… I should…'

His words were muffled as his hands covered his face and the sobbing began.

Although she had neither confirmed nor denied his question, Kim's failure to reassure him the woman was still alive had given him his answer.

'Mr Brady, you need to stop thinking about that, right now. Can you tell me how it happened?' she asked again.

'I can't think. It was all so quick. She just appeared from nowhere. I'm going to lose my job, aren't I?' he asked, sobering.

Kim was amazed how quickly self-preservation kicked in. Right now she had no clue who was to blame for the woman's death but she wondered if he'd be so quick to think about his pay cheque if she took him back and showed him the victim's wounds.

'Mr Brady, would you mind?…'

'Do I need a lawyer?' he asked, suddenly. 'Am I being charged with murder?'

'Mr Brady, I need you to calm down and stop getting ahead of yourself here. I'm simply asking you what happened.'

Suddenly, his face closed down. 'I think I'm going to keep quiet until…'

'Were you speeding, Mr Brady?' she asked, hoping for an answer before he shut her out completely.

'Excuse me?' he asked.

She was happy to clarify. 'I'm sorry, Mr Brady, but the impact of this accident at forty miles per hour is not making any sense to me,' she said, truthfully.

He looked from her to the red circled traffic sign staring at them.

'You don't think… I wasn't… my speed…' he stumbled, trying to get his point across.

She shrugged. 'The severity of the damage to your vehicle and the victim for a walking pedestrian at forty miles per hour doesn't seem to compute.'

Travis sidled up beside her as the van driver shook his head.

'No officer, you've got it wrong. She didn't walk into the path of my van. That lady was pushed.'

CHAPTER 29

17 October 1989

Jacob James had no clue what time of day it was.

The darkness cloaking him was stifling. Constantly he found himself fighting down waves of panic.

He had no concept of how long he had been in the room. At first, he had tried to keep a rough idea but the darting thoughts had interrupted his count.

Next he had tried to focus on Adaje. What was she doing right now?

He pictured her normal day. Still sharing the family home with him during the last year of university. Just the two of them for more than ten years. She would thunder down the stairs, grab a piece of buttery toast, kiss his cheek and run. And then pause at the front door to shout back, 'Love ya, Dad.'

The thought of those three sweet words, called to him every single morning, ripped at his heart. Those words used to pull him through the darkest days.

In the evenings, she would return. Some nights he would cook; some nights she would cook, and sometimes they would do it together, attempting to recreate her mother's jerk chicken and green beans followed by ginger spice bulla cake. They were never successful but the effort kept the memory of his wife alive for them both.

What was Adaje doing now? What was she thinking? Was she frightened? Was she in danger? Yes, she was now a young woman but she would for ever be his little girl.

If only he could answer these questions. If he could know for sure his daughter was safe. The other questions in his mind were secondary to his daughter's safety.

Suddenly Jacob heard a metal key in the door. A bright light shone in his face. He instinctively raised his bound hands to cover his eyes.

Fingers grabbed at his upper arms. Voices, the smell of alcohol, the sensation of warm skin grabbing at his cold flesh, bewildered him.

'Stand it up,' said one voice.

'Yeah, let's have a look,' said a second.

He felt himself being hauled to his feet. Fabric was placed over his eyes and tied at the back of his head.

'Let me go,' he cried. The words croaked from his dry throat.

He flailed his arms like a dervish but he was being held firm.

'Behave yourself, mud boy,' said the first voice.

Jacob ignored him and continued to try to pull himself free. He kicked out in front of him with his bare feet and met with something hard.

'Get your fucking hands off…'

'Hey, pack it in,' said a second voice, kicking him in the back of his knee.

His injured knee. He cried out in pain as his left leg buckled.

'What do you want?' he asked, trying to twist and turn out of the hands that gripped him.

'Calm down, fella. This will all go better for you if you don't struggle.'

'My clothes?' he asked. 'Where are my clothes?'

'You won't be needing them right now,' said the second voice.

A third voice sounded from behind him.

'Here's the bottle.'

'Time for a little drink. You're sounding a bit dry. Open your mouth.'

Jacob did as he was told. The plastic landed on his bottom lip and cold water filled his mouth. He swallowed greedily as the liquid quenched the arid thirst in his throat.

And then he bucked forward, causing the bottle to crash to the ground.

'What the fuck?…'

The distraction enabled him to pull his right arm free. He immediately reached for the hand clamped at his left elbow. This might be his only chance to escape.

He squeezed hard on the fleshy fingers and managed to prize them free before hands landed all over his body.

'Not so fast, fella,' said voice number one.

Suddenly he felt a hard slap on his bare behind. 'Just look at that fucking arse,' said the second voice.

Jacob heard laughter, the voices seeming to surround him.

'Best not let the boss hear you say that,' said another. 'He ain't here for that kind of entertainment.'

'Yeah, but…'

He was nobody's entertainment, Jacob thought as he tried again to pull free. The panic was driving down into his chest, taking away his breath. He had no idea what they were planning on doing with or to him. He had to try and get away.

'Calm down, eh? We ain't like that,' said one before sniggering.

'Got some fight, hasn't he?'

'Yeah, he's a good one. Should be a good night once we…'

'Shh… the boss is coming,' said the third voice.

From the words around him he suspected this was some random attack. He had been abducted by chance. Chosen for something. And as terrified as he was, he was also relieved. If these men didn't know who he was, Adaje was safe.

Suddenly his limbs began to dissolve as a feeling of weakness overcame him.

He felt his legs begin to buckle beneath him as a numbness stole over his flesh like thousands of crawling insects.

The water, he realised, too late. They had put something in the water to drug him.

The hands that were grabbing him pushed him against the wall, and Jacob began to slide against it.

A vent grate in the wall grazed his back on the way down. He barely felt it as his eyes began to close.

'Is this him, boss? Is this the right one?' asked one of the voices.

Jacob felt his chin loll forward onto his chest as a new voice replied:

'Oh yes. He's the one.'

CHAPTER 30

Stacey could feel the tension as her colleagues walked through the door. She looked from one to the other to work out who it was attached to.

Dawson appeared to have too much colour in his cheeks, and Bryant's jaw was hard and set.

'Everything okay?' she asked, automatically.

'Just peachy,' Dawson grumbled. 'Gary Flint, the neighbour from hell, is downstairs, just waiting to tell us how much he hates anyone that's not British born and cotton white.'

'Let it go, Kev,' Bryant advised.

Dawson battered his computer keys and seemed surprised when he failed to log in.

'Yeah, well you were hardly hero of the fucking hour,' Dawson muttered.

'Speak up, Kev,' Bryant replied. 'If you've got something to say…'

Stacey sat back in her chair and frowned. Most cases prompted a touch of antagonism between the two of them but, right now, the air was thick with resentment.

Dawson sat forward, rising to Bryant's challenge. 'You said fuck all to him, not a bloody dickie bird. How the hell could you be so calm around such a poisonous, vile?…'

'Kev, did you really think that was a mind we were ever going to change?' he answered, patiently.

'Yeah but…'

'Listen, I hate everyone who thinks it's okay to drink and drive. I hate everyone who thinks it's okay to have sexual feelings towards children. I hate every man who ever thought it was okay to rape a woman. The list goes on, and I hate them all but I can't pin every one of them up a fucking wall, can I?'

Stacey's eyes widened at the curse from her colleague. Bryant's voice had risen steadily throughout his explanation. There was something unnerving about seeing him losing his cool. His unruffled manner normally held them all together.

What the hell was going on between these two? Stacey wondered. And where was the boss to sort it out? She could normally defuse the tension between them with one sentence.

'Who's interviewing him?' Stacey asked, trying to refocus their attention on the case and away from each other.

'Me,' said Dawson.

'I am,' said Bryant at the same time.

Yeah, that had worked out well for her. From where she was sitting, either one of them would be a disaster. This Gary Flint had managed to aggravate them both.

'How about I do it?' Stacey asked.

'Not a fucking chance,' Dawson shot back.

Stacey felt the irritation bubble inside her.

'Well, you clearly cor,' she observed, as his hand clenched around his pen. 'He's managed to rattle you, already.'

'Sorry, Stace, but you're not going anywhere near him,' Dawson repeated.

Stacey bristled at the finality of the statement. He had no bloody right to tell her what to do. Yes, he was a sergeant and she was a constable, and officially he outranked her, but they had never played that way.

'Kev, I'm a bloody police officer who—'

'And he is a filthy piece of shit who should be lobotomised and then boiled like a lobster,' Dawson offered.

'Bryant?' she appealed.

He shook his head. 'I'm with Dawson on this.'

Bloody great, she thought. The one time they decided to agree, it was against her.

She threw down her pen. 'This is because he's a racist pig?' she asked.

They looked at each other and said nothing.

'You're trying to protect me against a bigot that hates black people?'

'Stace, he's not just a bigot. He's vicious…'

'Then where the hell were you when I was five years old, Kev?' she stormed. 'Cos there's nothing more vicious than a group of kids making monkey gestures at you every day.'

The memory still burned, almost twenty years on.

'Stace, we just don't want…'

'Kev, listen to me,' she said, as Bryant answered his phone. 'I dow even care about people like Gary Flint. Although I find his views sickening and repulsive, I appreciate his honesty. He cor hurt me because his opinion means nothing to me.'

She picked up her pen and stabbed the desk with it. 'Do you want to know what really gets my goat?' She didn't wait for an answer. 'It's all the people who claim they're not racist and qualify the claim with "my best friend is black" or "my boyfriend's sister's partner's next-door neighbour's cat is black". I hate the way people search around their social circle for a token black person on which to pin their declaration. Now *that* annoys me. Not the overt, mouthy bastards shouting loudly that they're racist, but the stealthy ones who constantly claim they're not.'

Kev looked at her aghast. 'You prefer Gary Flint to…'

'I prefer people that are consistent in their views and stand for their convictions, however warped they might be. People who refuse to order a Chinese takeaway or won't use the corner shop for a pint of milk because it's owned by a Pakistani family. These people are idiots but you can spot 'em a mile off.'

'Jesus, Stace, not everyone is…'

'Kev, how did your parents react when the first black or Asian family moved into your street?' she asked, pointedly.

He frowned and shook his head. 'They weren't at all bothered,' he said.

'At all?' she pushed.

'Well, they were cautious. Understandably.'

Stacey felt the sad smile creep onto her face.

'Why cautious and why understandably?' she asked, quietly.

She could see the colour seeping into Dawson's face as he realised how easily and naturally he had accepted his family's suspicion of a 'foreign' presence. And agreed with it.

Stacey held his gaze for a moment before looking away.

'No one is interviewing Flint,' said Bryant.

His words thundered between them.

'His alibi is watertight. He was at work all night. And as he's no longer part of Henryk's investigation, Woody has passed him on to another team to question him about the threats to the family. He wants our focus completely on the assault case.'

Stacey nodded and reached for her handbag.

She had to get out of the office. And she knew where she had to go.

Something had shifted between herself and her colleague. Something she would struggle to define.

As she passed by his desk, she paused.

'Kev, it's people like you I fear, way more than Gary Flint.'

CHAPTER 31

Both Kim and Travis were silent once they got back into the car.

The male victim had been rushed away in an ambulance while the medic was still working to keep him alive. The female was en route to the morgue and the van driver was being checked over in the second ambulance.

Traffic officers had cordoned off the road and got vehicles moving again, while uniforms had begun corralling all potential witnesses. More CID officers had arrived, relieving them, and a specialist RTA investigative team was just a couple of miles out. They hadn't left until the scene had been in order.

'You wanna go back to the station?' she asked, starting the engine.

They had just dealt with a traumatic incident, Travis more so than her.

He shook his head and focussed on a spot of blood on his thumb.

'You want to pop back for anything?' he asked.

'Nah, I'm good,' she said. She was surprised he'd asked. It was the closest he'd come to being human with her since they'd started this case. Part of her wanted to take this opportunity to address the issues of the past. But now was not the time. Detective Inspector or not, the adrenaline was still surging around his body trying to moderate itself back to normal. What he needed right now was to be left alone. And for once she was happy to oblige.

* * *

It wasn't until she turned into the drive of Donnay Hall, on the outskirts of Bromsgrove, that she offered a little whistle.

It was a property she had passed many times and assumed it was a National Trust site, not a family home. The pristine gravel separated two lush green lawns and appeared to lead directly to the front door that was set at the centre of the Elizabethan mansion.

As she progressed towards it, the trees lining the driveway gave way to an open view of the oversized fountains on either side. Symmetrical dolphins spouted water at each other across the front entrance.

Had Bryant been in the car beside her they would have played their 'guess the value of the property' game. Her opening bid would have been a little shy of 8 million.

Jeez, how she missed Bryant.

She briefly considered confessing to the crimes herself if it would end this investigation, and her torture, quicker. With good behaviour, she could be out just before she died.

Kim parked her car between a brand new Range Rover and a motorcycle. Although, Kim knew from one glance it was no ordinary motorcycle.

A man appeared from the side of the house, trailed by two black Labradors. He raised his hand to shield his eyes from the low November sun and then began to move towards them.

There was an assurance in the stride that Kim detected immediately. His casual attire of jeans, jumper and gilet said 'gardener'. His confidence said 'Owner'.

He held out his hand and smiled. 'Bart Preece,' he said, simply.

Kim returned the handshake while introducing both herself and Travis. His touch was cool and firm, not unpleasant. She appreciated his omission of any qualification, or explanation, just simply his name. She'd already met the older brother at the gravesite, and the similarity between the two was breathtaking.

'Thank you for the flowers that you took to the grave,' Kim said.

He was as handsome as his brother, but his face was open and relaxed. His black hair fell just over his eyes.

He shrugged in a 'least I could do?' kind of way.

'Nice bike,' she said, nodding backwards.

'It's okay,' he said, casually.

'It's an Ecosse,' she clarified, in case he didn't realise. 'Titanium, 2,400 cc billet engine with 225 horsepower at the rear wheel.'

He laughed out loud. The sound was pleasant.

'I'm sorry, officer,' he said. 'Please excuse my manners. I didn't mean to be rude, I just didn't expect that.'

She smiled at his apology. People rarely did expect her motorcycle knowledge. Especially men. She also knew that it was the most expensive production motorcycle ever made and cost roughly three hundred thousand pounds. Only thirteen had ever been produced. Not many people could afford more than a quarter of a million for a motorbike.

'Want to take a closer look?' he asked, as Travis sniffed his displeasure beside her.

Oh boy, did she ever. She would love to inspect the predominantly carbon fibre material used to keep the weight low. She ached to stroke the hand-crafted Berluti leather seat.

She shook her head. 'Not right now,' she answered. She was here to do her job.

'I assume you're here about the discovery on Cowley's land,' he said, turning serious.

'Well, your land,' she said.

He smiled. 'We don't really see it as ours any more. They've been there for so long.'

The dogs milled around his legs, wagging their tails but not stepping forward.

'We'd like to get a bit more information about the family; dates, that kind of thing,' Kim explained.

'Of course,' he said, turning to the door. 'That'll be my brother you want.'

Kim kept pace with Bart while Travis lagged behind.

Bart leaned towards her, conspiratorially. 'As the younger brother, I am spared the minutiae of the business. I prefer the great outdoors,' he said, with a smile.

'So, your role is?'

'I tend the grounds, Inspector,' he said. 'Well, to be fair, myself and a team of seven,' he admitted. 'And to be even fairer, they do most of the hard work.'

Despite his magnanimous attitude towards his staff, she was guessing he did his job very well. The estate grounds that she could see were immaculate.

'How much land does the property have?' she asked, following him inside the house.

'Twenty-seven acres,' he said, passing through the hallway as he spoke. The dogs followed faithfully behind.

He passed without a second glance at the stained glass panels embossed with family crests or at the life-size portraits of what must be his ancestors lining the walls.

Unaffected was the word that came to Kim's mind when describing the man guiding her. Even amongst the grandeur through which he strolled so nonchalantly, Bart's thoughts appeared to remain outside.

'We have an orchard, an ornamental lake, a seventeen-peg fishing lake, and fallow deer woods at the southern edge.'

There was a great deal of pride in his words.

Bart paused before a dark wooden door that looked heavy. He tapped lightly and then pushed it open.

The Labradors charged through the door.

'For goodness' sake, Bart, get those mutts out of—'

The man stopped speaking as he saw them.

'My brother, Dale,' Bart said, waving them through and ignoring the chastisement.

'We've met,' Kim said, entering the room.

Seeing the two of them together, Kim noted that Dale Preece was as dark as his brother but with an extra few pounds. She reminded herself of the difference in age. She knew it was only a couple of years but it appeared greater, due to the severe business suit and annoyed scowl of the older Preece.

Dale Preece offered a small kick to the Labrador closest to his feet. There was a small yelp before Bart called Ant and Dec back to him.

Kim ignored the frisson of irritation within her and continued to appraise the man before her whose blue eyes were serious, intense.

Bart nodded in her direction as he ushered the dogs out and closed the door after him.

Handsome and rich; Kim could only imagine the time these boys had had in school.

'Mr Preece, now is the time we need to speak to you about the discovery on your land,' she said.

He nodded absently as he sat and pointed to two chairs, indicating they should do the same.

As she sat she glanced beyond him to the view. Two rows of fruit trees formed an archway that travelled far into the distance. A figure with warm blonde hair appeared to be strolling and pausing occasionally to tend the trees.

'Of course,' he said, shortly. 'I've been on the phone with the solicitors half the morning.'

'Why?' Kim asked.

'To clarify our culpability as owners of the land, of course.' He moved some papers around forcefully. 'I pay them enough for a straight answer,' he said.

'The only person "culpable" is the person who committed the crime,' Kim said, wondering if that answer was straight enough.

'Thank you, Inspector but if you don't mind I'll take that under advisement.'

Suit yourself, Kim thought, feeling a little irritated by his manner.

'So, if you could ask your questions as quickly as possible,' he said, without looking at them. 'I'm a very busy man.'

'And we're just shooting the breeze trying to find out who buried multiple bodies on land that *you* own,' she answered shortly.

Travis covered his mouth and coughed beside her.

She ignored his covert warning about her manner because finally she had Mr Preece's attention. A clutch of papers had stilled, mid move.

He slowly lowered them back down to the desk as he spoke.

'I thought it was one person, one skeleton?'

'It was until it was discovered that there were two bodies, and most likely a third.'

'Jesus Christ,' he said.

'How long have you owned the land, Mr Preece?' Travis asked.

Kim allowed him to interject, as her attention was again drawn to the garden.

The woman's upper body had come into view. She appeared to be pushing something.

'We've owned that land for over ninety years. It was bought by my great-grandfather from a First World War widow. He paid double the market value for land he did not want.'

'And how long have the Cowleys held the lease?' Travis continued.

'Charles Cowley and my grandfather agreed a deal back in the sixties. Jeffrey Cowley had just been born. Charles Cowley turned the land into a successful farm. At its height the farm was turning over one and a half million pounds in revenue with a net profit of around four hundred thousand.'

Kim wondered how Dale Preece knew the Cowley's financial situation in such detail.

'My grandfather was an investor in the farm,' he explained, reading her expression.

'The farming industry died a literal death in the nineties with the BSE outbreak. The farm was hit hard. Jeffrey worked alongside his father; the staff were fired, and their entire stock was burned. They lost everything. The Cowley girl and boy were pulled from private school and shoved into the local comprehensive.'

She found his description of the Cowley children offensive. 'You mean Fiona and Billy?'

'Of course,' he said, impatiently, not understanding her point at all.

Travis coughed, and she allowed him to continue.

'Go on,' he urged Dale Preece.

Kim could now see that the woman outside was pushing a wheelchair.

'Jeffrey's wife left him, and his father died of pneumonia six months later. Ever since, it's been just Jeffrey and the children.'

They were hardly children any more, Kim thought, remembering the figure in the ambulance and the officious woman at the hospital.

'Never tempted to sell the land?' Travis asked personably, surprising Kim. That sounded dangerously close to an investigatory question. She would check him for fever later.

'My grandfather won't hear of it,' Dale Preece said.

From his tone, Kim guessed that Dale would sell at the earliest opportunity and turf the family out on their ear.

'Insists it was a gentleman's agreement made back in the day and he will not renege on it, regardless.'

Kim guessed the insistent grandfather was the elderly male being pushed around the garden.

'Paternal or maternal grandfather?' she asked.

'Maternal,' he said, as the woman outside smoothed the blanket over the old man's knees.

She saw Bart approach from the left, followed by the faithful Labradors. He bent his head slightly, addressing the older man. The grandfather did not respond or lift his head. Kim guessed he must be extremely frail. Bart looked to his mother, who reached across and touched his arm before he strode away.

'Do you all live here?' Kim asked.

He nodded. 'My brother, mother, grandfather and I each have our own wing. We occasionally meet for dinner.'

She moved her gaze from the window to the man before her, searching for a trace of humour in his words. There was none. He was stating a simple truth.

Dale Preece appeared to joke even less than she did.

Travis leaned forward. 'Are you aware of the Cowleys having any work done to the property – any building or excavation?'

He shook his head. 'They would need our permission for that, and no request has ever been received.'

'But you wouldn't really know, would you?' Kim interjected.

'We carry out an annual inspection of the property,' he said.

'Every year?' she asked.

'Most years,' he countered. 'We have a substantial portfolio of properties.'

'So, the last inspection was done in?…'

He clicked on the mouse a couple of times, spurring the enormous Apple flat screen into life.

He frowned and clicked again.

'It was in 2011,' he said, doubtfully, checking again.

Kim was not surprised. Within their vast empire of land and property, the Cowleys and their farm were no bother to anyone.

'So, no one has been to check for over five years?'

'It appears so,' he frowned, still clicking as though some new information would appear.

Five years is a long time, Kim thought, as the woman and the wheelchair went out of view.

'And you now run the family business?' Kim asked.

He nodded, his expression saying *who else is going to do it?*

She remembered that a boating accident had claimed one of his parents and had the sudden, inexplicable feeling this man could have done with having a father.

'Well, thank you for your time,' she said, standing.

In all honesty she was eager to get out of the room. The office was not to scale with the rest of the building. The small space was full of heavy wooden panelling from floor to ceiling. A wrought iron fireplace dominated the shorter wall. The window pointed north, away from the cold sunshine.

'I'm sorry I couldn't be more help,' he said, offering his hand again. This time Travis took it. 'But I do hope you find out what happened to those poor people.'

'Thank you for your concern,' Travis said, as Kim headed towards the door.

She paused, remembering something he'd said.

'Sorry, just one last question, Mr Preece,' she said, turning. 'You used the word "regardless" when referring to your grandfather's refusal to sell the Cowley's land. "Regardless" of what?' she asked

Dale Preece frowned deeply. 'Regardless of the fact they've paid no rent in almost thirty years.'

'Put your face straight before the wind changes,' Bryant said, as they chose another camera. It was something his grandmother had always said if he was sulking.

They had been in the CCTV viewing room at the rear of Sedgley Police Station for more than an hour, and Dawson hadn't spoken once.

From this location they had access to 187 cameras around the borough. Less than half were public space cameras covering high streets and car parks. A quarter covered local housing estates, and the rest were monitored on behalf of organisations like Centro.

'You still bothered by the thing with Stacey?' he asked.

'Leave it, Bryant,' he said, selecting another bank of cameras and typing in the date and time of interest.

'Why has it bothered you so much?'

'Because I'm not a fucking racist,' he snapped.

'Jesus, Kev, she knows that. She was just making a point.'

'Yeah well, her point has pissed me off,' he said.

Bryant knew better. Stacey's words had forced him to consider something about himself, and he didn't like that one little bit. Dawson didn't mind introspection, but on his own terms.

'Fucking waste of time,' he raged, pushing the mouse halfway across the desk. 'This guy is invisible.'

Bryant retrieved the mouse and nudged Dawson to the side. With a few taps he was back to the view of the car park entrance at the time the figure exited. He continued backwards for fifteen minutes to the time the attacker skulked around the building and into the car park.

'Now, is there any indication of his direction of approach? It may help…'

Dawson shook his head. 'We only see him against the wall. He could have come from anywhere.'

Bryant allowed the tape to continue playing.

'Okay, let's consider this logically—'

'Hang on, what was that?' Dawson asked, grabbing the mouse from Bryant's hand.

Bryant frowned. He hadn't seen anything.

'Watch this,' Dawson said, going back to the point Bryant had chosen but set to play at a slower speed.

'See that?' he asked.

Bryant shook his head.

'Look again. A second before Marie enters the car park.'

Bryant leaned forward and for the first time didn't focus on their witness.

'A flash,' he said.

Dawson nodded as he rewound again.

'A torch?' Bryant asked.

Dawson shook his head. 'Too quick. Didn't Henryk say something about the attacker wanting him to close his eyes. Could it be linked to that?'

'Not a clue,' Bryant said, dumbfounded. Interesting, but it still gave them nothing further in being able to identify the perpetrator.

'We need a better shot of him,' Bryant said. 'The camera at the end of the high street didn't pick him up in the time frame, and there's no footage of him at the bus station. So, what's left?'

'The church,' Dawson said. 'He must have cut through the graveyard.'

Bryant agreed. Not a popular route in the dark, but attractive if you were on the run.

'So, what's on the other side of the church?' Bryant asked, forcing his colleague to interact.

'Traffic cameras, both sides of the road,' Dawson said, excitedly.

They swapped to another menu and found the area they wanted.

Dawson typed in the time, and waited.

They both stared hard at the screen. Nothing.

'Try the other one,' Bryant said.

Dawson flicked to the other camera, and gasped. There he was.

They'd got the figure of a man walking at speed towards the camera, and watched as he continued to come close. But his head remained bowed.

Dawson squinted at the screen, and frowned. 'He's looking at his phone.'

'What the hell for?' Bryant asked. 'He's just beat a man almost to death.'

'Well, he's not hunting bloody Pokémon,' Dawson replied.

Bryant sat back in his chair. 'This guy has just beaten someone to within an inch of their life and literally two minutes later he's checking Facebook. What the?—'

Bryant stopped speaking as his phone rang. It was a number he didn't recognise.

'Bryant,' he answered.

'It's Keats,' the voice said. 'Your boss seems to be tied up on something else so I'm coming to you. I've got a body – and I can tell you now, it isn't pretty.'

CHAPTER 33

Stacey adjusted the satchel across her body as the bus pulled away.

The doubt was already crawling all over her, and right now she had no idea whether to listen to it or shoo it away. She was very rarely out in the field and never without direct instruction from her boss, or someone else higher up.

Somehow, it felt both wrong and right at the same time. Wrong that no one knew where she was or what she was doing, but right that she was acting on a compulsion in her belly.

There was no obvious crime; Justin Reynolds had definitely committed suicide, but there was something in his letter that would not let her go. She knew she could be courting trouble for herself. She didn't know how Kim would react and had been fighting that thought throughout the bus journey.

But, wasn't this what she'd been trained to do? she asked herself as she turned into Aston Drive.

Only when she saw the small, tidy, semi-detached property did she question the actual logistics of her actions.

Behind that door was a grieving family. A mother who had lost her son in one of the most horrific ways imaginable. What if she was about to walk into a house full of well-wishers, family members, comforters, all trying to bring a moment's relief from the pain?

Stacey slowed as she neared the property. Only a small Citroën was parked outside. A couple more vehicles were dotted around the kerb but no others close to the house.

What exactly was she hoping to achieve? Stacey asked herself critically. She had nothing to offer this family, nothing to ease the grief. And yet she was still being propelled forward.

She wondered, briefly, if her own boss ever questioned herself quite so rigorously before acting on her gut instinct. She suspected not.

Bravely, she tapped the door and ignored the part of her that hoped the knock went unanswered.

Too soon, she saw a shape looming closer towards the glass-panelled door.

It opened to reveal a woman in her early to mid-forties. Her frame was slight and no colour graced her cheeks. Stacey had not met Justin's mother properly on the day of her son's death; she had been flanked by paramedics checking her over and neighbours offering words of solace. Today, she wore jogging bottoms that had room enough for two and a grey hoody. It took Stacey a second to realise the woman was wearing her dead son's clothes.

'Mrs Reynolds, my name is Stacey… I mean, Detective Constable Stacey Wood.'

She fumbled in her satchel, and then dropped her ID card on the ground. She scooted down and retrieved it, holding it up to the woman's questioning gaze.

Mrs Reynolds looked past the card and frowned.

'You were here the other day, when…' The words trailed away.

'Yes, I was. I'm so sorry for your loss,' Stacey said, trying to ignore the awkwardness.

This was a mistake. She should never have come. She wasn't used to this. She wasn't the one asking questions in the face of someone's pain. She was the one making the tea. Her curiosity would have been best left in her head.

Perhaps this was a good lesson on the thin line between curiosity and instinct.

But the damage was now done. She had knocked on the door. She had interrupted the woman's grief. If she turned and walked away now, Mrs Reynolds would definitely be making some kind of call to Halesowen Police Station.

'May I come in?' she asked.

Mrs Reynolds stood aside as Stacey stepped into the narrow hallway.

The woman closed the door and Stacey followed to the lounge.

'Is this some kind of official visit?' Mrs Reynolds asked, wrinkling her nose in confusion.

'No Mrs Reynolds… it's not. I'm just here to…' Her words trailed away as she fought to find the right words.

'I'm sorry, officer, but I think I'd quite like you to explain yourself.'

Her tone of frustration was understandable. Stacey was still trying to make sense of it herself.

'I read his letter,' Stacey said, as if that explained everything.

'And?' she said, coming to a stop in the lounge.

Stacey was faced with condolence cards resting on every surface. Her intrusion into this woman's grief slapped her around the face.

'I'm sorry, I shouldn't have come,' Stacey offered, wishing she never had.

'But why did you?' the woman asked, lowering herself onto a single seat. She stroked at the fabric of the jogging bottoms.

Stacey perched on the edge of the sofa. She was already envisioning the letter of complaint that would be sent in regarding her conduct. There was no way back for her now.

Naked honesty was her only hope.

'Mrs Reynolds, when I read that letter from your son, I felt something.' Stacey tapped her chest. 'It started here and ended here,' she said, touching her stomach. 'I really can't explain it,' Stacey said, feeling every angle of inadequate.

'But there's no doubt, is there?' she asked. 'I mean…'

Stacey shook her head. 'No, Mrs Reynolds, there is no doubt that Justin took his own life but I'm curious to know why.'

The tears sprang into the woman's eyes. 'I can barely live with the fact that I'll never know.'

Stacey ached to reach out and comfort her, but she kept her hands in her lap.

'It's that one line,' Stacey said. 'Do you have any idea what he was sorry for?'

Mrs Reynolds shook her head as she wiped furiously at her cheek.

'It's the question that has kept me awake since his, since he—'

'Have you spoken to his friends?' Stacy asked, to prevent her from saying the words her mouth was struggling to set free into reality.

'I barely even know who his friends are any more. I don't think he was in touch with many of his old school friends. They drifted away after…'

'After what, Mrs Reynolds?' Stacey asked.

'The accident,' she said.

'Go on,' Stacey urged.

She swallowed deeply. 'Two years ago, Justin's father and sister were killed in a car accident.'

'Oh, I'm so sorry,' Stacey said, wondering how much pain one woman could take. When the body was being pounded with physical blows the flesh eventually checked out. Major organs began to close down. But the heart was different. How much loss and grief could the body take before it finally gave up?

'After that he closed down completely. He lost his job, got into some fights, refused to leave his room. Eventually his friends stopped calling and texting, and he seemed okay with that. But recently he seemed better. He'd started to go out occasionally. He was looking for another job.'

She shook her head.

'But that still doesn't explain the comment about being sorry for what he'd done,' Stacey said, gently.

A flicker of understanding came into Mrs Reynolds' eyes, as though a question had just been answered.

'Actually, officer. I think it does. He was there, you see. Justin was in the car. His father and sister were both killed instantly in the front of the car. Justin walked away with barely a scratch.'

'But he still wasn't responsible for the accident or either of the deaths,' Stacey said. 'It wasn't anything he did.'

'Oh, but it was,' she said, nodding vigorously. 'Because he gave the front seat up for his sister.'

CHAPTER 34

After circling the car park at Russells Hall three times, Kim took a spot reserved for maternity parking.

'You shouldn't really do that,' Travis said, disapprovingly.

She took the keys from the ignition and held them out towards him.

'Here, feel free to drive around all night while I go in on my own.'

He ignored the outstretched hand and got out of the car. Yeah, with evening visiting fast approaching, she didn't think so.

'So, you want to lead this one or are you happy to let me do all the work?' The words did not sound as conciliatory in the air as they had in her head.

'As ever, our perception of events is completely different,' he said, bitterly.

She hadn't meant for the simple comment to fuel the animosity that still sat between them like a pungent smell. Five years of hostility could not be erased by one traumatic incident earlier that day.

'Still blaming everyone else, Tom?' she shot out.

He ignored her, and they made the walk to the ward in silence.

They were buzzed through, and Travis almost collided with the food trolley that was being wheeled into position at the end of the corridor.

Kim held her smile in check as Travis sought directions from the ward sister.

She followed him through an assortment of smells that signalled the distribution of the evening meal. Oh yeah, hospital food was sure to cheer the patients right up. Vegetables fit for a hockey match; mashed potato that had lived in hope of a sprinkling of salt and a piece of unidentifiable meat. Or if you were lucky, a brown MDF sandwich. No wonder people were so desperate to escape.

Kim was more surprised to see Fiona sitting beside the bed than Fiona was to see her. The set expression was already on her face.

'Miss Cowley, Mister Cowley,' Travis said, nodding at them both. Fiona Cowley offered a slight incline of the head. Billy Cowley did not.

Kim could see why. The dressing on the left side of his neck was as padded as a newborn baby's nappy.

Travis moved to Billy's left-hand side. Both Billy and his sister eyed her colleague suspiciously. Kim remained at the foot of the bed.

'It's good to see you looking better, Mr Cowley. May I call you Billy?' he asked, gently.

Billy hesitated then nodded.

'Probably a stupid question but I'm going to ask it anyway. How are you feeling?'

Billy opened his mouth but the answer came from his sister.

'He can't speak due to his injury,' she said, as she took Billy's hand in her own. 'And yes, it is a stupid question.'

Travis smiled disarmingly at Fiona, accepting her rebuke.

Kim stood and watched with interest. This was a side of Travis she hadn't seen for a very long time.

Travis continued to offer small talk, while Kim observed the siblings. Billy Cowley looked younger than his twenty-six years. His fair hair flopped over warm blue eyes that were busy darting between his sister and Travis.

Fiona, on the other hand, looked older than her twenty-eight years. There was a grey pallor to her skin that reached into the temples of her dark brown hair. But it was more than just her severity in both appearance and manner. The relationship between the siblings presented more as parent and child.

'So, can you tell us a bit more about the shooting incident, Billy?' Travis asked.

Kim liked the way he continued to aim his questions at the victim despite his sister's determination to dominate.

'It was an accident,' Fiona said, squeezing her brother's hand.

'Oh, I see,' Travis said, amiably. 'And he told you this?' he asked, subtly calling her on the fact he couldn't speak.

Kim saw the panic in Billy's eyes.

Fiona recovered quickly. 'My father told me what happened. He saw the whole thing.'

'Really?' Travis asked, surprised. 'We arrived before the ambulance, and your father told us he was alerted by the sound of a gunshot but hadn't actually seen a thing.'

A smattering of colour flushed her cheeks. 'It had just happened. He was in shock. He remembers it now,' she said.

I'll bet he does, Kim thought.

'No problem,' Travis said, agreeably.

Not what Kim would have said. She was sure 'barefaced liar' would have been in there somewhere.

'We'll need to confirm that with your father. Get a bit more detail and take the necessary statements. Obviously, ballistics will match the bullet to the gun, and we can leave it at that. And I'm sure the residue on your brother's hands will confirm that he was the one holding the gun.'

Okay, Travis's way of calling her a barefaced liar with the added undercurrent of *we're gonna catch you out* was more tactful than Kim's way. And still the pleasant smile remained on his face.

Kim saw Fiona's tongue pass over her lips.

'It's a very simple test,' Travis continued. 'The residue on Billy's hands will be made up of burned and unburned primer combined with residue from the surface of the bullet, cartridge case and lubricants...'

'But you can't do it now, can you?' Fiona asked.

Travis nodded, pleasantly. 'I'm sure we could. All I'd need is an alcohol wipe and I could pop that into one of these...' He opened his wallet. On the left-hand side were pockets holding business cards, pens and small evidence bags. '... and we wouldn't have to bother you again.'

'He can't give his permission,' she said, frowning.

Damn, Kim thought. It hadn't taken her long to recover.

Travis nodded. 'But that shouldn't be a problem, should it? I'm sure you could do so as you'd want us to corroborate his story as soon as we can.'

She shook her head vehemently. 'He can't give permission as he is unable to speak and I am not prepared to do so on his behalf.'

Kim saw another squeeze of the hand. Billy Cowley looked terrified.

Travis nodded. 'No problem. We'll ask one of the techs to come and take the sample once we've obtained permission from your father.' He shoved a hand across the bed. 'Thank you for your time, and I'm sure we'll speak soon.'

Kim nodded to both of them as she followed Travis out of the ward.

'Do we have the bullet?' she asked.

He nodded. 'Gibbs got it last night once it was removed from Billy's neck.'

'Jesus, slow down,' she said, as they entered the main corridor.

'Not my problem if you can't keep up, Stone,' he threw behind.

Two more paces and she was level.

'What's the rush?' she said, as they hit the outside crowds.

'Think about it,' he said, sidling behind a group of smokers obscuring the 'No Smoking' sign.

She looked at his head towering above the plume of smoke. 'If we're supposed to be hiding, I suggest you duck down a bit.'

He moved further into the wall.

Kim peered through the smokers. If Fiona had been lying to them she would now have to cover her tracks, quickly. She would need to get home and tell her father what he'd seen. Travis had deliberately stated their next course of action to flush out hers. She would have to get to her father before they did.

'And there she goes,' Kim said, as Fiona sprinted over the crossing right in front of a taxi.

Travis started walking towards the maternity car park at speed.

'Hey, Travis, it's almost six. Aren't we getting past your curfew?' she asked. 'I mean, I'd hate to see you turn into a pumpkin.'

He shot her a frosty look. 'I'm not going anywhere, Stone. Just need to make one call.'

Kim started the car as he took out his phone and stepped away from her.

She felt a smile fighting its way onto her face.

Now, it was feeling familiar.

CHAPTER 35

Bryant parked behind Keats's van at the mouth of Buck Tunnel on what was known locally as the Codsall estate.

Bryant remembered football matches as a kid on Bearmore Bank, the playing fields right next to the Burton Delingpole factory manufacturing flanges and fittings. He remembered the evening siren that sounded right before black-faced men spewed out of the building and headed home for a warm meal.

Bryant wasn't naïve enough to view the past through rose-tinted glasses. He didn't believe there had been fewer problems for families in the seventies and eighties. Just a different kind. Many of the factories and foundries of that era had been responsible for thousands of health problems still being identified today. The average life expectancy had increased by more than ten years due to better working practices. Yet when he recalled the camaraderie he'd witnessed at the mass exodus of the workers at night, he felt saddened at its loss.

The factory had closed in the mid-eighties and been replaced by houses, the occupants of which were already formed into small groups on both sides of the road. They could see nothing, but it didn't spoil the entertainment of speculation.

He shook his head as one of the constables handed them plastic shoes and nodded towards the incline leading up to the railway track that was about halfway between the train stations of Cradley Heath and Old Hill.

As he trudged through knee-high grass, he took a few deep swallows. Even though Keats had warned them that the scene was gruesome he could not have prepared himself for what he was about to see.

He heard Dawson curse behind as he slipped on the already frosted vegetation. He considered turning to offer his hand but thought better of it. The kid's ego would not thank him.

At the top of the slope temporary floodlights bounced off the sea of reflective jackets of clusters of railway workers, police officers and crime scene techs. There was little movement and Bryant could feel the shock and horror in the air.

His colleague appeared beside him and began dusting the dirt from his knees.

'Oh Jesus,' Dawson said, mid swipe.

Bryant followed his gaze and almost gagged.

The body of a young male was sprawled across the rails. His head was two metres down the track.

Keats turned and smiled as he saw the two of them.

'Finally, a pairing I can live with,' he said. 'Care to make it permanent, boys?' he asked.

'No,' they said, together.

Keats shrugged away his disappointment.

'Come closer, for goodness' sake,' he chided.

Bryant realised they had both stopped short a good three metres from the decapitated victim.

'Suicide?' Dawson asked. A question not as stupid as it sounded. They had both attended scenes of death by train. Most times the person would throw themselves from a bridge into the path of an oncoming train, giving the driver no chance of slowing down.

Others did it as the train was pulling into a station; rather than jump, they would simply fold and fall into the train's path.

Personally he felt they were selfish bastards. He had met train drivers suffering from PTSD, depression, and other devastating conditions as a result of someone else's choice to end their own life.

Keats leaned down in response to Dawson's question and pointed to the remnants of string that had fallen inside the track, along with most of the victim's fingers. The cleanliness of the severed flesh instantly brought to mind the picture of a meat slicer used in a butcher's shop.

'Even the most determined soul can't bind both hands,' Keats answered.

'With help?' Bryant asked. He'd heard of stranger assisted suicide cases than this.

'Oh, he had help all right but I don't think it was wanted. Look at the footprint between the shoulder blades.'

'To hold him in place while the train passed by?' Dawson asked, echoing his own thoughts.

Keats shook his head. 'No, because the perpetrator would have been too close to the train.'

Bryant forced himself to look closely at the severed stump of the man's neck above the shoulders. A pool of blood covered the gravel between the tracks where the head had been sliced off. He was reminded of the cheap magic tricks with a guillotine and a basket. Except this was no trick and the head to his left was not made of latex.

Keats then pointed to a length of green garden string enmeshed in the pasty white flesh.

'To tie his neck in place?' Bryant asked.

Keats nodded. 'I suspect to make sure he was facing the right direction.'

He nodded east.

The track continued from the body approximately twenty metres before disappearing around a bend. The train driver would have had no hope of stopping the train.

'He didn't have a bloody chance,' Dawson breathed. 'Train needs more than two hundred metres to stop at just sixty miles an hour.'

Bryant shuddered. The victim would have heard the train in the distance, hurtling towards him, waiting for it to come into view, praying the driver would see him before it was too late. And then it would have been there, thundering towards him. All the time he had known what was coming.

He shuddered again and glanced sideways at his colleague, who had suddenly gone quiet.

He followed Dawson's pensive gaze over the baggy, low slung jeans and bright orange trainers.

A colourful piece of cloth peeped out below the blue North Face padded jacket.

'Kev, you okay?'

Dawson ignored him. 'Keats, has the head been moved yet?'

'No, it's the next job,' he said.

'Can we do it now?' Dawson asked, moving towards it.

'Oh my, this new partner of yours poses it as a question,' he said, nudging Bryant as he walked past. 'This one's a keeper.'

Bryant ignored the pathologist's dig at his boss and followed in his colleague's footsteps.

Like Dawson, he stared down at the severed head. The light brown hair ended unnaturally, like a blunt fringe turned upside down.

Keats beckoned one of his assistants and slowly they turned the head face up. The eyes were closed but the mouth was partially open. His peaceful expression did not reflect the barbaric horror of the last few seconds of his life. The ashen skin was covered in white chalk marks and grazes where the head had bounced along the gravel.

Bryant was surprised by the lack of blood on the pallid skin but his colleague appeared to be surprised by something else.

'Bloody hell,' he said, hoarsely. 'I fucking know this kid.'

CHAPTER 36

Stacey closed the door of the café and allowed the relief to wash over her. This was familiarity. This was normal. This was not out of her comfort zone, like going to people's houses and invading their grief.

Mrs Reynolds had appeared satisfied that she had discovered the source of her son's pain. Stacey was not so sure. It had been two years since the death of his father and sister. And although that was a loss that a teenager would never properly recover from, two years would have brought some level of healing.

Even so, Mrs Reynolds had allowed Stacey to take Justin's computer away with her, which told Stacey there was an element of doubt still lingering in her mind.

She moved one place up the queue when a woman left after being told they'd stopped serving hot food.

Priscilla spied her in the queue and turned to place a teacake onto the grill. Stacey didn't feel like eating but she appreciated the familiarity of the gesture.

By the time she reached the front of the queue, the steaming teacake and drink was waiting for her.

'You okay?' Priscilla asked.

'Rough day,' she said, turning around. She had hoped a seat would have become available, but the stragglers from market day still nursed lukewarm drinks before heading off in their product-laden vans.

'Come with me,' Priscilla said from beside her.

Stacey followed the woman just past the toilets to a single table by the 'Staff Only' door; currently it was covered in folders and paperwork.

Priscilla scooped it all into one pile.

'It's our break table. Have your teacake in peace.'

Stacey smiled gratefully as she folded herself into the cramped space.

She buttered the teacake before pushing the plate to the side. The golden mound turned to liquid and disappeared.

She placed Justin's laptop on the table and opened the lid. Unfortunately, his mother had no clue to her son's password but Stacey had extracted enough information about him to start with the obvious.

Despite online warnings about the strength of passwords, people still opted for something simple to remember using their own personal information. The most common was a derivation of the person's name with digits added.

She tried Justin's name and his date of birth but she got nothing.

She tried a few variations of both name and birthdate using capitals in key places.

Her hands flew over the keys. The more passwords needed the simpler the construction. Few people could recall numerous passwords to an array of social platforms. Shockingly, some people still opted for the word 'password' as their password.

She reached absently around the laptop for her drink as a hand clamped her shoulder.

The drink almost flew to the ground.

'Fuck's sake, Kev. What the?…'

'Hey, easy tiger. I was just passing and saw you in here.'

'Kev, you're a liar,' she said, as her heart began to slow down. 'No one can see me back here.'

He looked around. 'You ain't kidding.'

'So, what do you want?' she asked, easing down the lid of the laptop.

He ignored the question.

'And how was your day, Kev?' he asked himself on her behalf. 'Well, Stace, thanks for asking. We were called to the body of a young kid on the railway tracks. Pretty harrowing if you want the truth,' he answered himself.

Stacey sat back and watched the show.

He continued. 'A kid I recognised as well, since you ask.' He stopped and looked down at her plate. 'You eating that?'

She pushed the plate towards him. He lifted a piece and bit into it. Two chews and a swallow. Kevin Dawson ate the way he did everything else; quickly, eager to move on to the next thing.

'Which clearly bothered you enormously,' she said, pointedly. 'So, other than my teacake, what do you want?'

'You left in a hurry, earlier. Where did you go?' he asked, glancing at the laptop.

'None of your business. Now get lost, I've got goblins to kill,' she said, following his gaze to the computer.

He shrugged. 'Just wanted to check on you. You know, how mates do.'

She didn't try to keep the disbelief from her face. 'Dow treat me like a donkey, Kev. We are many things but we ain't mates.'

'Stace, I just—'

'For the third time, what do you want?'

He put the teacake down and fixed her with a stare.

'Stace, I am an arsehole. We both know that's true, but what happened earlier…' His words trailed away as he shook his head and looked back at the teacake.

It took Stacey a moment to catch up. She couldn't believe it was still on his mind. He was right when he admitted to being an arsehole; but he wasn't a nasty arsehole. He often gave the impression that nothing penetrated his cocky exterior but sometimes, just occasionally, something got through.

'Oh, Kev, ignore me. I didn't mean anything by it.'

'So, why say it?' he asked. 'You know there's not a racist bone in my body.'

She shrugged. 'Sometimes your arrogance needs a bit of a shake, Kev. You think you have all the answers all the time. It riles me, because you leave no room for improvement.'

'Huh?' he said, as he reached again for the teacake.

'Everything changes over time; things grow, adapt, learn and become more. Except you. You're the same person I met two years ago.'

He offered her a chewy smile. 'But don't you love me just the way I am?'

'No, Kev, I don't,' she said. 'Because I think you can be more.'

She watched as the top of her teacake disappeared completely. He rubbed his hands together above the plate to dust off the crumbs.

She touched her own cheek to demonstrate the ones he'd left behind. He brushed and they were gone. A smile bubbled somewhere within her. Sometimes he really was just like a little boy.

'What was it like, Stace?' he asked suddenly. 'What was school like for you?'

She was about to brush him off with a flippant comment until she saw the humour in his eyes had been replaced with gentle curiosity.

'Difficult, Kev,' she said, honestly. 'I was surrounded by two different types of people. People that were horrible to me because of my colour and people that were overly nice to me because of it, trying to prove to themselves and to me that it didn't matter. Often expecting gratitude because they "didn't care",' she said, sighing. 'Anyone who is different in any way is fair game for the bullies.'

These were not memories she wanted to relive. Suddenly she remembered something.

'Weren't you the fat kid?' she asked.

He nodded. 'Oh yeah.'

'So, to some degree you get what I mean,' she said. 'So, what did you do?'

'I lost weight,' he said, quietly, as a measure of understanding came into his face.

She raised her eyebrow in response. No amount of weight loss would have changed the colour of her skin.

'Got it,' he said, smiling. But not before she saw the wave of sadness pass over his features.

But, as pleasant as his impromptu visit was, she was eager to get back to Justin Reynolds's laptop. She took a quick look at her watch.

'Bloody hell, Stace. You been taking subtlety lessons from the boss?'

'No, I didn't mean…'

It was exactly what she'd meant and he knew it.

'So, we're all good?' he asked, sincerely.

'Yeah, Kev, we're fine,' she answered.

'Okay, see you tomorrow,' he said, tapping her right shoulder.

She didn't respond, as he was already out of earshot.

As far as Dawson was concerned racism was as simple as a black-and-white negative; racist or not, bigot or not. To explain the shades of grey that existed between the two extremes would take far too long. And right now she just didn't have the time.

She opened the laptop lid and the log in screen flashed into life.

It suddenly occurred to her that many people used the name of a loved one instead of their own.

She tried variations of Justin's birthday and his mother's name. Nothing.

She tried Justin's dates with the name of his father.

Nothing.

She tried Justin's dates with the name of his sister.

Still no joy.

Suddenly she looked around to find the café had emptied around her. Priscilla was busy with a mop and bucket.

Finally, she tried his sister's name and the date of her death.

She sat back as the screen flashed into life.

Bingo. She was in.

CHAPTER 37

Every light shone from the farmhouse, guiding their path to the rest of the parked vehicles, and once again highlighting the squalor and filth of the property. Rusted pieces of machinery were propped against the walls of the outbuildings. A pile of straw covered in excrement sat ten feet away from the side of the house. Half-opened bags of cattle feed were strewn everywhere.

A cordon stretched from the drainpipe on the side of the farmhouse to a tree at the end of the gravel drive, approximately ten feet from the bloodstain where Billy Cowley had been shot.

Kim cringed as she saw a well-fed rat scurry unashamedly across the mud towards the old barn.

'Even though it's a shit hole, Travis, I'd like to know why they've paid no rent for so many years,' Kim said, with disgust.

'Yeah, not even a token amount,' he agreed, as they headed towards the cottage.

Unsurprisingly, Fiona was waiting for them at the front door.

They had been held up by a poorly parked taxi collecting a very frail, elderly man. By the time she'd managed to exit the hospital, Fiona was long gone and had certainly made it home in time to feed her father the story she wanted him to tell.

Her red Jaguar was parked at the very edge of the property as though she didn't want it contaminated.

Kim could understand it. She counted six other vehicles: four ranging in age from seven to fifteen years, and two techie vans.

Kim recognised the brogues of a masked technician named Ben who had worked on many of the cases she'd been involved in.

'Hey,' she said, standing beside him as he took fresh evidence bags from the rear of the van. 'Anyone being obstructive?'

He removed the mask and smiled. 'Just attentive,' he said, nodding towards the doorway.

Yeah, she could believe it.

'Special attention to the fibres, if you can, Ben,' she said, remembering Doctor A's recent discovery.

'No probs,' he said, as she headed towards the house.

'That was quick,' Kim said, as she stepped past the scowling woman into the home.

'You can't just—'

'Yes, we can,' Kim answered. This woman had obstructed the investigation enough. The warrant had been served while they were at the hospital and Fiona Cowley knew who they were. There was no need for further explanation, and Kim was in no doubt that this woman knew more than she was letting on.

The open door led straight into a dark, poky kitchen with a small north-facing window. The wall cabinets were plain and square and badly painted. Two doors still bore the old wooden frontage, as though someone had realised part way through that their efforts to update or modernise were a total waste of time.

An Aga took up most of the wall opposite the window. Kim had no idea if it was functional as the top was a storage area for an electric kettle and tea canisters. A bean-stained camping stove sat next to it. A black plastic bin dominated the corner, spewing burger wrappers and pizza boxes all over the floor. The smell of stale refuse was a slight improvement on the overpowering odour of damp that weaved through the house.

She turned to Fiona, who was shadowing right behind them. 'If you don't mind giving your address to Travis,' Kim said. 'We may need it later.'

Fiona looked surprised, but began dictating it to Travis, who opened his leather folder.

Of course Fiona didn't live here. It wouldn't look like this if she did. The woman was clean and smart and wouldn't tolerate it. Hell, she didn't even want her shiny red Jaguar getting too close in case it caught something.

Kim took the step down into the lounge that could have been the heart of the home with the original features that were expensively emulated in modern homes. The brick fireplace and oak beams were lost amongst the mismatched furniture and heavy patterns that jarred against each other. The room was lit by a single naked bulb glaring yellow from the middle of the room.

The pleasant space had been filled with heavy, dark furniture from at least seven or eight different decades. The walls were dripping in pictures of farm animals and brass horseshoes mounted on leather strips.

The three seater sofa was purple with worn patches on the two end cushions. The back of the seat rose up to a fan shape in the middle. Foster family two had owned one back in the late eighties.

Mr Cowley stepped past three techies working by torchlight as he entered the lounge from the other end, leaving what looked like some kind of utility room.

'Mr Cowley, good to see you again,' she said, stepping forward. Kim could sense Fiona behind her but she continued speaking directly to him. 'Thank you for your permission in swabbing Billy's hands. I'm sure we'll be able to put this shooting matter to bed shortly.'

Kim heard Fiona's sharp intake of breath. He hadn't told his daughter he'd given his consent.

As soon as Fiona had careered off the hospital car park, Kim had called Mr Cowley direct to reach him before his daughter did and obtained his permission.

'The forensic technician should be with him now.'

He nodded in her direction. He didn't look at his daughter but his gaze narrowed. She could see his hand fidgeting in his trouser pocket.

'Your daughter mentioned that you remembered some details about your son's accident,' she said. 'Not least that you actually witnessed it,' she added.

Again he nodded. The fidgeting in his pocket continued.

'So, could you tell us exactly what you saw, Mr Cowley?' she asked.

'Yes, I was putting out the rubbish, and I saw Billy messing with the gun over by the bar. I called out to him…'

'Slow down,' Kim said, having already learned three key facts: firstly, the rubbish was still in the kitchen and hadn't been put out in days, possibly weeks; secondly she could smell the alcohol on his breath, and finally, he wanted to get this story out as quickly as possible.

Before he forgot what he was supposed to say, Kim thought.

Travis took a seat on the stained sofa, and she silently applauded his bravery. Until she realised exactly what he was doing. A memory threatened to bring a smile to her face but she kept it in check. He hadn't forgotten everything.

'So, you were putting out the rubbish?' she asked.

'Yeah, we always just leave it outside the front door.'

That explained the healthy looking rodent she'd seen outside.

'And what drew your attention towards Billy?' she asked.

She wasn't sure his son over by the cowshed would be too far out of the ordinary.

'I don't know. I think it was that he was holding the gun.'

'It's a rifle, isn't it?' she asked.

Normal hardware for a farm.

'Yes, he was turning it around and I remember thinking…'

'So, you stopped to watch him because he was holding the gun or twirling the gun?' Kim asked, slowing him down. The script was scrolling through his head and he was eager to follow it. She didn't enjoy the harsh line of questioning but she needed to distract him from the autocue in his mind.

'I think he was just holding it but I thought something was going to…'

'You thought that from your son just holding the gun?' she questioned. Mr Cowley was far too eager to get to the accident part. 'Is he not to be trusted with a gun?'

The man ran his hand over his bald head.

'No, no, it's not that,' he said, defensively. 'It just looked strange,' he said, getting flustered.

Kim had no choice but to capitalise on his confusion. She turned to the side so that Travis was in her peripheral vision.

'Shall we go outside and take a closer look at where it happened?' she asked. It wasn't Mr Cowley's reaction she sought. It was the slight nod from Travis she was after.

Fiona led them out of the lounge, through the kitchen and back outside.

'So, you were standing here?' she asked, pausing right in front of the open doorway.

'Yes, as I said. I was putting out—'

'The rubbish. Yes, I know,' she finished for him, while pointedly looking around for the missing rubbish bag.

'And Billy was over by the barn?' she asked.

'Yes,' he said, as his pocket began to move again.

'And he was holding a shotgun?' she said.

'Yes.'

'And a shotgun is how long?'

'About two feet,' he answered. 'Maybe a little more.'

Kim looked around. Her eyes fell on a thin piece of stump wood.

'May I?'

Mr Cowley nodded and stole a quick glance at his daughter who watched pensively, arms folded.

Kim placed the piece of wood against the wall. She brought her foot down and cracked it.

She picked up the longer piece. 'About this long?'

'Yes,' he said.

'Could you just remain where you are, Mr Cowley?' she asked. He nodded.

She walked towards the area where Billy had been standing.

Travis was now right behind her.

She lowered her voice, so only he could hear.

'So, Billy's twirling the gun and manages to shoot himself in the back of the neck. Let's see how that works out, shall we?'

She began twirling the stick like a baton.

'So, the trigger would be about here?' she asked Travis.

He nodded. She looked around for something to mark it.

'Lipstick?' he asked

'Have you met me?' she shot back without looking at him.

She reached down and retrieved a piece of slate from the ground, praying that the fat rat was long gone. She scored the wood and put her finger on the groove.

'Are they watching?' she asked.

'Oh yes,' Travis said.

Good. She wanted them to see how ridiculous their claim was, and if that meant a bit of play-acting from her, then so be it.

She stretched her arms, keeping one finger on the trigger mark. The gun wavered before settling beneath her chin. The suicide position. She adjusted the angle and the end moved further along her neck.

She changed position and fed the piece of wood up and over her shoulder.

'That's about the closest,' Travis said.

'Yeah, but I can't keep my finger on the trigger.'

She handed him the gun. 'You have longer arms.'

He took it and repeated her movements as she watched.

'Possible but more likely to be a graze or a flesh wound rather than the bullet entering the body.'

And they both knew it had.

They were currently reliant on the report from ballistics to confirm the bullet had come from that gun. Until then she couldn't run up to them and scream 'liar, liar'.

She sighed and took a step back towards Fiona and her anxious-looking father.

Her phone signalled a message. She took it out and read the short sentence. She turned to Travis with a smile and then strolled back to the family members.

'Was there anything you saw us do just then that looked familiar, Mr Cowley?'

'Yes,' he said, eagerly. 'Over the shoulder. I think Billy was putting the gun over his shoulder.'

Fiona stepped forward. Kim was surprised she had stayed silent for this long.

'Officer, what does this have to do with the discovery of bones on the land? There has been no crime committed here. My brother had an accident as he has already confirmed.'

'That you confirmed for him,' Kim reminded. She had yet to hear Billy Cowley speak.

'But my father…'

'Is recounting everything you told him to,' she said coldly.

'How dare you?'

'How dare you.' Kim replied. 'How dare you blatantly lie to us? Did you think we would take your word for it with a firearm involved?'

'It's the truth,' she growled.

Kim took a deep breath. 'So, despite it being almost a physical impossibility, and the fact we've just confirmed with the hospital there was no gunshot residue on your brother's hands or neck, you still insist your story is that it was an accidental shooting?'

Fiona faced her squarely. 'Yes, Inspector, that's our story.'

CHAPTER 38

Kim paused before pulling away from the Cowley property.

'Travis, what the hell is going on here?' she asked, trying to understand their determination to stick to a sequence of events that simply didn't happen.

'I thought you were going to arrest her,' Travis said.

'I was,' she admitted.

'For what?'

'Smugness,' she replied.

She would swear that a chuckle almost popped out before he smothered it with a cough.

'So, did you get anything?' she asked.

When they'd worked together in the past, Tom had had a thing for checking sofas. He maintained that whatever was down there was not even known by the owners. Nine times out of ten he came up empty, but just one time he'd found the missing earring of an assault victim who claimed she'd been raped and held hostage. The forty-seven-year-old male had denied all knowledge. Until Travis had found the earring hanging on to the lining of the sofa.

'Something fell onto my hand,' he said, reaching into his trouser pocket.

She pulled over into a bus stop.

A jagged, torn off piece of paper was in his palm.

Travis blew away the hair, fluff and sofa debris that had attached itself to the scrap.

'You know you should have bagged that and left it with the techies,' she observed.

'It stuck to me,' he offered lamely.

The murky colour of the paper told her it had been there some time. It was the size of a medium envelope, bank-statement size. One side was blank, and the other had printed capital lettering.

A brown stain coloured the top-left corner. A chunk was missing from the centre. Her eyes skimmed back and forth over it a dozen times trying to mentally insert the missing words.

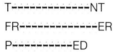

```
T-------------NT
FR------------ER
P----------ED
```

'This could be anything,' she said, shortly

'And yet you're stuffing it into your pocket,' he said, ruefully. 'When it was my find.'

He had a point but she had no intention of giving it back.

Silence settled between them but for a while, a short while, it had been very much like old times.

'Where to?' she asked.

'I'd like you to take me home,' he said, zipping up the wallet.

She sighed heavily. 'Tom, are we ever going to discuss what happened back—'

'No, Stone, we're not,' he said, emphatically.

'Fuck's sake, Tom. How long can you hold a grudge?' she cried, at his stubbornness.

'You never even said you were sorry,' he shouted back.

'Because I'm not,' she snapped.

The silence was more deafening than the shouting because it was final. While the accusations were flying between them there was a chance they could stumble upon some common ground. And the silence confirmed they never would.

After a few moments his steady voice broke the tension.

'I'll say it once more before I get out of the car and call a taxi: I'd like you to take me home.'

Kim knew any further attempts at conversation were futile. She drove towards Kidderminster without speaking.

As she pulled up outside the house she voiced what had been building in her mind.

'Tom, as this is a joint investigation, I'd like to lead the briefing tomorrow.'

She had expected outright refusal. Tom Travis was a proud man. But his hesitation gave her hope.

'I'll think about it,' he said, as he got out of the car.

Kim sat still and watched the curtain twitch as it did every night. Well, if the man was on a curfew, he was going to get punished tonight.

As she pulled away she tried to leave the sadness at his doorstep. Part of her wished she had not caught a glimpse of the man, and more importantly, the police officer, she had once known. The last few years had been filled with so much bitterness and animosity that it was sometimes hard to remember that she had once respected and liked this man – and even on occasion trusted him with her life.

But she knew now that they would never be able to get past what happened back then.

And that fact bothered her more than it should.

CHAPTER 39

'Come on, boy, help me out here,' Kim said, looking down at Barney.

She had showered and changed and now sat astride the Kawasaki Ninja, her bare feet resting on the pedals as she surveyed the wipe board that occupied a full wall of her garage.

Barney returned her gaze. If big brown eyes and a wagging tail could assist, she'd have the puzzle sorted by now.

The whole day had stuck to Kim like marker pen and had taken some scrubbing away. But now she had something to focus on, the negative began to fade. She had copied the letters, spacing and placement of them on the paper onto the wipe board to study. With the missing letters it was pretty much impossible to fill in the gaps. She felt as though she was playing a heavily biased game of Hangman.

And yet the structure was familiar to her. The letters had been centred across the page.

Damn it, had this been her own investigation she would have had this displayed prominently in the office so they could all ponder it. Four heads were most definitely better than one – depending on who the four heads were.

Kim knew she wasn't adjusting to the dynamics of the joint investigation as well as Woody would like. Every hour that she managed to endure was a victory of fist-pump proportions.

The worst thing wasn't even being stuck next to a man that hated her more than most of the folks she'd put behind bars. It was the slow, methodical approach to every piece of information. It felt as though Travis was constantly trying to find an operating theatre in the middle of a battleground. Sometimes you just had to get down in the mud and crack on.

And, God help her, she missed her team. Never would that thought see the other side of her lips. It was hard enough admitting it to herself. But she knew them. She could land a case and immediately visualise the best way of dividing the work. She knew that Stacey would not stop digging until she unearthed what she was after. She knew that Dawson would follow his own instinct and find good solid leads. And Bryant, well his brain would complement her own instead of slow it down.

She wondered if she was going soft in her old age, as now and again she even missed Woody.

She sighed and turned her attention back to the puzzle. There was something trying to make itself known to her.

She growled as her phone rang, then rolled her eyes when she saw the caller.

'Frost,' she said, swinging her legs back and forth on the bike.

'I wanna know what you're doing,' she said without greeting. 'What progress have you made? Have you identified any suspects?'

'Bloody hell, even you're normally more subtle than this,' Kim observed. 'You know I'm not going to comment on—'

'Are you kidding, Stone?' Frost said with an unusually thick voice. 'This is no ordinary case, and if you treat it as such I'll make your life—'

'Frost, calm down,' Kim instructed as her legs stopped swinging. 'What the hell are you talking about?'

Old bones in the ground should not have turned the reporter into this near-hysterical fishwife on the other end of her phone.

Stunned silence met her ears. 'You don't know?' Tracy cried, disbelievingly.

'Know what?' Kim asked, easing herself off the bike.

'Bubba, my trainee, dead…'

'Bloody hell, Tracy,' Kim said, placing her hand on the petrol tank for support. 'I'm so sorry. What the hell happened?'

'His head became separated from the rest of his body on train tracks earlier today.'

Kim stood still, trying to digest what she was hearing. Not only dead but murdered.

'Tracy, I'm sorry… I…'

Kim didn't want to admit the inconceivable truth; that she hadn't known.

'Well, what are you lot doing about it?' Tracy asked, choking back a sob. 'Whoever did this needs stringing up by the balls. Bubba was a good kid who didn't have it easy. I hope you're gonna pull out all the stops to catch this bastard.'

'Tracy, you know the police force will do everything they can—'

'Don't speak to me like a press liaison officer, Stone. If you tell me you're going to catch the person, I'll believe you, but get your two to pull their fingers out their arses and—'

'My two?' she asked, frowning.

'Bryant and Dawson. They attended the scene.'

The line fell silent as Frost worked it out.

'You didn't even know that, did you?' she asked, aghast. 'What the hell is going on with you and your team, Stone?'

Kim tried to work the tension from her jaw.

'Frost, I'll call you tomorrow but I'm so sorry for—'

'Save it, Stone. I'm clearly talking to the wrong person this time.'

The line went dead in her ear.

Kim didn't move for a full ten seconds as her mind tried to process everything she'd just learned.

Bubba Jones was dead.

A reporter that they knew had been viciously and horrifically murdered earlier that day.

And she didn't know about it.

Her next thought echoed Tracy Frost's accusation.

What the hell was her team playing at?

CHAPTER 40

Kim had called a 7 a.m. briefing, so was not surprised that her team was assembled and waiting. What did surprise her was the Post-it note name tags they were all wearing.

She screwed up the one marked 'boss' and launched it into the bin. On another morning it might have been funny.

Now she had their attention.

'How the hell did I not know that Bubba Jones had been murdered?' she asked, looking from one to the other, waiting for an explanation.

Her gaze finally rested on Bryant.

'Guv, you're working on another—'

'I have a phone, email, text. Jesus, you could have sent a bloody pigeon so that I wasn't blindsided by Frost at eleven thirty last night.'

'It was all over the news,' Dawson mumbled.

'And that's how you think I should have found out, Kev?' Kim raged.

If this was Dawson's attempt to protect his colleague it was both misguided and untimely.

She turned on him. 'Forgive me for taking an hour for myself after a fifteen-hour shift. Maybe tonight we'll have a briefing right here at ten o'clock so we can catch up properly.'

Her response was not strictly accurate – she had been studying the paper found by Travis – but she resented the inference that she should be informed of her team's activities by watching the bloody news.

'You're right, guv,' Bryant said. 'I should have let you know. It was down to me and I didn't do it.'

The apology was both sincere and genuine, and she accepted it with a nod in his direction.

This was new territory for them all. A different dynamic had been forced on them, disturbing the natural rhythm of their well-oiled machine. Right now they were all feeling their way.

The fact that Stacey had remained silent throughout told her that the constable had not been involved in the process either.

'So, where are we with it?' she asked, reaching for the coffee that had been waiting for her.

Although she had not met the lad personally, he had been responsible for Dawson almost losing his job a while back. The trainee reporter had managed to convince her colleague to act against her direct instruction, and it had resulted in a mountain of false leads and hours of wasted manpower.

'You cleared it with Woody?' she asked. Any prior involvement with a murder victim had to be logged and explained.

'Last night,' he answered.

'And?'

Formal permission was required to continue working the case.

'Cleared,' he answered.

For once Dawson appeared to have followed the rules.

'Tied to the tracks with his neck literally on the line,' Dawson continued. He made a cutting sign at the throat. 'Gone.'

'Family?'

'Care kid, boss. Got no siblings and last foster family haven't seen him for years.'

Kim couldn't help the wave of sympathy that stole over her. That there was no family to grieve for the young man's death saddened her. As a care kid herself there were few people from her past that had made it to her present.

'Keats finally removed the body at around eleven,' Bryant offered. 'Forensic techs are on-site but it's a bloody mess up there. That bank has been a shortcut and a hangout spot for as long as I can remember.'

Kim could only imagine the volume of debris that would need to be combed for clues.

'Woody has been on to Lloyd House for additional manpower, which will be used for door to door on the Codsall estate. We'll be focussing on Bubba's associates,' Bryant continued. 'Trace evidence isn't gonna solve this case any time soon.'

Kim agreed and offered him a half smile.

'Woody spoke to you yet?' she asked.

'Yeah, last night.'

'Acting DI?' she asked.

He nodded.

'Congratulations, Bryant,' Stacey offered with a wide smile.

'Are you joking?' Dawson exploded, glaring at Bryant.

'Calm down, Kev. It's just a title,' Bryant said.

'And quite right,' Kim offered, catching Dawson's eye. 'Bryant's skills are best suited for leading this particular case but your time will come.'

'Fair enough, boss,' Dawson said, nodding in Bryant's direction.

It was the obvious and correct thing to do, not only from a procedural point of view; Woody could not have a murder investigation headed by a DS. The only person who didn't think Bryant should hold a DI rank was Bryant himself.

She was satisfied that everything had been covered. Except informing her. But it was time now to let that go.

'Before you do anything this morning you arrange to meet with Frost, got it?'

'Got it,' they said together.

'So, how's the Henryk Kowalski investigation going?' she asked Dawson. The case had originally been his.

'Got a suspect on CCTV messing with his phone about two hundred metres from the scene. Caught him again scurrying past the supermarket on Manor Way but lost him at the Shenstone Island.'

'Any personal enemies?' she asked.

'Oh yeah, guy next door is a real charmer who has sent the family foul messages but was unfortunately accounted for during the attack.'

Dawson's tone told her he was seriously wishing that hadn't been the case.

'Respectable-looking kind of guy until you spend more than two minutes with him,' Bryant added.

'His social media accounts are not blocked, and he makes no secret of his racism,' Stacey said. 'Proud of the fact he's a member of the National Front and has participated in more than one EDL demonstration.'

'Criminal record?' Kim asked.

Stacey nodded. 'Assault charge in his teens got him a two-year suspended sentence, and he served eighteen months for harassing and threatening a family that moved into the next street.'

Kim raised an eyebrow questioningly.

'Asian,' Stacey confirmed.

She was beginning to agree with Dawson about this guy.

'Thing is, boss,' Stacey added, 'if Flint had anything to do with the assault on Henryk Kowalski, I reckon he'd come right out and say it.'

Kim nodded her agreement. 'Cast your net out a bit on this one, guys. A serious assault and a brutal murder with no key witnesses? Someone somewhere knows something.'

'Flint seemed to hint that there was more to the Henryk situation,' Bryant offered.

'Well question him harder and find out what he knows,' Kim said, feeling as though she was stating the obvious.

'We need to get to Tracy Frost first, and Gary Flint will be released on bail at around nine thirty.'

Kim was confused, 'So?'

'We can't do both, boss,' Dawson said, colouring.

Kim frowned. 'Wake up, Kev? Stacey can interview him.'

'But he's a full-on racist,' Dawson said.

'So?' Kim asked, as Stacey's face formed into triumph and a quiet 'thanks, boss,' came from her mouth.

'I doubt very much if he's got anything to say that Stacey hasn't heard before, and first and foremost she is a police officer and can handle this interview. If she is uncomfortable doing so, I trust her to let me know.' She looked at the detective constable. 'That right, Stace?'

'Yeah, boss,' she said, grinning.

She looked back at the young sergeant, who was staring hard at his nails.

'Kev, I get it but there are also a lot of misogynists and chauvinistic pigs out there as well. Should I throw every one of them your way?'

'I got it,' he said, and she suspected that he had.

'How's the joint investigation going, boss?' Stacey asked.

'Far too slowly for my liking,' she said.

'And Travis?' Bryant asked.

'I was taught that if you have nothing good to say...' she said, and then remembered the events of the previous day. 'But there are moments he is the copper I remember.'

Bryant offered a half smile.

'Okay, guys,' she said, taking a last swig of coffee before reaching for her coat. 'Be good while I'm gone.'

They all murmured their assent as she headed out the door.

She had chosen not to share with them that her finger had hovered over Woody's number the previous night. The words had been formed in her mouth. A demand to return to her own team to head the Bubba Jones murder investigation.

She would have been able to make a viable case and Woody would have authorised it.

Except it would have been at the expense of her team. By requesting her own return she would have been, effectively, declaring a motion of no confidence in the people she worked with every day. Stating to her boss that they couldn't manage without her.

After this briefing, she was pleased that she hadn't quite pressed that button.

CHAPTER 41

Dawson watched as Stacey stood and gathered up the Gary Flint file and a notepad.

'See yer later, boys,' she said, passing by his desk.

'Ouch,' Dawson said, once she'd left the room. He faced Bryant's wry smile. 'Don't know about you but my arse is still smarting.'

Bryant nodded. 'Oh yeah, but we deserved it,' he said, philosophically.

'For trying to protect her?' he asked.

'She's not ours to protect, Kev. She's a highly competent police officer, not our little sister.'

Dawson opened his mouth to speak and then closed it again. Bryant was right but it didn't stop the feelings he had when he thought of her sitting in the same room as that piece of shit.

'So, I gotta call you boss now or what?' he asked.

'Yeah, and I'd like you to use my full title, which is "acting detective inspector for the least amount of time possible or until the real boss comes back", if you don't mind.'

In spite of his irritation, Dawson laughed. Added authority did not sit well on Bryant's shoulders. It wasn't a rank he'd ever aspired to or sought. It was time to give the guy a break but the odd needle wouldn't hurt. Just for sport.

Bryant sighed and reached for his phone. 'Suppose we'd better start trying to track down our favourite local crime—'

Dawson cut him off. 'She was on the phone to the boss at midnight. You really think we're gonna have to go running to her,' he said, just as his phone started to ring.

He looked at the screen and smiled when he saw the contact name 'Frosty' flashing at him. 'Talk of the devil and she is sure to appear,' he said, pressing the button. 'Frost, we were just talking about you,' he said, pleasantly.

'Taking your bloody time, aren't you?' she barked in response.

He opened his mouth to respond.

'I mean, it was you and Bryant that attended the crime scene of my colleague up on the railway tracks almost ten hours ago now, wasn't it?'

'Calm down, Frost, we were just—'

'If this is the speed you're working at without your boss no wonder Bubba was—'

'Bubba was what, Frost?' Dawson asked.

'Nothing, never mind,' she snapped. 'I'm gonna be at Costa top of Merry Hill for the next twenty minutes. I suggest you get here before I'm done with my coffee and panini, or you guys are gonna regret it.'

The line went dead in his ear and he growled out loud. Dawson couldn't stomach the woman at the best of times but to him that had sounded like a definite threat.

CHAPTER 42

Stacey breathed a sigh of relief once she was away from Dawson and Bryant. On one hand she was pleased that the boss had checked in with them and had treated her like the police officer she was, instead of the intimidated black woman that Dawson thought she was. The change was refreshing. This wasn't her first interview, but it was her first time taking the lead. And yet her boss's faith and support gnawed at Stacey's guilt that she hadn't been honest about looking further into Justin Reynolds's suicide. Especially after her reaction to being left out of the loop on Bubba Jones.

Realistically she hadn't lied but omission felt just as grubby on her skin right now.

'All set?' she asked Sergeant Denny Rudd. Currently deskbound following an ankle injury, he'd been volunteered to assist in the interview.

He was a tall, thin, humourless man with a set expression that never changed.

'Yep,' he answered, nodding towards the door of interview room one.

Stacey pushed down the door handle and strode into the room.

God help her, the first thought into her head was that he absolutely did not look like a racist. And she knew better than anyone that racism didn't carry a badge and had no uniform.

But there was an element of safety in the assumption that hatred and bigotry came from predictable sources. Skinheads sporting swastika tattoos and crude knuckle lettering were one thing, but reasonable, educated people with such foul values was another thing entirely.

She suddenly thought of the films like *Borat* and *Four Lions*. It was acceptable to enjoy the humour in these films, as the opinions were always presented from the viewpoint of an ignorant, stupid, uneducated person.

She placed her folder on the desk and caught his wry smile. As though she'd been sent in here just to aggravate him.

'I am Detective Constable Stacey Wood, and I'd like to ask you a few questions.'

'About what? I've been charged, bailed and should now be free to go.'

'The details of your bail conditions are just being finalised. My questions are not related specifically to the messages you sent to the Kowalski family. It concerns a comment you made to my colleagues when they placed you under arrest.'

He sat back in his chair, draped his right arm lazily across the back of the vacant chair beside him.

'Oh yeah, what's that?'

There was a playfulness in his eyes that stoked the nausea inside her.

Oh, how she wished he had been held in custody, but the bastard had calmly and rationally admitted his guilt to the judge and had been remanded on bail until his trial. Stacey guessed that no trial would take place. There was barely enough room in the prisons for people who committed violence, never mind the sickos that just threatened it.

'It's a pity you have to find somewhere else to live,' Stacey said, trying not to respond to his arrogance. One of his bail conditions was to stay at least 500 feet from the Kowalski family.

He shrugged and Stacey knew even this wasn't a major inconvenience to him. The house was rented, and he'd soon find another.

'The street had gone downhill anyway,' he said, meaningfully.

'Excuse me?' she said.

'Too many new families, foreign families,' he said, pointedly. 'Where are you from?' he goaded.

'Dudley,' she replied.

'No, I mean, where are you really from?'

'Now just a—'

'It's okay,' Stacey said, silencing the sergeant's protests beside her.

'As I said, Dudley,' she repeated, pointedly. For the first thirty seconds of entering the room even she had wondered if this was a good idea but the more she looked at this man the more he diminished before her eyes.

She was not sitting in this room as a cowed black woman.

She suddenly remembered her first day at infant school. She had been one of the first in the classroom to take a seat. Other kids had filed in and seated themselves at the tables furthest away. As more children entered the room she could see them being guided towards the table she occupied alone. She had felt the heat in her cheeks as her excitement at school had ebbed away.

As kids had struggled to fit two to a chair before being instructed by the teacher on where to sit, Stacey had found herself smiling apologetically that they'd been forced to move.

It wasn't the only time she had found herself apologising for being black.

She was not apologising any more.

She was a police officer and a detective. And a good one at that.

'Mr Flint, much as your views appear to be very important to you, they are of no consequence to me and have no bearing on our discussion today.'

She was surprised at the strength in her own voice.

'What really interests me is the comment you made to my colleagues about something bigger. What did you mean?'

Again the shrug.

'Nothing in particular,' he said.

'I doubt that, Mr Flint. You don't seem too big on idle chat.'

'Let's just say that some people don't stop at text messages to get their point across.'

'You're talking more violence?'

He leaned across the table. 'I'm not talking about anything, except the fact there's a lot of hate out there to be exploited.'

Stacey felt her insides recoil at his proximity but she didn't move a muscle.

'And that's all I've got, constable,' he said, sitting back. 'Except to say, you should probably be careful.'

'Are you threatening me, Mr Flint?' Stacey asked, as a chill worked through her.

'Not at all. I'm giving you a piece of advice.'

Stacey noted his exact words on her pad.

That's not what it had sounded like to her.

CHAPTER 43

Kim took her place at the front of the room. She didn't mind Travis's silent objection by sitting in his office. From the corner of her eye she could see that he was staring at his computer screen but his hand on the mouse was still.

He was listening.

'Okay,' she said, claiming their attention. 'We learned yesterday that the Preeces have not inspected the Cowley property for years. That much is obvious. The place is a shit tip, and the chance of the techies finding anything to link the family to the bodies is hopeful, at best.

'We did, however, find this,' she said, handing out copies of the half note.

Five pairs of eyes frowned at it much the same way as she and Travis had the previous day.

'I don't know if we can gain anything from it but if anyone wants a stab…'

'Me,' said Penn at the back.

She noted his headpiece was a black and white polkadot design today.

'I'd like to give it a go.'

'Crack on, then,' she said. 'We visited Mr Cowley junior in hospital yesterday but were blocked at every turn by his sister. Now, she is currently trying to be everywhere at once so she can't stay by his side indefinitely. I'm wondering if we should…'

'How about I visit him?' asked Lynda.

Lynda was a young attractive woman, and the best chance they had of teasing some information out of the young man.

'Aren't you working on CCTV for the attempted abduction, and the RTA yesterday?' Kim asked.

'I'll carry on with that while she's gone,' said Lewis, shooting up his hand.

'Okay, thanks Lewis. Great idea, Lynda. His sister still insists it was an accident and that he can't speak.'

She raised her eyebrows to indicate her feelings on both scores.

'I'll check on Mr Dhinsa while I'm there as well,' Lynda offered. 'Still unconscious at eleven last night. Oh, and breath test on the supermarket driver was negative. Witness statements still being taken,' she added. 'And the post mortem on the female will take place later today.'

'Lynda, would you?…'

'I'll get right back on it once I've been to the hospital,' she said, brightly.

Kim smiled in her direction. Jeez, this girl was keen.

Johnson leaned forward, frowning.

'If Lynda's at the hospital, should we maintain a presence back at the Cowley house while the techies are still searching? Pile on the pressure to see if anything gives?'

'You volunteering?' Kim asked.

He nodded his shiny bald head.

Kim felt the excitement in her stomach.

'Okay, field trips sorted. This Cowley family is hiding something and we need to know what it is. They haven't paid rent to the Preeces in years, and I think we should dig as far as we can with this family. Do they have any other land? Why are the Preece family so accommodating to the Cowleys?

'And someone needs to chase ballistics and see what we have on that bullet.'

Gibbs held his hand up, taking responsibility for that task. 'And I'll work with Penn on matching the description of our male to the mispers reports.'

Kim nodded, satisfied. It was a two-way exchange, feeding off each other's energy. She felt good, energised, hopeful.

And then she spied Travis standing in the doorway.

She just hoped she could maintain it.

CHAPTER 44

'Why the hell is she sitting outside?' Bryant asked, as his colleague pulled on to the car park.

'A break from the fiery furnaces,' Dawson quipped.

His question was answered as she lit a cigarette.

'Didn't know you smoked,' Bryant said to Frost, getting out of the car.

'Near-death experiences and dead colleagues can cure a ten-year abstention,' she said.

Only two shiny silver chairs were placed around the table, and Tracy's designer handbag was occupying the second.

Bryant pulled two chairs from the next table when it became clear her handbag was staying seated on the chair beside her.

'Spare me the details, but did he suffer?' she asked, spearing Bryant with her eyes.

He would swear he saw some evidence of tears having escaped those slightly swollen lids.

'No details,' he said, kindly. The true horror of what they'd found would be withheld from the press. She didn't need the picture in her head. No one did.

'Any leads?' she asked, shortly, as Dawson scraped the metal chair across the slab as he sat.

'We're working on it, Frost,' he answered.

'Well, do it quicker, will you?' she snarled. 'He was a good kid.'

Bryant was surprised to see the emotion that she hid with a cough.

'Did you know him well?' he asked.

'Been working with him for a few months now. Keen as mustard and not bad at reading people,' she said, glancing at Dawson.

'For his own ends,' Bryant responded. He felt slightly defensive of the way the lad had manipulated his colleague, through vanity, into going against the boss's wishes. 'Any enemies you know of?'

Tracy shook her head and blew out a stream of smoke before pounding the cigarette into the ashtray.

'Surprisingly, despite our charm and wit, us reporters are not the most popular people in the world. But I can't think of anyone who would want to decapitate him.'

So she knew that much about Bubba's death. Bryant decided not to pursue how she'd found out.

'Have you spoken to his boyfriend yet?' she asked, testily.

'Boyfriend?' Dawson asked, looking his way. Bryant shrugged. He'd never even met the young reporter.

Frost looked incredulous. 'Really, Dawson? The shirts didn't give it away?'

'Truthfully, Frost, I've never judged a man's sexuality on the colour of his shirts.'

She shook her head as she took a pad and pen from her handbag on the seat beside her. She scribbled for a few seconds and then ripped off the piece of paper.

'His name is Nigel, and you'll find him here,' she said.

'Nexus?' Dawson asked, raising one eyebrow.

'New club opening next week off the Stourbridge ring road. He's the Manager.'

'Serious boyfriend?' Bryant asked.

'About a month; so, practically married,' she said.

Bryant held her attention. 'Was he working on anything likely to get him hurt?'

Frost coloured and shook her head.

'Do you want to elaborate?' Bryant asked.

'No,' she answered, reaching for her handbag.

'Come on, Frost,' Dawson said, leaning forward. 'You hinted at something on the phone. Sounded like he was working on something. What was he investigating?'

'You guys,' she answered.

Bryant looked to his colleague. 'Us?' he asked.

'Don't flatter yourself, boys. Not you two in particular but changing police attitudes in general. He was exploring the notion that many less serious incidents are not getting the attention they deserve.'

'I don't get you,' Bryant said.

'Well, let's be honest, there are sexy cases and ugly cases for you guys. Anything with the word murder, assault and violence shoots to the top of your in trays. Lesser incidents are constantly pushed down the list.'

Bryant began to shake his head but Tracy held up her hand.

'We're never gonna agree, but that's not the angle he was going for. He felt that some reports aren't even making it to your desks and are being blocked at the door, especially the ones not target driven.'

'Oh come on, Frost,' Bryant said. 'You and I both know that national targets were abolished five or more years ago.'

'Ha,' she said, derisively. 'Check the recent report that says burglary, vehicle crime and robbery are still target driven, and just because the targets have been removed at the top doesn't mean individual forces aren't still working to them.'

Bryant began to shake his head in denial.

'I covered a shoplifting case recently. Twenty-eight-year-old male arrested for two joints of lamb from Asda. Caught on CCTV and bang to rights. When searched, he had a bag full of goodies pilfered from seven other shops. How many offences do you think he was charged with?'

Bryant could already guess the answer.

'One, Bryant. Just the stolen meat, so it wouldn't increase the number of offences. His crime counts as one statistic even though he'd nicked from eight different shops.' She paused. 'So, yeah, I think the kid was on to something.'

'And you encouraged it?' Dawson asked. 'And here's me thinking you might have grown some scruples following your recent near-death experience – which, incidentally, would have been an *actual* death experience had it not been for us.'

Bryant shivered as he remembered how close Tracy Frost had come to losing her life to a twisted individual hell-bent on childhood revenge. Had Kim not been so doggedly determined that the woman had been abducted, in the face of everyone else's doubt, Tracy Frost would not be sitting here right now.

'Don't you dare throw that at me, Dawson. Your boss saved my life and for that she gets a bit of latitude and a lot of respect. If you think that encompasses the entire West Midlands police force, you can think again.'

Bryant stepped in. 'So, the story he was covering?…'

She turned away from Dawson and nodded in his direction. 'To be honest, it looked like it could go somewhere. He got the idea after speaking to Aisha Gupta and I think…'

'Who the hell is Aisha Gupta?' Dawson raged.

Tracy shook her head. 'Jesus, guys, you're kinda proving Bubba's point here.'

They waited for her to continue.

She rolled her eyes and lit another cigarette. 'Aisha Gupta is a seventeen-year-old Indian girl from Hollytree. Last week she was accosted by some weirdo, and she reported it to the police. She didn't get a great response.'

'Was she hurt?' Dawson asked.

Tracy shook her head and blew out a plume of smoke.

'Was she touched inappropriately?'

'I don't think so,' Tracy said.

Bryant was confused. 'So what did the weirdo do?'

'He forced her to the ground, took out his phone and told her to close her eyes.'

CHAPTER 45

Travis had been writing in his notebook during the whole journey to the hospital. He closed it as she turned off the ignition. She waited for him to make a move. It was obvious that any progress they'd made yesterday had been erased.

He continued to stare forward.

'Do you ever consider that sometimes you're not right?' he asked, suddenly.

She considered for a moment. 'Rarely,' she said.

Had they progressed or even maintained that brief harmony of the previous day she might have been tempted into honesty. But now she would continue to act in the role she'd been given.

'There are times when you just get it wrong, you know.'

'Did I do something in the briefing?' she asked, defensively.

'No, the briefing went well, I thought,' he said, rendering her speechless.

He unbuckled his seatbelt, and looked at her.

'I'm just saying that sometimes you're wrong and people suffer.'

'Travis, what the hell are you going?—' She stopped talking when the passenger door slammed shut in her face.

She shot out of the car and faced him across the roof.

'Travis, what was that supposed to mean?' she snapped. Either he wanted to talk or he didn't but baiting her with obscure comments and questions was just downright annoying.

'Either consider it or don't. I'm saying nothing more.'

Right now that was a bloody relief if all he was going to offer was cryptic one-liners.

They walked through the hospital hallways in silence. Kim pushed her way into the morgue and greeted Doctor A.

'Nice to see you, Inspector and the sergeant too,' she said pleasantly, as Travis's expression soured. Kim knew she shouldn't have found it funny, but she did.

As she watched Doctor A pull on a pair of blue gloves Kim noticed the freshly applied nail polish. Red and gold on alternate fingers.

She could only wonder at the de-stressing rituals of a woman handling cadaver bones by day and painting her nails by night.

'Inspector, I think you are going to love me a lot when I show you this,' she said, handing over a sheet of paper containing a photograph with measurements noted beneath.

The subject of the photograph at the centre of the page was a bullet.

'From the pit?' Kim asked.

Doctor A nodded.

'Is it here?' Kim asked.

'No, it is gone to ballistex,' she said.

'What, the cold sore cream?' Travis asked smartly.

'Yes, because that would make perfect sense,' Doctor A said, cuttingly.

He closed his mouth.

'Marina thought it was a bullet but I didn't want to tell you before I had chance to clean it properly.'

Kim couldn't help her excitement. Ballistics would be able to detail the composition of the bullet. Some were made of soft material, like lead, designed to expand on impact. Steel based bullets penetrated further into thicker targets.

Any information could help them potentially age it. Newer bullets used materials such as aluminium, bismuth, bronze, copper, plastics, rubber, steel, tin and even tungsten.

'And I have some information about our first victim,' she said, moving to gurney one. Kim could see that the other two skeletons were beginning to fill out, and another box of bones was waiting on the side.

'I think this gentleman here was Negroid.'

Kim knew the other two anthropological classifications were Caucasoid and Mongoloid. A term to describe a broad division of humankind native to Asia but had been turned into a sickening insult over the years.

'Do you see here?' she said, pointing with a pencil. 'The skull is high and square. The face is straight and the eye socket is triangular.'

Kim did see a definite disparity between the skull of the victim on gurney one and gurney two.

'Also, Negroids have proportionally longer arms and legs and their femurs are straighter.'

Kim accepted the woman's expertise.

'These characteristics diminish in mixed-race people but are significant here.'

Kim looked to Travis, who, for once, wasn't writing the detail down. She was grateful for the information. It would help narrow the search on missing persons.

Kim walked along the bottom of the gurneys holding the other two victims.

'Nothing to indicate any more victims?' she asked, hopefully.

Doctor A shook her head. 'I think three is our final count.'

Kim paused at the end of gurney three.

She lowered her head and peered closer at the fibula bone. The thinner lower leg bone lay beside the tibia but there was a marked difference in the texture of the two bones.

The tibia appeared smooth and even, whereas the fibula displayed dozens of nicks and grooves along its entire length.

Kim pointed. 'What are these marks?'

Doctor A rolled her eyes dramatically. 'Further inspection is one of the seventeen next jobs I have to do, Inspector.'

Kim ignored the dig and smiled. 'Anything you can tell us would be helpful.'

Doctor A placed her hands on her hips. 'And once I'm done I'll go and solve this crime for you,' she said.

'Feel free, and I'll stay and finish your jigsaw.'

Her mouth began to twitch. 'Inspector, you better get out of here before I…'

'I'm going. I'm going,' Kim said, heading for the door.

Travis was already on the phone, giving his team the updated information.

'How the hell did that woman get the job?' Travis asked when he'd ended the call.

'Because she is very intelligent, dedicated, knowledgeable and bloody good at her job,' Kim replied.

'With a very poor bedside manner.'

'Her customers don't mind that too much,' she offered, drily. 'But since you mention her bedside manner, Tom, I'll give you an insight. She was once the attending tech on the body of a nine-year-old boy found in the grounds of a listed building in Romsley. He was discovered late in the evening on New Year's Eve and we couldn't get him removed until early the next morning.'

She paused, remembering that night four years earlier.

'I left around eleven and she was still there. I got back at seven in the morning and yep, she was still there. Right alongside her sleeping bag and a flask of chicken soup.'

He looked unimpressed. She shook her head. She supposed it was difficult for a clock-watching man like himself to understand that, dead or not, Doctor A just hadn't been able to leave that young boy on his own.

She sighed heavily. 'I think we need to head straight back to the station,' Kim said. 'Trying to identify a missing black male anywhere from the last thirty years is a task too big for just Penn and Gibbs.'

Travis nodded and glanced in to the main reception as they passed by en route to the car.

She realised why and stopped walking. 'Wanna go and check on him?'

You didn't just forget the life of a man you'd helped to save. The fact that the road traffic incident had been passed to another investigation team would not stop Travis from seeing the man's face in his mind's eye for a long time to come.

He shook his head. 'Intensive Care,' he answered. 'On life support.'

Kim nodded, and they carried on walking.

'You know, I shouldn't be surprised that you've already—'

Kim stopped talking as Travis's phone began to ring.

Travis listened intently as the voice talked on the other end.

He stopped at a bin and rested the leather wallet expertly on the top with one hand and began to write. Kim tried to see but his fist was in the way.

'Good work, Penn,' Travis said, ending the call.

'No need to return,' he said, with a flash of pride. 'Our first victim has been identified.'

Kim couldn't help but be impressed. Finally, victim one was about to get a name.

CHAPTER 46

18 October 1989

Jacob James woke to a sniffling sound coming from the other side of the room.

It took him a few seconds to think through the groggy haze in his mind and realise that this whole thing was no nightmare. He was still naked, bound and cold in a pitch-black room.

He heard a sob somewhere to his right.

There was someone else in the room with him.

'Hello,' he offered tentatively.

A sharp cry of surprise came from that direction. He realised the voice was female. He had no idea if it was a girl or a woman.

'Please don't be frightened,' he said as gently as he could manage. He wanted to reassure her immediately that she was in no danger from him.

'O… okay,' she said, timidly.

'What's your name, love?' he asked.

'D… Devorah, Devorah A… Abramovich,' she answered.

Jacob wondered if it was the fear making her voice sound young. He hoped so.

'How old are you, Devorah?' he asked.

'S… seventeen,' she stuttered.

'Did you get taken too?' he asked.

'Y… yes, I think so. I remember leaving shul…'

'School?' he asked.

'No, no, synagogue. I was studying away from college for the day and… oh… tell me what's going on, please,' she said as the panic clutched at her voice.

'My name is Jacob,' he said. 'And I was taken as well. I'm not sure how long I've been here. Have you been given anything to drink?'

'No, they took me from the van and threw me in here. I didn't see…'

So they hadn't drugged her yet.

'Were you conscious for the journey?' he asked. He had been knocked out. They had obviously felt no threat from this young girl.

'Y… yes,' she answered.

He wondered if he could glean any information to help him clarify how long he'd been in this place.

'Devorah, can you tell me what time you were taken?'

'I left the synagogue at about two o'clock. Please, tell me, what are they going to do to us?'

Jacob closed his eyes and shook his head. He wished he knew.

What he did know was that he'd been taken around 6 p.m., which meant he had been gone for almost twenty-four hours. Adaje would have missed him by now. She would have raised the alarm but what details would she have been able to offer? She hadn't even known he was going to get fish and chips.

The hopelessness settled heavily on his heart.

'Did you hear them say anything when you were in the van?' he probed, gently.

'No… oh wait… no, I heard the word "appetiser" but they were just talking about food,' she said and then began to cry. 'I just wish I knew what I'd done,' she sobbed. 'What do they want us for?'

He ached to move forward, but his own nakedness prevented him from trying to offer her comfort. There was something obscene about moving his bare body closer to this poor, terrified girl.

From her voice he guessed they were just about fifteen feet apart. He began to move closer towards her.

'Hold out your hand,' he said.

She moved to her left, and he stretched his bound wrists towards her. His hand found hers in the darkness.

A pang of emotion shot through him at the sensation of the small, soft hand encased in his own.

Adaje, his beautiful Adaje.

A tear forced its way from his eye and travelled down his cheek as he wondered if he would ever see his daughter again.

'It's okay, Devorah. Everything will be okay,' he said, soothingly.

He stroked the flesh of her hand with his thumb as he had done many times with his own daughter. Her cries began to subside.

How quickly a bond had been formed between himself and a young girl who he would probably never have met, if not for the bastards that had plucked them both from their lives.

They sat in companionable silence until the key sounded in the lock.

'Jacob?…' she whispered. The panic dripped from that one word.

He squeezed her hand as two torches shone into the small space.

'Grab her,' said a voice.

'No,' Jacob cried, launching himself to his feet, clumsily. His body still fighting the effects of the drug he'd been given. His bound hands restricting his movement.

He lunged forward into the torchlight, not sure what he was hoping to achieve but he had to try and stop them taking her away. He couldn't even imagine what they were going to do to her.

'Fuck's sake, this one's a liability,' said one of the voices.

Jacob felt himself being pushed back to the ground.

'Don't be too eager to get out there, fella. Your time is coming soon enough.'

The door closed behind the voice but not before Jacob heard Devorah's sickening screams and pleas receding into the distance. His shackled fists met with the wall in frustration at being unable to protect her.

'Damn you, you fucking bastards,' he screamed into the darkness.

CHAPTER 47

Stacey had the sudden urge to close the office door. Justin's computer was open and positioned to her right. Someone would have to come close to see what she was doing, and yet she still felt as though she was doing something wrong.

She wondered, for the hundredth time, why she hadn't just mentioned to her boss that she wanted to dig around a little on Justin Reynolds. But she knew why – if the boss said no, she would have no choice but to let it go. This way, she was not going behind the boss's back. Not really, she told herself.

She could see from the front screen that Justin had an icon for every app available including Snapchat and Pinterest. But the one she really wanted was Facebook. Still the most widely used sharing platform, people treated Facebook like it was their lounge or bedroom. Users felt comfortable posting their entire lives on what they thought was their personal space.

The globe icon told her Justin had almost two hundred notifications. She clicked in and began to scroll through them. The majority were dated since Monday. The day he had died.

The earliest ones were expressions of disbelief. Pleas for Justin to make contact. The newer ones were expressions of grief and RIP posts. None of these posts had made it to his timeline, because of his privacy settings. Stacey had implemented the same on her own page. She had never liked that people could tag her in a post which automatically appeared on her timeline, especially after a less than flattering photo of her throwing some drunken moves at her cousin's twenty-first birthday bash.

Clearly Justin had felt the same way.

She clicked on the message icon. She saw that the top message was from someone called Floda. No last name, just Floda. She frowned. What kind of name was that?

She briefly considered continuing the message stream but guessed Floda would be freaked out if he suddenly got a message from a dead friend. But the last person Justin was in contact with was definitely someone she'd like to speak to.

She opened her phone and sent a friend request from her own Facebook account. Once they responded, she'd explain exactly who she was and see if they could tell her anything about Justin, and especially about his state of mind in those last few days.

She was about to click on the message when the one below caught her attention. And then the one below that.

She began to scroll down and the frown on her face deepened.

A whole batch of angry messages screamed 'unfriended' followed by angry emojis. Some just said 'wanker'. As she scrolled through them she counted some seventy messages that were all abusing Justin with one-word insults. The abuse went on for weeks prior to his death. None of the messages had been replied to or even opened – except for one. From a girl named Kirsty Littlejohn.

Stacey opened it. Unlike the others, this one asked for an explanation and pleaded for a reply. Possibly an ex-girlfriend, she wondered.

She scrolled back up to the first message and the only one he'd responded to. She opened it, and read, from the beginning.

'Are you coming on the 19th?' asked Floda.

'Yeah, can't wait,' replied Justin.

'You know you need the photo to get in?' Floda asked.

'Oh yeah won't be a problem,' replied Justin.

'Will we meet?' Justin had added as a separate message.

The question had remained unanswered.

Stacey knew that this Floda person was the one she needed to speak to. From what she could see it was the last person Justin had had any type of conversation with.

She had no choice but to wait. She could send Floda a message from her own account but it would automatically be sent to his other folder to gather dust.

She clicked onto Justin's timeline. Maybe she could learn more from what he'd been posting. Perhaps she could discover what had caused so many people to send him abusive messages.

She began to scroll down, and her blood turned cold at what she saw.

For a moment, she couldn't turn her head from the screen. Only when her phone beeped did she lower her eyes.

She'd received a notification.

Floda had rejected her friend request.

CHAPTER 48

Kim spotted the property she was looking for. The small boutique was located on the Soho Road, nestled between a fruit and veg store and a small coffee shop.

'Bloody hell,' Travis said as they reached the store, which was awash with brightly coloured garments and accessories.

Kim had always loved the vibe of Handsworth, located north-west of Birmingham city centre. It had become the hub for Birmingham's Afro-Caribbean community following a post-war demand for both skilled and unskilled workers. But the area had suffered from racial tensions since the sixties, and different riots over the years had damaged its reputation. Despite all that, the carnivals and parades that passed through the community were a celebration of life and joy.

Kim took a deep breath before pushing open the door.

The old-fashioned type bell dinged their arrival above her head.

The explosion of colour continued inside the store, but the clothing was arranged artistically, showcasing each individual piece on the wall with room to breathe. The shop displayed traditional Jamaican women's wear of dresses and skirts and shirts, mainly constructed of calico. Many of the garments were variations of the green, yellow and black of the national flag while others were infused with flashes of bright red. Kim hated small shops that tried to fill every available inch of retail space in a 'You will like something you see' kind of way. These garments said 'enjoy me'.

She approached the small single till area located halfway down the shop.

A woman in her mid-to-late forties smiled pleasantly in her direction. She wore one of the colour blocked dresses hanging in the window with a traditional headscarf.

The look turned suspicious when she spied Travis trailing behind.

'Adaje James?' Kim asked, removing her identification.

The woman tucked her straightened ebony hair behind her ears, revealing a small gold studded earring in her lobe.

'I used to be. I'm Adaje Sumner now,' she said, holding up her left hand.

'Daughter of Jacob James?'

She nodded, slowly.

'Is there someone else here?' Kim asked. They needed her full attention.

Mrs Sumner shook her head. 'Not for another hour or so,' she said.

'We really need to talk without interruption,' Kim said, looking towards the door.

'Have you found him?' she asked, softly.

Kim looked again towards the door. This was not a conversation she wanted to start while there was the possibility of customers disturbing them.

Mrs Sumner stepped around the desk, revealing a quad screen CCTV system behind.

She turned the sign on the door to 'closed' and slid the bottom bolt.

'Please, follow me,' she said, heading to the back of the store.

Kim followed past a row of curtained changing rooms to a door marked 'Staff Only' and then left into a small but tidy break room. A square wooden table sat in the centre.

They all took a seat around it.

Mrs Sumner's fingers laced together.

'Have you found him?' she repeated. Her eyes stayed on Kim.

'Possibly,' Kim said. 'But we need to ask you a few questions.'

The woman leaned her forearms on the table as though grounding herself, bracing for impact.

She nodded.

'Did your father have any old bone injuries?' Kim asked. Doctor A had established two potential indicators of a positive identification.

'The bone in his left arm?' Kim continued.

'Was broken in a football match in his early twenties,' she said. 'It was just after I was born.'

Kim felt the familiar sensation of excitement mixed with dread, as she asked the second question. 'Any injury to the knee?' But she already knew the answer.

'An accident at work in the late eighties,' she confirmed.

'And when exactly did your father go missing, Mrs Sumner?'

'October 17th in '89.'

'And it was you who reported his disappearance?'

She nodded. 'There were only the two of us, officer,' she said, quietly. 'My father came from Jamaica in the fifties. The work situation was dire, and he was unskilled. He got a job in a printing factory and worked hard. He met my mother there. They married, and I came along in '67.'

The woman's smooth skin belied her forty plus years.

'I lost my mum in '77 to leukaemia. There was a street party outside the day she died,' Mrs Sumner said.

'A street party?' Travis asked.

'Queen's Jubilee,' she answered. 'That left just me and Dad. He carried on working at the printers. Never had one day off sick,' she said proudly. 'Right until it closed in '85. After that he went from labouring job to casual work, unable to find anything steady.'

'What about when he disappeared?' Kim asked. 'Had there been any issues? Anyone he was having problems with?'

'What are you saying?' she asked, frowning.

'We just need to understand events close to his disappearance before—'

'You have found him, haven't you?' she asked. 'Those two questions have confirmed it or else you'd be gone by now.'

Like many relatives of missing people, Mrs Sumner may have held on to the belief that her father was still wandering around somewhere. There was a thin line between hope and delusion.

'We think so, Mrs Sumner,' she said, honestly. This woman had waited long enough, and Kim was suitably convinced they were talking about the same man.

The tears gathered in Mrs Sumner's eyes but she blinked them away.

'I had no real hope, if I'm honest,' she admitted. 'So many years. As each one passed I tried to remain hopeful, but I knew he would not have stayed away so long. We were very close.'

Kim nodded her understanding

'How did he do it?' she asked, unsure.

It was clear that this woman wanted to know details – but also didn't want to hear them.

'Do what?' Travis asked.

'Commit suicide,' she answered, as though it was obvious.

'What makes you think your father took his own life?' Kim asked.

'Because he left of his own accord. He was depressed; he couldn't find work. He was in dreadful agony but still he searched for work every day. I've questioned myself every day if I should have done more. How could I have prevented it? How did I fail him?'

Kim was caught off guard. This woman had spent more than two decades coming to terms with the fact her father had left her and taken his own life. And now she had the task of opening that wound and salting it.

'Mrs Sumner… I…'

'Adaje,' she said. 'Please call me Adaje.'

'Okay, Adaje,' Kim said, gently. 'Your father didn't commit suicide. He didn't leave you all those years ago, and there's nothing you could have done.'

Adaje began to shake her head slowly, trying to erase all the questions, regret and blame of the last twenty-seven years.

'I don't understand,' she said, licking her lips. 'Some kind of accident?'

Kim shook her head. 'It was no accident, Adaje. I regret to inform you that your father was murdered.'

Travis just about caught her before she fell sideways to the ground.

CHAPTER 49

'I can understand that must have been quite a shock to you,' Kim said, once Adaje had taken a couple of sips of water.

Travis's quick thinking had prevented the woman suffering a nasty tumble to the ground. He had held her firm until she had come back around.

'I know everyone says this but my father wouldn't hurt a fly. He was a quiet, unassuming and very gentle man. He was softly spoken, never got ruffled or stressed or angry and, believe me, I tested that in my early teens. He would always walk away from an argument. He hated conflict of any kind.'

'Was there anything at all that you can remember from the days immediately before he went missing?' Kim asked again.

Adaje shook her head. 'The day before he disappeared he'd been out job hunting. He'd run into "the boss" as he still called him.'

'The boss?' Kim queried.

'Yes, the man for whom my father was working when he had his accident. My dad said he'd been offered five hundred pounds to drop the case,' she said, nodding as the memory cleared in her head.

'He had politely refused the offer. The solicitor had told him to have no contact with his old workplace. The sad thing is, if they'd offered him his job back, he would probably have accepted, even though they were at fault.'

'Wait a minute, Adaje, your father was suing the company he worked for?' Kim clarified.

She nodded. 'Well, company is a bit of a stretch, but yes, they were negligent. Gave him a pair of faulty ladders to climb onto a barn, and he fell and badly injured his knee.'

'A barn?' Kim asked, stealing a look at Travis.

'Yes, my father was a labourer on a farm.'

'And the boss's name?' Kim asked, fighting the dread in her stomach.

'Oh yes, I've never forgotten. The boss's name was Mister Cowley.'

CHAPTER 50

'Bryant, don't you think our time is better spent heading for Nexus?' Dawson asked, wishing he'd never given his colleague the keys. Had he been working on his own, he wouldn't have allowed himself to be baited or sidetracked by Frost, and he'd be on his way to Stourbridge to talk to Bubba's boyfriend. They were going to talk to a young girl who had no physical injuries, instead of the partner of a man whose head had been severed from his body. He wasn't getting the priority.

'We're two minutes away. It can't hurt to have a quick word,' Bryant answered, exiting the shopping complex. 'You don't find it strange that this closing your eyes thing has come up twice now?'

'Just coincidence,' he muttered, as Bryant turned into Hollytree.

It didn't help that Dawson had not been back to the Hollytree estate since that night.

He felt a slight tremble as Bryant drove further into the belly of the estate. The council houses around the perimeter were like a skirt. Inside them were the maisonette blocks like a petticoat, covering the flesh which was the row of tower blocks at the centre.

'You just missed the turn,' he advised Bryant.

'Bloody place is like a maze,' Bryant said, taking the next left.

Bryant had been driving around this estate for more than twenty years but his little 'mistake' would mean they would not drive past the exact spot where Dawson had been attacked. The place where he'd thought he was going to die.

An image flashed into Dawson's mind. Curled on the floor, trying to protect himself from the four pairs of feet pounding him. The shame brought colour to his cheeks. Yes, there had been four of them, and yes they'd had a knife.

And yes, he was eternally grateful that Tracy Frost had come along when she had, saving him from further injury, but still he couldn't look at the woman without remembering that night.

'You do know I'm not as stupid as I look,' he said to his colleague.

'That's a bloody relief.' Bryant said, parking the car. 'So, which one is it?'

Dawson nodded towards the end property and headed towards it.

The door was opened by an Indian woman, of slight build, whose hair was tidily encased in a yellow headscarf.

'Hello, Mrs Gupta,' he said, showing his identification. 'We're here about Aisha. May we speak with her?'

Mrs Gupta hesitated for a minute, and then nodded and stepped back, away from the staircase that led up to the second level of the property.

Both he and Bryant shuffled in past a collection of coats fighting for space on two hooks.

'Please, go through,' she said, before calling her daughter.

A colourful picture of Guru Nanak above the fireplace told him he was entering a home that followed the Sikh faith.

Dawson knew a little about the religion: that it hailed from the Punjab region of India and followed the teachings of eleven gurus. A couple of years before he had accompanied his girlfriend to the wedding of one of her colleagues and had made it his business to disabuse himself of his ignorance.

'You are not the men we spoke to at the police station,' Mrs Gupta said, suspiciously.

Dawson lowered himself to the sofa, even though he had not been invited. He felt imposing towering over her petite frame.

'We are from another department, Mrs Gupta. We're detectives.'

'I asked to see detectives on Friday,' she said, as Aisha entered the room.

Dawson guessed the girl to be sixteen or seventeen. She was dressed in jeans, a plain jumper and a bright red headscarf.

He knew that women did not have to wear turbans but were urged to cover their heads. Unlike her mother, Aisha did not have her hair tied up. Instead it flowed over her shoulders and peeped from beneath the scarf, uncut as a symbol of her faith.

'Are you from Brierley Hill?' Mrs Gupta asked.

'Well, no, we're from Halesowen but we all do the same—'

'I don't understand why you are here,' she said.

'We think what happened to your daughter may be linked to an investigation of ours,' Bryant offered.

'So, now you want to listen to her?' Mrs Gupta asked. 'Instead of dismiss what happened to her as a prank.'

Her voice had risen and the words were shooting from her mouth.

'May I ask Aisha some questions, Mrs Gupta?' he asked quietly, hoping his low tone would bring down her agitation.

She pursed her lips but nodded.

He turned to the young girl and spoke gently.

'Aisha, can you tell me where exactly the incident happened?'

'The car park at Asda. I'd finished work and was on my way home.'

Dawson knew the area. 'Main road or shortcut?'

'Shortcut,' she said, apologetically. 'It was cold.'

Dawson smiled. The overspill car park was poorly lit and deserted at ten o'clock.

'Go on,' he urged.

'I never even heard the footsteps behind me,' she said, shaking her head. 'He turned me around—'

'To face him?' Bryant butted in.

She nodded but then lowered her eyes. 'He was wearing a hoody, and it all happened so quickly.'

'Aisha, did the man touch you in any way inappropriately?' Dawson asked, resuming the interview.

She shook her head.

'Did he try to grab any… part of you?'

Again she shook her head.

'Did he hit you?'

She hesitated and then shook her head.

'He grabbed my arms when he pushed me to the ground.'

'Then what?' he asked.

She frowned. 'He told me how to lie. He wanted me to bend my arms and legs at strange angles. He kicked at my knee when I couldn't do what he wanted.'

'And then what did he do?'

She swallowed.

'He told me to close my eyes.'

Dawson nodded for her to continue.

'And when I opened them he was gone.'

He glanced towards Bryant with a triumphant expression. He'd been right. They'd learned nothing new at all but perhaps Bryant would now accept this had nothing to do with their current caseload.

He made a move to stand.

'But I did see the scar,' Aisha said, quietly.

'A scar?' he clarified. 'Where?'

Aisha indicated a spot on her cheekbone.

The mention of a scar sparked some distant memory that his brain couldn't quite catch. Something he knew he should remember but it wouldn't quite come.

Dawson was convinced there was no way this random act of stupidity could be linked to the murder of Bubba Jones or the assault of Henryk Kowalski. This was probably just some kind of prank. A dare.

Although his gut was no longer as sure.

CHAPTER 51

'Do not keep telling me to calm down,' Kim said, as she jumped on the brakes in the centre of Smethwick. 'Give me one time that telling someone to calm down has actually inspired them to calm the fuck down.'

There were approximately eight miles between her and finding out exactly what the Cowley family had been up to.

'Then stop gambling with our lives at every set of traffic lights,' he snapped.

'Oh Tom, either grow a pair or shut your eyes,' she said. Even Bryant wasn't this bad.

'You don't even know their involvement. So, we know our guy worked there. There were probably many more that worked…'

'And we have two more bodies to identify,' Kim said, testily.

One of the first things they'd be wanting from the Cowleys was a full list of ex-employees.

'So, who exactly are you going to arrest?' he asked, mockingly.

'The first person to piss me off,' she answered. It was a pity right now that Travis wasn't an option.

'So, that'll probably be Fiona,' he said. 'Even though she's way too young to have been involved.'

'Details, Travis, you're always caught up in the details.' She took a brief look at his closed expression. 'But, can you tell me that she doesn't know something about something. She's been lying since we first met her at the hospital.'

'Not a crime.'

'Unless it's *about* a bloody crime,' she said, gripping the steering wheel, hard. 'And Travis, are you trying to piss me off even more with these stupid questions?'

'Probably,' he admitted.

'Why? Are you trying for suicide by cop driving erratically?'

Bryant would have just left her alone.

She took a left, sharply, and then straightened quickly.

The irritation that crossed his face was reward enough. Childish, yes. Worth it, absolutely.

'Thank the lord for that,' he said, as she pulled on to the Cowley's farm.

An earlier storm had reduced the area at the front of the house to a mudbath. Kim parked her Golf next to Fiona's Jaguar.

The door was opened by Jeff Cowley before they had reached it.

They'd had a call to confirm that the last tech vehicle and Travis's guy, Johnson, had left half an hour ago.

'May we come in, Mr Cowley?' Kim asked, stepping past him.

'Miss Cowley,' Kim said, striding past the kitchen. 'Would you mind joining us in the lounge?'

Normally she resented the woman's presence and interference, but today she welcomed it. This time they'd had no time to practise. Fiona's need to control the situation and her father's propensity to panic could be very interesting.

'Mr Cowley, Miss Cowley, does the name Jacob James mean anything to you?'

'Never heard of him,' Fiona said.

'Yes, he worked here,' Jeff said.

Kim folded her arms.

'Well, one of you is lying. Shall we try that one again.'

She turned to Jeff Cowley.

'I prefer your answer, Mr Cowley, so shall we start with you?'

'He's confused,' Fiona said, stepping forward.

'He doesn't seem very confused to me, Miss Cowley. It would appear that *you* are confused, and if you'd give your father a chance to speak for himself I'd like to hear what he has to say.'

Kim knew her voice had risen, and the colour had fallen from Jeff Cowley's face.

'Mr Cowley?…'

'Can't this wait?' Fiona asked. 'We were about to go and visit my brother in hospital.'

'Please feel free to leave us, Miss Cowley. We can drop your father off once we're finished.'

It was an empty offer on Kim's part. She knew there was no way Fiona was going anywhere.

She took a seat on the sofa and Kim instantly sat beside her, leaving Jeff Cowley nowhere to sit but the single chair. On his own and away from his daughter.

'You were saying, Mr Cowley?' Kim pressed.

Mr Cowley ran his hand back and forth over his bald head.

'Jacob James did some casual work on the farm, more than twenty years ago. The kids were very young, they wouldn't remember him,' he said, trying to excuse his daughter's premature denial.

'My father's health was beginning to fail, and I couldn't do all the work myself. We were busy then, successful,' he said. 'Jacob worked with us for just a couple of months.'

Kim waited for the rest of the story.

Fiona stood. 'There you are,' she said. 'You have your answer, now…'

'Please sit down, Miss Cowley,' Travis said, with authority.

She sat.

'Is there anything else?' Kim pushed.

'No, I think…'

'Why did he leave?' Kim asked, losing patience.

'He fell down. He couldn't work.'

'You mean he fell down a faulty pair of ladders you supplied for him to work on top of the barn.'

'Dad, don't—'

'Was that you or your father?'

'My father gave—'

'Your father gave an employee faulty equipment to use?'

'Dad—'

'Well… he didn't know…'

'And the ladders broke, didn't they?' Kim asked. She didn't particularly like this method of questioning but if she waited for too long Fiona would find some way to intervene.

'Yes,' he answered.

'And Jacob James shattered his knee in the fall?'

'He was hurt, yes.'

'He couldn't work, could he?' she pushed.

'Well, I don't know…'

'Dad…' Fiona warned.

'And he instructed a solicitor to act on his behalf.'

'I don't recall—'

'Jacob was suing your family, wasn't he?' Kim asked.

'I'm sorry but—'

'Tell me, Mr Cowley, who was it that met with Mr James and tried to buy him off?'

Fiona protested again. Just as Kim's phone began to ring.

Damn it, she'd been on the verge of getting something out of him. Now her momentum had been broken he would have time to recover.

'Doctor A,' she said, sharply.

'Untwist your knickers, Inspector. I have something you might wanting to know.'

Kim excused herself and stepped back into the kitchen.

'Go on,' she said.

'I thought you should know that the bullet is a match,' she said.

'So the bullet from Billy Cowley's neck definitely came from the gun at the scene?' she clarified.

'Absolutely not, Inspector. The bullet did not come from the gun at the scene.'

Kim was momentarily confused.

'So what is a match?'

'The bullet that came from Mr Cowley and the bullet that came from the grave.'

Kim gripped the phone harder. The incidents were almost three decades apart.

'Are you sure?' she asked.

'I will try not to be insulted as I assume you ask me that out of shock.'

Kim apologised, thanked her and ended the call.

There was only one person who could have been present for both.

Kim strode back into the lounge and stood before Jeff Cowley.

'Mr Cowley, I am arresting you for the murder of Jacob James and for the attempted murder of your son William Cowley. You do not—'

Fiona Cowley's screams drowned out the rest of her words.

CHAPTER 52

Stacey felt the disgust crawling all over her.

She had read Justin's posts from six months ago. A few selfies, a couple of meal photos, Justin at a few pubs and clubs in Stourbridge.

And then the posts had begun to change.

The first few were from Britain First. Particular stories exploited from a sensationalist point of view. Stacey often saw these posts floating around her own Facebook timeline and tried to ignore them. And yet she still took note of the people who shared them.

A few of Justin's friends began commenting about the 'rubbish' he was sharing.

Eventually, the comical clips from places like UNILAD died out altogether, and the posts from Britain First gave way to posts from the EDL and then onto posts so offensive to minority groups she could barely calm her stomach enough to read them.

But she had read on and by the time she reached the top of his feed, she saw the final post which had caused most of Justin's friends to abuse him.

Justin had shared a video clip of a young mixed-race couple being terrorised and eventually beaten by a group of masked youths while their toddler had screamed and cried in the background. Stacey remembered seeing the clip on *Crimewatch* and the wails of the child had stayed with her for days. Justin's header had stated 'wish I'd been able to join in with this'.

That last offensive post had been placed on the twelfth, two weeks ago.

Something stirred in her stomach.

A date that had stuck in her mind.

She clicked back into his activity log and saw why the date had mattered.

It was on the twelfth that Floda had sent Justin a friend request.

Stacey had a sudden idea.

She grabbed her phone and set to work.

CHAPTER 53

Kim watched as a West Mercia squad car left the Cowley property with Jeff Cowley on board.

'Hopefully our time together is almost at an end,' Travis said.

'Do you think?' she said, ruefully. 'We don't have a confession, and two bodies are not yet identified.'

She started the car and headed to the narrow track that led away from the property.

Fiona continued to watch her from the doorway.

Kim entered the main road traffic and drove slowly, before she pulled into a petrol station and killed the engine.

'What the hell are we doing now?' Travis asked.

'Waiting,' she said, simply.

She stared into her side mirror until the red Jaguar passed behind.

'Bingo,' she said, starting the engine. Fiona had wasted no time in leaving the family home.

'I don't get it,' Travis said, as she pulled into traffic two cars behind Fiona. 'She's probably heading to the station to be near her dad or to the hospital to see her brother.'

'Maybe,' Kim replied, but Fiona Cowley was rattled. And people thought differently in heightened states of emotion. They took risks.

At every opportunity she had acted like a human gag around her father, attempting to silence every word. Any involvement or control from her was impossible now that Jeff was in police hands, but Kim was curious to know what the woman would do next.

'You know this is some form of harassment, don't you?'

'Absolutely. But I still want to know where she's going,' Kim said, simply.

'Yeah, I'm quite interested too,' he admitted.

'So, which one of them pulled the trigger on Jacob James?' she asked as a third car pulled in behind Fiona. 'Jeff or his father?'

'We don't know that either of them did.'

'Tom, have you forgotten how police work is? You're given dots and you have to join them up. Jacob James disappeared over twenty-seven years ago. His skeleton is found on Cowley land with a bullet hole and a bullet that matches the same one removed from Jeff's son. You don't think these dots are begging to be joined up?'

'Not until we've got the gun that fired both bullets,' he said.

'But who else could it be?' she asked.

'The person that has the gun.'

Kim gave up. She wasn't sure they could agree on the time of day even if they were smack bang in the centre of Greenwich.

'Well, that's the hospital out,' Travis said as Fiona ignored the left turn that would have taken her towards Russells Hall.

'Not too concerned about her dear brother, then?' Kim observed.

Even Travis was watching the car intently now.

'And we should have taken the first exit to head towards Kidderminster,' Kim said as two cars exited left at the island.

Only a Land Rover Discovery separated them now.

They continued to follow Fiona in silence until she indicated a turn to the right.

Kim continued driving past.

'Well, I wasn't expecting that,' she said, as the car disappeared from view.

CHAPTER 54

'So what was that in there?' Bryant asked, as he directed the car away from Hollytree. 'You reacted to the scar that Aisha mentioned?'

Dawson shook his head. 'Not sure yet. It might be something or nothing. Let me think on it.'

Bryant shrugged.

They saw the sign for club Nexus being erected as Dawson pulled in opposite a car dealership on the Hagley Road. Two vans were parked right outside the premises which had once been a high street bank.

'Left, left, up, more,' shouted a man wearing black trousers, purple polo neck jumper and high-visibility vest.

'Nigel Townsend?' Dawson asked as they approached.

The man turned and scrutinised them. It took just a second for him to register they were police officers.

He nodded and removed his hard hat, revealing thick black hair that tumbled down on to a handsome face.

'Please, come inside,' he said, stepping inside.

Bryant cast a cautionary glance up before stepping underneath the neon sign hovering precariously between two ladders.

He followed the reflective figure through the darkness of a building site, weaving around piles of ceramic tiles and timber.

'In here,' he said, turning left into the male toilets. This area had been tiled in plain white oversized squares. Four urinals and two toilets had been shoved against the wall in the corner to make room for a desk.

'Only place I can access right now,' he explained, perching on the edge of the desk and offering Bryant the chair.

As Dawson took a seat on one of the toilets, Bryant had to wonder at the ridiculousness of this situation.

'It's one of those things that I'll laugh about when it's over. Just not right now,' Nigel said.

'We're here about Bubba,' Bryant said.

'Of course you are; but please don't call him that. His name was Brandon. Bubba was a name he gave himself, pretty much like everything else.'

Bryant was not surprised to see the lower lip of the good-looking man tremble.

'What do you mean?' Dawson asked from the corner.

'You must know his background. He grew up in foster homes. Even his name was given to him by the vicar on whose doorstep he was left. Brandon had no clue about his parents or background so he made it up himself…'

'He mentioned his grandmother to me,' Dawson said.

Nigel shook his head. 'Someone's grandmother, officer, but certainly not his.'

'May I ask how you found out about his death?' Bryant asked.

'A call, just ten minutes before it scrolled across the ticker tape of the twenty-four hour news channel. Short-term boyfriends don't take priority, it seems.'

'Who called?' Bryant asked.

'Frost?' Dawson added.

'Does it matter?' he asked. 'It doesn't make him any less dead, does it?' He swallowed deeply. 'You must think I'm a complete arse being here the day after…'

'Actually, I don't,' Bryant said. Keeping busy was his way of dealing with grief too. 'But do you have any idea who might want to hurt Bu— Brandon?'

Nigel shook his head, sadly. 'You know he was gay?'

'Of course, but…'

'No, I mean, *really* gay.'

Bryant tried to keep up. 'I'm sorry but I don't know what you mean.'

Nigel sighed heavily. 'I've known I preferred men since I was eleven years old, officer. I make no apologies for my sexuality but, guess what, I want the same things as your young colleague over there. I want to find someone to love, get married, maybe have children and lead a productive life. Brandon just wanted to be gay.'

'So what did that mean?' Bryant asked.

'He was aggressively homosexual, officer. I am a rainbow-flag flying member of my community too but Brandon wanted to challenge everyone who disagrees with our lifestyle.'

'And you don't?' Dawson asked, leaning forward.

'I want to live my life too. I refuse to hang on to hate and negativity, but Brandon thrived on it, invited it any opportunity he got. He would grab my hand or kiss me in public to provoke a response and then confront it.'

'I don't get how that is wrong,' Dawson said from the corner. 'Why isn't he allowed to express his affection in public? Fair play to him for challenging the bigots.'

Nigel smiled. 'If only the rest of the world agreed with you, officer.'

'Did he have any particular enemies that you're aware of?' Bryant asked.

'Oh please, he was a homosexual newspaper reporter. Take your pick.' He paused and shook his head. 'I told him,' he said, wiping his eyes. 'I bloody told him that kind of stuff would get him hurt but he was a gay man that liked to be noticed.'

A dozen thoughts began to swirl around Bryant's head as an unwanted notion screamed in his mind. He pushed the chair back and stood. He needed to get out and think, try and put these thoughts together.

He held out his hand. 'Thank you for your time, Mr Townsend, and we are deeply sorry for your loss.'

He smiled as the tears finally spilled from his eyes. 'Thank you, officer. That means a lot.'

Bryant turned to walk away as a feeling of dread began to form in the pit of his stomach.

'Nice guy,' Dawson said, catching up with him.

Bryant nodded.

'What's up, Bryant? You've gone a funny shade of sickly green.'

Bryant leaned against the car and took a breath. 'Put it together, Dawson and include Aisha Gupta in your thoughts,' he said, as his colleague shook his head.

'Look at our victims. I think what we've got here is a sudden rush of hate crimes.'

CHAPTER 55

Stacey sat back in her chair and admired her work. Aaron Holt was one angry young kid. He was eighteen years old and unable to find work because all the foreigners were taking the jobs.

He had liked every offensive right wing, white supremacy group he could find and had started agreeing and commenting and sharing his own experience.

It sickened Stacey that Aaron Holt had received seventy friend requests in under an hour. The pity was that a post spreading peace and love wouldn't have attracted anywhere near as much attention.

She'd added a few photos of pretty girls, some music tastes and a couple of games. Aaron Holt was beginning to look like a real person. And she didn't like him one little bit.

Stacey felt herself moving further and further away from her initial reason for investigating Justin's suicide. When she'd seen Justin Reynolds lying in a pool of his own blood she had been transported back to her own teens, to the day she'd held a handful of pills in her left hand and a full glass of water in her right.

It was the day after Janie Powers had kissed her. And she'd liked it.

Twenty-four hours had mixed the fear, repulsion, confusion and shame into one boulder that bounced around in her head. She felt permanently changed by the experience, as though it was printed on her face or a gigantic speech bubble above her head.

Her whole day at school had been spent looking around her, staring at anyone who laughed, convinced they were talking about her, and avoiding Janie Powers.

She had returned home to an empty house that had been both a blessing and a curse. At least her mother hadn't witnessed the panic attack that had seized her and brought her to tears.

Her only thought had been to escape the feelings inside her. Their confinement in her own mind had expanded them to insurmountable proportions. All her life, she'd dealt with being different. Her skin had hardened against many of the insults over time. But this was yet another obstacle between her and anything resembling 'normal'.

As she opened the packet of tablets she'd realised there was only so much 'different' a girl could take.

Luckily her mother had returned early from work and caught Stacey as the first tablets were hovering around her mouth.

Her mother's expression of fear and horror would stay in her mind for ever. The words had tumbled out of her, making no sense, but her mother had been able to clutch at the issue.

'So you want to die because you might like girls?'

Stacey remembered shaking her head and then saying the words that had almost broken her mother's heart.

'No, I want to die so I don't have to tell *you* that I might like girls.'

Stacey saw the hurt in her mother's eyes before she was gathered into a hug and a barrage of reassurance. *And that reassurance has been there for me ever since*, Stacey thought with a smile. They had made a pact that day that no secrets would exist between them, and Stacey had kept her word. Now and again her mum would ask if there was any 'special someone' Stacey would like to bring around. Sadly there hadn't been but she wouldn't hesitate when there was.

Looking back now, it was hard for her to believe that she had considered ending her own life because of her burgeoning sexuality, but at the time it had been all-encompassing and what she had sought was an escape.

And that was what she had recognised in Justin's letter. She had wanted to understand him, to reassure his family that it wasn't their fault.

But now, Stacey knew that the tide had turned. She had begun by leading this investigation and, with apprehension, she realised that it was now leading her.

She had expected to uncover an angst-ridden teenager, weighed down by depression, fear or emotional baggage. But as she looked once more at the profile of Justin Reynolds, she realised she had found something a whole lot darker.

CHAPTER 56

'How much longer are we going to have to wait for this bloody brief?' Kim asked, pacing around Travis's small office.

'It's been fifteen minutes, Stone,' Travis said, closing his folder and reaching for his phone.

She sighed heavily. It felt much longer since they had tried to question Mr Cowley, who had demanded a solicitor immediately.

She sat down opposite Travis.

'What's his daughter up to?' Kim asked, thinking aloud. Although they had Mr Cowley in custody, it was Fiona Cowley that held the key to this case. She knew something about these bodies in the ground, and Kim wanted to know what it was.

'Do you think we should haul her in as well?' Travis asked.

Kim was tempted to glance behind her. He couldn't possibly be asking her opinion. The silence and his impatient expression told her that he was.

Kim shook her head. 'Let's see what we get out of her dad first. It might be a good thing to threaten him with though.'

Travis nodded his agreement. 'Yeah, I was thinking of dropping that into the—'

'Boss, do you want to take a look at this?' asked Penn from the doorway.

They followed him to the wipe board on the side wall. It looked similar to her own in the garage. Only, his game of Hangman had small underscores in between the letters they already knew.

'So, based on the lettering of each line and the different font sizes I think we can estimate how many of these spaces are characters or spaces but...' His words trailed away as though his initial excitement had been extinguished by the hopelessness of the task, now that he looked at it in the cold light of day.

'Keep going,' Kim said, walking towards the board. She was impressed with his initiative. 'Tell me what you think,' she said.

'I think it's an invitation,' he said.

Kim looked at Travis, and they both approached the wipe board.

'Go on,' Kim said, with interest.

'I think it's definitely an invitation of some kind,' he said, springing back into life. His thoughts echoed her own.

'I think the first line is the announcement of what it is, like a wedding, a funeral. Something like that,' he said.

'Make a note to the side in red,' Kim suggested.

He did so.

'Second line down is the date,' he said, noting that to the side.

'I think the third line down is an instruction.'

'Maybe bring something?' she offered.

'If it is some kind of invitation, there is one vital piece of information missing,' she said.

The constable's eyes ran over the board once more.

'Location,' he cried out.

'I'm thinking so,' she said, as he wrote the word at the end of the last line.

Travis stepped forward as Kim was about to open her mouth.

'Good work,' he said, nodding his head appreciatively. 'Bloody good work, Penn.'

'Sir?' said a constable from the doorway. 'The brief for Mr Cowley has just arrived.'

He nodded his thanks and then turned to her. 'I'm leading this one, Stone,' he said.

'Why? You know I was getting to him back at the house?' she asked as they headed from the squad room.

'Precisely,' Travis continued. 'His brief is here now. We need a slightly different approach.'

There was a part of her that agreed with him.

'Less goading,' he said, heading out of the office. Kim cursed silently; he just had to finish with that.

She followed him downstairs to the interview rooms, and entered room one.

All conversation stopped as they stepped in.

The brief was in his late fifties and a few stone overweight. His hair was totally white and plentiful. His chubby face was clean-shaven and his clothes were top quality.

He stood and offered his hand.

'Leonard Cameron, solicitor to the Cowley family,' he offered, pleasantly.

Travis shook the hand while Kim sat. She hated happy briefs. It meant they weren't worried. And she wanted this brief to be worried. Even Jeff Cowley was looking more relaxed than he had at the house.

She felt her insides begin to turn as she realised they were not going to get anything from him, no matter who was asking the questions.

Travis switched on the tape and listed the date, time and persons present. Jeff Cowley had not looked at her once.

'So, Mr Cowley, I'd like to begin by talking about your son's accident. You maintain that it was an accident?' he asked, pleasantly.

Mr Cowley looked to his brief, who nodded.

'Yes, my son shot himself accidentally.'

'And you saw this?'

He nodded.

Travis pointed to the tape recorder. 'Please speak your response, Mr Cowley,' he said.

The man leaned towards it. 'Yes,' he said.

'And you saw him actually contort himself into such a position that he could shoot himself in the back of the neck?'

'Yes,' he said.

'Would you be able to demonstrate exactly how that was?'

'Umm… well… not… it happened so fast that…'

'Could you explain how, once he got himself into that unbelievable position, he could shoot himself with a gun that we haven't yet found?'

'It was right there,' he said.

'But it wasn't the gun, was it, Mr Cowley?'

He shrugged.

Travis looked to the recorder.

'I don't know.'

'You don't know how the bullet in your son's neck came from a completely different gun to the one you saw him messing with?'

'Your results must be wrong,' he said.

So, Kim thought, his brief had told him to stick to his story. Every question they asked would be met with the same response.

'And how do you explain the bullet in your son matching the one found in a mass grave containing one of your ex-employees?' Travis asked.

'It's a lot of land,' he answered.

'So, persons unknown came onto your land, dug a hole, buried three bodies, left again and you know absolutely nothing about it?' Travis asked.

'That's correct,' he answered.

Kim was growing weary of these non-answers.

'And what can you tell us about the accident Jacob James had on your property?' Travis continued.

'I don't remember it very well. It was a long time ago.'

'It was caused by defective ladders, wasn't it?'

'I think so,' he answered.

The brief smiled in her direction. He clearly thought the interview was going well.

She didn't smile back.

'And that accident left Jacob James unable to work, unable to support his family?'

'I wouldn't know about that.'

The man was unflappable. Gone was the cowering, terrified man they'd seen at the house. Mr Cowley now bordered on smug.

'Did you see Jacob James again?' Travis asked.

'Not that I recall.'

Kim realised they had lost the element of surprise. He knew every question they were going to ask and had a non-committal response ready and waiting for every single one of them. None of the questions were eliciting an emotional response that they could read and capitalise on.

'So, you weren't the Cowley that offered Jacob James a paltry amount of money to drop the lawsuit?'

He shook his head and almost smiled.

Kim nudged Travis beneath the table. They needed to see his response to a question he wasn't expecting.

'Mr Cowley, I'd like to ask just one more question if I may. It's about your daughter, Fiona.'

For the first time, Cowley looked her way.

'Can you explain why she would have visited the Preece residence immediately following your arrest?'

The colour drained from his face, taking all remains of smugness with it.

'No comment,' he answered with a tremor in his voice.

CHAPTER 57

It was late afternoon when they headed back into the squad room. Bryant pretended not to see Stacey push down the lid of the laptop. If she was doing some personal stuff at the end of the day, that was her business.

'Bad one, guys?' she asked as Dawson slumped down in his chair, and loosened his tie.

'Yeah, Stace,' Bryant answered.

Dawson's fatigue travelled across the room and found him.

He glanced at his colleague, who looked away.

'What?' Stacey asked. 'Did I do something?'

Bryant thought it was a strange question.

'It's hate crimes, Stace,' Bryant said as Dawson kicked at something under the table.

He saw the emotion flash in her eyes.

'And?' she asked. He could hear the controlled rage in that one word.

'It's just…'

'Just what, Bryant? Why am I suddenly being treated differently? What the hell are you two trying to protect me from?'

Bryant knew she was right, and yet something inside him didn't want her anywhere near this case.

'Do you try and shield me every time a woman is murdered – cos believe it or not, I'm one of them too. Do I try and protect you when a Caucasian male is killed or assaulted?'

Bryant shook his head. The controlled rage in her voice was no longer controlled.

'Do you think I've not come across hate crimes before, guys?' she asked. 'I wasn't born into this team. I experienced a whole twenty years before I met you. Trust me, I've seen it out there.'

'It's just that we find it so abhorrent...'

'Don't find it abhorrent because it's a black guy or a gay guy or a Polish immigrant. Be pissed off because someone lost their life or got hurt,' she said.

'But to be targeted because of—'

'Bryant, don't talk to me about that. I was the kid dragged into the stationery room when I was five by four kids with a scourer. Surprisingly, it didn't come off,' she said, wiping at the skin on her forearm.

'Stace, I'm—'

'No, Bryant. You want to know something about hate crimes? Well, listen to this. Say Dawson's house gets done-over tonight and all his stuff is taken. He may never get his stuff back but he can safeguard against it happening again. He can fit cameras, lights, alarms. Hell, he can even pay a guy to sit on his front lawn. He can prevent his stuff being taken again, but guess what, I'll still be black in the morning and there's no way I can safeguard against that.'

There was so much Bryant wanted to say but everything in his mouth sounded trite.

'Every day I have to wonder if I'm going to be the victim of a "knockout game" because of my colour.'

Bryant knew of these random, vicious, unprovoked attacks that were plastered all over the Internet. It was a relatively new fad that had followed 'happy slapping'. The aim was to knock out an unsuspecting victim with a single sucker punch. He'd lost count of the deaths that had resulted from the stupid phase, and some offences had been classified as hate crimes.

'And do you realise that most hate crimes are committed by ordinary members of the public? Oh yeah, the hate groups recruit, just like cults, by lying and brainwashing, and turning folks into vicious little hatemongers – but still the majority of attacks come from people acting alone. What did a young Asian girl in Derby do to deserve being doused in acid last week? But it's not just against blacks or Asians. It's goths, moshers – anyone who is different either by choice or design.'

Stacey stopped talking and shook her head as she began to gather up her things.

'And yet, guys, none of this hurts me,' she said, pushing back her chair. 'It angers, frustrates, enrages me but it doesn't hurt me.' She stood. 'What does hurt me is that, on a case where I could offer more than data analysis, you guys chose to freeze me out.'

Bryant shook his head as Stacey passed by his desk.

'That went well,' he observed once his colleague had left the room. 'And the worst thing is she's absolutely right,' he said, shaking his head. 'We could really use her help on this about now.'

He glanced at Dawson, who was busy tapping away on his keyboard. Bryant was eager for this day to end. He wanted to make a short detour on the way home to check that the Kowalski family was safely back at their address, following the issue of the restraining order preventing Flint from going anywhere near the property.

'So, Dawson, tomorrow, we get Stacey involved, right?' he said, reaching for his coat.

'Yeah, yeah, whatever you say, boss,' Dawson said, absently, while reading the screen.

'What is it, Kev?'

'Something Stacey said.' He looked over the top of his computer screen. 'I think you'd better come and have a look at this.'

CHAPTER 58

'I swear to God, Travis, if he says "no comment" one more time I'm gonna…'

'Hold your tongue and stay calm,' he said.

'But, we're getting nothing from him.'

'Yeah, since you mentioned his daughter,' Travis snarled.

'But it was the only reaction we got.'

Travis shook his head. 'And then the next twenty questions you asked about his daughter rattled him even more, and then the brief shut you down. At least while he was answering there was the opportunity he'd trip himself up, but we're now down to two-word answers and it's the same two words.'

She knew he had a point.

'Jesus, why do I feel like this case is going on without us?' she asked, leaning against the same wall as Travis.

They were only waiting for Cowley's refreshment break to end before having another crack at him.

'I can't go back in,' Kim said, honestly. 'Take one of the others in, or I'm going to do something I'll regret.'

His head turned sharply.

She shook her head. That hadn't been a dig.

'I think it's a good idea,' he said.

'Can you get a lift home?' she asked.

'Of course; I never asked you to be my chauffeur.'

Kim ached to respond to his snarkiness, but a picture of Woody came into her mind.

'I'll pick you up in the morning,' she said, walking away.

* * *

She headed out of the building right into the cold air and a man dressed from head to toe in leather.

'Inspector, just the person,' said Bart Preece, removing his helmet.

She looked beyond him to the Ecosse parked beside her Golf.

What the hell was one of the Preece boys doing here?

'Surely you're off-duty now,' he said with a lopsided grin.

'You're joking?' she asked, walking towards the bike.

He shrugged as he placed the helmet under his arm and reached for the keys. 'You seemed to appreciate it yesterday. Thought you might like to take it for a spin.'

Kim laughed. 'Yeah and you might never see it again.'

She appraised it beneath the street light in its full titanium glory. Oh, how she would love to place her behind on that gel seat and feel the MotoGP spec Öhlins suspension.

He laughed with her. 'Inspector, you are an officer of the law. I trust you to bring it back.'

She leaned down to get a closer look at the front wheel.

'A brake pad for each piston?' she asked.

He nodded. 'Handles like a dream,' he said, touching the handlebar.

She walked around it, appreciating the beauty.

'Multi adjustable riding position,' he said, tipping his head. 'Best experience you can have on two wheels.'

Kim nodded. She didn't doubt it.

'You got one?' he asked.

'An Ecosse?' she asked with her eyes wide open.

He laughed out loud. 'A motorbike.'

'Ninja,' she said, stroking the seat.

'Nice,' he said, nodding appreciatively.

She looked for signs of condescension and found none. Yes, the Ninja was a nice bike but the difference between the two was like a Timex and a Rolex. They were both watches and they both told the time. And there the similarity ended.

'Okay, just start her up and let me hear…'

Her words trailed away as the doors to the station opened behind her.

Travis appeared with a constable.

He stopped dead as he took in the scene before him.

'I'm heading to Russells Hall,' he said, urgently. 'Our accident survivor is conscious.' He looked to Bart and then back to her. 'He's asked to see me. Feel free to join us when you're done.'

He sprinted towards a squad car.

She looked to the bike and groaned. Not that she would have taken it for a ride but she wasn't quite done looking at it yet.

'Sorry, I've got to…'

'Of course,' Bart said, reaching for his helmet.

She began to walk away and then turned. 'But thank you. It was a lovely thought.'

He nodded and clicked down his visor.

As Kim got into the Golf and started the engine she took one more look at the bike, strangely relieved that they had been interrupted.

Her gaze moved to Bart Preece, standing lazily beside the bike.

Yes, very relieved indeed.

CHAPTER 59

Stacey forced back the tears into her aching throat.

It wasn't the issue about her colour. She was black, proud and happy with herself. It was the fact that, in trying to keep her out of something, Dawson and Bryant had inadvertently started treating her differently, excluding her. That was something she'd suffered all her life.

She jumped on the bus and took the last window seat available. The next stop was right outside a trading estate well known for low-level drug deals. She placed her arm over Justin's laptop protruding from her bag and edged closer to the condensation-covered window.

She looked away as a line of people streamed onto the bus. Eye contact could be viewed as an invitation, and she didn't feel like company right now.

Her eyes immediately began to fill again. She didn't even acknowledge the form that slid into the seat next to her.

She sniffed back the tears.

'Hey, are you okay?' asked a gentle voice beside her.

She turned and saw the pleasant smiling face of a man in his early thirties. He wore overalls and a beanie hat. He placed his jacket between them so their thighs didn't touch.

'I'm fine, thank you,' she said, thrilled that she had showed this stranger her watery, bloodshot eyes and snotty nose.

'If it helps any, I've had a shit day too.'

'It doesn't, but thanks anyway,' she said, hearing the tremor in her voice.

Stacey felt frustrated by her own emotions. It wasn't only her colleagues – she knew that. It was their insensitivity, in addition to the vile, disgusting articles she'd been posting all day. She tried to remember a day that she had felt less of a minority.

'So, the boss says to me, "that new clutch you fitted is slipping".'

Stacey hadn't realised the man beside her had continued speaking. And more importantly, he was explaining about his shit day at work. She ignored him and turned back to the window. Attractive or not, she wasn't in the mood for small talk.

It didn't help that her boss wasn't around. Kim would have banged her colleagues' heads together and they would all have got on with the case at hand. Her colour would not have been mentioned again, and it wouldn't have needed to be.

'So, I test the car and my boss is having a laugh. There's nothing wrong with that clutch plate but he wants me to spend four hours stripping it back down.'

'Mmm…' Stacey said, to avoid being totally rude.

'So, do you know what I did?' he asked, nudging her conspiratorially.

She shook her head and edged more against the window.

'I lay underneath the car with a spanner. Every few minutes I made a noise or swore but I was checking the football scores.'

'Clever,' she said, without emotion.

This good-looking stranger had picked the worst possible day to strike up a conversation with her.

'Dickhead road-tested it and said it was— hey, mate watch out,' he said as an older male walking down the aisle fell onto him. Consequently, he pushed Stacey even harder against the window.

'God, I'm so sorry,' he said, touching her arm. 'Are you okay?'

Stacey nodded and turned away, cutting off any contact between them. Right now she just wanted to be in her nice, small, familiar flat.

Two stops later, the male got off the bus. Stacey sighed with relief. Maybe on another day she might have been interested in engaging in conversation, but only negative thoughts were running around in her mind.

She allowed her generous bottom to readjust itself now it had possession of the double seat. Only two more stops and she'd be home herself. Into the shower, a frozen pizza for tea and some warm, comfy pyjamas. She'd probably share a few more poisonous posts, comment on another couple and then immerse herself in *World of Warcraft* for a couple of hours before bed.

The tension began to ease from her body as she stared at the night ahead.

The woman behind pulled on the metal topper of Stacey's seat to raise herself to a standing position. Stacey followed suit. It was her stop too.

She reached for her handbag on the seat and felt around, but her fingers knew just a second before her eyes registered the truth.

Justin Reynolds's laptop was gone.

CHAPTER 60

'You sure this guy is gonna still be here?' Bryant asked as they reached the Derbyshire Constabulary in Ripley.

The force was responsible for an area of around 1,000 square miles, with a population of just under 1 million. It was split into two: the more rural north covering the Peak District, and the more urbanised east and south encompassing the city of Derby itself.

The glass-fronted building was the Operational Support Division and housed the Road Policing Unit, Air Support and Armed Response, as well as Uniform Task Force.

'He said he'd wait,' Dawson said as Bryant pulled the car to a stop.

'Yeah, and we said we'd be here by half past seven,' Bryant observed.

The first half of the fifty-six-mile drive had passed quickly using the M6 toll road but a build-up around Burton-on-Trent had added forty-five minutes to their journey.

They sprinted across the car park. Bryant's hand was on the door.

'Hey, you after me?' said a voice from behind.

They both turned to see a man standing beside a Ford Sierra, smoking a cigarette.

They walked towards him.

'You had until I'd finished this one and then I was off,' he said, throwing the cigarette to the floor, demonstrating just how close they'd been.

'Thank you for waiting,' Dawson offered, quickly.

'You the guy I spoke to on the phone?' he asked.

Dawson nodded and held out his hand. The detective inspector they knew as Wilson returned the handshake.

The man bore an uncanny resemblance to Boris Johnson, Bryant thought as the fringe of his unruly blonde hair fell over his eyes.

'So, you got something going on down there in the Black Country you think might be linked to an incident up here?' he asked.

It was clear to Bryant this conversation was going to take place on the car park. They could hardly complain, given how long he had waited for them to get there.

Bryant allowed Dawson to lead. He was the one who had made a possible connection and contacted the man running the case.

Dawson nodded. 'Yeah, we've got some incidents that are looking like a spurt of hate crimes. Potentially three in a short space of time.'

Wilson shook his head as he lit another cigarette. Bryant remembered the days he'd been a thirty-a-day man. And after four years the occasional pang still took him by surprise.

'Doesn't match what we know about the attack on our girl,' he said.

'Can you tell us about Shay Chakma?' Dawson asked, thrusting his hands into his jacket pockets.

'Pretty girl, from a family well respected in the Bangladeshi community. Parents came here when she was two years old. Two brothers, older, more traditional than Shay. She worked at a call centre for a power company. No bother at all, did her job and got on well with everyone.'

Bryant wondered why Wilson had already decided this was no hate crime. It was beginning to sound like an unprovoked attack to him.

'Except, her parents had just chosen a husband for her from another Bangladeshi family. Problem is, Shay's been seeing one of her shift supervisors for the last seven months. Left work on Tuesday night a few minutes late and got two litres of sulphuric acid thrown all over her.'

Bryant was still unconvinced that the incidents were not related.

'You ever seen an acid attack?' Wilson asked, suddenly.

They both shook their heads.

'Only photos,' Bryant said.

He shook his head. 'Not the same. I saw Shay twenty minutes after it happened.' He stared into the space above Dawson's head.

'It was like someone had taken a blowtorch to her skin. It was like her face had melted down onto her neck, like an old candle. Witnesses said her face took just seconds to swell up like a balloon and then shrink again. The doctor explained that skin is sixty per cent water, and sulphuric acid doesn't like water. As the acid interacts the temperature rises very quickly giving the victim a hot sensation, before agonising pain.'

Bryant closed his eyes against the nausea whirling in his stomach.

'Jesus,' whispered Dawson.

Wilson returned to the present. 'Stuff got into her stomach and lungs as well.'

'Poor kid,' Dawson said.

Bryant wondered if they were looking at the work of one man. Had their perpetrator widened his net? Travelled to another area to spread his attacks apart?

'Still could be linked,' he said.

'We're treating it as an honour attack, lads,' Wilson insisted. 'We got no other crimes like yours around here, and what with her secret boyfriend and all, we gotta treat it as we see it. We're focussing this investigation on her family.'

'But how did they feel about her having a boyfriend?' Dawson asked.

He shrugged. 'Didn't seem too upset by it but I'm not so sure about her older brothers.'

Bryant couldn't help what his gut was screaming at him even though Wilson's suspicions were plausible.

There was only one way to be certain.

'Look, will you just let us speak to her – make sure?' Bryant pleaded.

Wilson shook his head. 'Sorry mate, but no can do. May be a blessing in disguise, but Shay Chakma died half an hour ago.'

CHAPTER 61

Travis was already beside the bed of Mr Dhinsa when she entered. Kim wondered if the man had any idea how hard her colleague had worked to save his life at the roadside.

The nurse had not needed to offer the stern look accompanied by the finger to her lips for Kim to understand that the ICU ward was full of desperately sick people. It wasn't the first time she had visited. And she was betting it probably wouldn't be the last.

There was an attitude, an ethos, in the ICU ward that reminded her of the library. Everything was performed calmly and as quietly as possible, the interminable silence broken only by the low hum of the life-saving equipment stationed next to most of the beds.

'How is he?' she whispered.

The man's young face was smooth in repose. His black hair stood up in tufts and part of his short beard had been shaved to allow for stitches and a dressing. Kim easily recalled the trauma sustained to the body of his companion. Mr Dhinsa had been the lucky one, although he might not realise that for some time yet.

'Coming and going every few minutes,' Travis answered. 'So far, he's asked me where he is and why. His lower legs are in a bit of a state,' he said, looking down the bed to the plaster casts that stretched from the toes up to the knees of both legs. 'Doctor says he's off the critical list now they've ruled out permanent spinal injury. They're dosing him with steroids.'

Kim had a horrible thought as Mr Dhinsa opened his eyes and looked straight at Travis.

'Where's Trisha?'

And there it was. He had been so badly out of it he had no idea.

'Don't think about that right now, Mr Dhinsa. Just concentrate on getting—'

Travis stopped speaking as Mr Dhinsa closed his eyes once more.

Kim stepped around to the other side of the bed and sat down on the plastic chair. It had the potential to be a very long night.

Mr Dhinsa opened his eyes again.

'Did you save me?' he asked.

Travis nodded.

The eyes closed.

'Are you going to try and ask him anything?' Kim asked. The last they'd heard, his partner had been pushed in front of that delivery truck and the only person seen around was him.

'Yeah if he stays with me long enough. It's a bit like trying to have a conversation with you.'

Kim was surprised to see that the comment hadn't been accompanied by the usual hard line to his lips. Surely he hadn't been trying to have a chuckle with her?

Eyes open.

'Mr Dhinsa, was Trisha pushed?' Travis asked, getting his own question in first.

'Blue van,' he answered.

'He's too confused,' Travis said, looking her way. 'The van was white.'

Kim shook her head. 'He's just groggy and fighting the drugs. Try him again.'

Eyes open.

'Trish got in the way,' he said, as his eyes rolled. And then rolled back again.

'He wants to tell us, Travis,' Kim realised. His short answers were revealing in sequence as much as he could manage at a time.

He was trying to tell them exactly what happened.

The shadow of a nurse loomed behind them. 'I think that's enough for now,' she said, quietly.

'Please, just another minute or two,' Kim said. She didn't want this man to have expended all this energy for nothing.

'Please…' Travis added.

'Two minutes,' she agreed, glancing at his vital signs on the machine.

'Men tried to take…' Mr Dhinsa said.

Eyes closed.

Kim's gaze met with Travis's across the bed. They were running out of time. They had to help him put this together.

Kim turned to Mr Dhinsa and hoped he could hear her before they lost him to sleep altogether.

'Mr Dhinsa, are you saying there were men in a blue van who tried to take your girlfriend?' Kim asked, corralling his previous statements.

He nodded and then shook his head as his eyes opened once again.

'No, Trisha stopped… they were trying to take me.'

CHAPTER 62

Stacey paced her small lounge once more. Since returning home she had cooked, thrown food away, tried to vacuum, tried to watch television, walk, stand and sit.

'Damn it,' she shouted, kicking at a dining chair. The screech of metal on the laminate flooring was satisfying.

She collapsed onto the sofa and buried her head in her hands. What the hell had she been thinking?

Part of her wanted to ring the boss and offload, confess to all the stupid things she'd done, take the bollocking and then move on.

Yeah, that might help her right now. She'd feel better once she'd passed all responsibility up the chain, but it wouldn't help her in the long-term. Not only would she be demonstrating that she couldn't use her own initiative effectively but that she couldn't sort the worms once she'd opened the bloody can.

'Damn it,' she said, again. She'd involved herself in a case that hadn't needed solving. She'd invaded the personal space of a grieving mother, taken the suicide victim's property, not logged it in officially, and now it had been stolen.

Stacey shook her head. At this rate they were already preparing her cell in Guantanamo.

The tempting factor in making the call was the knowledge that, after a fit of rage, her boss would help her to sort this whole mess out. She'd witnessed it with Dawson a hundred times. But Kim had never had to do it with her. Dawson was the one who fucked up. They all expected it. Hell, even Dawson expected it.

But not her. Stacey was the good girl, teacher's pet, as Dawson sometimes called her. And she was. She enjoyed being good old reliable Stacey. She prided herself on being no bother to anyone.

But she trusted her boss, implicitly. She would know what to do.

Stacey picked up her phone and swiped. She scrolled down to the contact called 'boss'. Her thumb hovered above the handset icon. She pictured the disappointment on the boss's face as she recited the litany of mistakes.

Stacey threw the phone on the sofa. No. Whatever she'd got herself into, she would have to resolve it on her own.

CHAPTER 63

'So, what the hell is he talking about?' Kim asked as they left the ward.

Travis shook his head. 'Your guess is probably as good as mine,' he said, rubbing his forehead. He turned left, and she turned right. She enjoyed the irony of the moment.

'We'll pick it up in the morning,' he said, and he was right. It was almost ten and it looked like Barney was going to be having a sleepover with Charlie from two doors down.

'Okay, see you in the morning,' Kim said, offering a half wave as she turned away.

She made a detour to the cafeteria to grab a strong, long coffee, and spotted a familiar ombre head bent down studiously.

Kim grabbed a coffee from the vending machine and stood opposite Doctor A.

'Mind if I join you?' Kim asked, tapping the wooden chair.

'Of course not,' Doctor A said, smiling. 'What are you doing here at this time?'

'I could ask you the same thing,' Kim said, before nodding towards her phone. 'I don't want to disturb your work.'

Doctor A turned the phone towards her. '*Pet Rescue* game, my saviour.'

'Really?' Kim asked. It wasn't what she'd imagined the scientist doing when she wasn't working.

'Well, if you want the truth, I prefer to read about quantum physics and the theory of the universe in my spare time but just now and again the pandas are calling me.'

'I bet you were a fun kid,' Kim said.

'I absolutely was,' Doctor A said, smiling. 'I was what you would call a tommyboy. I liked jumping, fighting and playing with mud. My father was in the army, leaving me, my mother and my brother.'

'Did you fight?'

Dr A's expression said, *of course*.

'Did you win?'

Her expression remained the same.

'You really okay?' Kim asked. Despite the woman's animation, the smile remained below her nose. She looked tired, drained.

'My glass is always half full, Inspector. But not right now. Marina is on her way with the last box.' She shook her head. 'We will not have all the bones.'

Kim understood. There was a sadness that the bodies would remain incomplete.

'We will survey again tomorrow to be sure, but the grave is now empty.'

'You been getting any sleep?' Kim asked, noting the dark circles beneath her eyes.

'Have you?' she asked with a tired smile.

Kim opened her mouth to offer well-meaning advice but closed it again. She could only wonder at the woman's mash-up of the pot and kettle analogy.

'It is the why that is bothering me,' Doctor A said suddenly. 'What did these people do to deserve such disrespect? What was their crime?'

Kim thought about victim one, Jacob James. A hard-working, mild-mannered family man. There was nothing to suggest anything in his past deserving of such horrific treatment. All accounts noted him as a decent hard-working guy.

Doctor A's phone vibrated on the table.

She checked it then stood. 'Walk and talk, Marina just arrived.'

Kim knew herself to be a quick walker but there was little chance of keeping up with the tornado that was blazing a trail through visitors, hospital staff and internal post trolleys. Conversation had become impossible.

Kim just about managed to keep an eyeball on her until Doctor A took a left into the staircase that led down to the morgue.

'Training for something, Doc?' Kim said, as she just about caught the doctor at the entrance doors.

The woman she had seen earlier in the week at the gravesite offered her a nod as she removed the lid from the plastic box.

Kim glanced again at the collections of bones that grew less detailed as her eye cast across the row of gurneys. It sickened her that only one yet had a name.

From the corner of her eye Kim could see individual plastic evidence bags being removed carefully from the box.

Sadly, Kim knew there were not enough bones to complete the gaps in front of her.

She remembered a documentary on the identification of bodies following the attack on the World Trade Centre. Some families had buried nothing more than a tooth or a bone fragment.

'Hey, Inspector,' Doctor A said, turning a bag and holding it up to the bright, white light.

Kim turned.

'Did you know that the human hand is eerily similar to that of a bear's front paw?'

'Problematic if I was looking for Yogi,' she said.

Doctor A frowned. 'What?'

'Never mind,' Kim said. Some things were just not worth the time.

'Aha, I was hoping to see you,' Doctor A exclaimed to the bone in her hand.

All signs of fatigue were gone as the woman began moving frantically around the room.

Kim understood it. Progress fuelled energy. She was exactly the same. Forward motion brought its own shot of adrenaline.

Doctor A moved to the side of body number two and placed the bag at the pelvis area. She nodded to no one in particular.

Kim already knew that the pelvis was the most reliable way to sex a body.

'I suspected number two was male from the distinct ridges on the skull but this pelvis is a fit and it is definitely male.'

'Age?' Kim asked, hopefully.

'The bone loses calcium and becomes less dense with age. If malnutrition and diseases like osteoporosis are not factors, I would age this male between thirty and forty at the time of death.'

Kim committed the information to memory. Penn could feed that into his database and try for a match.

Doctor A stood at the foot of the gurneys between Jacob James and victim two.

'These two souls are almost complete so I am hopeful that the rest of the bones will help with our other soul at the end.'

Kim looked towards gurney three and silently applauded Doctor A's optimism.

Doctor A followed her gaze.

'Once we are complete with the bones, we shall begin extracting DNA.'

Kim nodded her understanding. The only problem was they would need someone to match it against. She sighed heavily. These victims were not giving up their secrets as quickly as she would have liked.

'Well, Doc, I'll…' Kim stopped speaking and paused as she passed by the counter to the left of the door.

'What's that?' she asked Marina, who was removing an evidence bag the size of a credit card.

Marina pushed it towards her. She held it up to the light.

It was a triangular piece of paper.

CHAPTER 64

Bryant waited until the three of them were seated before trying to catch Stacey's eye. She hadn't yet looked at him once.

He had expected her to still be pissed off but refusing to look in his direction meant she hadn't simmered down one little bit. He'd considered flowers, even chocolates and yet he'd known that any grand gesture on his part would not be accepted in the manner it was intended.

There was only one way to resolve this.

'Stace, I want to apologise for not giving you the respect you deserve as a police officer and a detective.'

Finally, she looked at him.

'It won't happen again,' he continued. 'But we really need your help on this case.'

She nodded her acceptance, and then looked to Dawson.

'Ditto,' he offered, distractedly.

Bryant shook his head but caught the wink he gave his colleague.

'Okay, Woody has lined up an expert at Lloyd House for us to go and speak to. His name is Inspector Frederick Windsor bee ess see hons, it says here,' Bryant offered, reading out the initials that came after his name.

'Yay, let's go see the middle-aged white guy and learn all about hate crimes,' Dawson said, sarcastically.

Stacey chuckled and some of the tension fell from her face. But all too quickly, it was back again.

'Stace, can you look into the backgrounds of all our victims? Either we have three separate random attacks that just coincidentally happened in the space of a week or there is some kind of link somewhere.'

She nodded.

'Really dig around with 'Bubba' Brandon Jones. He liked to live loud. It might be interesting to see what kind of attention he was attracting on social media…'

'Ahem,' she offered.

'And I'll now stop telling you how to do your job,' he said. 'Once we've finished with our expert I want to go back to the families; start at the beginning and interview them all again.' He handed her a piece of paper. 'And just do some digging on this young lady.'

'The acid attack victim?' she asked.

Bryant nodded. 'Died of her injuries yesterday. Derby are treating it as an honour killing but see if there's anyone she upset on social media.'

He turned to Dawson. 'You're unusually quiet this morning, what's up?

'Still thinking about that scar that Aisha Gupta mentioned. I feel like there's something there, in the back of my—'

'What scar?' Stacey asked, frowning.

'Aisha said the male who accosted her had a scar, right here,' he said, pointing to his cheekbone. 'And there's something in my—'

'Justin Reynolds had a scar right there,' she offered.

'Who is Justin Reynolds?' Bryant asked. It wasn't a name he recognised.

'That's it, Stace,' Dawson said, slapping his hand off the desk as though he was the one that had made the connection.

Dawson turned his way. 'Teenager that committed suicide a few days ago. Stace and I attended.'

He turned back to Stacey. 'I can't see there being any connection but would you?…'

'I'll do some digging,' she said, staring at her computer.

'Okay, let's get started,' he said, reaching for his jacket.

Dawson stood and Bryant tossed him the keys.

'Start her up and pick a radio station.'

One of the numerous things they'd argued about was Radio One versus Radio WM.

Dawson smirked and Bryant realised just how much managing a team resembled raising a child. Discipline and reward.

'Hey, Stace, I meant what I said. I was wrong and I'm sorry.'

She offered him a weak smile. 'And I meant it when I said get over it and move on.'

He stole a quick glance back from the door.

Stacey's head was resting in her hands.

CHAPTER 65

Kim pulled up at the kerb outside Travis's house and took a deep breath to ready herself for the battle ahead. She had visions of that one breath circulating around the inside of her vehicle and insulating her against her passenger.

Normally he was at the door within seconds of her arrival. She saw the curtain twitch and counted backwards from three.

On one, the door opened but it wasn't Travis who appeared.

His wife stood in the doorway wearing a cardigan around her shoulders and an anxious expression.

Kim immediately got out of the car as the woman began walking towards her. They met on the drive.

'Is everything okay, Mrs Travis?'

She shook her head but said nothing as she touched the delicate chain at her neck.

'No, everything is not okay?' Kim clarified.

'No, I'm not Mrs Travis,' she said as she swallowed deeply and looked around as though she might get caught. 'Would you step in for a moment? Do you have time?'

Kim tried to hide her confusion. She had seen the man hug this woman every morning. 'Is Tom inside?' she asked, following not-Mrs Travis through the tidy box porch.

'No, he left early. He said there were some things he wanted to prepare for the briefing.'

Kim stifled her irritation that he had not bothered to let her know. Not even a simple text message.

Kim paused on the threshold into the hallway.

'I'm sorry but what am I?...'

'I hope you don't mind, but there is something I think you should see.'

The tremor in the woman's voice caused Kim to close the door behind her, and follow her into the lounge.

The room was surprisingly stylish, in shades of biscuit and cream. The corner sofa was velour with a couple of scatter cushions. The one-piece sofa ended in a recliner that was occupied by a pleasant-looking woman with brown hair and a striking resemblance to the woman still standing in the doorway.

'*This* is Mrs Travis,' she said quietly. 'This is Tom's wife, Melissa. I'm her sister, Carole.'

Melissa smiled at her warmly.

'You didn't tell me Frannie was coming today, Carole,' she said, patting the seat beside her.

'Sorry, sweetie. I forgot but I just need Frannie to come help me with something in the kitchen first,' Carole said.

Kim followed her back to the hallway.

'Frannie is Tom and Melissa's daughter. Cot death in '98,' Carole explained.

Kim felt the sadness growing heavy on her heart as she followed Carole through the house. She hadn't known. Tom had spoken little of his private life and neither had she.

'May I ask what?...'

'Melissa suffers from early onset familial Alzheimer's Disease. It's the most aggressive form and can start in the thirties, forties, sometimes even in the twenties. Melissa's symptoms started when she was forty-three. The normal forgetfulness and difficulty in completing familiar tasks at home.

'She managed to hide it from Tom for months. Our father had it, you see. He died only two years before Melissa's symptoms began.' Her eyes filled with tears. 'She knew what was coming.'

Kim had the urge to reach across and touch the woman's arm. If this condition was hereditary then Carole must be living with the same fear every day.

'Eventually she could hide it no longer, and Tom returned home one day to find her distraught on the sofa because she couldn't remember where the kettle lived.'

Kim swallowed the emotion in her throat.

'He promised her they would get through it. He would be her memory for as long as he could. He devised all kinds of lists, instructions and reminders to help her get through the day.'

Kim said nothing.

'I wanted you to know,' she said, gently. 'I remember when you two worked together before. He respected you. I know you had some kind of falling out, but he's a good man.'

'Who hates me,' Kim observed.

Carole smiled. 'He doesn't hate you. He just prefers to pretend he does. He wants to, don't get me wrong. But there's a part of him, a part he won't admit even to himself, that has enjoyed working with you again this week.'

The woman's eyes were full of emotion.

Kim understood. 'You love him, don't you?'

The smile disappeared but the tenderness remained.

She shrugged. 'It wouldn't matter if I did. He's my brother-in-law and Melissa is my sister.'

Kim thought about the awkward embraces she had witnessed at the door each morning.

'And he loves you too,' she said.

Her look said that she knew that and it still didn't make any difference.

'As I said. He's a good man.'

Suddenly the leather wallet made sense to her. He wrote everything down. Just in case.

Something else was beginning to make sense to her.

'Carole, how long ago was Melissa diagnosed?'

'Four-and-a-half-years,' she said.

Kim thanked her and headed out before the rage began to show on her face.

She sat in the car for just a minute as that final scene played out in her mind.

Back then she hadn't had Bryant to rein her back in, calm her down, help her see reason, tell her when she'd acted too hastily.

And it was clear to her now that she had.

Because now it all made sense.

CHAPTER 66

Stacey rubbed her forehead, trying to ease the tension away.

Why the hell had she not just come clean about Justin Reynolds when she'd had the chance? She had been so surprised by Dawson's reference to the scar she had blurted out his name in case Dawson had made the connection himself and then asked her why she'd never realised.

This situation was becoming far too complicated to continue.

She understood that her colleagues were investigating hate crimes, and Justin Reynolds had obviously been racist – but there were thousands of kids like Justin Reynolds floating around social media. He would not have any connection to their case. And the reference to the scar was nothing more than coincidence. It had nothing to do with Justin. It couldn't have.

But she was now more convinced than ever that she had to let the Justin Reynolds thing go. After posting a particularly offensive message over breakfast from her dummy account, the gravity of what she'd done had almost brought the Weetabix to the back of her throat.

Her instinct had been wrong, born of being not busy enough. Her senses had been given the opportunity to run riot on their own. And that had resulted in disastrous consequences. She had learned nothing.

And she'd managed to lose property that didn't belong to her in the process. Good job, Stace, she silently congratulated herself.

She had already decided that she would come clean with the boss once she was back with them. She would just be honest, explain what she had done, her reasons why and then take the consequences.

With the decision made, and a plan of action formed she pushed aside her mobile phone and focussed on the four names on her notepad.

HENRYK KOWALSKI
BRANDON BUBBA JONES
AISHA GUPTA
SHAY CHAKMA

Time to do what she always did: work methodically and pragmatically. She would start with the first victim and work her way through.

She entered a search for Henryk Kowalski into Google as her phone vibrated on the desk.

Damn it, she observed, she was still logged into her dummy account after that last article she'd posted over breakfast.

She swiped and clicked on the notification.

Floda had sent her a friend request.

CHAPTER 67

Kim slid into the briefing and sat at the back of the room. Despite the drive, she did not yet trust herself to speak to Travis.

He stood at the top of the room, his jacket draped over a spare chair. He was pacing back and forth in front of the wipe boards.

Five bodies were leaning forward, waiting, engaged.

'So, we desperately need a reason to keep Jeff Cowley in custody. He knows more about this than he's letting on.'

'Should we question him again, guv?' Johnson asked.

Kim was thinking *yes* as Travis nodded. An overnight stay in custody may have loosened his tongue.

'It's worth a shot to see if he'll crack. Ask him about his daughter. That seems a particularly sensitive point for him.'

Johnson nodded and made a note.

'Gibbs, track down Fiona Cowley. Find out where she is and let us know. I think we need to speak to her again. She's covering for someone in her family, and we need to know who.'

'Okay, guv,' he answered.

'Gibbs, I want you to work with Lewis on trying to identify the second male at the morgue I've just given you the details of.'

Kim had texted the basic vital information she'd gleaned from Doctor A regarding their second male victim to Travis as soon as she'd left the morgue the previous night. As usual he had not replied, and this was the first confirmation she'd had that the information had been received.

Travis's glance in her direction drew the attention of the team to her presence.

She nodded in response.

'Lynda, can you phone the hospital and see if Billy Cowley has rediscovered his voice yet,' he said. 'And I want you working with Johnson on trying to identify a blue transit van in the area of our road traffic incident. The victim claims two males tried to abduct him.'

Lynda frowned. 'Boss, Mrs Umgabe, the lady you sent me to see the other day, said the exact same thing. No closer with tracing the van, though.'

'Stay on it, Lynda. That's two attempts in one week. Whatever they're doing, they're gonna get lucky soon. And put it out again to the uniforms, refresh their memories. We can forget the delivery van driver, traffic officers have ruled out speeding so it appears he's off the hook but I want the witnesses interviewed again to find out exactly how that poor woman ended up in front of the van. This incident escalated from a road accident to potential kidnapping and manslaughter.'

Lynda turned away and started scribbling notes.

He nodded towards Penn. 'And, I think the detective inspector has a present for you.'

Kim stood and took the photocopy from her pocket.

He looked at it and then at the board. 'Part of that note?'

Kim nodded. 'I think so. It's faded and dirty but you might be able to figure something more from it.'

He rubbed his hands feverishly. 'Cool, thanks.'

'And Wilma goes to Lynda today,' Travis said, moving the plant across the room.

'Thanks, boss,' she said, placing it next to a photo of a Great Dane puppy.

Bodies began to lift and move as the energy and purpose took hold.

'Ready?' Travis said from beside her.

She nodded and followed him out of the door.

'Well, thank you for allowing me to conduct my own briefing today,' he said, smartly.

Kim didn't respond. Oh yes, she'd allowed him to speak all right.

She was only waiting until they reached the car.

And then it was her turn.

CHAPTER 68

Bryant acknowledged that Lloyd House, located on Colmore Circus at Queensway, had to be one of the ugliest buildings he had ever seen.

West Midlands Police headquarters lived in a plain, rectangle box with eleven rows of identical windows and concrete reaching up into the sky.

The revolving doors guided them into an airy space of light wood, glass and a circular reception desk that reminded Bryant of a health club.

As Dawson introduced them, Bryant pictured the first impression of Halesowen Police Station. Poor old Jack, the Custody Sergeant, stared at his own reflection in reinforced glass for his whole shift. But of course this wasn't a police station. This was HQ.

They took the journey through the metal detectors and headed for the second floor.

At the top of the steps was a sign. They followed the arrow towards intelligence, and almost missed a door on the right bearing the nameplate of the man they sought.

Dawson tapped twice and the door was opened immediately, as though the person behind was waiting for them. As the door opened further, Bryant could understand why. The desk and chair were forced into a small office also bearing cardboard storage boxes that rose six feet from the floor. It was a very short journey from the chair to the door.

'Fred,' the man said, thrusting out his hand. He fell short of Bryant's own six feet height by two inches. His fair hair was thinning atop a ruddy, flushed expression.

Dawson introduced them both.

'If you don't mind, we'll head down to the cafeteria where we can sit comfortably.'

The man looked to Bryant's left, and Bryant followed his gaze. He was clearly in the way of something. He stepped forward as the man reached around him and retrieved a single crutch.

'Wouldn't you prefer to stay?…'

'It's a permanent injury, but thank you for your concern,' he said, matter-of-factly.

Something in Bryant's brain shook free as they all bundled back out of the small space. He took a few steps forward and walked alongside the man who moved remarkably well.

The rolled-up shirt sleeves revealed a line of scars along his forearm, like a tally score. If pushed he'd say razor blade.

Bryant cursed his own forgetfulness.

'You're *the* Fred Windsor,' Bryant said, as Dawson frowned. 'The one that was held by the National Pride hate group ten years ago.'

'Eleven, to be exact, but yes that was me.'

Bryant felt bad for their assumption back at the station that this man could offer them nothing.

He now remembered it clearly. Fred Windsor had worked undercover in the hate group for years, gaining their trust, learning of their plans, their motivations. Two months before he was due to be pulled out, he was sussed by someone he'd lifted for shoplifting as a constable. The group had held him captive for six days, torturing and humiliating him. Both his ankles had been shattered, ensuring he never saw active duty again.

'The scars?' Bryant said, unable to tear his gaze away as Dawson pushed open the door to the cafeteria.

'One for every day I lied to them,' he said, tonelessly.

'And how long were you undercover?'

'Seven hundred and twenty-two days, exactly.'

Bryant hated to think what lay beneath those clothes.

'Mr Windsor, I'm—'

'Hey, I'm still just Fred,' he offered, with a smile.

'Okay, Fred, let me get the drinks,' Bryant offered.

'Sit down,' he said. 'The lovely Sophie will be over in a second.'

A young, slim red-head wearing a plain blue overall had already clocked them and was heading towards them with a small notepad.

'Inspector?' she said.

He rolled his eyes. 'Just Fred, please. I'll have my usual and?…' he looked towards the two of them.

'We're fine, we just need a few minutes.'

'If you're going to understand anything at all, Sergeant, you're going to need more than a few minutes. I suggest you have a drink.'

'Latte,' Bryant said.

'Orange juice,' Dawson said.

'Thank you,' they said together.

'Okay, let's get started. A hate crime offender's hostility is triggered by their perception of the victim's ethnicity, race, national origin, religion, sexual orientation, disability or gender.'

Dawson nodded. 'Yes, yes, we—'

'Young man, if I have to focus on what you might or might not already know we will be here for days. It is best I just tell you what I've learned in my twenty-two years of experience, and you may then disseminate it at your will.'

Bryant nodded for him to continue. The mild rebuke in Kev's direction was thoroughly deserved.

'To hold prejudiced attitudes is not a crime. To constitute a hate crime there must be two components: the actual offence, like assault or harassment, and evidence that the perpetrator's actions are motivated by prejudice against the group represented by the victim.

'The majority of hate crimes are aimed at individuals from social groups that have been historically subjected to institutionalised discriminatory treatment – but that's a subject for another day.

'And then there are hate crimes against hate crimes. Indian kids beating up black kids. Jewish girls attacking goths.'

Bryant shook his head. 'But how does it all start, Fred?'

'It often starts with low-level abuse; verbal, malicious gossip, intimidating looks, being ignored and isolated, all the way up to violent assault and murder.'

'How does name-calling escalate to murder?' Dawson asked. 'Every kid got called something cruel at school. It's a breeding ground for isolation, but how does it become particularly targeted towards minority groups?'

He smiled and shook his head at the same time. 'Racial hatred is not like picking on a kid at school because he's fat.'

Bryant saw Dawson wince at this. Fred could have offered no example that was closer to home for his colleague.

'There are socio-economic factors to consider. Successive generations of white residents create environments that are hostile towards minority ethnic residents. Add in the groups and even political parties spreading hate. In this country we have the BNP, EDL, Combat 18. Some operate like conventional parties to gain power through the ballot box, like the BNP. Others favour an activist street movement, like EDL, but one thing they all have in common is intolerance.

'All these groups promote xenophobia. They want people to be fearful of those from another country.'

He paused and looked from one to the other.

'So, now we understand some of the areas hatred can come from, you're going to want to ask me what type of person commits such crimes?'

They both nodded eagerly.

'And that's where we have our first problem.'

CHAPTER 69

'Why the fuck didn't you tell me about your wife, Tom?' Kim screamed once they were in the car.

She'd hoped to be off the car park before she started talking, but her mouth hadn't read the memo.

He spluttered like a thirty-year-old car.

She could not wait for him to get his mouth in order.

'I've met her and—'

'Don't talk about it, Stone. I'm warning you,' he said, finding his voice.

She hit reverse and then headed out of the car park.

'Where you gonna go, Tom?' she asked. Even he wasn't stupid enough to try and escape her by getting out of a moving vehicle.

'It's none of your damn business,' he raged.

'Oh, but it is, Tom. The rumours of what happened around that time have followed me too.'

'It didn't affect my work,' he said.

'Like hell,' she cried.

'It had nothing to do with… what happened.'

'Why are you still lying? It was four-and-a-half-years ago, wasn't it? Exactly the same time as—'

'I do not want to talk about this,' he growled.

'Oh, but you're going to,' she said, turning into a garden centre car park. 'I've questioned everything about that day, Tom. Everything,' she hissed.

He refused to look at her, and she knew why.

'Let's get it out, Tom. You were too rough with that boy. He was fifteen years old and you were pushing him around like a prize fighter.'

'He was selling drugs, Stone. To kids.'

'I bloody know that, but we don't choose who we get to treat professionally and you know it. Or at least you did before that day.'

'He talked in the end,' he defended.

'Not because you'd roughed him up. He talked because his mother gave him a clip round the ear and told him to come clean.'

He turned accusing eyes on her.

'Why didn't you report me?'

'Because I knew there was something wrong. You were clearly—'

'Not for that, Stone. For the other thing. For what happened later?'

There it was. Now they were getting somewhere.

'You mean when I challenged you about the kid and you punched me in the mouth?'

The memory of the pain had nothing to do with her lip.

Shame flooded his face but he kept contact with her gaze.

'Come on, why didn't you report me assaulting you. Was it so you had something on me?' he accused.

She shook her head. 'No, it was clear that something wasn't right.'

'Get off it, Stone. You were young and ambitious. You put the information in your back pocket to use at a later date, didn't you?'

She allowed the horror to show on her face. 'Is that really what you think? Or is it what you've told yourself to think?' she asked.

'You used that incident to get a step up. You threatened me with taking time off. You left me no choice.'

'You needed some time away, to cool down, sort out whatever it was that was needling you.'

'I didn't want time off. I wanted to do my fucking job,' he raged, punching the dashboard.

'You needed to be at home,' Kim said.

'It's no use saying that now. You didn't know about Melissa then. You just wanted me out of the way. You wanted to further your own career at my expense. You knew sick time would count against me.'

'Can you even hear what you're saying?' she cried in disbelief. 'Assaulting a teenager and then smacking me would have counted a lot more if I'd wanted to affect your promotion, Tom. You took the leave—'

'You left me no damn choice,' he growled.

'You came back after two weeks and you couldn't even speak to me. We both went for promotion and you missed out. Fuck's sake, Tom, we came up through the ranks together. You'd have had my vote for DI, and neither what happened with that boy or what happened later in the locker room was ever repeated to a soul by me.'

Silence fell between them.

'I'll never understand why you didn't tell me what was going on,' she said.

'And I still don't get why you didn't report me?' he said, quietly.

She thrust the car into gear and headed off the car park.

'You'll never understand if I tell you.'

'Try me,' he said. 'If it wasn't to further your own career or have something to hold over me, why didn't you file a formal complaint?'

She felt the hurt as though it was only yesterday. The way he'd looked at her when he came back. The way he'd treated her. The rumours he'd spread about her ruthless ambition.

She packed the hurt away and offered him the only thing she had. The truth.

'I didn't report you, Tom, because I thought that we were friends.'

CHAPTER 70

Dawson couldn't help the feeling of hopelessness that washed over him each time Fred Windsor opened his mouth.

There had been a time he'd felt that there was only one kind of racist, and the picture had been clearly defined in his head; skinhead, tattoos and a swastika sign somewhere upon his person. His initial assessment of Gary Flint had been coloured by his outward respectability. His first instinct had been doubt that such vile threats could have come from such a man.

Fred continued. 'You need to understand that hate crime offenders differ in age, education, family background and the underlying causes of their acts and the type of hate motive expressed. You have serial offenders and one-off perpetrators. There is no simple profile of a hate crime perpetrator. The educated and middle class are well represented in the hate movement.'

This kind of insight scared the life out of him.

'Hatemongers once had to stand on street corners and hand out leaflets. Extremists now use mainstream social networking sites. The Internet is an invaluable tool. Far more insidious is the ability for many to psychologically affiliate with hate groups without physically joining and attending formal meetings. The Internet makes it much easier to hate.'

'But how do normal, reasonable, educated individuals get turned towards racism?' he asked.

Fred smiled at him. 'You're making the assumption that all perpetrators are "turned" by a hate group,' he offered. 'There are families that have been raising and training their children from birth.

'The years between the ages four to ten have been identified as the optimum chance of becoming a dangerous racist if exposed to prejudiced ideas. People are not born bigoted. They are made that way. I won't bore you with all the theories of social learning etc, but nearly forty per cent of hate crime offenders are under the age of twenty-five. So evidence suggests the most common offender is a teenager or young adult acting in a group for excitement.

'The second highest percentage are what we call "defensive" and covers about a quarter of incidents. This covers the hate crimes that are committed to protect a neighbourhood.'

'So many different types and motivations,' Bryant observed.

Fred nodded his agreement and continued. 'Retaliatory hate offenders make up a third aspect. They typically travel to the victim's territory to retaliate against a previous incident.

'And then there are the "mission" offenders. The fully committed "haters" who commonly have far-right leanings. Their allegiance to an ideological bias is much stronger than the other three. The smallest percentage but the most dangerous. Mission offenders mean business.'

'But you're saying that these hate groups are made up of totally different types of people, educated, upstanding members of society and yobs?' Dawson asked.

'And everything in between, Sergeant. We've come to understand that the groups can be made up of four types of people, especially for thrill hate crimes. You have the leader who is normally a mission offender, then the fellow traveller who joins in, the unwilling participant and potentially the hero who tries to stop it.'

Bryant sat back and shook his head, seemingly overwhelmed by the information that was hitting his brain.

'And then you have the lone wolf in extremis – such as Anders Behring Breivik who killed sixty-nine people on the island of

Utøya in Norway. Eight people had already lost their lives at his hand before he even got there.'

Suddenly Fred turned towards him. 'If you take one thing from this meeting, it's this: if you continue to stick to your narrow-minded views on the appearance of a hate crime perpetrator, more people will die. And you can mark my words on that.'

CHAPTER 71

Kim wasn't sure if she was imagining the grudging peace that had settled between them. A few spores of animosity seemed to have dispersed, despite the silence.

She had never told a soul what had happened between them in the locker room or the events leading up to it. That day had been totally out of character for the man beside her. She had known there was something wrong with him. His mood had been pensive but contained, until that cocky fifteen-year-old had spat at him. Most police officers Kim knew preferred to be hit than spat at. But it hadn't warranted her colleague pinning him to a wall and punching him in the stomach. More blows would have followed had she not pulled him away in time. Back-up had arrived seconds later. He had refused to offer any explanation as he'd driven them both back to the station.

Had she known the truth, perhaps she wouldn't have followed him into the locker room, demanding answers. Maybe she would have given him the space he'd asked for, begged for, before lashing out.

She parked the car and, in what had now become a familiar pattern, Travis began walking away before she'd locked the doors.

But two steps later, he paused and waited.

'Listen, about…'

His words trailed away as her phone began to ring.

'On our way,' Kim said after Doctor A's name flashed onto the screen.

'Where exactly are you?' she asked, breathlessly.

'Walking into the hospital,' Kim said.

'Then I suggest you stop walking and run.'

Doctor A ended the call, and Kim quickened her step. Travis did not follow. She looked behind.

'Listen, Stone, I need to say something.'

And much as Kim wanted to hear what Travis had to say, it would just have to wait.

Doctor A's request was urgent.

CHAPTER 72

18 October 1989

Jacob had heard nothing since Devorah had been taken from the room.

He was guessing it had been about an hour but time was doing strange things in his head. The darkness around him seemed to have infected his mind, burrowed in through his ears and left a dark mist of confusion.

He hadn't had a drink since the drugged water, and he wasn't even certain now when he'd last eaten. The only thing he knew for sure was that his body was rebelling against him. Exhaustion, hunger and fear had sapped every last ounce of energy from his muscles and yet he knew he had to be prepared for whatever opportunity might appear.

Eventually they would come for him, and he had to be ready.

He pushed himself to a standing position and shook his legs one at a time. He raised his bound wrists high above his head to stretch the tension from his back and shoulders.

He brought his right knee up towards his chin, trying to shake the fatigue from the muscles.

He pictured the Rocky films where Sylvester Stallone used every basic method at his disposal to train for a big fight. All he had was a floor and four walls. How could he prepare his body for a fight in a square box?

He could move, that's how, he told himself. He could walk; he could bend; he could flex and stretch. Or he could do nothing.

He paced forward in the darkness.

His right foot met with something on the floor. He reached out and felt in front of him. There was nothing. He had not hit the wall.

His mind registered that the object was not hard or cold like the brickwork surrounding him. It was fabric.

He moved his foot around, as though stroking the object.

There was something solid beneath the cloth. He prodded it with his toe.

Nothing.

He dropped to his knees and began to feel around. His hands landed on something firm beneath the fabric. He squeezed.

'Oh no,' he whispered into the darkness.

He felt his way to the end of the material.

He reached a sewn in cuff at the bottom of a trouser leg, and then flesh.

His stomach travelled up to his throat as his mind seized on a horrific possibility.

'Devorah?' he whispered.

No response.

'Devorah?' he cried out.

Nothing.

He grabbed the ankle hard and began to shake it.

'Wake up, please, wake up.'

There was no movement.

How had they brought her back when he'd been conscious since she'd been dragged away? Hadn't he? He was no longer sure of anything.

His touch landed on something cool and hard. A shoe. He used both hands to feel around it. Leather upper, no heel and bigger than the average female.

The person lying in front of him was a man.

'Mate, wake up,' he said, shaking the leg.

He worked his way up the body, pushing and rocking as he went.

Was this another victim? Had this poor soul been snatched too? Perhaps he'd been drugged by the water just like him.

Come on, he prayed silently as all kinds of scenarios flashed through his mind. With two of them, they had a chance.

'Mate, you gotta wake up,' he called out as his hands worked across a broad set of shoulders. The figure was half lying and half sitting against the wall.

He shook the man forcefully. He felt the weight of the head loll sideways.

An unwelcome thought began to form in his mind.

His fingers travelled up from the shoulder blades to the neck and stayed there, praying for a pulse.

He waited, while silently willing to feel something.

He moved his fingers around and waited again.

There was nothing.

The man before him was dead.

Jacob felt the threat of tears at the back of his throat. He hadn't cried in years. Not since losing Freya to leukaemia but right now he was struggling to hold them back.

For just a few moments, hope had surged within Jacob. Hope that he could escape. Hope that he would be reunited with his daughter. The hope had been sudden and unexpected and now cruelly ripped away.

He had no strength, no weapon and no clue as to why he'd been snatched from his life.

But he now knew with certainty that he was never going to see Adaje again.

The sudden sound of the key in the lock startled him.

Whatever it was that he'd been chosen for, whatever use they had for him, had arrived. The only things in this room were himself and a dead man, and there was little more they could do with him.

'Where's the girl?' Jacob asked, as three torchlights shone right at him. 'Where's Devorah?'

'None of your fucking business, now get to your feet.'

Jacob stayed where he was.

'Just tell me, what's happened to her?' he asked.

The men laughed in a way that chilled Jacob to the bone.

'It's all right fella, you're about to find out.'

CHAPTER 73

'What's the urgency?' Kim asked, stepping through the doors.

Kim immediately noted that Doctor A looked paler than she had all week. She looked to the gurneys.

Doctor A came to stand beside her.

'That is all the bones we are having,' she said quietly.

Kim looked along the row. She knew victim one to be Jacob James. Victim two was an unidentified male around the age of thirty.

'Victim three?' Kim asked.

Doctor A shrugged. 'Without more bones we may never be able to sex…'

Her words trailed away as Kim nodded her understanding. On what they had, the third victim may never be identified.

'But, I can confirm that victim number two was disabled.'

Kim felt the ground begin to move beneath her feet.

'Wh… What?' she asked.

Doctor A nodded. 'I'm afraid so. Our second soul suffered from osteomalacia which caused me confusion as he was not an elderly—'

'Back up, Doc,' Kim said. 'What's osteomalacia?'

She thought for a moment. 'In children you would know it as rickets. Osteomalacia presents in adults due to inadequate mineralisation of the bone. Maybe insufficient calcium absorption or lack of Vitamin D. More commonly in elderly adults who are housebound or in nursing homes. No exposure to the sun,' she explained.

'So, restricted mobility?' Kim asked.

Doctor A nodded. 'This man would have had joint and bone pain, especially in his spine, pelvis and legs and most definitely difficulty walking.'

'So running away would have been a real fucking problem?' Kim asked.

Doctor A nodded, displaying a tension to her jaw that Kim had never seen before. She realised she hadn't heard the worst of it. That was not the news Doctor A had been waiting to share.

'I found some other marks on victim two last night but I didn't want to share until I knew what they were,' she said, moving away from the victims.

Kim followed her to the computer in the corner of the room.

Doctor A clicked on the screen.

It exploded to reveal a full-screen picture of a metal contraption that resembled an open, gaping mouth, full of metal teeth. At its centre, like a tongue, was a pressure plate.

Kim felt the saliva drying in her mouth.

'Animal traps?' she whispered, hoarsely.

Doctor A nodded slowly.

Kim knew that the sickness was coming. Travis cursed under his breath.

She understood what they were being told.

Their victims had been hunted.

CHAPTER 74

Kim just about made it outside before she threw up.

The retching continued long after her stomach had emptied.

'Here,' Travis said, handing her a tissue.

She wiped roughly at her mouth before kicking the wall, hard.

'Fuck, fuck, fuck…'

'Shhh…' Travis said, looking about. 'There are sick people around—'

'You're fucking telling me,' she raged. The facts she'd just learned refused to let go of her nerve endings.

'How the hell? I mean, how could anyone treat a fellow human being this way? How could they even think of doing such a vile, sick?…'

Words failed her as she kicked the wall again.

She paced, trying to work the rage from her system.

'I wanna hit something so bad,' she cried.

Travis stood right in front of her, blocking her path.

'Hit me,' he said, seriously.

'Piss off, Tom,' she said, trying to get around him to take another swipe at the wall.

'I mean it. Hit me. I owe you one and now seems good for it,' he said.

'Aren't you bloody angry?' she asked, frustrated by his calm control.

'Of course I am but your need to express it is greater than mine right now.'

'It's not a shared emotion. We can both have it at the same time,' she snapped.

'Yes, and then we'd kick the absolute shit out of the hospital, which wouldn't help anyone.'

'But it's fucking despicable…'

'It is.'

'That someone could be targeted because of their colour or race and, on top of that, someone who can't bloody fight back.'

'Absolutely.'

'And to hunt these people like damn animals…'

'Is the sickest thing I've heard in many years. So, we can either stay here and kick shit out of the wall, shouting about how reprehensible it is, or we can go and try to find these bastards.'

Kim looked at him, then back at the wall.

She wanted the people responsible, and she wanted them badly.

She thrust her hands into her pockets, forced her response through her gritted teeth.

'Okay, Travis. Lead the way.'

CHAPTER 75

Stacey knew she should be concentrating on the task given to her by the guys, but the friend request from Floda had reignited the churning in her stomach.

Once she'd accepted the request, she'd received a message with a link to a website. Was this what Justin had received from Floda? And did it have any bearing on his decision to end his own life?

There was a delay with the link before exploding into a header page bearing the St George's Cross flag and a swastika.

Stacey felt her fingers begin to tremble as she pressed to enter.

The title of the page was called 'Keep England Pure'. Stacey swallowed the horror down as she tried to focus. The menu across the top read 'Publications, Mission Statement, Chat, Scoreboard and Events'.

Stacey found herself biting the inside of her lip. She clicked on to publications and was assaulted by a range of extremist-titled books. Hundreds of books about Hitler were mixed with offensive joke books and links to further reading websites.

She instantly clicked out and moved the cursor across. She didn't need to read the 'Mission Statement'. There would be more words but the general theme of 'spread as much hatred as possible' was close enough.

She hit on the chat button. The top three threads were live. The second one down had received the most posts. She clicked onto the subject line 'The Event'.

She scanned down and saw the majority of posts were simply displaying their regret at not being able to attend something that was going on. She suspected some kind of rally.

She exited the chat boards and entered the scoreboard section. Her blood began to chill as it ran through her veins.

A grid opened up to reveal a key to the left. In order it read 'Black, Asian, Muslim, Jew, Queer, Foreigner, Cripple and Other'. Across the top was an emboldened heading of the month. Beneath that were more headings: 'Vandalism, Assault, Attempted Murder and Murder'.

People typed in their username at the boxes that intersected the two criteria.

'JJLucy' had put their name against almost every box.

Beneath was a hall of fame, and 'JJLucy' topped the charts most days by the looks of it.

She took out her phone and began taking photos. Sites like this could be gone within hours. She backtracked through all of the pages, capturing as many names as she could.

Satisfied she'd got all she could see, she returned to the scoreboard. Three people had posted in the murder column. They all got a screenshot each so she could include the headings too.

She opened up the last tab, marked 'Events', as her phone dinged a message.

She quickly took a look at the 'event' screen. The date screamed out at her. There was something happening tonight.

Stacey suddenly knew that this was too much for her alone. This was not a can of worms but a drum of electric eels, and she could not contain them without help. She had to let someone know what she'd found. Yes, it would mean coming clean about her activities and the laptop but this needed to be investigated; right now.

She checked the message that had come through on her phone. It said simply:

The laptop is outside

Stacey frowned. The sender was 'unknown'.

What did it mean? Outside her home? Outside the station?

Her finger hovered over Bryant's number, desperate to share what she'd found. But if there was a chance she could get the stolen laptop back she had to take it.

She stood and headed out the door. If the laptop had been returned, no one would ever know she'd lost it. She would ring Bryant the second she had it in her hand.

She tore past reception and out of the building.

She looked around the perimeter of the wall, nothing.

She took a few steps forward, her eyes scanning every inch of the car park, and kept moving, increasing her field of vision with every step.

Something to her far right caught Stacey's eye.

There was a kerb that gave way to a small planted area. A silver shape protruded from the shrubs.

She began to head towards it, taking her around the side of the building.

Each step confirmed to her that it was indeed the stolen laptop.

She inched, crab-like, past a blue transit van parked too close to a Renault and retrieved it.

A relieved smile began to tug at her lips – just as a sudden pain on the back of her neck caused Stacey to fold to the ground.

CHAPTER 76

Kim tapped impatiently as they waited to gain entry to the hospital ward. The nurse's station was unmanned. Kim prepared to buzz again, as an auxiliary appeared at the door.

She pressed the button to release it.

'If you just wait over by the counter, a nurse will be with you in a sec.'

Kim ignored her and carried on walking.

She'd had enough of waiting. It was time to make Billy Cowley speak. Unlike Bryant, Travis didn't try and soften any of her pointy edges. He didn't apologise on her behalf or explain or justify her behaviour.

She rounded the wall into the ward. The curtain was around Billy Cowley's bed. She experienced a moment of panic but then she heard his voice and it sounded loud and clear, like a petulant child, as he cried: 'Aarrgghh, that hurts.'

Kim looked to Travis, who smirked in response. Damaged vocal chords indeed.

She guessed the staff were changing the dressing on his neck.

He cried out again, and Kim had to stop herself from laughing out loud. She glanced at Travis, who was having the exact same problem.

Another shriek and Kim had to step away. She had known braver three year olds. Even the woman tending him sounded like she was losing patience.

Suddenly the curtain opened and a stressed-looking nurse appeared.

'May we?' Kim asked, holding up her ID and nodding towards the curtain.

'Absolutely,' she said, pushing back the second curtain.

Kim saw Billy Cowley's eyes fill with panic. He looked around but there was no one to hold his hand this time.

Kim took the left side of the bed, while Travis took the right.

'Good to hear your voice is back,' Travis said, sarcastically.

Like Kim, he was obviously sick and tired of people thinking they were clever by trying to hide the truth.

'Which is good because we really need you to answer some of our questions.'

Travis ignored the seat and sat on the edge of the bed with his back to the rest of the ward. Kim took a seat in the easy chair so she could see them both.

'Before I start asking questions I'd just like to make sure we are understanding each other.'

The quietness of his voice did not detract from the steely note of authority he exuded. Billy's eyes were fixed on Travis's face, and Kim was ready to watch with interest.

'Billy, I know you're not stupid, even though you're acting pretty dumb at the moment. You know that we've found bones on your land, and do you know what? I like you, so I'm going to give it to you straight. Three bodies we've found, Billy, did you know that?'

Billy continued to look ahead but his rate of nervous blinking had increased.

'Now, we've just discovered there's a good chance these victims were hunted like wild fucking animals. Do you understand what I mean?'

Billy nodded slowly. He reminded Kim of a child being told a bedtime story, except his jaw was not slackened with wonder but fear.

'Now, what's interesting is that we think at least one of the victims was killed with the same gun that shot you in the neck.

Isn't that just weird? But we'll come back to that,' Travis said in true Columbo style. 'Now, clearly you didn't shoot yourself in the neck, and your father has been arrested for—'

'He didn't shoot me,' Billy offered swiftly.

'Well, thank you for that clarification and, although it's nice to finally hear your voice, you may have spoken prematurely.

'We haven't arrested your father for your accident. We've arrested him for murder.'

Billy visibly paled, and the blinking went into overdrive.

'Because we think he put them there.'

Billy began to shake his head.

'You don't know that for certain though, do you, Billy?' Travis asked. 'And seeing as you won't share what you *do* know, we're forced to draw our own conclusions.'

'Have you arrested my sister?' he asked.

'Now, why would you ask us that, Billy?' Travis asked. 'Why on earth would we arrest your sister?'

Kim had a sudden thought. She raised herself from the chair, as Travis continued speaking, and headed back to the nurse's station. The harassed woman who had tended to Billy was busy rubbing someone's name from the board. Kim hoped it was because they'd been released.

'Excuse me,' she said. 'Could you tell me the last time Fiona Cowley was here to see Billy?'

The nurse shook her head. 'Not for a couple of days, now,' she said.

'Are you sure?' Kim asked. Fiona had been fiercely protective of her younger brother.

'Trust me, officer, I feel like I've barely left the place myself for the last six days except for a few hours' sleep. If she'd been to visit, I'd know.'

Kim thanked her and headed back towards the bed thoughtfully.

'… can you even begin to imagine the pain of one of those traps snapping around your ankle?' Travis was asking, making a grabbing gesture with his fingers.

The horror was written all over Billy's face.

'Officer, I want to speak to my sister.'

Yeah, Kim thought, *funnily enough, so do I.*

CHAPTER 77

Bryant threw his jacket and scarf onto the spare desk and headed to the coffee machine. It was the same sludge they'd left a few hours ago but it would be wet and warm while they waited for Stacey.

'So what did you think of Fred Windsor?' Bryant asked.

Dawson had been quiet while they'd fought their way out of Birmingham city centre.

'Brave guy,' he said, staring at Stacey's empty chair. 'He's been through it, I'll give him that, but I feel like there's no hope.'

Bryant, for once, actually knew what he meant. And agreed.

The job they did, the energy they expended, was all based on hope. Hope they would rid the streets of bad people. Every person they put away was a grain of sand but it was an actual grain of sand. It was one fewer. It was tangible.

A person committed a crime, you caught him, put him away. Job done, tidy. But how to contain hate? How do you lock up an ideal that spreads around like a common cold? If it was true that no one looked like a murderer, then it was doubly true of a hatemonger.

They had learned that much from both Gary Flint and Fred Windsor.

He was reminded that Stacey had already warned them that real danger was not necessarily from the racists in plain sight.

'Where the bloody hell is she?' Dawson asked, taking out his phone. Bryant took a sip of his drink.

'Ringing and then voicemail,' he said, holding his phone in the air.

Bryant glanced at her desk. She hadn't gone far. Papers were scattered over it, and her satchel was parked on the floor by her chair.

'Canteen?' Dawson said, pulling his chair back.

Bryant nodded.

Dawson sighed and left the room.

Their discussion with Fred Windsor had left them more in the dark than before. Having nothing back yet from forensics meant they were reliant on any type of snippet from Stacey. Why had these particular individuals been identified as hate crime victims? How had they been identified and chosen? Was there any link between the victims and the perpetrators?

Bryant realised how often they were in this position during big cases; relying on Stacey to uncover something that would point them in the right direction.

'Not there,' Dawson said, from the doorway. 'Sheila hasn't seen her all day.'

'Try her mobile again,' Bryant said, but Dawson's phone was already out of his pocket.

'Voicemail again,' he said.

Bryant grabbed his office phone and called down to the front desk.

He put the phone on loudspeaker. 'Hey Jack, you seen DC Wood today?'

'What do you think I am?' he asked in his customary grizzly manner that was not reserved only for arrestees being booked into the cells.

'Jack, it's important,' Bryant pushed.

'Tore out of here about an hour ago,' he said. 'Don't know how long she was gone. Missed her coming back in.'

Bryant swallowed. 'So, you don't know if she actually came back in?'

'Listen, mate—'

'Thanks, Jack,' Bryant said, ending the call.

Bryant followed Dawson out the door. They raced down the stairs and out of the building.

Dawson turned right, Bryant turned left; both scoured the area looking for anything that might offer them a clue.

They met at the rear of the building.

'Nothing,' he said.

'Ring her phone again,' Bryant said.

The panic was churning his stomach.

'Rings, then to voicemail,' Dawson said. 'So, it's not switched off. So, maybe she can't answer it,' he added, confirming Bryant's worst fears.

He began walking forward, away from the building and towards the road. There was a part of him that thought he might spot her walking towards him with an armful of sandwiches.

He looked left and right. Nothing.

Dawson was still holding his phone.

'Fuck, Kev, where the hell?—'

'Shhh,' Dawson said, sharply.

Bryant stood still.

Vaguely, he could hear the theme tune to *Game of Thrones*. Stacey's ringtone.

It stopped.

'Ring it again,' Bryant said, as the dread grew more sickly in his stomach.

The ringing sounded, and Dawson held out his phone as though it was some kind of homing beacon.

'Over here,' Dawson said, heading towards shrubbery at the edge of the car park.

The ringing grew louder.

'Got it,' Dawson said, pointing to an area of dirt at the edge of the kerb.

'Oh, Jesus Christ, no,' Dawson said, as Bryant followed his gaze.

The front of the phone had been smashed and it was covered in blood.

CHAPTER 78

'Gum?' Travis said, offering the packet of spearmint towards her.

She shook her head. She couldn't recall him being a chewing gum kind of guy.

Gum was one of life's mysteries to her. What was the point? You couldn't swallow it. It did nothing to satisfy hunger, so why bother?

He popped one in and began to chew.

Kim steered the car through the lunchtime traffic that was slowing her down. She hid her frustration.

'Remind me why we're going to the Preece home instead of going directly to Fiona Cowley's address?' Travis asked.

When something was biting at Kim's gut, she grew intolerant to everything that couldn't keep up with the speed of her thinking: motor cars, other drivers, traffic lights; *other people*, she thought, casting a sideways glance at a loudly masticating Travis.

'Because that woman has not yet been truthful with us once. Why did she head straight there after we arrested her father?'

He shrugged.

'If we ask her directly she'll be caught off guard, momentarily, but she will recover quickly and come up with some kind of cock and bull story that we can't disprove.'

'So, basically, you want the opportunity to call her a downright liar to her face.'

'Exactly,' Kim said, pulling up on the drive of the Preece home.

She parked between a Lotus and a Bentley convertible.

'Do you reckon she came to see Dale?' Travis asked, as they got out of the car.

Kim nodded. They crunched across the gravel drive.

'Those are the two powerhouses of these two families,' she said, as they stepped onto the stone walkway at the entrance.

Kim raised her hand to knock. Travis spat his gum to the ground.

'Charming,' she said, as her hand hovered over the ornate knocker.

She paused: shouting from within, and a scream.

She tried the door handle. It opened on to a scene of chaos. The elderly Robson Preece lay in a heap on the stone floor. His wheelchair was upturned beside him.

Mallory Preece stood to the side, her hand at her throat as Bart placed a hand under each armpit.

'Not like that, you damned fool,' Robson cried.

For a frail old man, his voice was stern and cutting.

'Turn me over, idiot,' he boomed. 'You're far too weak to lift me.'

Travis stepped forward to assist.

Robson Preece raised his head as Mallory put up a hand.

'Don't touch me,' he growled, trying to wriggle himself round the floor.

Travis met his gaze. 'Mr Preece, please allow—'

'Get out of my house, whoever you are. Get out.'

'I'm so sorry, Dad,' Mallory said, stepping forward.

'Stop snivelling, woman,' he shouted, and Mallory visibly flinched.

Bart leaned down again and touched his grandfather's shoulder. 'Gramps, just move—'

'Don't touch me, queer. Get your brother. Get me Dale.'

Mallory ran from the hallway.

'Gramps, I can do it,' Bart said, kneeling by his side.

'Get away from me, you fairy,' he said, as Dale came running into the hallway.

He registered surprise at the presence of Kim and Travis but his priority was the man on the floor.

She noted his casual attire of jeans and sweatshirt, rather than the austere suit he'd worn the other day.

'Get away, Bart,' he said, pushing his brother to the side.

Kim saw the flash of emotion in Bart's eyes. As if the dismissal from his brother was the final straw.

He said nothing but stomped out the front door.

'In fact, can you all leave, please?' Dale asked, kneeling beside his grandfather.

Mallory headed to the back of the house, while she and Travis stepped outside.

She spied Bart at the edge of the wall. His hands on the brick, staring down.

'Back in a minute,' she said to Travis.

'You okay?' she asked, tapping Bart lightly on the shoulder.

He turned and she saw the emotion had reached his eyes.

'I'm fine,' he said, trying to place a smile on his face. 'He likes to call me names sometimes. It's what he called me as a child. I made the mistake of showing I didn't like it. Made him worse.' He paused. 'And I'm not, you know,' he said.

'You're not what?'

'Gay,' he said.

'Does it matter?' she asked.

He shrugged. 'I just wanted you to know.'

'But he's your grandfather,' Kim observed. She had zero experience of grandparents but she was reasonably sure this wasn't normal.

'I'm a disappointment to him, Inspector. My grandfather is a man who believes that fair competition brings out the best in people.' He shrugged. 'He was always pitting us against each other. Who could climb highest, run fastest. My father hated it, but when he died we moved back here and my grandfather's selection process continued.'

'Selection process?' she queried.

He turned and leaned his behind against the wall. She followed suit so they were both facing the house.

'Survival of the fittest, *Hunger Games*, however you want to look at it but what he wanted was someone worthy to take over the business. And that someone is Dale.'

Kim tried to imagine being set against your own brother. She'd had a brother for such a short time but she couldn't imagine being forced to compete against him.

'Doesn't Dale mind?'

Bart shrugged. 'He's a good guy, don't get me wrong. Cast in the same mould as my grandfather but I love him. We're just beyond being any other way,' he said, as Mallory appeared in the doorway.

She spied her younger son and began moving in his direction. He offered her a look of disgust and walked away.

Perhaps her silence was one betrayal too far.

'You can go in, now,' she said to Kim, wringing her hands and staring after her younger son, although she made no effort to follow him.

Travis turned to the woman. 'Do you mind if I use the bathroom first?' he asked.

Mallory again looked flustered, and Kim realised it didn't take a lot.

'Yes, yes, there's a restroom at the top of the stairs.'

'I'll join you in the office,' he said, indicating she should continue without him.

Kim feared for his ageing bladder. He'd used the toilet before they'd left the hospital.

Mallory appeared torn, unsure who to follow. She opted for Kim, as Travis took the stairs two at a time.

Kim followed the woman, even though she knew where Dale's office was. Mallory knocked and waited for an answer before entering. Kim followed closely behind.

As she stepped into the room, she noted Dale Preece close the lid of the laptop.

His grandfather was seated beside him.

There was no evidence of the frail man lying on the tiled floor just moments earlier. Despite the wheelchair, his demeanour was upright, proud. The excess skin at his turkey neck was kept in check by a starched white collar and tie. His eyes were keen and focussed.

Kim recalled Bart's comments and found them easy to believe.

'Where is your partner, Sergeant?' he asked, officiously, looking behind her.

'It's Inspector, Mr Preece and he had to answer a call of nature.'

The irritation showed in his eyes.

'You have come to update us on your investigation, I assume,' he said, attempting to control the situation.

'Amongst other things,' she answered, taking a seat.

Dale sat back in his chair, his expression pensive. Clearly her conversation today would be with Preece senior.

'Mr Preece, could you explain to me the history of the lease between yourself and the Cowley family?'

'Absolutely none of your concern,' he said easily.

'I understand it's a long-term lease for a minimal amount of money that hasn't been increased—'

'It is none of your business, officer, and certainly not pertinent to whatever it is those animals have been up to. How many bodies have you found?'

Kim ignored his question. 'You seem convinced the Cowley family is responsible for our findings.'

He frowned and stared at her hard. 'Inspector, are you in charge of this case?'

'I am,' she answered, only half lying.

'Then I would assume that even you have mastered the art of adding one and one together to make two.'

Kim wasn't sure what the 'even you' comment meant.

'I have mastered the art of not jumping to conclusions which—'

'Aaah, perhaps now we'll get some answers,' he said, as Travis stepped into the room.

Robson Preece thrust his hand across the desk in Travis's direction. She was tempted to slap a cuff on it and arrest him for being a sexist bastard.

Travis shook the hand and nodded before glancing in her direction. She met his gaze. Her unspoken message said: *You just dare undermine me in front of this arsehole and I will crush your nuts with my bare hands*, or something along those lines.

He opened up his leather wallet and looked down.

He got it.

'As I was saying, Mr Preece, we rely on something called evidence. We struggle to make a case without it,' she said.

'But you've arrested Jeff Cowley, so you obviously have *some* evidence,' Robson emphasised, still looking at Travis. 'I don't see why you're complicating it, Inspector. The bodies were found on their land and—'

'But it's not technically their land, is it Mr Preece?' Kim asked, calling his attention back to her. 'It's *your* land, which is why we have to investigate all avenues.'

'Give me the name of your superior officer, miss,' he said, thunderously. His generous, unruly eyebrows had descended over his eyes.

She'd had enough of his condescension. She ignored his question and turned to Dale. 'Mr Preece, we need to know the purpose of Fiona Cowley's visit here yesterday.'

He swallowed deeply.

'Fiona Cowley, here?'

'Yes, Mr Preece, yesterday lunchtime,' she clarified. 'Fiona Cowley came here.'

He shook his head as colour suffused his cheeks. His gaze did not meet hers as he offered his answer.

'I'm afraid I haven't seen Fiona Cowley for years.'

CHAPTER 79

'But why would he lie?' Travis asked, as they closed the door behind them.

'I have no idea,' she said. 'But this woman is going to great lengths to stay out of our way. Get on to the team and get her address and…'

She stopped speaking when she realised he wasn't crossing the gravel beside her.

She turned to find him still standing on the clean stone entrance tiles.

He fished inside his jacket and removed an evidence bag.

She frowned as he reached down and removed his right shoe. He showed her the sole. It held a splodge of sticky pink chewing gum, covered in fibres.

'They just stuck to me,' he said, innocently.

Now Kim understood the walk around the house.

She smiled as she remembered the piece of paper from the sofa.

'Happens to you a lot, doesn't it?'

'Strangely, yes,' he said, hobbling across the shale.

Kim tried not to enjoy the idea of a hundred needles nipping into Travis's foot.

He got in the car and took out his phone. She did the same. There was something she wanted to know.

Doctor A answered on the second ring.

'Doc, I need a little help on something. The dig, the location, everything. Who exactly was it from the family that gave their consent?'

'Waiting one minute while I check my paper works.'

Kim drummed her fingers on her leg as Travis wrote down an address.

'I have it,' Doctor A said. 'It was authorised by Miss Fiona Cowley.'

Kim thanked her and ended the call. Three seconds later, so did Travis.

As she glanced sideways, she smiled at the evidence bag in his lap.

'You know we'll never be able to use that?'

He nodded. 'Yeah, but aren't there times when you just have to know?'

'Oh yeah,' Kim said, throwing the car into reverse. And right now, everything she wanted to know needed to come from Fiona Cowley.

CHAPTER 80

'Hurry up,' Bryant shouted in his ear.

'I'm trying,' he snapped, typing in the date. He was reminded of those dreams where body parts would not respond to the brain's command.

'Jack said an hour ago. Try from one fifteen.'

Dawson ignored the command and entered one o'clock dead. He would fast forward until he saw her. He'd spot those knitted Fair Isle tights anywhere.

'Go slow,' Bryant said.

'Shut up,' Dawson snapped, focussing on the screen.

There were three cameras that covered the exterior of the station. One was directly above the entrance, pointing down to capture all persons going in and out. The second was fixed to the east side, facing the front car park. The other was fixed to the west side, covering the rear of the building. That left two black spots that Dawson knew about.

Silence filled the room as the two of them focussed on the three images running alongside each other. Dawson dared not breathe in case he missed her.

He watched as officers came and went, two civilians entered and left.

'There she is,' Dawson said, as Stacey's familiar figure appeared on the front and west facing camera at the same time.

Dawson wasn't prepared for the lurch of his stomach on seeing her.

She took two steps forward, moving out of the view of the entrance camera, leaving only the west view on screen.

'What's she looking for?' Bryant asked, rhetorically.

Dawson watched her bowed head as she looked from right to left.

'No, Stace,' he said to the screen as the figure began to move to the east, away from the camera view.

If she walked around the corner, she would be beside the shrubbery and lost from view unless she reappeared at the rear of the building.

As she disappeared he clicked on to the camera that covered the rear.

'Come on,' he said, urgently, desperate to see her form again.

The timer continued to climb towards the moment they'd returned to the station.

Stacey didn't reappear.

She had never left the area where they'd found her broken phone.

For a long moment, they simply stared at each other. He saw every ounce of his own fear reflected in his colleague's eyes.

Dawson swallowed his panic as Bryant stood.

'We have to see Woody. Now.'

CHAPTER 81

'Stay in the car,' Kim said, as she pulled up outside Fiona's house in Fairfield.

Travis nodded. They really were going to have to head back to the office to get him a fresh pair of shoes.

The house was a detached property on a main road used by motorists wanting to avoid the A38. With its post office and general store the area had a village feel to it.

Kim didn't hold out any real hope of finding Fiona at home. The red Jaguar wasn't parked on the drive, and she spied no evidence of activity within.

Kim knocked and waited only a few seconds for a response before looking through the letterbox at a short hallway with stairs and two open doors. She listened keenly but there was no sound.

She turned to Travis, shook her head and pointed to the side of the house.

The waist-high fence was broken by a narrow gate, which stood open.

The back of the house was tidy, with a small lawn and a rockery. Three items of clothing hung on a rotary clothes line.

Kim touched them. They were sopping wet, but there had been no rain since the previous morning.

She tried the back door. It was locked. She stepped back and appraised the property. No windows had been left open.

'Damn it,' Kim said, peering into the kitchen window.

The room was tidy, with just a plate and coffee mug resting on the sink drainer.

She sighed. Much as she wanted to break in to the property, she knew she didn't have cause. Fiona Cowley was a grown woman, and Kim had no real grounds to fear for her safety.

She took a step and then paused. A scratching noise sounded from the garden shed. Kim stood still and listened again.

The sound of her mobile phone startled her. She took it out and cancelled the call. Now was not the time to update her boss. She would call Woody back later.

Again she heard the scratching. She put the phone back into her pocket and tried the handle of the shed door.

She opened it slowly.

'Jesus,' she exclaimed, as the source of the scratching became clear to her.

The entire left side of the space was occupied by an oversized cage that held an abundance of hay. She stepped closer. The hay was moving.

Suddenly a black-and-white head popped out and squeaked at her.

Kim rolled her eyes. A guinea pig. Beside the cage were containers of dried food and a row of bottled water.

She frowned as the thing moved to the far edge of the cage. Fiona had not come across as the animal-loving kind.

The creature began to suck on a bottle that made a clicking noise. The water bottle was empty. She looked closer. Only a few green flakes of something remained in the food bowl.

Kim rubbed her chin. A cage the size of a mansion, bottled water. Clearly, she loved this strange-looking creature. Kim opened the food container, took a handful of the food and dropped it into the dish. She unhooked the water dispenser and refilled it from one of the bottles.

There was only one explanation that made any sense to her.

Fiona hadn't come back because she *couldn't*.

'Stone… Stone… where?…'

She stuck her head out of the shed door.

'I think Fiona Cowley—'

'Forget that,' Travis said, holding out his mobile phone. 'Your boss wants to speak to you, right now.'

Kim frowned before taking his phone. It had been less than two minutes. He wasn't normally so impatient for an update.

'Sir?' she said, an apology ready in her mouth.

'I need you back here, right now. Stacey is gone.'

Kim felt her face pulling into a frown. What the hell was he talking about? Had the guys upset her so much she'd walked off the job?

'Sir, I'll give her a call and—'

'Not that type of gone, Stone. She's been taken, snatched, abducted from the bloody station car park.'

Kim felt the ground move beneath her feet. He wasn't making sense. If this was Woody's idea of a joke then she was waiting for the punchline. And it had better be a good one.

'Stone,' he growled into the silence.

It wasn't a joke and there was no punchline.

She began to shake her head in denial. 'No… no… sir, that's not…'

'Stone, get back here. I want every available body on this, now.'

The line went dead in her hand.

Stacey, *taken*? How the hell?…

'Stone, you okay?' Travis asked.

She slowly began to shake her head.

No, she really didn't think she was.

CHAPTER 82

'Bloody hell, Kev, take it easy,' he said, wishing he'd never handed Dawson the keys. He had done so only because he'd been on the phone to Woody at the time.

'And the guv said to head straight to Kidderminster.'

'We're almost there,' Dawson said, taking a sharp left and hitting the accelerator as the road opened up into dual carriageway.

'Kev, slow down,' he urged, as the car swerved around anything travelling slower than seventy miles per hour.

Dawson ignored him. He crossed the dual carriageway to enter the housing estate. A minibus sounded the horn. Bryant held up his hand in an apology. Dawson took the next left and a right before pulling up in a marked parking area.

'That one,' he said, opening the door.

He was heading up the path before Bryant had his seatbelt off. Dawson banged continuously on the door.

It began to open, slowly.

'Kev…' Bryant warned.

The second Dawson saw who was behind it, he pushed forward. His right hand reached up and clamped around the throat of Gary Flint.

'Where is she, you racist bastard?' he cried, forcing the man against the wall. A picture frame teetered and then clattered to the floor.

'What the… what are?…'

'Don't play dumb, you fucker. Just tell us where she is. You told us this thing was bigger so what the hell has happened to our colleague?'

A middle-aged woman came hurtling out of the kitchen with a tea towel in her hand.

'What do you think?…'

'Step away, madam,' Bryant said, assuming he was speaking to Flint's sister. It was her address he had registered, due to the restraining order preventing him living near the Kowalskis.

He moved around Dawson and prevented the woman coming any closer. She looked in horror at her brother pinned up against the wall.

Bryant turned his back on her shocked expression.

'Where is she?' Dawson repeated, giving him another shove.

Realisation dawned in Gary Flint's eyes.

'Your colleague, she's been taken,' he stated.

'And you know something, you bastard. Now tell me.'

'I don't know—'

'You knew she'd gone. Who has her? Where is she?' Dawson barked.

Bryant saw the smirk begin to form. Dawson saw it too. He tightened his grip on Gary Flint's throat.

'So help me, God, I'll squeeze the life out of you if you don't give me something.'

Bryant knew they were both risking their careers. Dawson with his hand on the man's throat, and his refusal to do anything about it. But this was Stacey. Bryant wanted Flint to talk as much as his colleague did.

'A name,' Dawson screamed in his face.

'Let him down,' the woman cried as his face began to flush.

'Stay out of it,' Bryant hissed.

'A name,' Dawson repeated, bringing his face closer.

'He doesn't know,' the woman said.

'Yes, he does,' Bryant said.

'One name,' Dawson said.

The colour in his face was deepening. A gurgle sounded in his throat.

'Let him down,' she screamed. 'He's going to die.'

'He might,' Bryant said.

'A name,' Dawson said, as Flint's eyes began to roll.

'He's killing him,' she cried. 'Make him stop.'

Bryant shook his head, despite the fact he was two seconds away from pulling him away himself.

'Let him down and I'll give you a name,' she shouted.

Dawson loosed his hold and let Flint drop to the ground.

'No... Miriam... don't...' Flint gasped.

Tears streamed down her face. Bryant turned to her expectantly. 'A name?' he said.

'Floda,' she said, quietly. Her eyes were fixed on her brother, heaped against the wall.

'That's all I know. The name is Floda.'

Dawson offered them both a look of disgust before leaving the house.

Bryant followed.

'What the hell kind of name is that?' Dawson asked. The rage inside him would only have been quashed if he'd beat the racist pig senseless.

Bryant's footsteps slowed as the name lit up in his mind's eye.

'Damn it,' he said, as they reached the car. 'Floda. It's Adolf spelled backwards.'

Dawson visibly paled.

'Bryant, I'm not afraid to admit I'm a bit scared right now. You?'

'No, Kev. I'm fucking terrified.'

CHAPTER 83

'Go,' Travis said, as they pulled up on the car park.

She nodded and sprinted into the building. Travis had immediately called all his team back to the Kidderminster squad room, and she had done the same with hers.

A quick scan of the car park told her Dawson and Bryant had not yet arrived. She would brief them separately but right now she had not a minute to lose.

Six pairs of eyes aimed straight at her as she entered the room.

'Guys, I need your help,' she said, honestly. 'A member of my team has been abducted.' She hesitated before admitting the truth. 'And I have no idea why.'

'What was she working on?' asked Penn, as Travis entered the room.

Kim tried to ignore the shame she felt as she shrugged and shook her head. She didn't know and she should. She'd only been away from her team for a few days but she'd lost touch. And somehow she'd lost Stacey.

Urgent footsteps approaching caused Kim to turn.

Bryant and Dawson appeared in the doorway. She couldn't work out who had the least colour. A few seconds of silence fell between them. One of their team was missing and they had to get her back.

She beckoned them in. 'My team,' she said. *Or what's left of it*, she almost added.

She made the bare minimum of introductions as everyone nodded in different directions.

Bryant held out Stacey's damaged phone.

She nodded towards Penn, who held out his hand.

'Can I just get a minute?' she asked Travis.

He nodded towards his office.

Bryant and Dawson followed.

She closed the door.

'Guys, what the fuck has happened here?'

She knew the guilt was increasing the volume of her words.

'Everything was fine this morning, guv,' Bryant said. 'She was looking into the histories of our hate crime victims while we were at Lloyd House.'

'And you didn't keep a check on her?' she asked, knowing she was being unreasonable, and Bryant's expression reflected it.

'Protect her, don't protect her…' he said.

She opened her mouth to respond when her phone rang.

'Go, share the case details with the guys,' she said, turning away from the door.

'Sir,' she said.

'Where the hell are you, Stone?' Woody asked. 'I have half the borough CID team at Halesowen waiting to be briefed.'

'I'm running it from Kidderminster, with Travis's team,' she said.

'No, Stone, you're not.'

'Sir, you wanted a joint investigation, well now you've really got one. I've worked with these people, I trust them. I know what they can do.'

'Stone…'

'Sir, please. Let me have access to Stacey's login and I can run it from here.'

She could hear the tension in his voice. 'Stone, are you disobeying a direct instruction?'

This was his opportunity to push the shit downhill. By disobeying a direct instruction, she would be held totally accountable for the events from this point forward.

'If you're issuing one, sir,' she said, honestly.

This was it. If he confirmed it, she was on her own. This single moment was about the trust that existed between them.

'Stone, we'll talk about your insubordination later.'

'Happy to do so, sir,' she said. Right after she got Stacey back.

'Okay, let me know what you need.'

'I will. And thank you.'

She sighed heavily and turned back to the door, which had been left open by her colleagues.

Had they heard her entire conversation?

She saw the slow, knowing smile on Travis's face.

Yes, they'd heard.

CHAPTER 84

'Are you in, Penn?' Kim asked.

Temporary access codes had been emailed to her, and she had typed them into the remote login.

He nodded.

'Listen, guv,' Bryant said. 'We have this name supplied by our racist lead, Gary Flint. It's Floda. Don't know who it is or what it means but this guy knows more than he's letting on.'

Penn's head snapped around. 'Floda?'

Dawson nodded.

'Adolf backwards,' Kim said, aloud. She turned to Dawson. 'And this name came up in connection with your current hate crimes investigation?'

Penn frowned. 'I've just seen that name on your girl's phone. Give me a minute.'

Kim looked from one to the other in confusion. It wasn't a name that cropped up often. 'Did you two pass that name to Stacey?'

Bryant shook his head. 'We only just got it.'

She looked at the sea of confusion around her.

They were all thinking the exact same thing.

What the fuck was going on?

CHAPTER 85

'Gibbs, Johnson, condense the Cowley case onto board one. Dawson, note bullet points from your hate crimes case on board two and mark up the last board as Stacey,' Kim instructed.

'Who is Justin Reynolds?' Penn asked, suddenly.

Kim could see he was still looking at Stacey's broken phone.

'Justin Reynolds?' she clarified. The name was familiar, but not immediately recognisable.

'Teenager from Sedgley,' Dawson said, stepping forward. 'Stacey and I attended the scene the other day and I asked Stacey this morning to do a bit of background searching on him.'

'Why?' Kim asked.

'Slim chance he might be involved in the incident with Aisha Gupta,' he said. 'The girl who was pushed to the—'

'I know who she is,' Kim snapped. Her information retention rate was pretty good, and Bryant had not made the mistake of leaving her out of the loop twice.

Penn frowned. 'You sure you asked her this morning?' he asked Dawson.

'Of course,' he answered, tightly.

'Well, your girl was paying a lot of attention to his Facebook page way before you asked her to.'

Dawson's eyebrows almost met in the middle. 'But how… I mean… his name hadn't come up before yesterday?'

Penn shrugged his shoulders.

'Guys?' she said, looking to Bryant and Dawson. 'What the hell has been going on?'

They both shook their heads. 'She never mentioned him.'

'So, why the interest? Did you two discuss him in front of her?'

'Don't think so,' Dawson said. 'There was nothing to discuss. We did our statements, clearly suicide. There was nothing there,' Dawson said, defensively, even though he'd done nothing wrong.

'Bryant, put in a welfare call to Mrs Reynolds. We need to rule this out, straight away.'

He nodded and stepped away.

'Wow, your girl some kind of racist?' Penn asked.

'Absolutely not,' Kim snapped. 'Her parents are from Nigeria.'

'Well, she set up a dummy Facebook account and posted all kinds of vile…'

'Let me see that,' Kim said, standing behind him.

He scrolled through a whole stream of offensive posts. Blacks, Asians, gays, Jews, the works. This Facebook profile hated everyone. Kim felt her mouth begin to dry up.

She knew these posts were not from her colleague.

'Guv,' Bryant said, ending his call. 'Mrs Reynolds wants to know when she can get Justin's laptop back.'

Kim staggered backwards and rested her behind on someone's desk.

Real fear for her colleague surged through her. Stacey had clearly been conducting her own investigation prompting her to set up the profile of a cruel, hateful person online. She had hidden her curiosity behind the wall of anonymous security. Only it hadn't stayed that way as demonstrated by the blood on her phone.

Kim knew without doubt that Stacey's life was in danger.

And that they were running out of time.

CHAPTER 86

'What the hell did you do that for?' Gary asked for the third time.

He swallowed deeply and stretched his neck. It was bad enough being forced to live with his sister. He hadn't liked her when they were kids, and he liked her even less now.

'He was going to kill you,' she said.

He stood. 'Of course he wasn't going to kill me, you stupid cow, he's a police officer being watched by another police officer with you witnessing the whole fucking thing.'

'You were turning a funny colour,' she said, as the tremor entered her voice.

He continued to move towards her. She took a step backwards.

'You gave them a name,' he said, feeling the rage burn around his body.

'I was trying to save you,' she whined, angering him more.

Her foot caught the bin as her body came to a forced stop in the corner of the kitchen.

He advanced. 'Do you realise what you've fucking done?'

His arm swept across the counter, sending plates, cups and a fruit bowl crashing to the ground.

She shook her head but her eyes didn't leave his face.

She knew what was coming.

'I said, do you realise what you've gone and done?' he repeated.

'What was I supposed to do, Gaz?' she pleaded.

'You could have jeopardised everything, you stupid bitch,' he said, punching her in the mouth.

She cried out and raised her arms in front of her face. The second blow landed in her stomach; his hard, powerful fist driving through the softness of her flesh.

She made a retching sound as her hands lowered to protect her belly.

The third blow landed on the side of her temple as she started to crumple to the ground.

'Please, Gaz, don't—'

'Shut up, you stupid cow. Do you think you won't be found out?'

He clenched his fist again. The throbbing in his knuckles felt satisfying.

He should never have told her anything. Yes, his sister shared his views but he should have kept Floda his own secret.

'I can't fucking trust—'

His hand stilled in the air as the doorbell rang.

'You know who that is, don't you?' he asked, as a deathly calm stole over him.

'It might be the neighbour or—'

'Keep your damn mouth shut,' he said, straightening his shirt and moving away.

The glass panel in the door told him the person who had knocked was a stranger.

But he already knew who it was.

CHAPTER 87

Kim sat on the edge of the table at the top of the room. The boards were almost complete.

'Anybody managed to find Fiona Cowley yet?'

Gibbs shook his head. 'Not been into work and no call either.'

Damn it.

'Guv,' Lewis said, quietly. 'Why did Fiona Cowley authorise the dig in the first place?'

'Bloody good question,' Kim answered. 'And one of the first ones we'll ask her once we find her.'

'And Jeff Cowley has just been released,' Travis said, coming back into the squad room.

'You're kidding?' Kim said.

He shook his head. 'Time's up. Not enough to charge him with anything. He won't be going far with Billy still in hospital. We'll get him back.'

Kim hoped so. He still had a lot of questions to answer.

'Okay, folks, to recap; Stacey, for some reason, has taken an interest in the suicide of a teen named Justin Reynolds. She has visited his home, spoken to his mother and taken the boy's laptop.

'It appears that Justin's accounts are full of racist posts, losing him most of his friends. Stacey has made a dummy account, which I can only assume is to get the attention of someone called Floda.

'That same name has emerged in connection with a rush of hate crimes being investigated by Dawson and Bryant and one of our bodies from the Cowley site is Jamaican,' she added, for the benefit of Dawson and Bryant. 'Who also bore physical signs of being hunted.'

Those words would never come easily to her.

Penn held up Stacey's phone. 'The account for Floda no longer exists but I have a text message telling her the laptop is outside the station,' he said. 'And I'm just working through some photos she took of a racist website. There appears to be some kind of get together happening tonight.'

Damn it, Kim thought. Stacey had been lured outside by someone who had stolen Justin's property and then promised it back. Unaware of the danger, she had foolishly gone looking. And someone had been waiting.

Lynda stood up slowly, and began walking towards the fourth board on the other side of the room.

'It is the invitation,' she said, to no one, as she picked up a red marker pen.

She silently began to fill in the gaps on the board.

The first line read 'The Hunt'.

She ignored the second line, which they had already assumed to be a date.

She hesitated at the last line in small letters. She wrote backwards as though trying something out.

Two words. The last one ending in 'ed'. She filled in the word 'required' and made a space leaving a five-letter word beginning with the letter 'P'.

'Photo,' Dawson called out.

'Proof,' Kim said.

'Hang on,' Dawson said. 'Remember our guy who beat up Henryk. He told Henryk to close his eyes. We saw footage of him messing with his phone.' He turned towards her. 'Maybe it's both. Maybe a photo is proof,' he said.

'If it's an event, it's proof of entry,' Kim said, as a wave of nausea circled in her stomach.

She saw Dawson's deep swallow before speaking. 'Aisha was accosted for one reason. To lie down and close her eyes.'

'Fuck. To look dead,' Kim cried out. 'That's the proof of entry. A dead body.'

'But the note is more than twenty years old,' Gibbs said. 'There were no camera phones back in the…'

'Polaroids,' Bryant said. 'Very popular in the eighties. I had…'

'The abductions,' Lynda suddenly cried out. 'The attempted snatches this week. First victim was West African and the second from the traffic accident was Asian. And you say Stacey is…' her words trailed away as every face in the room fell on her.

'It's a new one,' Kim breathed. 'It's a new event. A fresh hunt.'

Kim felt the trembling start at her knees.

Stacey was the prey.

CHAPTER 88

'Okay,' Kim said. 'Somehow, everything we've all been working on brings us back to the same place. We're all agreed that the rush of hate crimes is somehow linked to a live hunt, some kind of entrance into the actual event.'

She swallowed the bile that rose in her throat. Indulging her rage and disgust would not help her find Stacey.

'It's likely that Justin Reynolds was responsible for the assault of Henryk Kowalski and that Aisha Gupta was his first attempt. He was trying to get his entrance fee but he just couldn't finish the job.'

Despite her best efforts, she could not keep the bitterness from her tone. Any human life valued so poorly was horrific to her but the choice being made on the colour of someone's skin or sexuality made her want to hit something, hard.

'I still think—'

She stopped speaking as her phone rang.

'Go ahead, Doctor A,' she answered.

'I have the results of the soil samples,' she said.

'And?' Kim prayed this was going to give her something.

'Different levels of magnesium, potassium and—'

'Doc, anything that can help us?' Kim asked, urgently. Those bones had been moved like they were leftover scraps.

'Higher moisture content in the second—'

'The field,' Kim cried out as everyone turned and looked at her. 'Thanks, Doc,' she said, ending the call.

At least one of the mysteries had been solved. The bones had been moved when the camping field had flooded a few years earlier.

She explained the lab results to the others as, once again, it seemed everything brought them back to the Cowley family.

'I still think Fiona Cowley is the key to this,' Kim said. 'I don't know why. Dale Preece is lying about Fiona not visiting their property, and I want to find her.

'I need someone to check the CCTV around the Preece home to see if we can establish a direction of travel when she left.'

Johnson raised his hand and picked up the phone.

She turned to Lynda.

'We need to look into all property currently owned by the Preece family. The Cowleys may well have access to a list and are exploiting it. We need to know where this fucking event is going to take place.'

No way she could use the word 'hunt' when her colleague, Stacey Wood, was involved.

CHAPTER 89

Stacey opened her eyes and groaned. Her head felt as though it was being pounded with a jackhammer. She could feel the nausea biting at the back of her throat.

She blinked her eyes twice to make sure they were open. The dense blackness around her was unyielding. She blinked again to try to adjust her eyes to the light. Tried to make out a shape, a form, a silhouette; but there was nothing.

She felt the trembling begin in her legs. The blackness all around her was stifling, suffocating, as though she was being held down beneath a blanket. She took huge gulps of air.

A wave of dizziness threatened to engulf her. She opened her eyes wide and fought through it.

She tentatively lowered her hand from her lap to the ground beneath her and felt around, furtively. Neither her hands nor her feet were chained. Therefore there must be no chance of escape.

She fought to keep her centre of gravity. The darkness was disorienting.

She remembered a film where the prisoner had been perched on a ledge. A foot or two in any direction and they would have fallen to certain death.

With her eyes out of action, she tried to employ her other senses. She listened keenly but the silence thundered in her ears.

The darkness was swallowing her, cloying, clawing at her hair, enveloping her.

The ground beneath was cold to her touch. Bare concrete with a light dust covering that she could feel on her fingertips.

She inhaled deeply, causing another rush of dizziness. Her eyes closed to ward off the pain. There was a faint smell of something stale in the air.

But despite the fog in her brain she could sense something. She couldn't see, hear, feel or smell anything but there was a presence. Something else in the room.

She tried to remember any detail of her journey but the last memory she had was of bending down to retrieve the laptop.

She suddenly thought of her colleagues, her boss, and the emotion surged up inside her.

She could taste the regret of keeping her activities to herself.

A small voice questioned whether any of them had even missed her, but she knew it wasn't true. It was the voice of the child that had felt left out, abandoned. The adult police officer knew they had already noted her absence. That same realistic adult also knew there was nothing they could do.

She had told them nothing, shared nothing in her attempts to prove herself, and she had proved nothing – except she couldn't be trusted alone.

Stacey blinked back the tears as the gravity of her situation wove itself into the blackness around her.

She hitched forward on her bottom, feeling around her as she went. The effort of the movement brought fresh pounding to her head.

The stars swam in the darkness. She swayed to the left and felt herself falling sideways to the ground.

She knew she was losing consciousness when the sound of the key in the lock startled her awake.

She heard a man's voice, pleading, begging.

'Please, I won't say anything, I swear. Just let me go and—'

His words were cut off abruptly as she heard him being thrown to the ground.

The door slammed shut and a gust of air whistled around her body.

'Hello…' she said, tentatively. Whoever it was, they were in here together.

'Stay the fuck away from me,' he growled.

Her eyes were wide open in the darkness as she realised that she knew who it was. She hadn't recognised the begging tone but she remembered the aggression.

What the hell was Gary Flint doing here?

CHAPTER 90

Every person in the room was either tapping furiously or speaking on the phone.

'Stone,' Travis said, ending a call. 'Just checked with the hospital. Jeff Cowley signed Billy Cowley out of the hospital twenty-five minutes ago.'

'Damn it,' she said.

'Tried both their mobile phones. Switched off,' he added.

Oh yeah, she just bet they were. That family was in this up to their lying, deceiving eyeballs.

'Got her,' Gibbs shouted.

Kim stood behind him. He pointed to the screen and zoomed in on the number plate of the red Jaguar as it pulled in behind a blue transit van.

'Two thirty driving through the centre of Hagley. What time did you see her enter the Preece house?' he asked.

'About one thirty,' Travis answered.

'And this is about six miles away in lunchtime traffic so she couldn't have been there long.'

'Keep going,' Kim said, tapping him on the shoulder and walking away.

'Bryant, contact Stacey's mum. I want to know if she discussed anything with her over the last few days. Dawson, anything on the CCTV in Halesowen yet?'

Dawson didn't turn but shook his head.

There was a petrol station camera at the top of the road that ran in front of the police station. A council camera covered the traffic island at the other end. Dawson was trying to crossmatch vehicles that passed one camera but didn't pass the second, meaning they had pulled in somewhere. The travel time along the 40 mph stretch was seven seconds. It was a thankless, laborious task that would most likely yield nothing but Dawson had offered to do it anyway.

She stole a glance at the window and felt the anxiety kick up a gear.

'Guys, it's getting dark out there.'

A wave of acknowledgment travelled around the room.

She could feel the panic building in all of them.

She hit Woody's number on her phone.

'Anything, sir?' she asked.

He had dispatched teams to both the Cowley farmhouse and Fiona's home in case she turned up suddenly.

'No, Stone, both places are in darkness. She's not been there.'

'Okay, thank—'

'Stone, how's it going?'

'We're making progress,' she said, ignoring the empty feeling in her stomach.

'How are you holding?…'

'I'll speak to you soon, sir,' she said, ending the call.

'I've got four properties,' Gibbs called out. 'All of them have been in the Preece family for over twenty years,' he said, as the printer spluttered into life.

'A manor house in Bromsgrove. An old hospital site in Staffordshire. An army training ground in Wolverley, and a derelict trading estate in Walsall.'

'Any links to the Cowleys?'

'Still checking,' he said.

'Guv, got a sec?' Bryant said.

She moved away from the others and joined him by the door to Travis's office.

'It's not gonna help us to find her, but I think I know why she couldn't let this go.'

'Go on,' she said.

'Her mum was just very honest with me after I told her about the case Stacey had been working on. Apparently our Stace contemplated suicide in her teens. Her mother walked in on her, thank God, but it does explain why she went looking for answers.'

'Shit,' Kim said, taking a deep breath. 'That stays between us, yeah?'

'Obviously,' he said.

She turned to walk away but Bryant had stayed where he was. 'What?'

'I should have seen it, guv. Thinking back, I remember her closing her computer when we walked in. The sombreness of her mood was another clue but I thought it was this case. I should have—'

'Bryant, there's no point to this, especially now,' she said. She would have liked to offer him reassurance that it was not his fault, but she couldn't. Not right now.

'Jump on the CCTV with Kev,' she instructed. 'I want to know if there was a blue transit van anywhere near our station.'

'Got one,' Penn called. 'Got a link…' He paused. 'Shit, I've actually got two. Fiona Cowley was the marketing manager at the Brookmyre Manor House. The Preece family tried to resurrect it about five years ago but it failed. And Jeff Cowley served at the army base twenty-three years ago.'

'I've got the last sighting of Fiona's car, here,' Gibbs called out. 'Caught by the Esso services in Wordsley.'

Kim took a look at the car disappearing around a corner.

'Shit, guv, I've got one,' Dawson shouted.

Kim frowned. 'Hold that a minute,' she said to Gibbs, and turned to Dawson.

'Kev, play me your footage.'

Passing the Esso station was a blue transit van.

'Pause,' she said.

'Gibbs,' she said, calling him over.

He looked at the screen.

'Same one you got following Fiona Cowley's car?'

'Looks like the same age and model but without registration numbers…'

'Have you timed that one yet?'

Dawson shook his head.

'Do it now,' she said.

'Stone,' Travis said, phone in hand.

She turned.

'Checked your emails?'

'Not in the last twenty seconds,' she said, sarcastically. She'd developed whiplash from going desk to desk.

'The fibre found with the victims. It's a match for the bathroom carpet,' he said.

She nodded and frowned. 'Of course it is. We saw that carpet ourselves.'

It was the result they'd expected.

He shook his head. 'Not from the Cowley's. It matches a fibre in the gum on my shoe. The fibre in the grave came from a Preece.'

'We can't rule out that the two families are linked somehow. There's a history there and they must have been in and out of each other's houses,' Kim said. 'Fibres get transferred.'

She turned away, trying to process all the information as Dawson put up his hand.

'Seventeen minutes, boss,' he called out. 'Van was out of sight, and it went back the way it came.'

Everyone stopped working, and turned. They all knew.

That was the vehicle that had taken Stacey.

The sound of Kim's phone ringing shattered the sudden silence.

'Doctor A?' she answered, as people turned quietly back to their tasks.

'I have heard about your Stacey. I will not keeping you long,' she said, quickly. 'But those marks, the nicks you called them, on the legs of victim number three…'

'You know what they are?' Kim asked, standing up.

'Yes, Inspector. They are teeth marks. Dog teeth marks, and I counted one hundred and ten.'

'Jesus,' Kim said, closing her eyes for one second. The poor soul had been mauled to death by a pack of dogs.

'Thank you, Doctor A,' she said.

'Inspector… good luck,' said the scientist.

Kim thanked her again and ended the call.

There were few ways to die that could be more horrific than having the flesh ripped from your bones by a pack of hungry animals.

She could not consider such a horrific fate for her colleague. She would not.

Everything they had learned about this case meant nothing to her right now. The only thing that mattered was finding Stacey and getting her back. Alive and unharmed.

'Okay, everybody on CCTV. We want a registration number for that van, and we need to know where it went.'

CHAPTER 92

Bryant watched her move around the room, whirling from desk to desk, trying to pick out pieces of the puzzle that would take her where she wanted to go. Solving any case had been trumped by the need to find Stacey.

He was sure everyone in the room could see the growing tension in Kim. The fact that her hands were permanently clenched and her jaw was set rigidly. The occasional neck roll was a poor attempt to relieve the tension building in her shoulders.

What he did question was whether the others could see everything else that was going on.

Did they see the guilt she was feeling every time she scratched her upper lip? Did they see the responsibility she was feeling every time she cupped her chin in her palm? Or the sheer determination that coursed through her every time she thrust her fists into her front pockets? He knew the signs, because he was feeling it too.

But unlike him, she had learned responsibility at the age of six years old when she had felt accountable for trying to protect her weaker twin from their schizophrenic mother. And guilt when she had been unable to.

Right now, Kim stood in front of the three wipe boards, studying them for a clue, her arms folded across her chest.

She glanced towards the window and bit her top lip. It had been dark for more than an hour, and he could sense the panic clinging to her body.

But what the others wouldn't know was the cause and effect of her feelings of guilt and responsibility. She closed down and focussed. She turned every emotion in on herself and hung on to the steely determination that he had seen before. Except that rigid resolve also eroded her common sense and objective decisions. She would take any measures to get Stacey back. Whatever the risk to herself.

He stood and moved towards her.

'You all right, guv?' he asked.

The mask descended, hiding everything he'd already seen.

Her voice was measured and calm and emotionless.

'Of course, I'm all right, Bryant,' she said, offering him a look, before moving away and continuing to study the boards.

And in doing so, she confirmed he was right.

CHAPTER 93

Kim moved away from Bryant's prying eyes. At times like this it did her no good to know that he could read most of her thoughts, never mind her feelings. They were no good to her now. If she submitted to them she would find herself tearing out of the building and running the streets, shouting Stacey's name, convinced that she could find her better than anyone else.

'Okay,' she said, getting everyone's attention. 'We have two prime locations. Thoughts?'

'Looking at this manor house, it's huge, derelict, spooky and a great location…' Lynda's words trailed away when she saw the look on Kim's face.

'I mean, it's ideal for what we think they have in mind. Nearest property is a mile away. There are a few barns out back and…'

'Gotta disagree,' Gibbs said. All eyes turned to him.

'Before the Second World War, Denton Army base was developed by the Ministry of Defence as an ammunition dump. Basically, a storage facility for live ammo and explosives.'

He tapped a few keys and an aerial view showed on his screen.

'It has a buffer zone, a cleared area of two miles in the event of an explosion. All that land now belongs to the Preece family.'

'Why haven't they sold it on like the rest?' Travis asked.

'Developers prefer land where they have no chance of discovering an undetonated bomb,' Gibbs answered with a shrug.

Kim stood behind him as others wheeled in their direction.

He used his pen to touch the screen.

'There's a metal fence around the whole site.'

'What are they?' Kim asked, pointing to a row of humps on the east side.

'Igloos, sorry, bunkers for storing ammo.' He moved his pen along. 'I think those are pits to divert the force of the blast. And that over there,' he said, pointing to the top left of the screen, 'will be the destruction area: the demolition range used for burning or detonating defective, surplus or obsolete explosives.'

'And this?' she asked, pointing to a large structure at the centre of the site.

'Transit building for transferring ammo. There'll be a workshop, ammo repair space and facilities for the troops,' he said, knowledgeably.

She raised an eyebrow.

'Visited the derelict Bandneath Munitions Depot in Scotland a few years ago. Had its own railway distributing munitions to more than thirty warehouses. Denton is much smaller but with a similar layout.'

She stood silently for a moment.

This had to be the right call.

Bryant caught her eye. 'Don't they do that paintballing shit at these disused army places?'

Never did he let her down. He was sharing his thoughts without trying to make the decision for her. But now there was a picture in her mind of individuals running around with guns, hiding behind structures, ducking, diving, laughing.

'Denton it is,' she said decisively.

And silently prayed she was right.

CHAPTER 94

'Just tell me what you mean,' Stacey said for the hundredth time.

She had asked him what was going on, and he had told her she really didn't want to know. After that Flint had fallen silent but she could hear his breathing somewhere to her left.

If only he would speak to her they could find some way out of this, despite their differences. Were his racist views more important than his life?

'Look, if we work together, surely we can—'

'Don't you get it, you stupid bitch? It's over for both of us.'

Stacey opened her mouth to argue when the door swung open. His words had drowned out the sound of the key.

Damn it, they could have had a plan ready to execute next time the door was opened.

A bright light shone into her eyes and then moved left and right. She dropped her lids in defence but a thousand white stars danced in front of her eyes. She heard a groan as Gary Flint was hauled to his feet and taken from the room.

Stacey felt the tears sting her eyes. She suddenly thought about her mother's concern when she'd said she wanted to be a police officer. Horrific images and untold worry must have plagued her mother while constantly praying that she would rethink her decision. Stacey wondered if this was an image that had crossed her mind. A tear spilled over and rolled over her cheek.

Yes, she was a grown woman in her twenties, and yes, she was a police officer and a detective, but right now she just wanted to feel the warm embrace of her mother. She fought back the rush of emotion that prompted the tears to form. She swallowed them down.

Suddenly her mother's voice sounded in her head. And it wasn't pleased. Stacey had never been allowed to indulge in self-pity. Her mother had offered comfort when the situation warranted it, but had been equally fond of a stern rebuke too.

Snap out of it, Stacey, she would have said, with impatience on her face.

She had to stop thinking like a victim. She had to think like a grown-up. A police officer.

What could she do? What did she always do?

She looked for information. She searched for data. She explored for clues.

She moved her left buttock forward and then her right. The darkness had not lifted and still cloaked itself around her but perhaps she could find clues. How big was the room? Was there any furniture? Where was the door?

Each time she moved she swallowed down the fear. Sitting in the dense blackness was terrifying enough but moving around with no clue of potential hazards or dangers intensified her fear.

After each few shuffles of her bottom she paused and lowered her bound hands behind her. All she felt was the dusty, concrete floor.

She had no clue of the direction of travel. She could have been moving away from the door. She paused and began to inch backwards. She had been against a wall. Her mind began to work. If she edged around the perimeter, she could estimate the size of the room based on distance from corner to corner and, wherever she was, she would eventually reach a door. Inching around in the centre of the space would simply disorient her more.

Her back hit the wall and she suspected she was where she had started. She contemplated trying to stand but she recalled the ease with which she had fallen into unconsciousness earlier. She couldn't risk it again. She had work to do.

She began to shuffle sideways, which was much harder than moving forwards or backwards.

She hit the first corner after what must have been only a couple of feet.

She turned and began to head along the next wall.

Her shirt had ridden up her back and a cry escaped her lips as her skin scraped along a metal grid. A trail of blood began to ooze towards her buttocks. She felt along the wall until her fingers met with some kind of vent.

She continued her journey along the wall estimating she'd travelled approximately eight or nine feet.

She cried out as her foot met with something solid yet yielding at the same time, like a firm cushion.

She paused, before jabbing her foot at it once more.

It groaned.

Stacey felt her mouth run dry before she whispered into the darkness: 'Who the hell are you?'

The Denton facility was located three miles east of Wolverley, a village two miles north of Kidderminster.

She silently urged Bryant to drive faster. She had allowed him the keys only because her hands were busy with her phone.

Travis and some of his team had headed to the manor house in Bromsgrove to make sure there was nothing happening there. Given the outbuildings, and derelict nature of the building, she could not rule it out as a potential site for the despicable event, although her gut was still headed to Denton.

At the last minute she had grabbed Gibbs, given his knowledge and understanding of the layout of the facility. Due to the possibility that firearms were involved, armed response units from West Mids and West Mercia were en route to both locations.

Most armed response vehicles were unmarked converted Audi Estates with a top speed of 150 mph. The units carried taser guns, pistols, semi-automatic carbines and rifles.

She had managed to persuade Woody not to send in every available officer. Such commotion would drive this sickening event underground, and Stacey could be anywhere, hurt or worse.

Her main concern was the safety of her colleague but there was another issue; the people. The participants involved in this hunt were loathsome, vile, repulsive individuals capable of treating fellow human beings in a sickening way.

They now suspected that all people present had performed some kind of heinous act to gain entry. And damn it, she wanted them all.

'Any joy, Kev?' she asked but his silence said it all.

'Still no answer from the Cowley or Preece families,' he said. He'd been alternating between all the numbers non-stop since they'd got in the car. Squad cars were parked at both locations for when any family member arrived home.

'Half a mile out, guv,' Bryant said, turning towards her.

She nodded and took a breath.

'Okay, Bryant, time to stop the car.'

CHAPTER 96

Gary Flint stumbled over the door frame as he was pushed forward into the cold night air. A strong hand gripped each of his upper arms like a vice.

Floda walked ahead, while two heavies dressed in balaclavas aided his own forward movement.

'Please, let me go. I won't tell anyone. I swear,' he cried out as he tried to keep pace with his captor.

A small hope burned inside him. Perhaps Floda had decided to spare him, allow him to join the hunt. He'd paid his dues. He'd earned his entry. Although he hadn't killed anyone, he'd waited outside the police station and sent a photo of the police officer who was asking questions. The one who had been snatched for the main event. Surely that earned him the right to hunt.

The hood was suddenly ripped from his head.

He was standing beside a metal enclosure, approximately thirty feet square. Inside the metal fencing was a pack of dogs, snarling and eyeing him with interest.

He knew that he was looking at German shepherds, used by the police and military for their trainability. He'd seen them track until their pads bled. Normally good-natured, he knew any dog could be bred to hunt.

He also knew that Floda was not letting him go.

'No…' he said, as his mouth began to dry.

'They're hungry,' said Floda. 'Haven't been fed for days.'

Flint started to shake his head in denial.

'No, please… don't…'

He knew some packs were starved and then thrown live animals to train them. But he wasn't an animal. He was a person.

'I g… gave you the prey. I gave you the black c… copper,' he stuttered.

Floda grabbed Gary's arm and pulled up his sleeve. A knife glinted as it tore a slit down his forearm.

Flint cried out and tried to back away, but Floda was holding him tight. The throbbing of the wound was nothing compared to what he would suffer if he didn't get away.

'Please, I'm begging you,' he whispered. 'I hate these people as much as you do…'

'In you go,' Floda said, opening the metal gate.

Flint tried to plant his feet into the ground.

Floda looked to the figures either side of him.

'Don't do this… I've been loyal. I can…'

He stopped speaking as he felt himself being pushed forward. He tried to squirm and turn but the hands held him firm and then shoved him into the enclosure.

The gate closed behind him but he threw himself against it, hoping it would relent.

The dogs stared at him and nudged sideways against each other restlessly, impatiently. But they didn't advance.

The blood gushed from the wound on his arm. The dogs watched as it trailed to the ground.

Flint stood as still as he could manage despite the trembling that had taken over his body. He prayed his legs would not give way.

The dogs remained in the corner of the pen: seven or eight of them, he counted. Why were they not coming towards him?

He glanced over to Floda, who was watching with amusement, and he knew why they hadn't yet moved.

'Please,' he whispered, imploring his captor.

Floda smiled at him, before issuing the instruction that would set the dogs free.

'Eat,' he heard from behind him.

As the first set of teeth clamped on to his shin bone and another on the open wound of his arm, Gary Flint passed out and fell to the ground.

CHAPTER 97

Stacey squeezed and prodded the form, eliciting an occasional moan.

'Who are you?' she whispered.

No response.

She continued her journey up to the knee joint, feeling the cotton fabric as she went. Her fingers met with a hip, then a waist.

Just like sizing the room, she had to form a picture in her mind to continue to check for injury. She knew now that this was a woman.

'Talk to me,' she said, as her hands travelled up towards the shoulders, the hair.

The sound of a key in the lock close to her head startled her. She fell backwards, away from the figure.

Suddenly a bright light shone in her face, causing her to blink rapidly.

The inert form was hauled to a standing position but Stacey couldn't see by whom.

'Come on, it's time for the warm-up act,' said a male voice.

Stacey put her hand up to shield her eyes from the light.

She managed to force her trembling mouth to speak. 'Please… tell me…'

'Don't worry, Stacey,' the voice said calmly. 'I'll soon be back for you.'

CHAPTER 98

Kim slammed the boot shut.

'Everyone set?'

Dawson was still trying to attach one side of the bulletproof vest.

Bryant stepped in. 'Bloody hell, Kev, it's only Velcro.'

She heard the ripping sound of it being peeled away and then re-attached.

As detectives, none of them were used to the extra six pounds of weight, and Kim thanked the lord they weren't wearing the military issue type which weighed around twenty pounds.

The vests had been gathered from every nook and cranny of the West Midlands police force. Stab vests were plentiful but offered no protection against bullets. Ironically the ones they were wearing offered little defence against knives.

And even though they were under strict instructions not to enter either site without a firearms unit, she had to ensure that her team was safe. The ones she could see, anyway.

Hang on, Stace, we're coming, she thought to herself as they all piled back into the car.

'The main entrance is about half a mile along this road,' Gibbs said, viewing a picture on his phone.

He tapped on it and passed it forward.

Kim could see thick metal fencing between two brick pillars with a gatehouse to the left.

She passed the phone back. Gibbs tapped twice more.

'If we carry on along this road we're driving parallel to the perimeter of the site,' he said. 'In about a mile we should be as close as we're going to get to the hub, where the main building is situated; but there's no way in, obviously. The place is surrounded by metal fencing.'

Kim cast a glance backwards to Dawson. Even in the relative darkness of the car she saw his almost imperceptible nod.

Good. The others hadn't needed to know about their private conversation.

Her phone rang, startling them all. It was Travis, eleven miles away in Bromsgrove.

'Nothing here, Stone,' he said, without greeting. 'Searched the perimeter and the grounds of the manor house. Nothing happening.'

'Thanks, Travis. How long until you're here?'

'Twenty minutes or so. We're leaving right now.'

Kim heard the car engine fire up in the background.

She gave him directions from the main entrance and ended the call.

'Anywhere here,' Gibbs said.

Bryant drove another hundred feet and parked on the grass verge.

Kim got out of the car and listened.

Dawson stood beside her. 'Boss, what?…'

'Shh…' she said, holding up her hand.

Her initial sense check offered her nothing but silence, but she closed her eyes and focussed. Somewhere in the distance were voices, chatter, an occasional laugh.

Kim tried to loosen the tension in her jaw.

Bryant shone the torch around them, ensuring he kept it low to the ground. Weeds and grass grew both sides of the metal fence. Barbed wire ran across the top. An unlit street lamp lay approximately thirty feet beyond the boundary.

Her heart began to pound in her chest.

Suddenly the street lamp illuminated above them.

She stepped forward, right up to the fence and followed the line of lights. Every third light was now illuminated.

She heard a distant roar of excitement, and her stomach turned.

'Bryant, how long?' she asked.

He had been liaising with the armed response unit.

'Fifteen, maybe twenty minutes.'

She paced back and forth along the fence line, feeling like a tiger in a zoo.

As ever, Bryant could read her thoughts.

'Guv, you know we can't—'

His words ended as a shot rang out in the distance, stunning them all. A roar of barking dogs followed.

Kim looked to Dawson, who stepped forward with wire cutters in his hand.

'Shit, guv, you know you can't—'

'Bryant,' she said over the sound of the cutters snipping at the wire. 'Stacey is in there – so please, tell me again I can't.'

CHAPTER 99

All thoughts about the size of the room and the location of the doorway had fled from Stacey's mind the second the key had turned in the lock.

Who the hell had been in here with her and what had he meant about a 'warm-up act'?

She pushed herself back against the wall, hoping its solidity would stop the trembling. The coolness of the breeze block bit through her shirt and sent further shivers through her bones.

She thought about her colleagues and swallowed back the emotion. There was no team of people that she would want looking for her more than them but it was hopeless. There was no trail of breadcrumbs left behind her. She cursed the moment that it had felt like a good idea to not trust her team.

The sound of the key in the door obliterated the silence that was pounding in her ear. She backed further into the wall as the bumps that covered her skin rose.

The blinding light shone directly into her eyes, and she blinked rapidly to escape the glare.

A hand grabbed at her shirt.

She tried to move away, but the fabric was gripped tightly.

'No… No…' she said as the terror surged through her body.

She felt herself being yanked to her feet.

'Please. I don't…'

'Shut up,' said the male voice that she'd already heard.

Those two words stopped her dead. The tone was one of disgust, derision, as though talking to an unwanted animal.

The rage began to swirl around her body.

Her hands began to flail around her, seeking a direction of attack. She swallowed through the pain still pounding from the back of her head.

'Get off me…'

'Calm down,' he commanded.

She did the opposite and struggled even more, the anger surging around her veins.

'Take your hands off—'

Her words stopped as her foot made contact with flesh, and he cried out.

She tried to get a bearing of where he was. She wanted to aim her blows for maximum effect.

He slapped her around the face. Hard.

He then tried to turn her towards the wall, but she squirmed away from his grip.

She remembered her father trying to get hold of her to tickle her ribs, and the physical shapes she had formed to prevent it.

She ducked to the left, to the right, felt her face being pressed against the cold brick. Her top half was pinned against the wall. Her options were limited but she tried kicking out backwards. Her foot was hitting nothing but open space.

'Stop struggling you stupid…'

He cried out as the back of her head met with hard bone when she threw it backwards.

She would not go quietly, she thought, just as the torch struck the back of her head, reigniting the red hot pain of earlier.

Her legs faltered as the nausea travelled up to her throat, and she buckled to the ground.

She felt her right arm being lifted and pulled into some kind of garment that then went around her back. Her left arm was pulled through before she heard and felt a cable tie securing her wrists behind her back.

There was a rough dabbing motion on her shirt sleeves and then down the fabric of her tights before she felt the sensation of something warm and sticky penetrating the fabric onto her skin.

She had no time to think about it further, as she felt herself being dragged to her feet.

Suddenly Stacey knew only three things.

She was in the presence of Floda.

She was involved in some kind of sick game.

And her time had run out.

CHAPTER 100

Kim was heading in the general direction of the shot when Bryant appeared to her right.

'Guv, this is a bad idea.'

For once she wished he would tell her something she didn't know.

She stopped dead as Gibbs and Dawson almost walked into her.

'I don't have time for a pep talk, and I don't have time to make anyone's decisions for them. Stacey is here somewhere, now please yourselves.'

She wouldn't think anything less of anyone who turned back to the perimeter. Probably.

She turned and carried on moving forward.

'I meant all four of us moving together,' Bryant said. 'We need to split up.'

'Gibbs?' she said, calling on his knowledge.

'There's a collection of small structures to the west, the field site is to the east and the main building is about a quarter mile straight ahead.'

'Okay, Dawson and Gibbs head west. We'll go east and hope-fully we'll meet at the main building.'

The shot had come from the east.

'Try and keep off the road but watch out for those bloody animal traps,' she said. She'd seen first-hand the damage they could cause. Although the street lights would help their direction, they would also increase the chance of being seen.

'And if you get close…' she said, catching Dawson's eye.

He held her gaze for just a second before he nodded his understanding.

In this kind of situation, the risk assessment was ongoing, and changed minute by minute.

She knew what she was willing to give up for Stacey. She had no right to expect that from anyone else.

'Shit, watch out,' Kim said, pushing Bryant to the right.

She had stepped on to a metal grid covering a shaft that disappeared into the depths of the ground.

'Blast hole,' Bryant said, as they walked around it.

'You know, guv,' he whispered, as they moved east in the semi-darkness. 'If anything's happened to Stacey—'

'Shut up,' she snapped.

She wouldn't think about that. She *couldn't* think about it.

'Get down,' she said, grabbing his arm.

In the distance, she could see three figures walking towards them. Two had dogs straining at the leash and panting.

She pulled him behind a bunker that rose from the ground like a hobbit house from Middle Earth.

Torchlight beamed to the right of them.

'It went down here somewhere,' said a low voice.

'Did you get it?' another voice asked.

'My first shot went wide but I think my second hit.'

Kim felt the bile rise in her throat. She ached to jump up and grab these bastards by the throat. But that wouldn't help her find Stacey, and if she was injured she could bleed to death while she was diverted.

The torchlight continued to sweep and finally rested an inch from Bryant's foot.

'Listen, Floda said not to come this close to the road,' said a third voice.

'Yeah, but it'd be good to just finish the job,' said the first.

Kim could feel her own breath bursting to be exhaled from her body, but she dared not move a muscle.

For a few seconds, silence rested in the distance that separated her from the men.

Suddenly a siren sounded in three short bursts.

'Aah, never mind. Looks like we're ready for the main event.'

They began to move away, and Kim finally breathed.

'Did you hear that?' she whispered to Bryant.

'About the main event?'

She shook her head. 'About something or someone being shot here?'

She looked along the row of bunkers raised up from the ground like sand dunes.

It was the logical place for someone to try to hide.

'Bryant, you go left and I'll go right.'

He nodded.

She peered around the grassy mound. The males were a good forty feet away. She stayed low and crawled across the distance between the two bunkers.

She shone her mobile phone down at the immediate area. Nothing.

She crawled along to the next and shone again.

Nothing.

She lowered her hand to the grass to crawl again and felt a small pool of liquid around her little finger.

She shone the phone onto her hand and then onto the ground.

The sticky redness glistened right back at her.

For a second, her heart seemed to stop.

She pointed the phone down and spotted the trail. It lessened as it travelled. The person must have rested here for just a minute or two.

Kim swallowed deeply as she moved. Was she following a trail of Stacey's blood?

The trail deviated away from the row of bunkers and then back again.

Kim was reminded of a wounded animal trying to find somewhere to die.

She stopped crawling and paused to listen. Where was the moaning and groaning? Someone was suffering but making no sound.

Kim would not allow her mind to think the unthinkable as she resumed her search.

Halfway past the next bunker she looked forward and saw a shape in the distance.

One long continuous drone sounded from the building.

She waited for it to end before rushing across the final gap.

Her breathing was laboured as the light of her phone rested on a shoe, then a thigh, then a breast and finally a mouth.

She gasped as she looked into the face of Fiona Cowley.

She hadn't noticed Bryant crawl up behind her.

'Nothing down— Jesus, who?…' His words trailed away as he realised. 'The Cowley daughter?'

Kim nodded as she placed her fingers on Fiona's neck.

'There's a pulse,' she said. 'Faint, but it's there.'

'Fiona, Fiona,' she said in an urgent whisper. 'Wake up, come on,' she said.

'What the fuck?…' Bryant said in a hushed tone.

Kim followed his gaze to the foot her phone hadn't illuminated. The horror on her face matched Bryant's. The unforgiving teeth of an animal trap were clamped around Fiona's ankle.

Blood seeped from beneath the denim of her jeans over her bare foot. Kim didn't even want to imagine the torn flesh underneath.

From what she could see, Kim was guessing Fiona had not been shot. The blood loss was from the chewed limb.

'Fiona,' Bryant said, shaking her again.

Kim stopped him. 'Don't. The pain has sent her unconscious. Best she stays out of it. If she wakes, she'll likely be screaming her head off.'

Kim realised how petite and slight the woman was in reality. Her ferocious manner had made her appear somehow bigger.

She looked around. They were about two hundred metres from the perimeter fence.

'When the armed team arrives, they'll do a perimeter check. You need to get their attention and get her safe.'

'Guv, Forget it. I'm not staying…'

'You have to, Bryant. You have to keep her alive.'

'Guv, I'm not…'

His words trailed away as they both heard the sound of excited chatter in the distance again.

Kim looked at him imploringly.

He nodded. He understood.

He had to listen to her.

She had to go.

The hunt was on.

CHAPTER 101

Stacey stumbled over the door frame, into pure terror.

The hand that had steered her forward, clamped to the back of her neck, suddenly disappeared as the cold November night bit at the bare skin of her face.

Her wrists were secured together behind her.

She looked around. The darkness was not as dense as the room from which she'd been removed, and the blinding torchlight was no longer being shone in her eyes.

She blinked furiously as shadows turned to shapes in front of her. At first she doubted if they were real or shapes burned onto her retina from the torch.

In her mind she was trying to run, but her legs were not following the command. And where to? She had no idea of the best direction to go.

In the distance she could hear voices; a chant. Her body turned in that direction as her mind cried 'Help'. She took two steps forward and paused. It was a count.

'Ninety-three, ninety-two, ninety-one...'

What was being counted down, and why had she been freed right now?

The two questions merged in her mind as she heard the chant of 'seventy-eight'.

She stepped forward and found herself swathed in the glow of a street lamp. She quickly stepped back out of it, feeling more vulnerable in the light.

'Sixty-six.'

'Sixty-five.'

Would they be expecting her to run? Was that her best opportunity for escape? To just run as fast as she could? Her mind reasoned that, if it were possible to escape that easily, they would not be giving her such a head start.

'Forty-nine.'

'Forty-eight.'

'What do I do? What do I do?' she whispered into the darkness.

Her instinct was to shout for help but the only people here were trying to hurt her.

Please, someone help me, she prayed silently as her knees began to tremble.

The numbers were disappearing too quickly.

'Thirty-two.'

She had less than a minute to work out how to save her own life.

She took another few steps forward. Her brain had numbed with fear. No decision made sense to her. Nowhere felt safe.

'Twenty-three.'

She jumped as something rustled beside her. Bloody wildlife. Something was scurrying around her. A mechanical snap sounded to her left. Metal cracking. Something howled in pain, filling the silence between chants. Stacey wondered if some poor animal had been caught in a trap that had been meant for her.

'Nineteen.'

She realised that she couldn't step too far away from the lights for fear that she'd be caught by one of those traps.

'Ten.'

She had to think quickly. Had to work out what to do, where to hide.

Three successive shots rang out in the distance.

And she had just run out of time.

CHAPTER 102

The main building loomed up in the distance as the shots rang out.

Kim guessed that meant they were on the move.

She lowered herself to the ground and crawled towards the building. One single light illuminated from the second window along.

Kim wondered if both Fiona and Stacey had been held in this building. Fiona had chosen to run as quickly as she could and had somehow managed to get one hundred metres away from the perimeter fence before being snared in an animal trap.

Kim moved carefully, wondering how many of those things were lying around.

She surveyed the area as voices began to disperse in different directions.

She pushed her back against the wall, forcing herself further into the shadows, to think.

If Stacey had been set free from the building and she'd heard the countdown in the distance, would she have chosen to run as fast as she could, or hide?

Kim tried to put herself into Stacey's mindset and adopt her logical, pragmatic approach while factoring in the terror her colleague would be feeling. If Stacey understood the situation and knew the reason for her presence, she would also understand the countdown. Would she realise there was no possible way to get to safety, leaving little reason to run? Or would panic and instinct have taken over, causing her to move quickly?

Would she also consider that beyond this collection of buildings the dense blackness would be no friend to her?

'Stacey, what did you do?' she whispered, moving towards the doorway of the building.

A shadow moved across the open window. Just a head. Kim considered storming in and putting her hands around the throat of the first person she met. But that wouldn't help Stacey. Not when there were bastards armed with guns trying to kill her.

She ducked and moved away from the window. They'd keep.

Kim crawled slowly. The whole area was awash with shafts, traps and hazards. Each move she made, she expected to feel the teeth of a trap clamp around some part of her body.

She crawled past the open mouth of a tin building shaped like a semicircle.

Her left hand hit something protruding from the grass.

It was leather.

She looked closer.

It was an ankle boot.

She picked it up.

It was Stacey's.

Damn it, Kim thought. What if the bastards had already got her?

Kim raised her arm to launch the boot in frustration and then paused, as she had a sudden thought.

CHAPTER 103

Stacey rubbed at her arms furiously against the terror and the cold. She had tried to keep count since the three shots had sounded. She was guessing it had been just a couple of minutes.

Her only chance was to buy time – for what, she still had no idea, but the thought of running around the place with a target on her back sickened her. If she was going to die, she wasn't going to provide sport for a bunch of cruel, despicable racist bastards first. They could find her and shoot her on the spot. She would not be their fucking animal.

In an effort to get out of sight as quickly as possible she had ducked into a corrugated iron structure formed into a semicircle. She had quickly moved through its tunnel-like interior towards the thick blackness at the end.

The wet grass was soaking through her woollen tights and her skirt but she couldn't stand. She could only make herself smaller if she was on the ground.

She brought her knees up to her face and looped her bound wrists over the top.

Her cheek rested against her knee, and she closed her eyes. There was no change in the level of darkness.

Had it only been today that she'd stepped out of the station to retrieve a laptop she'd had no business having in the first place?

If she'd thought there was a case there, she should have passed it on to real detectives. They would have put it all together much quicker, and they wouldn't be sitting here curled in a ball, waiting to die.

She hated the self-pitying thoughts that were filling her mind but she knew her one little attempt at being clever would go completely unnoticed. She had left the simple sign in the vain hope that anyone was looking. Her one ankle boot pointing to her location. Realistically she knew no one would find it, but it had helped for just a second to do something.

She cursed herself for hiding but her brain had offered no other solutions. Hunters with guns put her at a definite disadvantage.

She cried out as a sudden gust of wind caught a loose piece of the corrugated metal roof. It flapped three times, raising her heartbeat with every rap. She pulled her arms tighter around her legs to still their trembling.

A hand grabbed her stockinged foot.

The terror rushed to her mouth and she let out a scream.

A hand clamped over her mouth.

Stacey shook her head and kicked out. Fuck hiding. Now she'd run. She wasn't ready to die.

'Stacey, it's me,' she heard, whispered into her ear.

The words stunned her into stillness; she knew who it sounded like but it couldn't be. There was no way. Not possible.

She began to shake her head.

'It's me, Stace. I've got you,' she heard.

'Boss?' she said, against the palm.

The hand loosened, and the boss's face appeared before her own.

'Listen, there's no time to explain but I got your message. The boot pointing this way.'

Stacey felt the tears gather in her eyes.

Her boss. Here. For her.

Hot tears spilled from her eyes. Somehow, this determined, ballsy woman had put it all together and found her. Never had she been so grateful for anything in her life.

'Boss…'

'Now, we gotta get going. The armed response team is here. They're closing in but we're at the centre of the site. We need to try and move out. Got it?'

Stacey nodded, still processing the fact she was no longer alone. Hope began to rise inside her, chewing away at the inevitability of death. Maybe she would make it out alive.

'Once we're out of here we stay low and head east, okay?'

Stacey nodded. She would follow any instruction she was given but there was so much that she wanted, needed to say.

'Boss, listen…'

'Not now, Stace,' Kim said. 'We'll talk later.'

She watched as her boss stood and then offered her hand. Stacey held out her bound wrists, and Kim pulled her up.

'We'll have to leave them for now. Can you move okay?'

Stacey nodded.

They tiptoed towards the entrance to the tunnel-like building. Her boss paused at the end and turned.

The shape and structure reminded her of Netherton canal tunnel. Her father had taken her there for Sunday afternoon walks, and she had never admitted to him just how scared she was of the one-and-three-quarter-mile trek but she had always been relieved to see the pinprick of light appear at the other end.

'You ready?'

Stacey nodded and they both lowered themselves to the ground.

'There are animal traps,' she whispered, remembering the poor animal's cries.

'I know,' her boss said.

'What's that?' Stacey asked, looking into the distance.

They paused as the figure came closer.

'Shit, it's Bryant,' the boss said, as she started to wave.

Suddenly Stacey realised she wasn't waving at all. She was signalling for him to get down.

Bryant slowed.

The boss waved again. Get down.

He shook his head, not understanding, and still advancing towards them.

'Bryant, don't—'

Her words were cut short as a single shot sounded.

And in slow motion, Bryant finally folded to the ground.

CHAPTER 104

Dawson turned to Riggs, the officer in charge of the Armed Response Unit.

'How much longer?' he asked, fighting the urge to break through the fence and get looking himself.

As he and Gibbs had reached the western edge of the site they had run right into six armed officers entering the site. Despite their protests they had been frog-marched to safety.

'You know the drill, sergeant,' Riggs said, humourlessly. 'There are protocols to be—'

He stopped speaking and held up his hand as he listened to something in his earpiece.

Dawson fought the frustration. Quite frankly he didn't give a fuck about protocols when it came to people he cared about.

And shots were still being fired. His eyes roamed to the rear of the Audi where the rear seats had been removed and a gun case fitted. Right now he wanted to knock this guy out and just grab the keys.

'We've pulled out seven individuals so far,' Riggs said, lowering his hand. 'I have one officer already injured in a trap and—'

'How far are your guys out?' Dawson interrupted, caring less about Riggs's team member than his own. Stacey was the one they were all after.

'About four hundred metres from the centre.'

'Can't they go any quicker?' Dawson asked, running his hand through his hair.

'Absolutely – and then miss one and someone gets killed. We don't even know how many are in there.'

His answers were not helping Dawson's mounting anxiety.

There was something very wrong happening in that compound. And his colleagues were right in the middle of it.

Gibbs put a hand on his arm.

'Dawson, we can't…'

'Listen to your pal, mate, and step away,' Riggs said. 'I can see the look in your eyes, and I dare you to try it.'

Dawson squared up. 'Oh yeah,' he said.

A hint of a smile touched the dour lips.

'Listen, buddy, I've got enough heroes in there already. My team is in there too, and you do anything to compromise their safety, I'll shoot you myself.'

CHAPTER 105

Kim's vision narrowed as her heart thumped within her chest. Little else mattered as she crawled along the ground. A nettle stung her right wrist and gravel dug into her stomach but her focus was on her colleague.

'Bryant,' she whispered urgently, as she neared the area where he'd dropped. She felt around in the shadows.

'Bryant,' she repeated.

'He's down here, boss,' Stacey hissed to her right. Kim scrabbled over a row of tall grasses and peered down.

'I heard him,' Stacey said.

'Bryant,' she called down into the pit.

'Here, guv,' he called.

The relief washed over her.

'You hurt?'

'Just my pride,' he called back.

That would mend, she thought to herself as she took a moment to analyse the situation. Armed officers were closing in all the time but their progress was slow. There were people in that building who could get away. And one of them had just taken a shot at her friend.

'How far down are you?'

'Ten, fifteen feet,' he said.

'Throw up your pocketknife,' she instructed.

She heard fumbling.

'Coming up,' he called.

The pocketknife flew into the air and landed about five inches from her knee. She grabbed Stacey's wrists. Two cuts and the cable wrap was released.

'Get that high-vis vest off,' she said to Stacey, as she began removing her own bulletproof vest.

'No, boss, no…'

'You'd better not be doing what I think you're doing,' Bryant called up.

Kim ignored it as she balled up the fluorescent vest and threw it far into the bushes, out of sight.

'Put it on,' Kim barked to the constable.

Stacey shuffled into the bulletproof garment.

Kim knew she was leaving herself vulnerable without the protection of the vest but she could keep moving. If Stacey and Bryant were discovered by the hunters, they would be trapped.

'Put your legs over the edge,' she instructed. 'Bryant, get ready to catch her.'

It was the only thing she could do. She couldn't risk Stacey's safety, and she couldn't get Bryant out.

They would be safer together, out of sight.

'Guv, you need to get down…'

'Ready?' Kim asked Stacey, while gently edging her forward.

Stacey nodded before pushing herself over the edge.

She heard a groan from them both.

'Okay?' she called down.

'Yeah, guv. You need to—'

Kim didn't hear the rest of his sentence as she was already crawling away.

CHAPTER 106

Kim paused behind a brittle brown grass mound and estimated that she was halfway between where she'd left Bryant and Stacey and the building where the light still shone.

The fifty metres she'd got left to travel was undulating grass without cover. Once she moved from her present position she would be on land that was open and exposed.

She listened keenly. A rustle to her left brought the tension to her jaw.

She wasn't alone.

And the good guys weren't here yet.

She stayed still. Every muscle now wanted to defy the instruction from her brain.

The sound was moving towards her. But it was higher. They were walking.

She silently edged from the gravel path onto the grass.

Crunch.

In almost any situation, Kim had always felt that attack was the best form of defence.

She thrust out her hand and grabbed at an ankle, pulled it towards her, forcefully. The figure fell backwards to the ground.

She rounded on it immediately.

The form had fallen into the glow of the street lamp.

She looked down into a face she knew very well.

CHAPTER 107

For just a few moments, Stacey felt safe, crammed against Bryant in the three feet square space.

'Do you hear that, Stace?' Bryant whispered above her head. She listened keenly. 'What?'

'The dogs, they're getting bloody closer.'

Stacey felt the panic surge back into her body. It hadn't been too far away. Whether she was with Bryant or not, they were trapped in the pit until someone came to get them.

'But they can't know we're here, can they?' she asked.

'Stace…' he asked in the darkness. 'What's that smell?'

'What smell?' she asked, before the penny finally dropped in her mind. 'Oh no, Floda… he rubbed something all over…'

Her words trailed away as she felt Bryant's hands already touching her in the darkness.

'Your arms, they're sticky,' he said, sliding down the wall. 'And your tights. What the…' He quieted for a second. 'Fuck, Stace. It's blood.'

'Oh no, oh no, oh no,' she said, touching her shirt sleeve and raising her fingers to her nose. 'What am I gonna do. They're going to come straight for me.'

'Stace, you've got to take them off. Now.'

She began to protest. 'Are you having a?…'

'We have to throw the clothes out of the pit,' Bryant said, urgently.

'But won't that just bring them right to us?'

'They're coming this way anyway. Because the clothing is in here, the dogs will come right to it. It's what they're trained to do. If the hunters realise we're down here, we are literally fish in a barrel. We need to confuse the dogs. Divert them from this blast pit.'

He paused to think as Stacey visualised the scene up top. She hadn't yet moved around the small space and was still against the wall that she'd half slid and half fallen down. Opposite were the bushes where she'd heard the spring of the animal trap.

'Stace, you gotta take 'em off,' Bryant growled.

She nodded and then realised he couldn't see her. 'I know,' she said, beginning to remove the bulletproof vest. He had daubed her shirt, skirt and tights. They would all have to come off. She knew she would be naked except for her underwear. She pushed the thought away. Against the thought of getting mauled by dogs or shot, she'd cope.

'If you put your foot on my hand, I can give you a bit more height and then you can launch them out as far as you can away from us.'

'Okay,' she breathed as the shirt dropped to the ground. The November air bit into her bare skin immediately.

But she'd rather be cold than dead, she thought, removing her skirt and tights together.

'Ball them up,' Bryant said. 'They'll travel further.'

She leaned down, gathered the clothing into a pile and wound it all up with her tights.

'Ready,' she said.

'Hurry up, they're getting closer,' Bryant hissed.

She bit into the ball of clothes and then felt along Bryant's arm to where his hands were clamped together.

She raised her right leg and placed her bare foot into his palms.

'Grunt when you're ready,' he said.

She used her free hands to help scale the mossy wall either side as he lifted. She grunted and Bryant lifted her up. She loosed her grip on the bank and grabbed for the ball of clothing from her mouth.

'Aaarrgghhh…' she cried as she began to fall to the side.

Bryant immediately lowered his hands to prevent her from toppling completely.

The ball of fabric was still in her mouth.

'Shit,' Bryant said. 'Get your balance with one hand on the wall before you try,' he advised.

Stacey couldn't answer him but she nodded in the darkness. She could hear the dogs baying in the distance.

She had to get it right. She wouldn't get another chance.

This time, he lifted her slowly until she was about three feet away from the opening. She could feel the strength of Bryant's grip.

She took a couple of seconds to steady herself before removing her right hand from the wall.

She slowly reached for the bundle in her mouth. The cloth had dried every drop of saliva. She swallowed dry air to try to moisten her throat.

She tentatively balanced the ball on the palm of her hand and placed it at her shoulder like a waiter carrying a heavy tray.

She counted to three in her mind, focussing every ounce of strength she had into her shoulder.

On three she launched the ball into the air as hard as she could, aiming towards the bushes.

'Okay?' Bryant asked, lowering her slowly.

'Y… yes…' she stuttered as the cold air seemed to invade her whole body.

Bryant rubbed at her arms with moss picked from the wall. 'Might help disguise the smell,' he said, before moving away. She heard his movement beside her as she tried to rub at her own freezing skin.

Within seconds, she felt his jacket being draped around her shoulders and fastened at the front.

Suddenly every inch of her being wanted to burst into tears.

Bryant placed a reassuring arm around her.

'You did great, Stace. You did great,' he said.

She looked up to the dark sky.

She'd managed to throw the blood-soaked clothes out of the pit.

She only prayed that she'd thrown them far enough. For both their sakes.

CHAPTER 108

The first punch landed square on his nose. Blood spurted and reached her fist.

'You fucking bastard,' she spat, as she landed another punch to his face, this time feeling the satisfaction of her fist in his eye socket.

'How fucking dare you?' she cried, smashing her hand into his mouth.

A tooth broke free beneath her knuckle.

Kim felt release in the anger that had taken over her body. It demanded an outlet.

'I… stop…'

'Shut the fuck up you vile, disgusting piece of shit. Who the hell do you think you are, Floda?' she said menacingly.

Any thoughts of her career were gone. This man had tried to treat her colleague like a piece of meat, and for what. What possible reason?

Her hand paused in the air as it itched to land once again on the face of Dale Preece. She suddenly remembered the scene in the hallway of the Preece house. The way old man Preece had called for Dale. Rejecting Bart.

The truth of the situation flew into her mind like a bullet. The disgust and disrespect from Robson Preece to his youngest grandson. The idle reference to the Hunger Games. Competition and survival. The attempt to distract her with the motorbike.

'Fuck. It's not you,' she said, as everything suddenly made sense. 'You're not Floda.'

Dale Preece began to shake his head, as she finally let him go.

'Please, don't hurt him, Inspector. He's still my brother.'

CHAPTER 109

'Who's the fucking queer now, Granddad?' Bart asked, triumphantly.

For once, he was in the position of power, his grandfather's chair bound to the old fixed grate.

'You backed the wrong son, Gramps.'

He watched the irritation flash in the cold blue eyes, just as he had all his life.

'Oh, I forgot. You hate that, don't you, *Gramps*? Wouldn't let us call you anything like that when we were kids. Too playful, too childish. You didn't want to be anyone's Gramps, did you?'

The irritation turned to hatred, and that was fine with Bart. He had waited a long time for this chat with his grandfather. And the gag in his mouth prevented him from talking back.

'But you *were* right, back then, Gramps. You said that competition would help us strive, make us better. And look,' he said, pointing outside.

'Look at what I did,' he said, taking a step closer. 'You think your precious Dale could have pulled this off? You think precious Dale could have reproduced what you did all those years ago with old Cowley?

'See, I didn't need any help, Gramps. I did it all on my own. *I* found the guests. *I* found the targets. Everything that's going on out there is because of me, and do you want to know why?'

'Why?' asked a voice from the doorway.

His head shot round towards the person who was daring to try and spoil his climax, the picture that had been in his mind for years.

'What the fuck are you doing here?' he snarled right at her.

CHAPTER 110

Kim took a step into the room and leaned against the door frame. She did not remove her gaze from Bart's.

She had already seen the rifle propped up against the far wall. She knew she had to delay him until help arrived. Her only aim was to keep that gun out of play.

'It's over, Bart,' she said, quietly, trying to inject calm finality into her voice. 'There are armed police all around the building. I came in to bring you out.'

He glanced towards his grandfather whose expression was as shocked as his own.

'But before we go out, tell us both why you did it, Bart. Tell us why you recreated the atrocity of your grandfather.'

She saw him glance towards the gun.

By her reckoning, they were equal distance away from it.

She had to keep his attention.

'It wasn't just for him, was it?' she asked.

Every fibre of her being ached to launch across the room and beat the shit out of him, but she wanted Bart alive. She wanted to see him on the stand. She wanted to watch every day of his trial. And she wanted to see him carted off to prison to personally face every single black, Asian or gay male the facility had to offer.

'I know why, Bart. It's because you agree with his racist, bigoted opinions, isn't it?'

He nodded slowly, and she saw the same coldness in both of their eyes. They were more alike than either of them knew.

'Of course I do,' he said, dismissively. 'How could I not?'

Kim understood that it had been bred into him. It was an attitude, a belief that he had been spoon-fed his whole life.

'That's why you chose that disgusting name?' she asked. 'An anagram of one of the most evil men that ever lived.'

Every sentence she spoke delayed his movement towards that gun. There was no point in debating his views. They were despicable and sickening, and she would not be able to undo a lifetime of conditioning in minutes, if ever.

'He knew what he was doing,' Bart said, as his face took on an ugliness she had not seen before. 'It's about purity. They're taking over, all of them. Don't you see that we have to do something?'

'And were you blackmailing the Cowleys, like he did?' Kim asked.

They had been allowed to stay on the land, rent-free. As long as they minded the bones.

'You shot Billy Cowley, didn't you?' she asked, and instantly regretted it, as he turned towards the gun.

'And you took Fiona?' she said, quickly, to bring his attention back. That's why Dale didn't see her that day. 'She came to demand action from your family after her father was arrested.'

'She needed shutting up, that one. She's probably bleeding to death somewhere…'

'She's alive,' Kim said. 'We found her, Bart. And my colleague is alive too,' she said, unable to keep the anger from her voice.

His frown deepened.

'So, you've actually killed no one yet,' she said, meaningfully. Although she had at least three counts as an accessory, the blood on his hands was currently on a latex glove.

A bitter laugh sounded from the old man in the wheelchair.

Bart turned and saw what she could see: derision, disgust and disappointment.

Kim watched the colour of his shame flood into Bart's cheeks. Damn it. He was a failure to his grandfather all over again.

'Fuck you,' he snarled at the old man. 'I'll show you how…'

His words trailed away as he lunged for the gun.

Kim did the same thing. And missed.

He grabbed at the gun with his left hand, while pushing her away with his right.

He lifted the rifle – and shot.

Robson Preece slumped forward in his chair.

Bart stood rooted to the spot for a second, staring at the blood bubbling from beneath his grandfather's suit.

Kim knew this was her only opportunity.

She had played for time – and lost.

She launched forward and used her body weight to push him to the ground. He had turned slightly in her direction and landed on his side.

The rifle was still in his hands.

'You stupid fucking…'

He tried to wrestle Kim off him, but her legs were clamped around his waist.

She grabbed for his arms to retrieve the gun, but he flailed them from her reach.

Kim managed to lift herself up his body and spread her legs over his backside to stop him from wriggling. If he managed to get his arms free with that rifle, it was game over for one of them; and the odds were not on her side.

Kim managed to clamp her left palm around the barrel of the gun. She punched him in the throat as she snatched the gun from his grip.

She launched it across the room, heard it skid across the concrete floor.

Yes, she could have tried to shoot him, but by the time she'd positioned the firearm he would have managed to wrestle it back from her.

Now, it was a fair fight.

'Move away from him, Inspector.'

She froze at the cold, emotionless voice.

'Dale, thank God,' Bart said, scrabbling to a sitting position. 'She tried to take the gun; it went off. She killed our grandfather.'

'So, you're a lying coward as well as a sick racist bastard, Bart?' Kim asked, breathlessly.

'Shut up, Bart,' Dale said, stepping into the room.

The rifle was poised at his shoulder.

Kim felt the fear in her stomach as she stared at the coldness in the face she'd beaten outside.

'I told you not to hurt him,' Dale said, pointing the gun at her.

'And I haven't, yet,' she said. 'I want him to face a jury. I want him to pay for what he's done. I want the world to know what a sick, racist bastard he is. And I want him to suffer for it.'

He met her gaze and nodded. 'I know you do.'

Kim glanced towards the old man. He was dead, and now she was the only thing standing between the brothers and some semblance of a relationship. Despite the competition that had existed between them, they had managed to maintain a deep bond. Throughout it all they loved each other. Their views and their young minds had been twisted out of shape like molten glass but they'd always had each other.

'Just shoot her, Dale,' Bart cried.

They would always protect each other.

'We'll blame all this on her and—'

His words ended abruptly as a shot rang out.

Kim waited for the bolt of pain, the feeling of her flesh being ripped apart by lead. It didn't come.

Bart Preece slowly crumpled to the ground as his brother lowered the gun to the floor and left the room.

CHAPTER 111

Kim parked the Ninja on the pavement to the right of the hospital doors. Despite the two degree temperature outside, she needed the solitude of the bike today. Too many people were still in her head.

She had spent the night staring at her bedroom ceiling, questions swirling around her mind. And there was only one person who could give her the answers.

She headed towards the surgical assessment ward. Her earlier call to the hospital had confirmed the location of her target.

She edged inside the ward as a patient was being wheeled out.

The reception desk was unmanned, and Kim did not have the time, patience or inclination to wait.

She found the person she sought in the second bay along.

Fiona's bed was nearest the window. Her head was turned towards the grey, featureless sky.

Her petite body was clad in a long cotton nightdress, which told Kim some member of the family had been by to bring her own things.

The dressing around her ankle and foot was padded and clean. A grey furry slipper was on her good foot, the spare one discarded on the bed.

'Hey,' Kim said, quietly, as she approached.

Fiona turned to her with a look of hostility, and then seemed to realise that she didn't need it any more. Her face dropped to neutral.

'Hey,' she said.

'How's the pain?' Kim asked, sitting on the easy chair.

She shrugged and nodded towards the machine on her left. 'Better because of this.'

'Morphine?'

Fiona nodded.

'What's the prognosis?' Kim asked, looking towards the bandaged foot.

'No promises, basically. The doctors don't know if it will be weight-bearing again, and if it is, I'll have a limp for the rest of my life.'

Kim thought about what could have been.

'I know what you're thinking, and I agree,' Fiona said, appearing to read her thoughts. 'Is your colleague okay?'

Kim nodded. 'Thank God,' she said, and then added: 'We searched for you. I never thought for a minute you'd been taken.'

'You thought I was in on it, didn't you?'

'Can you blame me?' Kim defended. 'You blocked me at every turn.'

Fiona tipped her head. 'Was it you that fed Gizmo?'

'Did I… oh, the funny thing in your shed?'

The first real smile touched Fiona's lips, followed by a grimace and a press of the button. For just a second it had lit up her face and offered a glimpse of the person inside.

'How many other people died last night?' Fiona asked, quietly. She'd obviously been told about Robson and Bart Preece.

'Is that what you were thinking about when I came in?'

Fiona nodded.

'Just one, and I'm not sorry for saying that he deserved it,' she said, honestly. The sight of his chewed-up limbs in the dog cage had been horrific to witness, but easier to bear when Kim realised that it was Gary Flint who had suggested her colleague as the main event, following the police interview. Stacey's snooping had simply played into Floda's hands. Kim guessed the theft of

Justin's laptop had been ordered by Floda, to search for anything incriminating, and then used to bait Stacey out of the station.

'How many hunters were there?' Fiona asked.

'Nine,' she answered.

'Did all of them actually kill to get into the?…'

Kim held up a hand to stop her. 'We don't know yet. They hail from six other counties. The investigation will be ongoing for some time yet.'

West Mercia had already formed a task force to conduct the interviews of the nine people who had been apprehended. The team included psychologists, behaviour experts, computer forensics and eleven detective inspectors. The photos Penn had retrieved from Stacey's phone would be invaluable in matching the person to their username. The website itself had disappeared an hour before the event had begun, and she had asked to be informed specifically when the killer of Brandon 'Bubba' Jones was identified.

Despite what they'd uncovered, Derbyshire Constabulary was determined to treat the acid attack on Shay Chakma as an honour killing. Kim only hoped that the poor woman got the justice she deserved.

'Explain the timeline to me, Fiona. How much did you and your brother know?'

Kim knew that Fiona would be questioned formally by West Mercia but this wasn't for the investigation. This was for her.

Fiona took a deep breath. 'The first one took place twenty-seven years ago. My grandfather mentioned the lawsuit of Jacob James to Robson Preece, who came up with the idea for a hunt. You know how foul and racist he was.'

Kim nodded.

'The second my grandfather agreed, he sealed the fate of us all. By the time he knew about the other two victims he was in too deep. He didn't take part in the event, but he did take the bodies and bury them in the lower field.'

'The one that flooded?'

'Yes. That's when the victims were moved, and my grandfather told my father everything. My dad wanted to go to the police, but his father wouldn't hear of it.'

'So, your father continued to babysit the bodies after your grandfather died?'

She nodded.

'You and Billy?…'

'Found out all this a month ago when Bart came to tell us he would be adding bodies to the grave. He threatened us that if we breathed a word to anyone the next bodies would be ours.'

'So, you authorised the training dig and directed the team?' Kim asked.

'I wanted someone to find the bodies, and that way none of us had actually said anything. Bart went mental on the day they found something but I told him I'd authorised it before his visit and couldn't change it. He went for me, and Billy smacked him down, threatened him with the police.'

The younger Cowley had shown more backbone than she'd given him credit for.

'So Bart shot Billy to shut him up?'

Fiona nodded. 'And to frighten us into silence,' she added.

'And you went to the Preece house to talk to Dale?' Kim asked.

'Yes, when my father was arrested I went to plead with him to tell the truth and at least limit the damage to my family. I never even got to see him. Bart hauled me into the transit and got one of his guys to follow in my car.'

'Did you really think Dale would help?' Kim asked.

Kim was under no illusion about that final shot. Although he had saved her life that had not been his motivation. Dale knew what life in prison would have been for his brother. He would have died a hundred different ways.

He had killed him because he loved him.

Fiona shrugged. 'There was no one else I could speak to. The grandfather was a cold, unfeeling bastard, and Mallory Preece has been psychologically battered into submission.'

Mallory Preece now had the unenviable task of burying both her father and her youngest son. Her remaining son would be spending the next fifteen to twenty years inside.

Kim marvelled at the strength of feeling between the brothers, despite the constant rivalry instilled in them. Robson Preece had destroyed many things but he hadn't destroyed that.

'You know that your father and brother are being questioned right now?' Kim asked, gently. No matter how much they had suffered as a family, others had suffered more. In trying to protect themselves they had risked the lives of many more innocent people.

'I guessed so and it won't be long until they come here, will it?'

Kim shook her head. 'Just tell them the truth like you told me. It's your only defence.'

Kim stood and offered her hand. However misguided Fiona Cowley had been, she had tried her best.

The woman returned her handshake and smiled her goodbye.

Kim turned and left the ward, satisfied that some of the questions in her head had been answered.

But not the ones that mattered.

CHAPTER 112

Kim saw the familiar figure standing at the entrance to the police station.

'You lost?' she asked.

Travis smiled. 'I didn't get a chance to speak to you last night.'

She nodded.

Dale Preece had walked out of the building right into three armed officers alerted by the sound of the first shot. He had offered no resistance and had made a full confession to Dawson.

'Everybody okay?'

Again she nodded. 'Thanks to you and your team. Without them we'd never have found her. Please thank them all for me.'

It was Gibbs who had offered invaluable insight into the location. It was Lynda who had put together the link to the abductions. Penn's database had identified the first victim, Jacob James, and given them a starting point. He had already identified possible names for the other two victims. Victim three possibly being a nineteen-year-old Jewish girl from Walsall.

'I already thanked them on your behalf,' he said.

He moved from one foot to the other.

'We could have had this conversation over the phone,' she said.

'That's not why I'm here and you know it. What I have to say deserves to be said in person. You are entitled to see the shame on my face.'

'Tom, don't—'

'Shut up, Kim,' he said, holding up his hand. 'What I did in that locker room was not only out of order, it was completely without excuse. You were trying to help me but I couldn't see that at the time. You should have reported me and you didn't. I still have a career and the means to take care of my wife.'

'Please, stop…'

'Kim, I'm sorry for what I did,' he said, earnestly. 'It's important to me that you know that.'

'I know it, Tom,' she said, and meant it.

She tipped her head. 'So, did you transfer because I got DI first?'

He smiled and shook his head. 'No, you deserved it but I wasn't going to tell you that.' He sobered again. 'I transferred because I couldn't bear to look at you after what I'd done.'

She shook her head. So much time. Surely they could have worked it out.

He coughed self-consciously. 'Okay, that's me done. Time to debrief my team properly.'

'On a Saturday?' she asked, when that was exactly what she was going to do.

'Yeah, it's not so bad now and again. Keeps them on their toes, and Carole is with Melissa for a couple of hours.'

Kim nodded as he stepped towards his car.

'Tom, about you and Carole. Melissa would never know.'

'Yeah, but I would,' he said, opening the door.

Kim understood and realised that Carole was right. He really was a good guy.

'See you around, Tom,' she said, as he got into the car.

'And I'll look forward to our next battle over a crime scene, Detective Inspector,' he said before closing the door.

Jack looked at her strangely as she entered the building, and she knew why.

For once, she had a smile on her face.

CHAPTER 113

Kim's smile had disappeared by the time she'd reached the squad room.

Her team waited for her. Silently.

Bryant tried to catch her eye.

Dawson coughed.

Stacey stared at the keyboard.

'Bowl, Stace,' she said, walking straight through.

Stacey followed her in and closed the door.

'Boss, I'm sorry—'

'Sit down,' she instructed. 'You need to be prepared for what's about to happen.'

Stacey looked petrified.

'I've had the heads-up from Frost that this whole story is gonna break later today, and everyone is going to be after you. Do interviews, don't do interviews. That's your call.'

Stacey looked sickened, and shook her head vehemently.

'But expect backlash from Mrs Reynolds. You took away her innocent son and gave her back a racist in the name of truth. She is not going to thank you for that.'

At least his mother had the knowledge that her son had felt remorse for almost killing Henryk Kowalski. There had been some remnant of a conscience in the young man.

'But I…'

'Hang on. You had no choice,' Kim said. 'The truth isn't ours to sanitise or censor. It is simply the truth – and much as it might be painful for Mrs Reynolds, there are families that now know what happened to their loved ones and why.'

Stacey nodded her understanding.

The fear in her eyes made Kim sit back in her chair.

She sighed heavily. 'Stace, why the hell didn't you just talk to me?'

Kim saw the tears form but the constable blinked them away.

'I don't know. I should have. I wanted to, but everyone was so busy.'

'Too busy?' Kim questioned.

Stacey thought for a second before shaking her head, honestly.

'No, I could have. I know that,' she shrugged. 'I think I just wanted to prove that I can do more.'

Kim laughed, ruefully. 'And by the same token, maybe I should have pushed you a little bit harder. Taken you out of your comfort level a bit. And for that, I'm sorry,' she said.

Stacey looked confused.

'Boss, am I gonna get the sack?'

'For what? Doing your job? You had a hunch and, for your own reasons, you followed it. It just so happens you were right and, much as I hate it because you were in danger, your actions have taken a lot of nasty racist bastards off the street.'

Stacey swallowed.

Kim knew she had to force out words that did not come easy to her but that the constable needed to hear.

'Stace, you followed your instinct like any good copper would. And that's what you are. And if it means anything, I am immensely proud of you.'

Kim could tell from her face that it did.

'Now, go on,' Kim instructed, nodding towards the squad room. 'I'll be out in a minute.'

Stacey opened her mouth to say more, but Kim shook her head. There was nothing else to say.

She had the feeling that this case had taught them all something. Her team had been through the wringer, and she wasn't sure they had come out intact.

Stacey had learned valuable lessons about teamwork, and had almost lost her life.

Dawson had finally learned how to work alongside someone else, and Bryant had learned that Dawson wasn't quite the arsehole he'd thought. Not quite.

And what had she herself learned? Kim wondered, looking down at the desk. That her team meant a bloody great deal to her. More than they should. All of them.

And now it was time to find out if her team was okay.

'Right, guys,' she said, stepping into the room.

'Sorry, boss,' Stacey said. 'Can I just ask one question before we start?'

'Go ahead,' Kim said, perching on the edge of the desk.

Stacey stared at Dawson.

'So, Kev, why are you the only member of my team that didn't come looking for me?'

He rolled his eyes. 'Stace, I've already explained this.'

'So, you let some brute of a guy with a car full of guns and countless rounds of ammunition keep you from me.' She blew air out of her mouth. 'Then we're clearly not as close as I thought.'

Kim shared a smile with Bryant. They both knew this was Stacey's way of letting Dawson off the hook on which he'd hung himself.

'Oh Stace, let me take you out for a meal to make up for it,' he offered.

'Nah, you're okay,' she said happily.

'You won't come out with me?'

'No,' she repeated.

'Stace, is it cos I'm white?' he asked with a wink.

'No,' she answered.

'Is it cos I'm a man?' he asked.

She shook her head.

'No, Kev, it's because you're an arsehole,' Stacey said.

Kim did not even try to contain the laugh that burst out of her.

She looked around as the chuckles travelled from one person to another.

Yep, her team was going to be okay.

LETTER FROM ANGELA

First of all, I want to say a huge thank you for choosing to read *Dead Souls*, the sixth instalment of the Kim Stone series.

This was a difficult book to write for reasons different to any other book I have written. There were moments that the research took me to a place of such disgust and despair I truly wondered if I should continue.

I have always wanted to understand the motivations behind people who choose to perpetrate Hate Crimes against any kind of minority group as it is a mentality so completely beyond my own comprehension.

When I made the decision to explore this subject in greater detail the relevance was not as timely or current as it is right now due to the political landscape developing around us. However, I have also been heartened by acts of support and solidarity in the face of hatred and will continue to hope for the day we focus on our similarities and not our differences.

As many of my readers know, I like to try and offer Kim Stone a different challenge with each new story and in this one I wanted to see how she would adapt to working with another team, in an environment where she doesn't get her own way every time. This also gave me an opportunity to explore Stacey's character a little deeper and to pair up Bryant and Dawson for their own investigation.

I hope you enjoyed it.

If you did enjoy it, I would be forever grateful if you'd write a review. I'd love to hear what you think, and it can also help other readers discover one of my books for the first time. Or maybe you can recommend it to your friends and family…

Thank you for joining me on this emotional journey.

I'd love to hear from you – so please get in touch on my Facebook or Goodreads page, twitter or through my website.

And if you'd like to keep up-to-date with all my latest releases, just sign up at the website link below.

Thank you so much for your support, it is hugely appreciated.

Angela Marsons

www.bookouture.com/angelamarsons

www.angelamarsons-books.com

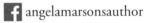 angelamarsonsauthor

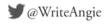 @WriteAngie

ACKNOWLEDGMENTS

First and foremost, I have to acknowledge the involvement of my partner, Julie. Although my name is on the books there is no doubt that the process is a team effort. From brainstorming to typing the first draft to two full readings she is beside me every step of the way. She is my partner in life, love and also my partner in crime.

I would like to thank the team at Bookouture for their continued enthusiasm for Kim Stone and her stories. In particular, the incredible Keshini Naidoo who manages to extract every ounce of creativity from me even when I feel there is nothing left to give. To Oliver Rhodes who has the expertise to know what to do with our books once the blood, sweat and tears have passed. And to Kim Nash who offers us tea, sympathy, professionalism and fierce protection on the journey.

A special shout out to the unbelievably ferocious and tenacious Lorella Belli who continues to sell the foreign rights to the Kim Stone stories and has conquered more than 20 territories to date.

I must acknowledge the growing family of Bookouture authors. Their enthusiasm for each other is genuine and provides an environment of friendship, advice and support. Thank you to the fantastic Kim Slater who has been an incredible support and friend to me for many years now and to the fabulous Caroline Mitchell, Renita D'Silva and Mel Sherratt without whom this journey would be impossible.

I am grateful to each retailer for their continued support for the Kim Stone series.

My eternal gratitude goes to all the wonderful bloggers and reviewers who have taken the time to get to know Kim Stone and follow her story. These wonderful people shout loudly and share generously not because it is their job but because it is their passion. I will never tire of thanking this community for their support of both myself and my books. Thank you all so much.

Massive thanks to all my fabulous readers, especially the ones that have taken time out of their busy day to visit me on my website, Facebook page, Goodreads or Twitter.

Made in the USA
Middletown, DE
26 September 2018